The Murder of Henry VIII

Simon Cann

Coombe
Hill
Publishing

Published by Coombe Hill Publishing
33 Melrose Gardens
New Malden
Surrey KT3 3HQ
United Kingdom
coombehillpublishing.com

ISBN: 978-1-910398-00-5 (paperback)
ISBN: 978-1-910398-01-2 (ePub)

25 June 2014

for Hope and Alacoque, a story without elephants

Thanks are due to many in connection with this book:

- Those who read the first draft—Anne Cann, Phil Rippingale, and Orren Merton—who all added in many different ways to what you are about to read. Thank you all.

- Cathleen Small for her firm editorial hand.

- Lawrence Rippingale (lozeng3r.com) for the cover art.

- Peter Baker (thejollypilgrim.org) for swimming the Bosporus many years before Montbretia.

one

"Asshole," Boniface mouthed, snapping his phone shut with a flick of his wrist. Had Trudgett taken lessons in how to be annoying, or did he spend all day planning how to exasperate?

Boniface straightened, turning into the room. So this was what hand-printed wallpaper looked like up close. Burgundy highlighted with a deep red pattern—a texture of repeating geometric shapes—overlaid with gold leaf.

Lots of gold.

Gold applied without restraint.

Gold applied without any consideration for taste.

Gold applied without any consideration for cost.

Enough gold to fund the debt of all developing nations, leaving sufficient change to embarrass the zillionaires in Silicon Valley.

To Boniface it looked like the wallpaper he saw in Indian restaurants, but this came at an eye-watering price tag—apparently into seven figures for this reception area alone. All that for something displaying the subtlety of a vulgar property developer or the restraint of an oil-rich sheik.

The three pairs of eyes that had been on him since he arrived were still locked on him, emotionless but judging. Three men: one behind the desk, two in front. All standing. Each with the confidence of a man who had, and was prepared again, to defend himself physically. Each with the posture of a man conditioned to the discipline of the military. Each, in addition to his manifest physical presence, with a sense of menace seeping through his pores.

Veronica had told him about Kuznetsov's ex-Spetsnaz bodyguards. Russian Special Forces who learned their trade under a regime that needed its soldiers to have near-superhuman powers, requiring them to succeed at any cost. And what weapon was issued to these human death machines? A shovel, apparently.

Whatever powers they had, whatever training they had received, they hadn't been taught how to make a guest feel at ease. Boniface was avoiding eye contact but could still feel his skin blistering where the fixed gazes burned into him as he self-consciously moved to one of the sofas, relaxing into its delicate embrace as he released his weight.

The furniture mirrored the wallpaper—well-stuffed chairs, covered in thick fabric repeating the pattern of the wallpaper. On the table in front of him—gold-framed, with a glass top—three newspapers had been arranged with architectural precision. In a room that was clearly intended as a defiant statement of opulence, the newspapers would usually have seemed somewhat incongruous, but these were a selection of newspapers owned by Kuznetsov and were left as a statement, not for information.

Without picking up a paper, Boniface scanned the headlines. The theme was similar—the continuing call for a referendum. Unsurprising, given that the man he was about to meet for the first time, Ivan Kuznetsov, was widely rumored to want to be the first British president, despite many unconvincing public denials, and it was his newspapers that conceived, launched, and supported the Referendum for Democracy campaign.

Boniface knew the argument he was going to hear when he got to meet the Russian: "The UK is a disgrace. You talk about being a democracy, but the head of state is only the head of state by an accident of birth. You have more influence over which singer gets chosen to keep singing on a Saturday night television show than you've got over who governs you. And this is the twenty-first century—why are you still voting on scraps of paper?"

The contradiction being that, as far as Boniface could tell, Kuznetsov had no interest in democracy.

Democracy was just a useful slogan to make a grab for more power and influence, and if that failed, then hopefully someone would be installed whom Kuznetsov could buy.

But it was still hard for Boniface to see a firm link between the task he had been hired to achieve—to handle the public relations for the launch of a book recounting, on the most flimsy evidence, the murder of perhaps England's most famous monarch—and an attempt to start the process to replace the hereditary monarch with an elected president.

The tallest of the three men flicked his eyes to Boniface, dismissively wrinkled his nose, and gave a nearly imperceptible nod of his shaved head to the other man standing in front of the desk; then closed his eyes as if to confirm his affirmation. The other man, whose face was lined with a scar, turned silently, walked to the elevator, punched the lower button, and departed.

As the sound of the descending elevator faded, the man with the shaved head turned to the man behind the desk—a swarthy man, with hair just long enough to start to curl—who started to turn as if to come out from behind the bombastically ornate desk. The opulence of this piece of furniture desk wasn't lost on Boniface, as he noted the massive pieces of mahogany, inlaid with rosewood and ebony, and with a corporate logo detailed in flamed maple.

The man with the shaved head looked at the swarthy man. Keeping his arm by his side, he lifted his hand as if telling a dog to stay, then walked to the elevators and jabbed the higher button. His boots, displaying a shine that only comes with many, many layers of polish applied with rigorous discipline, scraped through the thick burgundy pile with gold corporate crests.

The gold elevator doors opened, and the man with the shaved head glared at Boniface while gesturing into the waiting elevator. Boniface jumped up, hastily pulling together a few papers he had slipped out of his briefcase, and scurried over.

After a few seconds, the doors opened and Boniface stepped out of the elevator into the Observatory on the seventy-first floor of Kuznetsov's London re-creation of the Chrysler Building, the building Londoners called the Silver Spike. The elevator doors—on this floor, exotic hard-woods with delicate fretwork—closed on his escort, leaving Boniface alone.

Where he had sat in an enclosed lobby on the lower level, this whole floor was open. There were no internal walls apart from the elevator block running through the central core, which had become more prominent as the building tapered toward its eponymous spike. The dull electric light from ornate gold lamps on the lower floor had been replaced by muted daylight straining through the triangular windows arranged in a sunburst arc on each wall, giving an effect of a child's picture of the sun.

Boniface paused to take in the room. Apart from the large flat-screen television with a 24-hour news channel silently recounting the latest developments, one disproportionately sized chair, and a stand-up desk, the interior looked like a color re-creation of the black-and-white photos he had seen of the original building in New York.

Unlike the reception area, with its oppressive darkness and overly rich decor, this was a refined and perfect re-creation of the art deco interior, complete with starscape murals suggesting that the height of the skyscraper put the room into space, and with lights hanging like planets, in case you missed the allusion.

A slight shift in the shadows around the room alerted Boniface to the silent arrival of Ivan Kuznetsov. "Mister Boniface."

two

Montbretia had been quite clear in her instructions: "Wear the dark blue suit, the one we bought when I last stayed with you. No, don't wear pants. Sure, they're functional, but this is television: You get shown from the neck up—you're not going horseback riding."

She didn't stop there. "Wear a skirt because men will look at you differently. If you get interviewed by a man"—and 99 times out of 100, for a political piece Ellen was interviewed by a man—"then the interviewer will be a preening alpha-male type, or at least a wannabe alpha-male. He will want to stand in front of the camera and grab all the attention, so by definition he'll want to call the shots. And if he's that type, then he'll be kinder to you if you're wearing a skirt. Sexist, absolutely. But do you want to come across well on television, or do you want people to watch a narcissistic Neanderthal bullying you?"

The logic was sound, and Ellen couldn't argue with her sister. "So can I wear my cream suit?" she asked and was promptly told no.

"Wear the blue one. Very sober, very businesslike, and the skirt is such a good cut. It fits you perfectly. Wear your glasses, too. It gives you that whole repressed-sexuality vibe that the English men go gaga over."

And she continued without pausing. "Jewelry. One item and one item only. And something that doesn't make a noise; the microphone will pick up any rattling or jingling."

"So a brooch, then. Blouse?"

"Yeah, that would be good, sis. Not sure you're ready yet to get your whammers out on national TV, are you? Wait until you're a bit more famous, and then make some real money."

And she continued without a pause. "Make sure the blouse is one color. Avoid polka dots, stripes, and patterns—they all interfere with the cameras. Make sure it's cotton. Not silk. Silk looks like cheap polyester on TV. And wear heels."

"For the alpha-male interviewer?"

"No, because you're short."

"Not that short."

"But you're not tall. If you're standing next to someone who's taller, then the camera will only see the top of your head. Or if the others are giants, you'll just be a gap between two people." A day spent in any heel too high would hurt, so the agreed compromise was kitten heels. And as Ellen walked from Westminster tube, her feet agreed it was a sensible compromise.

She looked up and checked the time; according to Big Ben, she had five minutes to spare. Crossing the six lanes of traffic, she followed the railings around the Houses of Parliament and then crossed to College Green, which, as usual, was filled with several production crews. This was what passed for normal for Ellen these days—looking to figure out which TV crew she should be talking to.

Two years ago the book was published. The logic was simple. The logic was straightforward. The logic was perfect. It was a path trodden by many academics before her: Publish a book, sell a few copies—they talked about a print run of 2,000, so expectations weren't that high—cement your reputation as an expert within your field, and live out a quiet life in academia, but with your reputation assured because you've published a book, so you must be an expert. And that was what Ellen did, confirming her position as the leading authority on the English constitution, an ironic distinction given that she was an American citizen.

But then one of the newspapers had started agitating and had launched its Referendum for Democracy campaign.

The basic thrust of the argument was reasonable, and some of the ideas suggested were quite forward-thinking. In the twenty-first century, in a country that called itself a democracy, it wasn't that outrageous to expect the head of state to be elected by the people, was it? Other than to encourage tourists, there was no benefit in having a hereditary monarch.

As the campaign caught the media's attention, Ellen had been dragged from her cozy academic life and thrust in front of a television camera whenever producers felt they needed an expert to prove that their program was serious. So thanks to the newspaper owned by the Russian who had built the thing they call the Silver Spike because no one could pronounce its Russian name, this American had become what in common parlance was known as a media personality.

And boy, did she loathe it. The title and the role. The English constitution still fascinated her, but the media frenzy was a joyless experience—answering the same facile questions from overly aggressive, insecure, cardboard-cutout journalists who might look good on camera but who had absolutely zero skills when it came to intellectual rigor and recognizing, then dealing with, fallacious arguments.

If there was an upside, at least the book was selling well—more so since the publisher, Richard Sherborne, as overly familiar as he was over-weight, had become involved and demanded a substantial reprint while making sure that his PR people got behind the book. As a result, Ellen was scheduled for even more interviews.

She looked at her interviewer and cringed with a sense of what was coming. Did this interviewer care that she was a historian, not a political animal grasping for power? Ellen studied the past, noting each historical event and its implications for the current state of society. She was an expert on the historical basis of the English constitution—she wasn't a politician who was happy to answer any question, however ignorant of the facts they might be.

Ellen's phone rang, reminding her to ask Montbretia how to change the ringtone. She had understood how to use her last phone, but this new one? This was real space-age technology, but it was the one that Montbretia thought was best, and it did let her do a lot of things without needing to turn on her computer. As well as calling, she could email, check her calendar and to-do lists, blog, tweet, buzz, squawk, and do all of those other social-networking things Sherborne's PR people told her she should do to help promote the book. And not only did the phone let her leave her laptop at home, it also pinpointed her precise geographic location, and some clever gizmo then highlighted her current position on her website to show everyone that she was a real person who didn't spend all day in some ancient university.

At least that's what the PR people had told her.

"So what did Boniface say?" she asked, catching an angry glance from the producer. "Well, I'm not surprised. It's never going to sound good if you tell people you've just come from the police station... Look, I've got to go. I'll try and make it, but I've got another two interviews after this. I'll call you when I'm finished."

Calls from Nigel never helped when she was trying to focus, especially when Nigel was so excited. But what was his big secret and why did he want to tell her face-to-face? He was still buzzing after "helping the police," but the call was more than his usual combination of insecurity and desire to please, made worse by the arrogance that came from him feeling that he had finally been recognized for his expertise.

She checked her hair and added a few dabs of powder—a superstitious gesture to appease gods who would otherwise make her face look overly shiny in front of the camera—as the producer started counting down for the live broadcast.

three

Turgenev stood in the doorway to his office off the reception area and stared at the PR man who had just met with Kuznetsov. The Russian sized him up. Five eleven, one-hundred-and-sixty pounds, short hair—not military short, but long enough to suggest he bothered about styling, although the gray flecks suggested that at least he didn't dye it—blue pinstriped suit, a shirt and tie that the Englishman doubtless thought made him look superior to a former soldier, and shoes that only shone that way because they were new.

He snorted. The Englishman wouldn't make it past the first punch.

The man changed elevators, exiting the only elevator that could access the Observatory and Kuznetsov's private floors, exchanging it for one that would drop him to street level. The Russian made, and held, eye contact with Boniface, who seemed to wither in his gaze.

The doors closed on the PR man, and the Russian took the vacated elevator and ascended to the Observatory, stepping out to find Kuznetsov watching television and shaking his head in disagreement. He watched his boss, waiting for his cue to interrupt.

On the television, the short woman with blond, slightly curly hair; thick-framed glasses; and a blue jacket appeared to be an academic—Professor Armstrong, he thought the interviewer said. For some reason, the woman conducting the interview seemed to have taken against this academic and was singling her out for a metaphorical beating, while ignoring the male politicians flanking her victim.

Kuznetsov started talking at the television, his voice a rising crescendo that soon became a shout.

Turgenev maintained his silent vigil. The blond academic's comments were annoying Kuznetsov, but Turgenev wasn't sure what was particularly annoying him—was it what she said, or was it that she was too close to Sherborne? When Sherborne came up in conversation, Kuznetsov would usually start shouting, and this woman seemed to have something to do with Sherborne.

Turgenev watched the television, trying to listen to the conversation and ignore his boss's rants. "If I could correct you," said the blond woman, stopping the interviewer. Turgenev could feel the temperature plummet and cold wind blow out of the television. Silently, war had been declared. Even he knew that if you made an interviewer look stupid on live TV, they'd bring out the big guns.

And the interviewer did. "Look. It's a straightforward question for the country's leading expert. Could we have a straightforward answer, please?" And if the big guns didn't work, then the interviewer would cheerfully tear the professor to pieces with her bare hands.

The academic retorted, "It's not a straightforward answer. You're trying to bring many different and unrelated issues, and you want a simple answer. This isn't a binary issue...it's not yes or no. It's more a question of yes or no to a whole range of sub-issues."

The interviewer had seen weakness in her victim's response and went for the kill, but the academic fought back. Turgenev checked Kuznetsov. His face remained impassive, but the back of his neck was turning pink, then red, finally darkening to a raging purple, like a cartoon thermometer set to explode.

Turgenev continued watching. He still didn't understand what she was talking about, but he could see how the small blond professor was getting increasingly combative in her response, having seemingly decided to elaborate sufficiently in her answers to highlight the extent to which the questions she was being asked were matters that she thought any fool should understand. And like the balance on a set of scales, as her authority rose, Turgenev could see Kuznetsov's spirits seem to fall.

Kuznetsov spat out a few words, looking like a man both disgusted and disappointed. A man who could not be consoled. Turgenev went to speak but stopped himself, instead returning to the elevator.

four

"The man is a menace."

"And good afternoon to you, Boniface." Veronica's head remained down as she lifted her eyes to look up from her desk. "I'm busy. Can we do this later?"

The room was as Boniface remembered—the walls, painted a delicate shade of yellow, almost bordering on gold under a white ceiling, with lights hanging from the beams encasing the building's steel skeleton. Veronica sat in her corner office behind her understated but functional cherry-wood desk, positioned as if to brace the corner of the building. Her chair—leather, and the model of comfort—was backed into the outside corner.

Square windows to her left and right provided a view over the London's West End. For the second time that day, Boniface gazed at Big Ben. When he was with Kuznetsov in the Observatory, the clock tower beside the Houses of Parliament was more than 600 feet below them. Now, somewhere around 200 feet below Kuznetsov's Observatory, the change in perspective made the face of that most iconic landmark more readily visible, like a carriage clock on a low table.

Backed against one outside wall and obliquely facing the desk sat an armchair. Again leather. Again designed for comfort, but chosen so that whoever sat there was not placed at a psychological disadvantage. On the near side of the room was a meeting table, again made from cherry wood and surrounded by six leather-upholstered chairs, three on either side. Against the far wall, growing in large terracotta pots standing on the dark green carpet, three Acers—Japanese Maples—each about four feet high, were just coming into leaf. Mounted on the wall, squeezed in the corner diagonally opposite her desk and just inside the doorway, a television was showing 24-hour news on one of the Murdoch channels.

Boniface ignored his former wife's preoccupation. "He's a complete menace. This isn't a kid who likes to pull legs off spiders. This is a man who has grown up and wants to pull limbs off human beings. This is someone intent on the power play." He dropped his briefcase on the floor and slumped into the leather armchair across from Veronica's desk. "Call me Vanya, he says. Vanya. Russian for Johnny."

Veronica sighed as Boniface continued.

"Vanya. And then he says, 'When I am at home, people call me by my full name, Ivan Konstantinovich Kuznetsov, as a mark of respect, but my friends call me Vanya, so you should call me Vanya, too.' And apparently I'm Sasha. That's the diminutive of Alexander, you know. I tried to tell him that only my mother calls me Alexander, but that only seemed to set him off on another course—no, in Russia she would call me Alexander when she was scolding me. Then there's what's-his-name? The shaven-headed one with the big boots."

"Turgenev," said Veronica, making some notes on the document in front of her.

"Turgenev. Right bloody charmer he is. Head of Security? Yeah... thug-in-chief, more like. Stares at you through those eyes with no life, making it quite clear that if he wants you dead, then you're dead. And then there are his mates who all dress the same. I know you said Kuznetsov has security, but you didn't tell me he has a private army."

Veronica deliberately put down her pen and looked directly at Boniface. "New suit?"

"Yup."

"But still the same tailor?" She nodded as if confirming her approval. "Well, you're looking good for it. Just don't go and put on weight—or grow any taller."

Boniface leaned forward. "Kuznetsov does know this is an unwinnable war, doesn't he? He does know he's not going to get a referendum—and if he does get a referendum, he'll never win?" He tried to keep the exasperation out of his voice. "Am I meant to take him seriously when he says that he thinks *The Murder of Henry VIII* will, and I quote, *help to inflame the national consciousness*?"

Veronica reached to her right and pulled out two cut-glass tumblers from her desk. "Sure I can't tempt you back to the dark side?" Boniface slowly shook his head. "Or rather, are you sure I can't tempt you back into the light? You seem to have chosen to hide in the shadows since you stopped. But I guess that's where your demons live."

"Can we not have that argument again? Please." Boniface kept his voice calm.

Veronica's face softened as she filled the bottom of her tumbler and placed the bottle on her desk without replacing the cap.

"It's all about disappointment, Boniface. Don't disappoint the man." She took a sip. "And I mean don't disappoint him, ever. Don't think that because you've done exactly what he asked you to do—and more—he will be happy, because he won't be. For him, disappointment is measured in the moment. If something goes wrong and he thinks you're the one who disappointed him, then life is shit. Well, on a good day your life is shit; on a bad day..." she trailed off.

"So you've got me a job, and all I can do is disappoint this menace with his own private army of dead-eyed psychopaths." Boniface's throat tightened, his voice straining.

Veronica took another sip. "Look, we both do things for money.

We're two of a kind. You're unemployable, so you had to set up your own agency, and I'm working for the only person I can work for—there are no other options for me. The only way forward is to persuade the big man to carve out a new role for me overseeing several papers, and then I might be able to move up a few more floors."

She pointed to the ceiling as she walked around to the front of her desk and sat, her hands folded on her lap, holding her tumbler. "I got you the job because you need the money. You do still need money?"

Boniface looked down. "Lots." He blushed. "And fast. How quickly will they pay once I send my invoice?"

"What's gone wrong now?" she asked.

He sighed deeply, resigned to admitting his folly. "I borrowed money."

A look of disappointment spread across Veronica's face.

Boniface winced. "I wasn't that stupid, but I needed money to get the office, and I'm not a good risk for the banks given my...shall we say... history."

"What did you do?" Her voice was disapproving but resigned to acceptance.

"I borrowed what I thought was family money." Boniface felt the self-criticism twist his gut. "But my kindly lender was happy to take risks and liked to gamble, and one evening, finding himself rather short, he used my loan as a stake. Lost. And the winner sold the debt on to a gentlemen who has decided it's time to call in the loan."

Veronica raised her eyebrows. "When?"

"Today."

"No. I mean when do they want their money back?"

"Today." Boniface was more emphatic. "And to make sure I really understood the message, they put holes in my office wall, and now I need a new receptionist." He exhaled loudly. "But let's not dwell on that."

"Focus on the job, Boniface, and you'll get paid."

"But..."

Veronica stopped Boniface with a look that he knew she had honed over many years. He sat in silence as she took another sip before continuing. "All you have to do is avoid failure." She waited, watching, as if calibrating his understanding. "And as long as you avoid failure, everything will be fine. As you've said, how hard can it be to babysit a professor? You hardly need danger money, unless you count the danger of getting bored to death."

"Or annoyed beyond reason." Boniface recalled his conversation with the professor as he waited to meet Kuznetsov. "He's very annoying. You will visit me in jail if I can't resist the compulsion to ring his scrawny little neck?"

Veronica frowned, slowly tilting her head from side to side as if weighing up the request. "Look, Boniface, Kuznetsov is fighting this battle on many fronts—you just have to make sure that your front isn't the place where the enemy breaks through. The rest of us are out in the trenches too, each with our separate campaign. I'm trying to undermine the royals, and others are making the arguments for representative democracy."

Boniface laughed. "Like he cares about democracy."

Veronica looked hurt, narrowing her eyes at the unnecessary barb. "All you have to do is make sure the message gets out that Henry VIII was murdered and so all the so-called descendants are impostors and crooks, or whatever it is Kuznetsov wants to call them. Hold the party line and make sure that nothing goes wrong. Make sure you can't be identified as being the reason he couldn't get a referendum."

He looked down, staring at the carpet, and didn't notice the man walking in. "Oh. I'm sorry." Boniface looked toward the voice. He didn't know the man, but he recognized the type on sight—longtime journalist, probably quite good in his day, but drank too much and couldn't hack it, so now he had been given a courtesy title—deputy something that sounds important—to make him feel good, and he would stay in the office and remain employed until he ceased to be useful.

Since he wasn't out on the streets, he had become fatter, and the cheap suit—the same suit he wore every day with a jacket that lived on the back of his seat so it looked like he was in the office even when he was in the pub—was now so tight that his gut flopped over the top of his belt, which was open as far as possible. It was impossible for his shirt to circumnavigate his stomach, so it was always at least partially untucked. "I'm sorry. I didn't realize you were...er... Give me a call when you're, you know..." He turned and rolled away.

"What are you up to?" asked Boniface as the unhealthy specimen departed.

Veronica raised the side of her lip in a dismissive sneer and casually waived her hand as she stood.

"Your man had a picture of Oscar—Sherborne's kid, Oscar—on the top of the file he was holding." Boniface's ex-wife shrugged. "You can't go after him again, not after you accused him of being the father of that child and then had to print the retraction."

"You know that wasn't me, Boniface. I was on holiday when that broke."

"I know. And don't get me wrong, Oscar is a noxious little spoiled brat, and I spent years trying to bury Sherborne—you know—and you know that I still want to get him, and my new friend Vanya would reward me well if I could stab Sherborne in the back for him. And I'd take that job—Sherborne was the one that took me from broken-down alcoholic, to unemployed alcoholic, to unemployable."

"Unemployable and divorced. I know, Boniface." There was a slight coloration in her cheeks. "You will remember we were married at the time."

"I know. I'm sorry." He paused. "But for all he did to hurt me...to hurt us... I never tried to get at Sherborne by attacking his kid, or at least, the guy we think—but have never been able to prove—is his kid."

Veronica sat down behind her desk and stared at Boniface, seemingly willing him silent, before she carried on in a soft, measured voice. "We're going after Oscar von Habsburg, not because of any rumor about his daddy, but because after tonight we will have proof of his criminal business deals. We've known his partner is dirty for a while, but we also know that Oscar doesn't have the wit to stay alive in the drug trade. After tonight we should be able to prove that his club is taking a cut from the dealers it lets trade on its premises. Not only is this a great scoop, but it helps Kuznetsov." Boniface frowned quizzically. "We don't know for sure who his daddy is, but we know who mummy is."

Boniface's mouth dropped open as he tried to speak. "Heidi. Princess Heidemarie."

"And if we can find a way to embarrass the royal family through proof that the junior royals are...well, let's be frank, criminals, then I get a gold star from Kuznetsov. I'll get another gold star when you succeed, because I brought you in for the job, and I need all the gold stars I can get at the moment."

"Well, no one's giving me a gold star," said Boniface, rising from his seat. "However, they will send thugs with shaved heads and big boots if I don't get to Hampton Court to hold Nigel's hand at the launch. And then maybe Kuznetsov's guys could help me with the small matter of the outstanding loan?"

Veronica smiled. "I'm here all evening. As you've figured, I'm not going home until the snare has tightened around Oliver and the first edition has been put to bed, so call me if you want a chat. If I'm not around, it probably means I'm upstairs having something to eat with the big man. I'm in favor while I'm earning gold stars."

"Upstairs? The Cloud Club? Very impressive. Playing with the big boys."

"Indeed. Floor sixty-six." Veronica emptied her glass as Boniface left.

five

Turgenev was already walking to his office as the gold elevator doors opened. The boss was angry, and he should be the man to fix it for him. Kuznetsov's words had been clear and unambiguous, and had not required any discussion or elaboration, or even a response from Turgenev: "Professor Armstrong must cease to be an irritant to me."

This was an easy job and one where he could show what he could achieve and how he could be trusted. He paused. Should he check with the boss?

No.

It was time to move up, and an opportunity like this didn't present itself very often.

This was the smart strategy. Sure, he could ask for more responsibility, more pay, his own share, funding for a business, but why should he? And why should he force Ivan Konstantinovich Kuznetsov to consider such a request? Kuznetsov had already given him a position of responsibility, and he was trusted; to ask for more would be disrespectful. But if—through his own initiative and actions—he demonstrated that he could be more useful, then that took the risk out of the boss's decision.

Turgenev put on a pair of latex gloves; opened his safe; flicked through a stack of Russian passports, dropping one on his desk before he replaced the pile; and took out a pistol. He checked the magazine, firmly pressing it back into the gun, which he placed on his desk before closing and locking the safe.

With two clicks of a mouse, he had a travel website open. With a few key taps he had the flight to Moscow Sheremetyevo selected. He input the details of the traveler and his passport reference, clicked through to the payment page, lifted the receiver on his phone, and dialed a familiar number.

"Yuri. Mikhail. I need a clean credit card number...no, not much, two-hundred-and-thirty-three...pounds sterling... No, it must be clean and not traced back to us...a flight, to be taken tomorrow morning; after that I don't care if they find that the card was stolen." Turgenev input the card details and clicked the pay button. "Perfect. Thank you, Yuri. Payment authorized." He hung up and printed out the receipt and boarding pass, adding them to the pile with the passport and the gun.

He unlocked his bottom desk drawer, took out a set of car keys and a phone, then rummaged in the top drawer of his desk and pulled out a list of names and phone numbers. Halfway down the list he found the number he wanted; marking his place on the list with his left hand, Turgenev programmed the number into the phone with his right.

Turning back to his computer, he called up another website, entered the phone number, then clicked the mouse and waited. About fifteen seconds later, the phone beeped. He opened the SMS message, followed the instructions to acknowledge it, and turned back to his computer, clicking the maps link on the open webpage. A map of central London loaded with St Giles' Circus in the middle. An arrow appeared, moving toward the center of the map, coming to rest on the Silver Spike.

He placed the phone on his pile of unrelated objects, which was now beginning to look like a child's memory game.

One of the advantages of working for a man who owned a number of newspapers was intelligence—or as the newspaper staff preferred to call it, the Oracle. The papers kept huge databases about anyone who had ever blipped on the public's radar for whatever reason. Scoutmasters who liked little boys, sportsmen who liked white powder, and little old ladies who liked to grow flowers in their garden—they were all there with their details logged and cross-referenced with any and every other piece of information that the paper could get hold of, whether that be voter registrations, credit scores, or anything that came at a price. It all went into the database, and then all anyone had to do was click a button, and the data was there. And not simply there—it had been verified from multiple sources, making it as accurate as any information was likely to be.

In the case of someone like Professor Armstrong, it wasn't hard to pinpoint the individual Turgenev was looking for. First, there was the name. Check. The profession. Check. Recent media interest. Check. Publications. Check. Which all pointed to one person at one address. Turgenev looked back to his screen, opened Google Maps, and put in the address. Almost perfect, go west, drop south over Kew Bridge, into Richmond, and you were virtually at the front door. The route out was equally straightforward. Keep going on the main road into Kingston, turn right, go over the river, and then it was a pretty straight route to Heathrow.

GPS systems could be unreliable in the field. They broke; they gave the wrong route; they gave directions in English, which didn't help if your man barely spoke the language; they could be hacked and tracked; and most significantly, they left a history. They left a trail of breadcrumbs that could be traced, and if you were stopped, it was really hard to get rid of a whole GPS unit with the route stored deep in the memory. Paper was far more reliable, and if anything went wrong, the evidence could be destroyed. A single page could be burned or eaten—quickly and completely.

Turgenev went to his shelves and picked the top copy from his pile of London street atlases. It was an old and tattered edition, barely holding itself together. He checked the location in the index and opened to page 183, comparing the map to the image on the screen. He took a pen and marked "Professor Armstrong," putting an X to mark her house and writing the address on the page, then snapped the book shut and watched as a few loose pages fluttered to the floor. He picked them up, looked them over, and dropped them in the trash.

He grabbed a large envelope and delicately filled it with the gun, the atlas, the boarding pass, the phone, the car keys, and the passport, and then folded the top twice to close it before throwing his gloves into the trash on top of the discarded map pages. Then, with a click of his mouse, he switched off his computer.

six

Boniface was caught between the stone balustrade and the angry rush-hour traffic, threading his way through the directionless tourists meandering in the opposite direction over Hampton Court Bridge toward Hampton Court train station.

The sun-baked path was still radiating heat, and even after the early evening breeze skimming off the river had washed away some of the closeness, Boniface could still feel his shirt sticking to his back under his jacket.

Walking down from the bridge, he turned through the pillars of the outer gate—a lion on one side of the entrance and a unicorn guarding the other—to face Hampton Court Palace as he started on the path from the outer perimeter of the grounds to the main gate. He crunched down the broad stone track before spinning and returning to seek out the guard, who was bound to be in the hut by the outer gate.

He found him. A tall man in his seventies with good posture. Probably former military—in other words, a man who understood logistics and who could be reasoned with, but who wouldn't mess around. Boniface introduced himself and chatted for a few moments. The war stories started. Definitely an ex-soldier.

When it was polite to move on, Boniface asked his question. "We've got some cabs arriving to pick up our guests from the event tonight; they should be ready to leave around eight-thirty. Can you send them straight through to wait outside the Great Hall?"

"I'm sorry, sir. We don't allow vehicles through the main gate." Boniface waited to see whether a compromise was offered. "But what I can do for you is get them to line up on this side of the main gate. That space to the right, overlooking the river..." He pointed to the main gate to the Palace at the other end of the entrance drive. "If we do that, your guests only have to walk across the courtyard from the Great Hall, rather than come all the way out here."

Boniface stuck out his hand. "Deal." The guard shook it, and Boniface recommended the long walk to the main gate with the comfort that a cab would carry him back when he left.

As he reached the Palace and passed under the arch of the main gate, he checked the time on his phone—less than 30 minutes to make sure everything was in order—and looked up to see Nigel. How could he do it? How could someone so intelligent be so stupid? How could someone who dedicated his whole life to understanding and interpreting nuances miss the obvious? How could someone who had written extensively about how the outer appearance is a metaphor for the inner manifestation of power be so unaware of his own appearance?

Boniface remembered the conversation with Nigel, virtually word for word. "So you're going to get a new suit for the book launch."

"Of course."

"And you understand what this suit needs to do for you."

"I do."

"You understand that you need something classic. It shouldn't be on the cutting edge of fashion."

"Do you see me as male-model material, Boniface?"

"Equally, it shouldn't give off that dusty-professor-who-only-wears-tweed-that-he-acquired-through-inheritance type vibe."

"Believe me, I've met those professors, and I'm not like that."

"And it shouldn't be what you wear on a day-to-day basis."

"Like this jacket," Nigel had said, indicating the dull sand-colored corduroy jacket with patches on the elbows that he was wearing at the time. "It will be nothing like this."

"Great. But you do understand this is quite a tough balancing act. Modern, but not too modern, and certainly not fashion-victim modern. Showing personality, you don't want to be bland, but not showing too much personality. Serious, in no way frivolous or open to ridicule. It's all about getting the balance right."

"I understand."

Now this. Nigel had called him when he got his new suit. "I did exactly what you told me," he proudly confirmed, and Boniface had relaxed.

Mistake.

He should have checked the suit. He should have made sure someone was there when Nigel went shopping. No, that wouldn't have worked; he should have sent Nigel to his own tailor—that would have been the only way to keep control of this situation.

And who still sold suits like this? In the twenty-first century? Who still made corduroy? Surely these suits were banned by some sort of United Nations convention at the same time that landmines or biological warfare agents were banned. And what color was that? It certainly wasn't one that appeared in nature. It wasn't blue, it wasn't gray, and it wasn't slate, but there were elements of all. Equally, there were hints of green and brown in there, maybe even some red, but no single identifiable color, and no color you could name to suggest the tone. Perhaps it looked good in a nightclub or under the lighting that technicians had in those crime-scene programs?

But this was all irrelevant. There was a book to be launched; the guests had been invited and were on their way. And the first task was to deal with the grinning idiot in that repellent suit, and to stop him from talking about whatever stupid things he'd been up to today with the police.

The police.

That last conversation with Nigel—"I've been helping the police with their inquiries"—came flooding back to Boniface.

"Nigel. Good to see you." Like all good PR men, he could lie on cue. Heck, he didn't even realize he was doing it and didn't feel guilt or remorse. Boniface looked him in the eye; it was time to be reassuring and to calm Nigel's over-excitement, which was radiating like nuclear waste.

So what was the best strategy here? Probably best to lance the boil, let all the puss spill out, and then get some disinfectant and put a sterile dressing over the wound. "So tell me about your adventures with the police."

Nigel excitedly began recounting his day, and at the point where Boniface felt that the only two options were physical violence toward Nigel or returning to his life as an alcoholic, he stopped him. "Quite an adventure. Now look, for tonight—*just for tonight*—it's probably best that you don't mention this tale. There are going to be a lot of journalists—drunk journalists, drunk and lazy journalists—around here tonight. You mention that you were at the police station today, and the next thing you know...well, you can guess."

"But you haven't heard the best part," whined Nigel. "I have now seen the evidence..."

Boniface cut him short. "Whatever you have seen, we can't reprint the book within the next ten minutes, can we?" This was progress; Nigel no longer emitted unrelenting excitement. "We need to remember what we're here to do. And we're here to do one thing: to sell your book."

Nigel perked up; the subject had moved back to him. Boniface pushed forward before Nigel could start talking. "There's only one thing we need to think about for tonight, and that's your chat about your book."

"Yes."

"Now, please tell me you've got something prepared as we discussed."

"Yes."

"You've practiced it, and remembered it, so it feels like it's a natural conversation. This isn't a lecture; you're only saying a few words. Casually, off the cuff; only you and I need to know you've prepared."

"Yes, yes."

"And these informal and casual comments have no jokes."

"Well...you can't not have jokes."

"You can. Cut them." Nigel's rising enthusiasm seemed undaunted. "And you're sure that you won't speak for longer than three minutes."

"Yes."

"And you confirmed this by saying your speech out loud, including pauses for you to breathe and breaks to acknowledge audience feedback?"

"Yes."

Which probably meant no, but in reality Boniface knew that Nigel would most likely dry up after about 90 seconds. However, everyone who turned up to one of these events understood the rules. You got free food and free drink in an interesting venue, and you got to meet some other interesting guests and do a bit of networking. The price was that you had to listen to some tedious author meander through the story behind his book, then laugh and clap at the appropriate place. The PR would keep it short and jump in, as Boniface would do with Nigel if—or should that be *when*—it looked like Nigel was losing the audience's charity.

"Now clearly, the chat is your big piece, and I'll introduce you. But before that, you need to circulate. You want to meet everybody, and that means you need to keep moving. Don't spend any more than three minutes with any one person. For tonight, everything's limited to three minutes."

Nigel smiled. Good. He had got away with justifying the three-minute rule when all he wanted to say was: Don't spend more than three minutes with anyone, because you're a tedious dullard and everyone will want to wring your scrawny neck. But perhaps he could soften the blow: "You need to do enough to convince them that you're an expert. Move in, radiate gravitas"—he could see that Nigel liked that idea—"and then move on before you get into any in-depth questioning."

"But isn't this about the in-depth questioning?" Nigel seemed worried.

It was time to have the serious talk. "No. We don't do in-depth. Remember, drunk, lazy journalists looking for an easy story. They can only understand one thing. They think they're smart and they think they can multitask." Boniface shook his head firmly. "They can't."

Nigel seemed to be understanding the concept. "Give them one message and only one message. Don't confuse them by telling them what you know. Tell them what they need to know to write their story, and then your book will sell millions and you can buy another new suit...or perhaps a car. Do it right, and by the end of the week you can buy yourself a Ferrari."

"But I've got a car," Nigel was whining again. "A 2CV." Boniface knew what was coming. A history lecture from a historian about the worst car ever made. A car designed for French peasants and taken to their hearts by vegetarians. Great for French peasants, awful for London, where any crash would guarantee immediate death as the whole contraption dissolved into dust and a few rusty component parts. A few smart ads in the 1980s, but production had long since ended.

Boniface jumped at the only option he knew. "Then you can get another. Perhaps get a whole fleet. Get them restored. Pay for a garage to store them all."

He waited for Nigel to mentally process the image of a fleet of French vegi-mobiles and continued. "So you're happy? You know what we're doing?"

"Certainly." Nigel had given him this unwavering confirmation before, and what had happened next?

That suit.

"Then we've got radio tomorrow and the TV interviews the day after, and I'll be with you through all of these. But tonight is all about you."

Nigel beamed. "Now, where are we set up?" asked Boniface, looking for any excuse to get away from that awful suit, wondering where he could emigrate to in order to hide from his new friend Vanya, who was sure to be very disappointed very soon.

seven

The elevator reached street level and Turgenev stepped into the central concourse walled with flamed Moroccan marble. The triangular floor plan funneled people left, right, and forward, giving an immediate impetus to move.

He gripped the envelope containing the tools of the mission and headed out of the central entrance, as he always did casting a glance back to his left, the Porsche showroom, and behind him on his right, the Ferrari showroom. The Rolls-Royce showroom at the back of the building was of less interest, but perhaps he might acquire a taste once he had his own chauffeur?

The Silver Spike stood on its own island—which for some reason he didn't understand they called St Giles' Circus—and traffic found its way around, but with typical English town-planning priorities there was no clear path through this untidy conjunction of island and roads. A mishmash of bad compromises that black-cab drivers alone seemed able to divine how to navigate.

He checked the traffic and moved forward, finding gaps created by the panic of tired taxi drivers afraid to hit a pedestrian and lose an evening's income explaining the accident to the police. Reaching the far side, he walked up Tottenham Court Road through the mass of people, some heading somewhere, some heading nowhere, all moving slowly in the fading heat of the early summer afternoon. He passed the theatre, which was still showing a musical based on the songs from a famous 1970s rock band, and took the first right into the quiet of a side street.

Great Russell Street had a different character with a mixture of cheap construction crammed against decaying Georgian terraces, office fronts, and a few business hotels where the architecture had been sympathetically restored to follow the Georgian origins. Nestled about halfway down on the right was Sodom and Gomorrah, where the two doormen ushered him inside.

As Turgenev was subsumed into the belly of the club, he lost contact with daylight and any other outward signs that might suggest the time of day, or even that there was any world outside the sealed bubble.

The only sign of time passing was the women around him, who he could see visibly age as he watched. Years of extreme sun and tanning beds, frequent and cheap cosmetic surgery, cheap food eaten infrequently and at odd hours, diets to keep a figure, nicotine as a food substitute, alcohol, alcohol as a food substitute, party drugs, drug addictions, harsh chemical treatments in the name of beauty from skincare and hair products had aged these women. They were like the result of some bizarre Nazi research experiment where through inhuman treatment, twenty years of research data could be generated within three years of what passed for a normal routine.

Some of the younger ones had yet to develop the rhino-hide skin, but it was only a matter of days before regular moisturizing could no longer mask the accelerated passing of time.

While they fought the aging battle, they had already lost another battle: They were here. Some would be paying off family debt at home, others would have come for promises of bright lights and modeling careers. All would have been lied to. All would have been given enough drugs to become addicted. Most would have been beaten, and all would eventually work to start paying what was owed—and once the debt was satisfied, most then stayed in the only place where they could find some sort of security, with the twisted form of camaraderie that is shared between victims of a natural disaster or a terrorist outrage.

Turgenev knew better than to look into their eyes; the eyes would always sparkle back. But that was a conditioned response. When you looked closely, you could see that the sparkle was a cover, and usually the result of eye drops to combat the effect of air conditioning. Underneath there was nothing. Not life, not death; nothing. He had seen this before when he was a soldier. Even the new kids who got shipped in had the look of a broken and defeated conscript army. They had gone beyond the hurt, the loss, the bereavement, the fear, the terror, the anger, and they had reached nothing. Whatever had connected their soul to their body had snapped, and their body just moved around.

Turgenev had once dreamed of owning a club like this, and Kuznetsov would probably set him up in business if he asked for his help.

But not now.

Now he could see the cliché: pretty girls, fast cars, and people spending other people's money. Now he could see it would be like commanding another army of conscripts again. Instead, he wanted freedom. He wanted to break free from the ties of loyalty that, in truth, were ties of fear, and Professor Armstrong had given him a way to take that first step to establish his independence.

The pounding beat of 1980s hair metal was oppressive but useful, and while a Whitesnake power ballad played over the sound system, explaining unsubtle horizontal ambitions, no microphone would be able to hear his conversation.

He looked around the room; the men either wore business suits or boots, jeans, and leather jackets. Sitting in the far corner was the man with the scar across his face. Turgenev held his gaze, breaking when the man acknowledged the unspoken order.

"Get a room; I'm going to give you a private dance." The man with the scar turned and led Turgenev toward the back of the club. Two men with tuxedos and bowties stood guard over a narrow passage, not moving as the man with the scar approached. With a backward tilt of his head he indicated the higher power, stepping out of the line of sight of the guardians so they could see Turgenev.

"Room three," said the gatekeeper, stiffening as Turgenev passed.

As the two men walked into the burgundy-painted room, Turgenev shut the door behind him and looked up at the security camera on the wall above the door. "Put your jacket over that." The man with the scar complied, and in an exaggerated gesture, like an unctuous waiter, Turgenev offered a seat on the leather banquette spanning the back wall of the small room.

Closing the door had muffled the sound, making it slightly less bright but still as loud. Turgenev sat close to the man with the scar so he could be heard without needing to shout. "You're going home tomorrow morning, but I've got a job for you first. A job that must be completed tonight."

He unwrapped the two folds at the top of the envelope, pushed the sides so the mouth opened, and offered the aperture to the other man, who removed each object in turn, placing it on the only other piece of furniture in the room—a small table, still sticky with spilled drinks and whatever other fluids had been spilled by the previous occupants of the room. "Put the gun in your jacket. We don't want anyone getting a surprise, do we?"

When the man with the scar had sat down again, Turgenev continued. "Page one-eight-three in the atlas." The man with the scar opened the map book, put a finger to the name and address written on the page, and returned his concentration to the shaven-headed man. "Professor Armstrong must cease to be an irritant to someone who is very important to both of us. Professor Armstrong must cease to be an irritant permanently, and tonight."

The man with the scar nodded his affirmation.

"Listen. This is what you will do." The man with the scar focused on Turgenev. "Take the car: It's a little red Toyota, completely anonymous, no one will notice you. Drive to Richmond."

The man with the scar nodded, glancing back to the map and running his finger over the page.

"When the professor returns, complete the task. You're a good shot, but this is a residential area, so get next to the professor before you pull the trigger. You need to be fast, accurate, and achieve the outcome with the minimum of fuss. Shoot once, then leave. Drive slowly; you've got plenty of time before the flight. You're on the first flight that's available, but it doesn't leave until nine-thirty tomorrow morning, so you've got the whole night."

Turgenev cocked his head toward the map, holding his finger away from the page while pointing. "Drive out this way and then get something to eat. You can stop around here; there's bound to be somewhere suitable. I want you to stay close in case there are any other loose ends that need to be tied up. You've got the phone; I'll call you if I need."

The man with the scar gave a confident nod.

"When you've found somewhere to eat, then call the number that has been programmed into the phone. And you know the drill if you get caught: Eat the SIM card so that no one finds the number. The number is for some friends of ours. They don't know what's going to happen, but it's important that they are the first to find out about the professor's accident. They will then report the professor's sad demise."

Turgenev persisted. "When you've had something to eat, drive into Kingston. You see, it's a straight road. Go under the railway bridge and turn right." The man with the scar followed the directions on the map. "When you get to the bridge over the Thames, stop and drop the gun. Then it's an easy route to the airport."

The man with the scar on his face looked at the map, flipping pages as he followed the road to Heathrow.

"Leave the car on a street. Somewhere away from the airport. Somewhere away from CCTV. A quiet residential street, something like that. Then walk to the airport, but don't get there too early. Flights start landing from six in the morning, so after that time it should be much easier to blend in. Leave the phone under the driver's seat. We'll track it, get the car, and make sure everything is cleaned up."

The man with the scar nodded. "One other thing," said Turgenev. "They're very suspicious about people without luggage, so make sure you take a full bag. If there's anything you can't fit in or don't want to carry, leave it, and I'll get Sergey to send it."

Turgenev stood, and the man with the scar scrambled to his feet. "Thank you, my friend. Your dedication is appreciated and will be rewarded." The two men embraced. "Who is your favorite?" He tipped his head backward in the direction of the noise.

"Kristalle," said the man with the scar. "But her real name's Olga."

"Well, she is going to give you a very special going-away present. My treat to you my friend. Here's..." Turgenev took the cash out of his back pocket and started to count it. "Two hundred and fifty pounds. I will pay, but you can look like a hero to her when you give her a tip. And here's another fifty for your dinner tonight," he said, giving the man with the scar his last bill.

eight

The Great Hall, Hampton Court. Location of the first documented performance of Shakespeare's *Macbeth*, and tonight, the location of the launch of Professor Nigel Trudgett's new book, *The Murder of Henry VIII*.

Henry would be weeping with the decline.

Nigel had explained the theory several times, and each time Boniface cared less. There was no grave for Wolsey—Cardinal Wolsey, the King's chief administrator and trusted confidant—so any stories about Wolsey's death were simply rumors to explain away his disappearance. He disappeared so that he could metamorphose into the King. Not being within the line of succession, he couldn't become King by inheritance, so he had to take the role through a bit of sixteenth-century identity theft, which also involved a swift murder. As Nigel was forever saying: "Have you ever seen a picture of a slim Wolsey? But you've seen a picture of a slim Henry and a fat Wolsey? Okay, now join the dots."

Boniface looked up. He had been here as a kid, and looking at the ceiling he still found it stunning today. Even though he vaguely knew the building—and he had read the guidebooks and checked out Wikipedia's references to the *sumptuously decorated hammer-beam roof* when he prepared the invitations—as he stood right underneath it, breathlessly looking up, he marveled at how impressive it was, and how impressive it must have been for the thousands of people who ate under this roof when Henry reigned.

He stood, fixated on how the crossbeams appeared to have had their middle section cut out. Each end of the protruding beam was then supported by curved braces meeting the wall below, and the arched ceiling was balanced on top of these supported beams. The detailing was exquisite; Boniface could find no other word. It was like a doll's house but more intricate and bigger, much bigger—as in probably the biggest of its kind when it was built—and it had survived for more than 500 years.

Around the walls hung tapestries. Nigel had told Boniface that these showed the story of Adam and that they had been restored for a huge cost. Tens of millions spent on restoring something that, while it was hugely impressive, had been rendered pointless by central heating, Swedish furniture stores, and cheap labor in Vietnam.

His contemplation of the treasures of the Palace was disturbed by the caterer. Bloody prima donna. She stood in a room like this—self-obsessed and yet lacking the self-awareness to see her own lack of talent—and thought what she created was art. You put her next to true beauty and grace, and she just couldn't see it. At the planning meeting Boniface had lost interest. He'd said finger food; the managing editor had suggested finger food with a Tudor twist.

Boniface didn't even know what that meant. Swan vol-au-vents perhaps? Mini sparrow pies? Spit-roast stag, washed down with a flagon of the finest mead? Figuring the catering shouldn't affect how the book was reviewed in the papers, he left the catering arrangements to the managing editor, who had apparently delegated the task to her secretary—an arrangement Boniface was now regretting.

He turned away, trying to concentrate.

Time for a final run-through of the mental checklist. Most things seemed covered; there were stacks of books, and someone had even taken them out of the boxes and laid them on the table. A table...fabulous. A small raised stage, so everyone could see Nigel.

And where was he? People were starting to arrive.

It was stunning how someone so non-descript could be so completely defined by a single clothing choice. Nigel was five-foot-three and slightly built, made even slighter by his hunched shoulders. His hair, usually greasy, was only lank today, and like the rest of him, his clean-shaven face had no distinguishing features, but for Boniface, finding Nigel was as easy as finding an emergency beacon tied to the end of his own nose. "They like the suit," Nigel said, beaming like a six-year-old who has been told he looks exactly like Superman when he wears his underwear on the outside.

"Huh?" This wasn't the line Boniface was expecting.

"I was standing behind those people there"—Boniface looked at a cluster who had seemed particularly keen to get to the wine—"and the blond one"—the overly-peroxided one, thought Boniface—"said 'Love the suit.' And she must mean it because she didn't even realize I was there."

Boniface didn't know where to begin in the explanation of the concept of sarcasm, so he moved on. "Well, it just goes to show, doesn't it, Nigel? But remember, it's like a party dress—now that everyone's seen the suit, they shouldn't see it again, so you will wear something different for the TV stuff, won't you?"

Before Nigel could do much more damage on a one-on-one basis, it was time for him to address the gathering. This was the PR equivalent of crop spraying with highly toxic insecticide: necessary, but there might be casualties, although of course all appropriate precautions would be taken.

Boniface led Nigel to the stage and watched as the bravado, bolstered by the apparent positive perception about his new suit, crumpled, like the suit without Nigel's insubstantial frame to hold it.

Boniface surveyed the unintelligible hum of human interaction echoing around the room, waiting as a polite hush settled over the gathering, leaving whispers, a few clinking glasses, and the sound of a caterer performing her art. After a few gentle jokes, Boniface introduced Nigel and stepped away to allow the audience to focus.

Surprisingly, Nigel seemed to have prepared quite well and engaged the audience much more successfully than Boniface had expected. He touched on most of the points he seemed to mention every time he opened his mouth...Henry VIII was murdered...by Wolsey...with the lead pipe in the conservatory, perhaps...no, apparently there was now evidence of a plot with Anne Boleyn...

Boniface guessed he must have misheard. Nigel had told him the Wolsey/Anne Boleyn story several times, but it was always a theory; there was never definitive evidence. No matter, Nigel was on a roll, so Boniface didn't need to pay too much attention, and he casually moved next to the pile of books. This was the first time he had held a copy; until now he had only seen pictures of the cover.

He picked up a copy from the nearest pile, felt the weight, and flicked through a few pages. He was surprised: Somehow, it looked much more impressive than he was expecting. He turned to the back cover.

Henry VIII came to the English throne on 22 April 1509 at the age of 17, following the death of his father, King Henry VII.

The new King was a fit, good-looking, clean-shaven man with a passion for sport. He was a world-class tennis player, a skilled archer, and an accomplished horseman who would take on all-comers during a joust. He also enjoyed fishing and hunting.

He was well educated and spoke several languages, as well as being a devout Catholic and a scholar of the Bible. His (Roman Catholic) Christian belief was shared with his devoted (Roman Catholic) wife, Catherine of Aragon.

While he keenly embraced the pomp and ceremony of the monarchy, the affairs of State did not interest the young King, except when it came to war. He was well regarded as a soldier and led his troops in battle, in particular against the French.

When he first became King, due to his age his aunt, Lady Margaret Beaufort, acted as regent and performed the duties of the monarch. When Henry reached the age of 18 and the full power of the monarchy was vested in him, he still had little interest in the day-to-day business of the state. Instead, he left the administration of the country to his advisers, in particular the most trusted among their number, Cardinal Wolsey.

So why is it, in the twenty-first century, 500 years after this young man came to the throne, that Henry VIII has a reputation for having six wives, for being morbidly obese, for being little more than a tyrannical dictator who was ready to put his enemies (and some of his wives) to death, and for breaking with the Roman Catholic Church, which led to the founding of the Church of England?

Or is the man in our history books not Henry VIII?

A bit long and a bit wordy, but an interesting question. If Boniface hadn't met Nigel and didn't know what a twat he was, then sure, he might be interested in the book. Until he read it, of course... If it was written anything like Nigel usually talked, then he wouldn't get past the first page without wanting to throw the book across the room in anger and frustration.

Boniface glanced up and calibrated the responses. The mood had shifted. Nigel paused and Boniface took two steps forward, catching the eyes of two or three people in the small gathering. The audience understood the cue and started clapping. "Congratulations, Nigel. Great speech. They loved it."

"But I..." Boniface hustled Nigel back into the crowd, leaving the academic to move like a hunter finishing off the lame animals who didn't run swiftly enough.

nine

"Thank you so much. You were great in there." Ellen tried to focus on the producer but found herself distracted watching the other woman who was tightly gripping a cup of coffee but sloshing the liquid as she scratched the back of her other hand. "I am so, so sorry that we kept you waiting for so long. I hope you can forgive us."

"It's not a problem; I'm pleased to have been able to help, and if it sells more books..." Ellen felt sheepish, cringing at how commercially she was thinking.

"Well, it's your website you've got to thank. When I looked at the map and saw how close you were, I figured it was worth giving you a call."

"It's my sister that takes all the credit there," said Ellen lightly. "I don't understand all these gizmos, but she seemed to think it was easy: She took me to the shops and told me which phone to buy, did something on the website, and well...now you know where I am."

"Anyway, it was a pleasure to meet you." The producer seemed unable to focus on Ellen and was twitchily looking around the corridor.

"No, the pleasure's all mine. It was a joy to be interviewed by someone with a grasp of the subject. And if you need me again, well..." She looked down, her cheeks beginning to redden. "You've got my number and you know how to find where I am."

"Thank you. I'm sure we'll want to call you again," said the producer. "Let me show you the way out."

Ellen walked out of the studio and onto Millbank, following the River Thames upstream; checked her watch; silently cursed; and pulled out her phone. "Nigel, hi... Yes, I've just left my last interview. I'm at least forty-five minutes away."

Ellen was surprised that Nigel didn't seem disappointed. Not even vaguely annoyed. Instead, he seemed preoccupied. He was hyped up, but even by his usual standards of over-excitedness, there was something much more important preoccupying him. He was desperate to talk but didn't want to talk on the phone.

She checked her watch again. "It'll be quicker for me to go straight home; I should be there in under thirty minutes. Why don't you finish up there, then come 'round and you can tell me all about your evening and whatever it is that's exciting you."

She held the phone away from her ear as Nigel's babbling excitement seemed to ratchet up another gear.

"I can't be too late... Mmm, that's right. I've got to be up at some ridiculously early time to meet Montbretia at Heathrow... No, still don't know what we're going to do, but we'll figure something out. Call me when you get close."

She held the phone in front of her and started typing a text message. "Hi Monty, Nigel really excited. Perhaps he's found a pot of gold!?! I'll let you know. Maybe he'll let us spend it :-) So looking forward to seeing you tomorrow. Love E."

She hit the send key.

ten

By the third loop of the Richmond one-way system, the man with the scar on his face had figured out how it worked. It had been easy to reach Richmond, but he seemed to spend longer driving around the town than he had getting there.

The car was where Turgenev had said it would be. The route he had set out was simple, and once he got out of that bloody loop thing in the middle of Richmond, the route up the hill was straightforward. As he reached the top, the villas on his left side looked like they had been constructed as part of a BBC period drama, but he guessed these must be the real thing that had inspired the TV set designers. To the right the hill fell away, and at the bottom meadows ran down to a river that curved along the side of the lush grass. It was like a picture postcard of what England was supposed to look like, but he had only driven a few miles from the heart of London. From there it was a short drive to Ham Common, where Turgenev had marked Professor Armstrong's house.

The north and south sides of Ham Common were bisected by a main road—the exit route specified by Turgenev, which led first to dinner and second to Kingston, where he was to go over the river and dispose of the gun.

The professor's house was easy to locate on the north side of the common. It was on a road that ran parallel to the loop road, separated by a strip of land about sixty feet wide with grass and a few trees. The building was a small semidetached cottage in a row where there were houses on only one side of the road, facing out across the common.

Having completed his reconnaissance and double-checked his exit routes, the man with the scar found a place to park his car outside a church on the common's perimeter road, about 100 yards away from the professor's house. There was a certain irony in parking next to a church when he had come for such an ungodly act, but it was secluded, with the surrounding trees and bushes offering some cover, and with no street-lights to highlight his presence.

He waited for a man with a white terrier to pass, then took out the gun Turgenev had given him at Sodom and Gomorrah. By force of habit, he removed the magazine, confirmed again that it was loaded, and returned the pistol to his jacket pocket. He checked the phone—not that he was expecting any calls, but it was another habit to make sure that he had a signal and enough power.

Having checked his tools, he was ready to get in position before the light faded. Looking to make sure the man with the white dog had gone, he got out of the car and stretched, surprised at how relaxed he felt. Turgenev was right; Kristalle had helped him to clear his mind. He could now focus.

Across from Professor Armstrong's house, the common was wooded with dense, prickly undergrowth. The man with the scar found an old tree stump in the minor suburban jungle and sat, waiting under the protection of the natural camouflage, ready to be at the front door as soon as the professor returned.

eleven

Boniface and Nigel followed the last few stragglers from the Great Hall into the cobbled courtyard between the third gate—which was apparently called Anne Boleyn's Gate—and the Palace main gate, which Nigel made sure everyone knew was actually called the Great Gatehouse, not to be confused with the gate on the outer boundary, which was a modern construct.

"So why is it called Anne Boleyn's Gate? I thought it was called the Clock Tower." Boniface regretted his question immediately but remained stunned by the majesty of this third gate's architecture. In the dark, the two octagonal towers on either side of the gate were less prominent, but three floors above the archway was the exquisitely decorated astrological clock, now floodlit and now commanding everyone to stop and pay attention to its beauty. Kuznetsov could learn something about using gold for effect if he paid a quick visit here.

Before Boniface had the chance to slap himself for his stupidity, Nigel's phone rang. He watched as Nigel seemed to go through the whole range of emotions: excitement, enthusiasm, disappointment, hope, and back to puppy-dog enthusiasm building to unrestrained excitement.

As they walked through the Great Gatehouse archway, Boniface saw the line of cabs confirming that his chat with the ex-soldier on the outer gate had been worthwhile. He said his goodbyes and thanks to the last few departures and stood between the last cab and his corduroy-clad tormentor with his fingers crossed. "You live quite close, don't you, Nigel?"

The professor ended his call and looked down at his phone. "Yes. Thames Ditton Island." A flash passed across Boniface's face, his raised eyebrows acknowledging his approval and his slight surprise that Nigel would live somewhere so unique. "It's just over a mile or so if you walk, less if you want to swim."

"I know it," said Boniface. "Well, I know *of* it. It's on the bend behind the pub. I've seen it many times, but I've never been onto the island."

Nigel beamed. "But I'm not going home right now."

"So where are you going, Nigel?"

"Ham Common. My friend Ellen..."

"Oh, that's fine. I'm going to Kingston. Jump in. I'll get out at the bottom of Kingston Hill, and you can take it round to Ham."

Nigel grinned again like an inane child and continued on his line that Boniface had interrupted. "My friend Ellen. I've mentioned her before, and you've probably seen her on TV: She's the English constitutional expert. I want to tell her what I found out today when I was at the police station."

Boniface opened the cab door and Nigel scampered in, continuing to fiddle with his phone as he had been since his call ended. "Kingston, please," said Boniface to the cabbie. "Foot of Kingston Hill for me, and then could you take his nibs on to Ham Common?" The cabbie raised his eyebrows wearily.

"So is she your girlfriend?"

"Who? No." Nigel seemed to be encouraging his phone to perform an important task.

"But you'd like her to be?" Boniface didn't know why he asked these questions. It was probably some knee-jerk reaction from his journalist days, as hard to give up as the drink.

Nigel shifted awkwardly in his seat but managed to revert to his earlier subject. "As I was trying to tell you earlier, Boniface, the police called me because they had this guy who had found himself stuck in a hole."

"But you're an expert on history, Nigel. In particular Tudor history—you've written a book about Henry VIII. Why did the police need your expertise on people stuck in holes? Have you been keeping your talents with a pickaxe hidden from me?"

The cab jerked away, heading for the outer gate. "Tudor history is my thing, so when the police found an intruder stuck in a hole in Hampton Court, and with 'old bits of paper,' as the sergeant called them..."

"Old bits of paper?"

"What I call priceless documents, Boniface. They prove I was right, and that there is an heir to Henry VIII. This means the book is out of date, which is great news: The book's out of date because we've now got evidence, real documentary proof, of the aftermath of the murder. We just need to find some more of these documents to complete the story. This guy in the hole had some of them when he was picked up, and he wasn't telling us where he found them."

All Boniface could hear were Kuznetsov's words bouncing around his head. The point of tonight was to prove that the Royal Family had stolen the English crown, not to prove that there had been another heir to the throne.

He tried to calculate how many millions Kuznetsov had spent on his campaign to undermine the monarchy and to position himself as the obvious choice for first president, and figure how Nigel—who was still fiddling with his phone—had managed to subvert the whole campaign with his bumbling enthusiasm.

"You haven't told anyone about this, have you?"

"No. You told me not to when we spoke earlier."

"You're sure."

"Sure. I mean, obviously the police know."

And so it started. He had told the police the implication of the finding but was disappointed with their apparent complete disinterest—if they even understood the point he was making. The guy who got stuck in the hole had overheard this conversation and had said to Nigel that he could get more of these documents. Nigel had left Ellen some messages but didn't think he had given her details. "And I was about to mention it tonight, but then I remembered what you told me about reprinting the book."

So in short, lots of people knew—even if they didn't understand *what* they knew—and there was no way to get these worms back into the can. The only hope was that people hadn't been listening to Nigel and that what they had heard, they had forgotten.

The cab reached the end of Hampton Court Road, spun three-quarters around the roundabout, and headed over the River Thames into the Kingston one-way system. Boniface cursed under his breath. The driver. That was another person who had heard. Nigel looked up. "These photos are taking far too long to upload."

The comment begged to be ignored, so Boniface did, not that he even understood what Nigel was trying to tell him. Instead, he leaned closer to the academic and whispered, "Look. I can't explain here, but we need to talk tomorrow."

"Could you speak up a bit?" asked Nigel, drawing attention to Boniface's attempt not to alert the driver.

Boniface stared at Nigel, waiting for him to make and keep eye contact. Nigel flicked his gaze around the cab, finally finding Boniface's stare and locking onto it. A single shake of the head conveyed the response and the gravity of the matter Boniface was about to mention. He leaned in to Nigel. "Do not, I repeat, *do not* under any circumstances talk to anyone. Anyone. Not your mother, not your cat, and definitely not your friend Professor Ellen. Do not talk about your visit to the police station and what you found out. And," he lowered his voice further, "don't talk about a line of succession and this proof that could still be in Hampton Court."

Nigel's face took on a solemnity, like a seven-year-old trying to join the grown-up world.

"Not anyone," said Boniface, letting his voice reach a normal level, "including..." he lifted his eyes to indicate the cabbie and held up a single finger. "We will discuss this tomorrow, when everything will become clear."

"Okay..." said Nigel hesitantly.

"Okay," said Boniface, closing the subject.

The cab had found its way through the one-way system and was reaching the foot of Kingston Hill. "Drop me on the corner," Boniface called to the cabbie.

The cab pulled up, and Boniface let himself out. "Until tomorrow," he said to Nigel, lowering his head so he could look up for added emphasis. "You go and have a good evening talking about history. She's sitting there waiting for you, is she?"

"Should be," said Nigel, indicating to Boniface to come closer. As Boniface leaned in, Nigel whispered, "And tomorrow I'll tell you about the descendant of Henry. His direct heir...the true heir to the throne... He's living in London."

Boniface leaped back to see Nigel grinning. Subtly, he raised a finger to cover his lips; then pushed the door shut with a clunk.

He checked the meter and took a few bills out of his wallet without looking at the amount. "Thanks, mate. If you could now take my dear friend to Ham Common." The cabbie winked conspiratorially as he took the cash.

Boniface let the cab pass, feeling incapable of moving his feet and having difficulty putting his thoughts in order. How was he going to keep a lid on Nigel's discovery for long enough to keep Kuznetsov happy?

Standing by the side of the road wasn't helping. Curry might.

twelve

The man with the scar across his face identified the professor as the cab pulled up.

Why did all professors look the same? They were all uniquely different, but somehow they all looked the same. They always had lank, unkempt hair and slightly too-open eyes, and their sense of dress was always at least two decades out of date, even to the untrained eye. Even to the eye of a soldier who didn't understand fashion. And they all always dressed in weird colors. This one was dressed in a color that almost occurred in nature, but not quite. And in a weird material that looked like bits of string stitched together. It was almost what the man had heard called "peasant chic" but it still screamed "professor". He watched as the professor with the strange-colored suit made a big show of using his phone, like the taxi driver would care...

And as the taxi started to pull away, the man stood up and swiftly moved toward his prey.

■ ■ ■ ■ ■

"Hi Ellen, guess who? This call has gone through to voicemail, so you're probably on the phone. Anyway, I'm outside your house now, so if you're in, you can open the door. And if you're not in, then I'll try Hilda next door and see if she'll let me in. I've got lots to tell you. Ellen, you're not going to believe it; I've finally got the proof, and it was murder."

"Professor Armstrong?"

Nigel picked up on the thick Russian accent immediately. Or did the accent originate from farther south, from some other part of the Russian Federation? That didn't matter for now; all that mattered was giving the right answer, and that answer was obvious: Yes, this is her house, but no, I am not her.

Nigel trawled his brain for the right words. Da is yes. Dacha is a house... But can a dacha be a main home? Or is a dacha only a second home, sort of like a summer cottage? This was Ellen's home, after all, and not a summer residence. This house was a cottage, so perhaps it could be regarded as a dacha, or did the fact that it was the main home rule out that option? There was a lot Nigel needed to find out from his Russian and Eastern European colleagues when he was next at the university, or perhaps this fellow might tell him.

"Professor Armstrong?" repeated the man in front of Nigel, looking at him with an intimidating intensity. It had been a very pleasant evening, and now a big Russian—or at least someone who appeared to Nigel to be Russian—wearing boots, jeans, and a leather jacket, and with a large scar starting at his nose and crossing his cheek, was demanding to know whether he was Ellen. Clearly there was some misunderstanding.

The man stared at Nigel, his eyes insisting on an immediate answer, and Nigel hesitantly started to answer as best he could while he tried to find the right words to give him the answer in Russian: "Da..."

■ ■ ■ ■ ■

The man with a scar pulled out the pistol and placed one shot between the professor's eyes. With a single flowing movement, the gun had been removed, discharged, and replaced in his pocket. There was no need to check that the professor was dead or to put another bullet into his body. That one bullet, placed accurately, was sufficient.

His task now was to leave rapidly and without drawing any attention to himself. He moved swiftly and noiselessly through the trees, looking to confirm he hadn't been seen before he drove away, taking the road away from the professor's home and the lifeless body, following the perimeter of the common as it circled back to the main road.

At the junction he turned left and followed the route toward Kingston. As he crossed the end of the professor's road, he saw the man with the white terrier kneeling next to the fallen body. The man seemed torn between trying to help the professor and keeping his dog away from the body.

He continued to follow the main road, pulling off to park in front of a parade of shops, where he picked up the phone, selected the number that Turgenev had programmed for him, and notified the man who answered that Professor Armstrong had been shot dead outside his home on the edge of Richmond.

Grabbing the map book on the passenger seat, he flicked to page 183, ran his finger—again—over his route for departure, and, having fixed the image of the route in his mind, tore the page from the book. Dropping the book back on the seat, he opened his car door and set fire to the page with a plastic lighter he pulled from his pocket, twisting the burning paper to make sure every detail was caught by the flame, dropping the last unburned corner when every other detail had been obliterated.

His task complete, he looked up at the Chinese restaurant on the other side of the street.

thirteen

As every kid who has ever visited Hampton Court Palace knows, each resident changed something.

Cardinal Wolsey when he acquired the location from the monks, Henry VIII when he acquired the Palace Wolsey had constructed, each of Henry's wives, and every resident since has changed it. Some added bits. Some removed bits. Some replaced bits. Some changes were structural, others decorative. Some changes were gorgeous, others were hideous. But everyone changed something.

The end result is a complete hodgepodge.

There are odd angles and illogical layouts. Corridors end unexpectedly. Room sizes and dimensions don't make sense. Where there are new rooms next to old rooms there are gaps and crevices. Sometimes these are filled but sometimes not, and sometimes these are quite interesting spaces…if you're the kind of person who likes to find his way around.

And that was what Peter Winckley had been doing. It started more than a day ago, shortly before closing time at the Palace.

Pete had bought himself a ticket and started to look around. The public lavatories were not the most salubrious location in the Palace, but they were a useful place to hide if you were looking to get yourself *accidentally* locked in. Having succeeded, Pete only had to wait a few hours for the cleaning crew to pass through, and then he was free to roam. His only concern was to ensure that he didn't bump into the security staff, but those old soldiers were so noisy that he could hear them coming from a mile off. Whoever made those big clompy boots, he owed them.

There was a gap that Pete had wanted to look at for a while. He'd seen it next to a new wall—new as in several hundred years old, but newer than the older Tudor walls—which seemed to cut off one of the very old parts. This created a gap.

The gap was tight, but Pete was skinny and accustomed to a tight squeeze—literally and metaphorically. He had pushed into the gap and followed a right and then a left right-angle turn before a wall, built to the height of about five feet, cut the passage. But there was still a gap above the bisecting wall that he could scramble over.

As Pete had dropped over the wall, there had been a delicate ripping sound—like gossamer threads being pulled apart. He had switched on his light to find he was not the first living being to have had the idea of taking a look around. With each stab of light into the darkness of the room, it had become apparent that industrious spiders had spent several hundred years working on a very special project. Where some residents choose to paint their rooms and others choose wallpaper, the spiders had focused on soft furnishings and had attempted to cover every surface and all the space between with webs.

He had turned to look around the room and felt a clump of webs stick to the right side of his head. Reflexively, he had shaken his head and raised his hand to remove the mess—his ponytail had flicked more webs, and by the time his hand had reached his face, he had been wearing a cobweb glove.

They say dust only gets so deep. Pete had wondered whether there was a limit to the number of spider webs that could fit into one room as he had pulled his hands inside his sleeves and chopped through the blankets in front of him, and then kicked at the webs holding his legs.

Against the long wall on the other side of the room appeared to be some bookcases, and Pete had guessed the lumps were cabinets. Holding his light in his mouth, he had ducked his head and pushed forward to the nearest piece of furniture, a long table.

He had tried to move the gossamer blankets; each time he had picked up a web, he needed to flap his hand to try to drop the clump he had just grabbed, but he failed as it stuck to him. In frustration, he had pushed the morass to reveal the top of the table and what looked like some old pieces of paper.

It was no good; he was getting nowhere. He would have to come back, but with a stick or a saw or something else to cut through the mess. Five minutes on Google, and he would find the answer for dealing with spider webs, but for the moment he had done enough—he had maneuvered himself into one of the very old parts of the building, and he had found *something*. It still wasn't clear what the room was; it certainly didn't show up on any of the histories that he had read or in any of the floor plans he had seen. He had guessed it was an old storage room that had been split and permanently sealed when a new room was built, and on first glance there didn't seem to be anything of value that he could sell easily.

He had turned back to the wall he had climbed over to enter and then stopped himself, remembering the documents on the table. Cautiously, he had picked them up and returned to his exit.

Getting out, it had been harder to scrabble over the wall. Where it was five feet high on the outside, on the inside the drop was deeper, probably by another two feet or so, plus he had the documents and the spider webs still sticking to him.

He had balanced on top of the bisecting wall for some time, listening to boots trample up and down the passageway outside. It had seemed like there was a convention of security guards outside his crevice. When he finally was convinced they had left, he had dropped into the gap. On the second right-angle, he had wedged his foot in a place that, given what followed, could've been regarded as a bad place to put his foot.

Having put his foot in a less than ideal place to negotiate the corner, Pete had twisted his leg and fell sideways, wedging his body in the gap, which he had found narrowed toward the bottom, and had trapped his right arm underneath him. While his body had fit along the bottom of the gap, his head had stuck out into the passage, far enough to see that although he had thought there were no guards, he had been wrong.

After their convention the guards had dispersed, but they had left one of their number who had decided to sit down on a bench in the passage. He had been contentedly having a quiet nap when he was rudely interrupted by Pete's fall.

In a slight state of shock, having woken too quickly, the guard had overreacted. The control room, hearing his radio call, had picked up on the panic in his voice, and rather than simply calling for additional guards to assist, they had also called for the police. It must have been a slow night at the station, because the police had arrived before most of the guards.

As soon as the police had arrived, they had taken charge. This was unfortunate for Pete; if he had been dealing with the old men, he might have been able to talk his way out of trouble—or at least offer some plausible explanation as a delaying tactic while he pondered his next move. But this option hadn't been available to him.

Instead, the first policeman had taken the papers he had discovered, which he was still holding in his free left hand, as evidence. Doubtless, one or more of the guards would be admonished for letting these valuable new finds leave the Palace by the same Palace authorities that had hired old soldiers drawing their pensions as guards, knowing that they were cheap labor.

After making a cursory check to ensure that, as far as they could tell given the circumstances, neither his back nor his neck were broken, the remaining police had then dragged Pete from his resting place, taking special care to ensure that it was as inconvenient and humiliating for him as possible.

He had been bundled into the back of a police car and taken to the station, where, of course, he had become the butt of every joke. What sort of thief gets stuck in a hole?

The police didn't have much evidence. It's hard to suggest that someone is guilty of breaking and entering when there's no broken window or busted lock to prove that your suspect broke in, and the entry is to a public place. But still, his questioner had persisted.

And then the King of Corduroy had turned up.

Pete had watched the man in that horrible suit, the kind of suit that wasn't even fashionable in the 1970s. And what color was that anyway? The man in the suit, Pete had soon learned, was Professor Nigel Trudgett, a leading expert on the Tudor period. An expert who was sufficiently well regarded that he had published a book. A committed expert who lived and breathed his subject: He had even boasted that he lived on Thames Ditton Island and could see Hampton Court Palace from his back window.

The professor had become very interested, very quickly. This wasn't simple interest; this was a man driven, like a cocaine addict searching for his next fix. This was something big. The professor had become quite insistent that he should be allowed to try to find out where the documents came from, and then *bang*. He had mentioned it: valuable. These documents had value, and that value would be significant to someone like Richard Sherborne.

In the end, probably to shut him up, the police had allowed Professor Trudgett to sit in on the interview. "There's more," Pete had said to the professor. That was all that was necessary to get his attention in a brief moment when the police were distracted. "I'll show you." The deal had been sealed with the professor, and the academic had gone silent and remained silent.

Later, as Pete was going through the discharge formalities, signing pieces of paper for the return of his possessions—unfortunately, with the exception of the papers he found at Hampton Court Palace—the station started buzzing about the shooting. It began with a call about a shooting and, within minutes, news came in about Professor Trudgett's murder.

Pete was sad to hear about his death. He had liked the man. Well, perhaps *like* was too strong a word. He was impressed by the man's enthusiasm for his subject, and he respected his breadth of knowledge. The way he had been able to take new information—kindly supplied by Pete's hard work—and put it into context, linking it with other historical information, was impressive.

It was even more striking that the prof had been uninterested by the financial value, even though he seemed to know who would want to pay money for this 500-year-old information. He had been quite dismissive about that aspect and didn't want to soil his hands. Instead, there was something else in the papers that interested him more.

But now he was dead.

■ ■ ■ ■ ■

Pete walked out of the station, removed the elastic band holding his ponytail in place, shook his hair free and tugged out some more spider webs that were still stuck, then pulled his phone out of his pocket and called directory enquiries.

On the third attempt, he got lucky.

"Richard Sherborne, please." The voice at the other end was pompous.

He sounded like a Richard Sherborne, so Pete continued. "This is one of those 'you don't know me but...' phone calls." It was rare that he got to use such a clichéd line. "I've got some documents that I believe could be very significant for you." It took some time to interest Sherborne. "Definitely authentic. Verified by Professor Nigel Trudgett; I'm sure you know him."

Once interested, Sherborne seemed quite willing to pay money for the documents. "Of course, as you will understand, the documents are in a secure facility. I'll need a few hours to get hold of them, and I'll bring one or two samples to our first meeting so that you can appraise what's on offer."

Sherborne seemed quite open to this approach.

Pete hung up and went to find the next bus headed toward Thames Ditton. It couldn't be that hard to find Professor Trudgett's house on the Island. Once there, he was bound to find something he could sell to Sherborne—and maybe the professor had a suit that he could borrow for the meeting.

Hopefully his suits weren't all corduroy.

fourteen

As Ellen's cab pulled up, her phone beeped—a missed call and voicemail from Nigel. Ignoring the phone until she got inside, she continued to look through her purse for some cash and found a bill that she pushed through the glass to the driver.

"D'you wanna receipt, love?"

"Yes, please," said Ellen.

"There you are, my darling," said the cabbie, passing the receipt and Ellen's change. "Not sure what's going on over there." Ellen looked to where the cabbie was indicating: the path to her house. Several people were standing around, all looking flustered. Each seemed to be looking outward for the answer, as if they were expecting a knight to ride up on his trusty white steed.

It took Ellen a moment or two to realize that they were standing around someone, someone who seemed to be lying on her front path. She looked again at the faces; this wasn't just concern she was seeing.

This was shock.

This was panic.

As the sound of the cab's engine faded, she stood frozen, becoming increasingly aware of several sets of sirens, each with a different tone and character. Hilda Longthorne, her neighbor, came toward her.

Hilda was in her seventies, but despite being in apparently good health, she looked older: Dry, wrinkled skin; colorless gray hair; and an old brown floral dress with a faded green cardigan all displayed her age but hid her warm heart. Ellen looked into the old woman's eyes and could see a desperation to look sympathetic, but an inability to hide her horror. "Your friend," said Hilda, her old skin crinkling as she trembled. "It's your friend."

Ellen threw a look of panic. "Nigel?"

"Yes, dear. He's been shot." The siren from the paramedic's car drowned out Ellen's scream.

In the evening gloom, the flashing blue lights on the paramedic's green-yellow car gave the street the stop/go effect of a 1920s monochrome movie, slowing down time. Ellen watched as the paramedic walked over to where Nigel lay, getting closer with each flick of the lights, and knelt beside him.

As an ambulance arrived and shut off its siren, the sound of another emergency vehicle could still be heard in the distance, but nearing. "That'll be the police," said Hilda. "Now come on, dear, he's being looked after by the best people for the job. You need a cup of tea, or maybe something stronger."

Hilda took Ellen's arm and pulled her toward the shared path to their houses. "Look away, and I'll guide you through," said Hilda, but it was too late. Ellen had already seen Nigel, who had fallen onto his back with his head pointing toward her front window.

He looked as he always did, apart from the new suit and the round hole in his forehead where a small trail of blood oozed. Ellen looked up at the front of her house, a few feet away from where Nigel must have been standing when he fell, and noticed the splattering, as if someone had thrown a cup full of dark, sticky liquid mixed with shredded raw meat.

"Is he...?"

"I don't know," said Hilda, ushering her past Nigel and the paramedics, and through the older woman's front door.

"He is, isn't he?" said Ellen, starting to cry uncontrollably.

fifteen

"What and why?"

Veronica Rutherford leaned back in her chair, twisting her fingers in the end of her hair as she contemplated the woman standing in her office door.

What lipstick was left was badly applied; the rest had been rubbed off, hopefully only on a coffee cup. The lipstick that still clung on clashed with her fuchsia jacket, which exaggerated her peroxide-scorched hair. Burst capillaries—hieroglyphics that, when decoded, told a story of too much alcohol, too little sleep, followed by too much caffeine, all in the name of career, and some misunderstanding between career and self-worth—strained like gauze holding back the last remnants of youth, before the floodgates of age opened. And with age and experience came competence, so Veronica listened.

"Our bitter and twisted little man who Sherborne never appreciated, but who we are being kind to, called. Something is going on. Something has caught Sherborne's interest in a big way." She pursed her lips. "But we don't know what. All we know is that he's called in the big guns—outside muscle to keep him safe."

Veronica let go of her hair and slumped. "So what—precisely—has happened?"

"Difficult." The fuchsia jacket pondered. "As far as we can tell, Sherborne received a phone call from someone who he has apparently never met. He got excited by the call and is expecting the caller to get in touch with him later today."

"So...they're going to meet? What does this mean?" Veronica sat up, shoulders lifted, palms up. "Some sort of trade? Blackmail?"

"That was my least implausible conclusion." The fuchsia jacket sounded noncommittal. "Sherborne has called in the cavalry, which is how we got the tip. And he wants brawn, not brain, which tells us something, although I'm not quite sure what."

"So where is Sherborne at the moment?" Veronica knotted her eyebrows. "Where does he want the reinforcements? Home or the office?"

"Home. In Richmond."

"At home, protected by the redoubtable Ada. I'm surprised he feels the need for anyone other than Ada to defend him. Perhaps he's getting sentimental in his old age."

The fuchsia jacket's concentration remained fixed on her boss. "Shall we send someone to sit on him for a few hours? Perhaps see if we can recognize the source before he gets to Sherborne?"

"Let's do that. Send Whittaker if he's not still sulking." The fuchsia jacket frowned but seemed unwilling to ask for an explanation. "We're chasing a lead on Oscar—and before you say it, I doubt it's connected to this, but I guess we'll find out. Anyway, we've got a sting to catch Oscar, and Whitters doesn't look the part, so we sent someone else, and young Whitters..." She pushed her nose, putting a kink in it.

"Out of joint, big time." The fuchsia jacket smirked conspiratorially. "I see. I'll be gentle. I'll tell him that you handpicked him for this mission."

Veronica smiled broadly. "Thank you." The smile dropped. "Just make sure he gets that this is all about subtlety. I don't want Sherborne to know we're there. I don't want him to think that anyone's on to him. If he starts thinking that way, he's going to get paranoid, and if he gets paranoid, then he's going to start looking for spies. 'Traitors, dear Vron. Traitors, the damned blighters.'" She dropped the Sherborne mimicry. "And if he starts looking for spies...well, there's always a chance that he might suspect our bitter and twisted little friend. Even if he can't prove anything, we risk losing our source, so tell Whittaker not to be noticed. By anyone."

Veronica loosened the crick in her neck with a gentle twist of her head, then shook her hair free in an involuntary reflex. Her dark auburn mane convulsed and gently settled itself. "Sherborne may seem like a buffoon, and he is in so many ways, but he's not stupid. Remember, we don't know what security he had before the reinforcements, and much more importantly, we don't know who else might already be chasing this. The last thing we need is a branch meeting of the National Union of Journalists outside his front door."

"Aye aye, Cap'n," said the fuchsia jacket, saluting as she turned to leave.

Veronica sighed, reaching into her desk to pull out her whisky, and filled her tumbler, which was still sitting on her desk from when she had seen Boniface. She turned to her screen to skim the next day's layouts while taking the occasional sip.

There was a soft tap on her door, and she spun. The fuchsia jacket's tanned hide was looking pale. "I was passing the duty office on my way out..." She hesitated, a slight tremble audible as she continued. "Professor Ellen Armstrong was murdered tonight. She was shot dead outside her house in Richmond."

The room was silent. Veronica took a deep breath, held it, and then slowly exhaled while closing her eyes. "Is it confirmed?"

"The call came direct, and apparently the caller was certain about the identity. We haven't got a second source yet, but I've got calls out."

Veronica paused, moving her lower jaw from side to side. "Has anyone else got it yet?" A single shake of the head. "Then we'll run it. Check and double-check with whatever sources you can find, but unless Oscar makes his mistake soon, that's the lead story. Let's get it out to the TV stations; maybe we can get the lead on *Newsnight*. But try and get more information and a second verification before the presses roll."

"On it."

sixteen

Boniface stared at the wall on the other side of the restaurant.

He didn't want to be with people. He didn't want conversation—he had spent too much time with Nigel, too much time in a room with too much alcohol, and too much time had been wasted with half-drunk people he thought he had escaped from. Then, to put the cherry on the top, Nigel had blurted out that he had found the heir to Henry VIII living in London.

He wanted quiet. And if he couldn't have quiet—which was difficult to achieve in a restaurant that was open to the public—then he wanted to be left alone.

He couldn't stop fixating on the implications of what Nigel had said: If there was a living heir whose ancestry could be proved, then Kuznetsov's plan to undermine the monarchy on the grounds that they were frauds would be irrelevant, and his ambitions for a republic—with him as the president, becoming the de facto first tsar—were in tatters.

The last three, four, five, or however many years of Kuznetsov's pursuit of his ambition would all come apart as a direct result of the job that Boniface had been given. Sure, if there ever was a referendum, it would be virtually unwinnable, but now any failure to achieve a referendum would be directly attributed to Boniface rather than the fact that it was a stupid idea in the first place—and, as Veronica had so succinctly suggested, that would be a bad thing.

Boniface had been assigned one mission, and it was a simple one. But he had failed.

Someone was bound to have listened to Nigel. One of the cops would have taken him seriously and called the papers. The cabbie almost certainly heard. Nigel was bound to have told someone at the book launch. And then there was the guy who got stuck in the hole at Hampton Court, who had actually found the documents. He wasn't going to sit back, was he?

There were two questions that needed to be answered: How was the story going to get out and how angry would Kuznetsov be? Never-work-again-in-this-town type of angry, or send-around-one-of-the-guys-with-big-boots-and-a-worn-leather-jacket angry? Probably the guy with the scar across his face; he looked like he could be good with his hands, and if not him, then Turgenev, who would kill him just with his looks.

Boniface's stare remained fixed; he didn't even notice the annoying background sitar music. His empty plate sat in front of him, with the greasy yellow stains on the over-starched tablecloth proving that he was both messy at serving and messy at eating. But he didn't notice; he kept staring at the dark-red flocked wallpaper, which seemed far less tasteless than the wall coverings in Kuznetsov's reception.

"Mister Alexander, you're being very quiet tonight." The proprietor stood by attentively.

Boniface pulled himself out of his trance-like state. "I'm sorry, Shankar. Lots to think about, I'm afraid." He looked sheepish, still half-dazed with Nigel's revelation, when his phone rang. "Yes, that's me, and it's Boniface, please, no mister." His smile for Shankar turned into his fake reassuring business smile, and then dropped to reveal his un-faked worried look. "The police? How can I help you?"

Shankar shared Boniface's look of worry. "Yes, I know Professor Trudgett. I was with him until about an hour ago." Shankar's look of worry relaxed. "Dead?" Shankar took the form of a cartoon character, with his eyes out on stalks.

Boniface felt winded. The life force was being sucked out of him. He was supposed to be the expert on handling situations, and now he didn't know what to do. He was already dazed, thinking about how widely Nigel had spread his revelation, but now he sat and listened to the policeman, repeating back odd phrases like a three-year-old trying to say big words. "Shot...dead...his phone...I.C.E...in case of emergency, oh...my number...really, oh...no, I don't know why...oh...no, I don't know why anyone would want to shoot...did he...I mean...pain, suffer...doc says instant...oh...Ellen Armstrong...yes, his friend...no, never met her... shocked...she would be...they were at Cambridge, I think, together... doubt they were more, but I don't know...his publisher is my client..."

Boniface continued talking with the police, or rather listening and mumbling odd phrases. As he ended his call, he said "gotta go" to no one in particular and dropped a few bills on the table before heading into the cool night air.

seventeen

Ellen felt like she had been wailing forever.

In reality, she had been sitting, gently sobbing, in Hilda Longthorne's sitting room for less than an hour while Hilda kept vigil, silently offering support.

The room was typical of old-woman chic. Two old armchairs with an unpleasant floral design sat on the edge of a heavily worn carpet betraying its 1960s vintage and exposing old floorboards where the fabric rectangle didn't extend to the walls. The wallpaper was of a similar age, reaching up to a ceiling that had once been white and now wasn't, but did have numerous fine cobwebs thoughtfully hiding the cracks in the plaster. The television seemed nearly as old but was functional. The picture was on, but the volume had been cut when Hilda went to investigate the loud noise outside.

The police had asked to talk with Ellen, but Hilda had refused. She had politely offered tea to the officers, the paramedics, and the doctor who had arrived to confirm that Nigel was indeed dead, but no one had accepted her offer. Hilda had offered alcohol to Ellen, but Ellen was happy with a cup of tea as she sat motionless, apart from her tears, staring at her phone, looking at the message notification.

Eventually she pushed the button to retrieve her voicemail, heard it ring, and heard the computerized voice giving her the menu options. Too much. She couldn't go through with it and hung up, continuing to stare at the phone. She tried again but only got as far as the ringing before she hung up. On the third attempt, the voicemail system spoke to her: "Message one was received at nine-oh-five pm today from zero-seven..." It was Nigel's number. Ellen hung up without listening.

On the fourth attempt, she heard his voice: "Hi Ellen, guess who?" Ellen smiled at his goofiness and felt a new torrent of tears flow down her cheeks. She missed most of the message, only hearing the last line: "Ellen, you're not going to believe it; I've finally got the proof, and it was murder."

Murder, and then he gets murdered.

The police called again; a gentle tap on the front door was enough. Hilda sent them away again and returned. "Bob..."—she saw Ellen's confusion—"the man with the white dog. He saw a man parked up near the church earlier in the evening when he took the dog out for a walk. He thinks he saw the same man sitting and watching from the other side of the common for about an hour or so. It was as if he was waiting for Nigel to turn up."

"But he can't have been. I only invited Nigel 'round when I finished that last interview—I was meant to be at Hampton Court, not here, so he can't have been waiting for Nigel. Bob must be wrong."

"I don't know, dear. He's a very nosey man and tends to notice things. You may not want to pass the time of day with him, but he can tell you every car that has parked up the street, the time they arrived, and the time they left."

A silence fell over the room as the two contemplated the new information. The television flickered as the previews for the next day's programs flashed, and then the titles for *Newsnight* started running. In her stunned state, Ellen stared at the flickering screen. It was the very stern presenter tonight—the one with a reputation for tearing politicians limb from limb. On any other day, if he had been doing a political interview, it would be worth watching. But Ellen wasn't in a mood for blood sports tonight, not with the amount of blood that had been splattered over the front of her house.

Ellen's picture came up on the screen, and she snapped out of her daze. It was like she had been given a year to mourn, all the sleep she needed, and a refreshing bath. "Turn it up," she said to Hilda, suddenly regretting that she was commanding, not asking. "Why am I on television? I didn't talk to them today; why am I being featured?"

The presenter was in the middle of the sentence by the time Hilda found the remote control "... the sad news about the murder of Professor Ellen Armstrong, who initial reports say was shot dead at her south London home tonight. The professor has recently made several appearances on this program..."

Ellen stood, clenching her fists, every muscle in her body tightening. "Why do they think I'm dead when Nigel's dead, Hilda? Something must be wrong."

Hilda's face remained serene. "It's probably a silly mistake, dear, don't..."

"Don't what?" Ellen snapped, and then regretted the target of her anger, slapping her hand over her mouth. "I'm sorry." She hugged her neighbor. "I'm sorry." She released Hilda and looked her straight in the eyes. "Someone has told the media that I'm dead. You're not going to tell me that this is all a coincidence, are you? There's a man waiting outside my house, Nigel finds something, Nigel gets shot, and then they say I'm dead." Ellen found she was gripping the sleeves of Hilda's dress. "I'm sorry... It's..."

Hilda's voice was soft; her tone practical, matter-of-fact. "What can I do?"

Ellen released Hilda's sleeves and stood back. "I don't know, but I can't stay here—not if the killer knows where I live." Hilda listened intently as her neighbor continued. "I don't know why Nigel was shot, but I do know it's not good to know someone who's just been killed, especially if they tell you they've got a secret. People tend to think you might know the secret too, and want you dead or want to force you to reveal it. But as I don't know what he found out, I'm going to go to his house before anyone else gets there and have a look 'round."

"Go out the back. I'll hold off the police." Ellen frowned quizzically. "I have my ways, dear. I've learned a thing or two," said Hilda, picking a bottle of sweet sherry from her shelves, and snapping the seal as she twisted the lid before pouring herself a small measure. "Awful stuff. Why do people think that you'll like it because you're over sixty?"

She took a sip, pulling an exaggerated face, swilled the liquid around her mouth, gargled, and looked around as if she had lost something. Spotting a small African violet sitting on the windowsill, she picked it up. "Pah. Horrible stuff," she said, spitting the sherry onto the violet.

A mischievous grin came over her face as she put her fingertips into her glass and then dripped sherry onto her wrists, which she rubbed together and then rubbed on the side of her neck. "Dotty old bird... I can keep them talking for hours. They'll think I'm drunk..." she put her thumb into the middle of the V neckline of her dress, giving it a noticeable tug down "...and desperately lonely. That's the scariest thing for a young policeman."

She winked at Ellen, who was seeing a resourceful side of her neighbor she had never seen before.

"Go out the back. Hop over the fence." Hilda cocked her head and looked Ellen up and down. "That's not the best skirt for fence climbing, and those aren't the best shoes, but you're young, you'll manage. Bert's got the garden at the end. He'll be in bed by now, so he won't notice you going through. His gate is never locked, but he gets upset if it's not closed, so do shut it after you go through. Turn right, and you'll reach the main road. I'll keep them busy when they next knock, and when they get insistent, I'll tell them you're asleep upstairs. It should be hours before I have to tell them that you must have slipped out while I was getting some more sherry. And while they think you're here, so will the man with the gun if he comes back."

"Thanks, Hilda. I owe you."

eighteen

The old leather creaked as he leaned to replace the receiver. The leather creaked again, and the whole chair groaned as Richard Sherborne moved his bulk back to sit squarely.

Ada had arrived at her sister's, where she would spend the night.

In safety.

He had fought quite a battle with her. She was unquestioningly loyal and only agreed to stay at her sister's when he agreed to bring in two guards for the night. And now she was safe, so he didn't need to worry about her.

But safe from what? He wasn't quite sure—this was probably a setup. The question was who was doing the setting? The obvious answer was Kuznetsov, but it didn't have his usual fingerprints: a call from a phone where the number wasn't withheld, a call to him personally at a time and place where he wouldn't usually be, the sums of money didn't seem huge—but that could be a double bluff—a proposition that hadn't been rehearsed, papers verified by one of Kuznetsov's authors... Sherborne sighed; Kuznetsov would never be that obvious. There was a ring of truth somewhere in the dirt, and if the documentation was authentic, then it would be worth paying money. But all his intuition said it was fake.

And in case it was something else, then Ada was safely stowed with her sister, and the cavalry were here.

Sherborne pushed his chair back from his leather-topped desk and stood. With his expanding waistline, standing was becoming less of a straightforward task. It wasn't that he weighed more than he once had; after all, the tweed jacket he was wearing was at least 25 years old—Ada had done a splendid job with arm patches and stitching up the burst seams over the years—and his brown trousers were probably 20 years old. But they were both tight. The trousers, naturally, around the waist, although as his gut pushed them downward the constriction became less of an issue, but it did mean he needed to think about asking Ada to take up the legs. The jacket hadn't been buttoned up since 1980-something, and now it was getting tighter under the arms and across the back. This was a new and, to be frank, rather unpleasant experience.

Having managed to lift his bulk and balance on top of increasingly tired legs, Sherborne paused to catch his breath. He looked up and exhaled, then looked down. It was a familiar sight: an old checked, brushed-cotton shirt and a tie covering a large gut, but no feet in sight. He steadied himself on the chair with his right hand and leaned over.

Yes. His feet were still there, brown brogues as expected—old, but spit-and-polished to perfection by Ada. That was a relief and something that should be celebrated with a drink while he contemplated.

The drinks cabinet was on the left-hand side of the study. Sherborne placed a crystal tumbler on the dark wood; dropped in a few ice cubes; put in a good measure of gin; topped it up a bit further, and a bit further again; added a slug of tonic; and threw in a lime slice.

He took a sip and distracted himself by looking at the spines of his first editions, arranged conveniently just below eye level. He could see the contents of the first two shelves, but below that he needed his glasses or a chair to sit on, as bending wasn't a practical proposition. From the filled dark mahogany bookcases covering the left wall, he turned to the window looking across his architecturally ordered garden in the direction of the Thames. In the gloom he could see shadows, but no signs of any of Kuznetsov's men ghosting across the manicured lawns.

Walking around his desk, he dropped into his Chesterfield sofa with its back to the right wall, which was also covered in mahogany bookcases, like the others, filled to overflowing. On some shelves, books were stacked on top of books, and on others there were two rows, one behind the other.

Sherborne flopped his arm over the scrolled back of the sofa and stared up at the ceiling while he slowly sipped. Then he turned and placed his drink on a mahogany end table, exchanging his tumbler for the TV remote control.

He sat back and recalled his words during the strange conversation earlier that evening. "An offer I can't refuse? And yet somehow, I feel compelled to say no." That was enough to convince the individual to explain what he was about.

He checked his watch and clicked on the television, switching to *Newsnight*. He was shocked by the headline: Ellen Armstrong, his favorite historian, had been murdered. Shot outside her house less than two miles away.

He made a mental note to pay his respects in the morning. He didn't know whether the professor had any family in this country, what with her being American, but he would offer his condolences and any practical help—in particular by making sure royalties on her book were paid to the beneficiary in her will—where he could.

nineteen

Hilda had been right. It wasn't easy getting over the fence, but it was possible. Ellen would've preferred to have gone home and changed, perhaps slipped out of her skirt and put on some sensible shoes. Home wasn't that far—it was next door to Hilda, across a shared path with facing front doors—but that would have meant seeing Nigel, the remains of Nigel still over her house, the police, probably the press by now, and all of those other well-intentioned but ultimately annoying neighbors.

And she might have seen the man with the gun. And he, her.

So she had gone out the back way, climbed over the fence, skinned her knees but kept her suit clean, passed through Bert's garden, closed the gate as instructed by Hilda, and walked to the line of shops at the end of the road. There she had been fortunate and seen a cabbie who had said he had just come out of the Chinese restaurant. You couldn't usually find a cab for hire at that time, but tonight she had been lucky, and so she had been able to get to Thames Ditton in less than ten minutes.

Ellen asked the cabbie—a strange-looking man, who was balding but kept what hair he did have collar-length at the back—to drop her at the roundabout in the middle of the High Street, and from there she headed toward the river.

She walked up Thames Ditton High Street, a road she had always found cute in a Ye Olde English type of way. Given its history, Ellen always expected this to be a more substantial road. According to Nigel, when Henry first took ownership of Hampton Court Palace, the island—Thames Ditton Island—didn't exist. Instead, it was part of the bank on which the Palace stood. Supplies for the Palace would be brought up the High Street, and at low tide there was a ford to cross the river. If the tide was in and you wanted to get across, then you had to pay a ferryman.

To travel to the Palace, the King would be rowed up from Westminster. But Henry was dissatisfied with the lack of grandeur on arrival, particularly when he was receiving guests at this country Palace. So he had ordered the river be dug straight. The land that was cut off when the river was cut straight became a separate island. Ellen remembered how excited Nigel had always been, living somewhere created by Henry.

She reached the sharp bend at the junction between the High Street and Summer Road, and crossed, following what had been the route of the road into the ford, but which now led into two parking lots: the one on the left attached to a pub and the other a more informal space that doubled as a slipway into the river.

She stepped onto the footbridge, and at the security gate halfway over the river she punched in Nigel's code 1-5-0-9-4-7 and smiled: always the Henry VIII obsessive. Each resident on the island had their own security code for the gate—Nigel had been so pleased that he had been able to set his code to reflect Henry's period as King, 1509 to 1547. Or rather, the historically recognized period during which Henry was King. In reality, Nigel believed that Henry had probably been murdered sometime around 1530, so maybe he should have changed his entry code. Ellen wiped away a tear. It was too late to tease Nigel about that now.

As she hit the last digit, the lock clicked and Ellen pulled the gate, then strolled the short distance to Nigel's house.

Nigel had given her his door key several years ago. She wasn't quite sure why, and she had never reciprocated. She wasn't even sure whether the key would fit; she had never tried it, as she had never been on Thames Ditton Island without Nigel.

The key fit—of course, Nigel would have checked several times to make sure—and the lock turned smoothly and silently. Ellen removed the key and pushed the door open, remaining on the step.

There was an unpleasant stillness to the house. Perhaps it was always this way when Nigel wasn't there, or perhaps it was her thinking too hard. She reached inside to switch on the light, then waited as her eyes grew accustomed to the electric glare. When her pupils had stopped reacting, she craned her neck to look into the house before gingerly taking a step over the threshold and quietly shutting the door behind her.

twenty

What was this English obsession with sending the traffic in one direction? He had once heard them called one-way systems, and now tonight, the man with the scar on his face had found two, and both had confused him. Say what you like about the Soviet days, but central planning had some real benefits for its citizens.

When he arrived in the Chinese restaurant there was one other customer, a balding man with longer hair at the back of his head who was reading a newspaper while he ate his meal. This emptiness didn't give the anonymity that he had hoped for, but he was hungry and Turgenev had told him to stay near, so he stayed. The balding man soon finished his meal and was gone before the man with the scar's first course had been delivered.

When the meal arrived, he finished it swiftly, all the time reflexively checking the phone, then left, leaving a fifty pound note on the table. Following the map in his mind, he drove in the direction of Kingston, reaching an intersection immediately before the railway line where the road fanned into three lanes. He took the right-hand lane, ready to turn right as he went under the railway bridge.

As he came up from under the railway line, he was surprised to see that the three lanes all flowed to the left. To his right, in the direction he wanted to go, was a large pedestrianized area, with another road heading in the direction of the bridge on the far side. Driving over pedestrians was not the sort of low-key exit he had been instructed to make.

He followed the three crowded lanes as they went left, finding himself blocked, confused, and intimidated in his small car as he tried to figure out how to get back on track. The three lanes then curved right, and he found himself in the left lane, approaching a junction, where he was again surprised, this time to find his lane filtered left. For a country that prides itself on its freedom, the UK didn't seem to give its motorists much freedom of choice, and he was now going away from the river, although this road did at least go in both directions.

He spun the car and headed back to the last junction, taking the road that would have been the first right turn. This was a two-way road but narrower than the other roads he had followed since he had turned left. He followed it until it came to an abrupt end.

Cursing under his breath, the man got out of the car. In front of him were some red phone boxes, about ten in total, but apart from the last one they had fallen over like a series of toppling dominoes. On the other side of the phone boxes were some railings preventing him from driving through to the road that he guessed was the road he should be on.

The man with the scar across his cheek took out the map book and flicked through, looking for his location, then swore again—the pages were missing. He threw the atlas across the street, its remaining pages coming unglued and scattering, before getting back into the car, feeling the gun in his pocket niggling him that it should have been at the bottom of the river by now.

Nagging him that he had already made too many fuckups and needed to sort out his fuckups.

Immediately.

And ideally before Turgenev found out.

twenty-one

Ellen stood with her back to the front door, which she had shut as she stepped in, looking around a large, open plan room.

On her left, toward the front, was an L-shaped kitchen area following the outer wall. Nigel was never much of a cook, but at least there weren't any dishes left or any evidence of rotting food. The room was bisected by two high-backed armchairs facing French doors that looked out from the other side of the house and over the river, the chair backs facing the kitchen area. In front of the chairs was a low coffee table, positioned so that you could reach it while sitting but still walk around the other side and open the French doors to access the small back lawn separating the house from the river.

To her right there was a small bathroom. Ellen looked in quickly and decided there probably wouldn't be any clues in there. In the back-right corner was Nigel's bedroom. So, where to start? Kitchen or bedroom?

Ellen took the coward's option and started to open the kitchen drawers underneath the counter.

There was nothing of interest. Knives, forks, assorted cutlery, a can opener, a wooden spatula, and some other cooking implements that were old but didn't show signs of heavy use. In one drawer, there were some candles and matches together with some string—brown string on the left and white string on the right—a bottle opener and some folded supermarket bags. In another, opened bills, a few rubber bands, two screwdrivers, a selection of rusty screws, a pair of pliers, an adjustable wrench, and several sets of keys—car keys and the keys for the back door, Ellen guessed.

Moving past a washing machine, she opened the first cabinet. Nothing seemed out of place. Cleaning supplies—bleach, dish washing liquid, laundry detergent and softener—were as expected in the cabinet under the sink. The sink was placed squarely under the front window so Nigel could look out at his neighbors on the other side of the island as he did his dishes.

The corner cabinet had a stack of plates showing a faded blue floral decoration and a collection of assorted mugs. She pulled a mug out: "Tudor Historians do it..." Enough. Too tedious. She put it back without finishing the pun, closing the cabinet door.

Turning the corner, the final cabinet had a stack of old, worn pots and pans, and a burned frying pan on the top shelf with plastic food containers jumbled on the bottom. Ellen closed the door and stood up. On the counter a kettle with coffee, tea bags, and a jar with sugar stood ready to offer refreshment, and above that a cabinet hung on the wall. Ellen opened the cabinet: food. Nothing special, a few cans and some packets. Nothing suggesting Nigel had hidden the greatest secret of his life there.

Next to the end cabinet was an electric cooker, old but clean. Ellen opened the top oven and looked at the grill pan that had been pushed in and then opened the bottom oven, which was empty. The kitchen ended with a fridge freezer. She pulled the top door. Again, it was clean and largely empty, only having some milk, butter, cheese, ham, and a bottle of lemon juice. She closed the top door and opened the freezer door, pulling out each drawer in turn. Frozen peas, frozen bread, what she guessed was chili but could be Bolognese.

Nothing dating from the Tudor era.

She closed the freezer and turned to face the room. What had seemed like a burning sun when she first switched it on now revealed itself to be a dull, glowing low-energy bulb with a dirty shade.

The room was beige; there was no other way to describe it, in terms of both color and character. The walls were flat and featureless, without pictures, ornamentation, or any form of decoration or personalization. The carpet was old, and the two chairs reminded her of Hilda's chairs, both reflecting a certain age of furniture and the solitude of the owner. But whereas Hilda was happy to live alone, Nigel's solitary life had been less of an option and more of a consequence of Darwinian natural de-selection.

Ellen slowly and carefully surveyed the room. From her recollection of previous visits, nothing was out of place. Well, there wasn't much there that could be out of place, and nothing new had been added. Certainly no pile of papers with a nice sign saying, "In case of my death, this is the important stuff that you should read first."

She felt a shudder. She was intruding, digging through a dead man's house less than two hours after he had been shot on her doorstep. Shot for a reason she didn't understand. Shot after having found something that he thought was very important, but that he wanted to tell her about in person. Shot by a man she wouldn't recognize.

Over the ten years since she had first met Nigel, she had never had a conversation with him that touched on anything of a sexual nature. A few times she had wondered if he was trying to make an advance, but he had always seemed to feel even more uncomfortable raising the topic than she had been rejecting his inept, naïve overtures, so she had steered the conversation in a different direction, and the subject had not been raised for many years.

But Ellen had always wondered.

It was impossible to believe that he was completely asexual. It was easy to suppose that he couldn't sustain a relationship, and she understood how few friends he had, especially female friends, of whom she was the one and only true friend. But just because he didn't have a girlfriend, that didn't mean he wasn't interested. Perhaps he used prostitutes? Perhaps he kept a crate full of porn? Perhaps he kept that porn collection in his room? Perhaps he was into kids and that was the simple and straightforward reason he was murdered?

Ellen had been into Nigel's bedroom once, when she first visited the house—as an observer, not a guest, and had remained standing and fully clothed with no bodily contact. As she stepped in, the room was as she remembered, with closets along the wall shared with the bathroom. On the back wall was a window, and the other two walls were filled with shelves loaded with books. Somehow a bed had been fitted into a space between the shelves on the far wall, and an old desk had been slotted into a gap on the near wall behind the door.

On the desk was a moderately new computer. Ellen looked for the power button and pressed it. The computer buzzed and beeped, whirring to life, and while it clawed its way to consciousness and performed whatever checks and tests computers feel they have to perform in the five minutes before they are happy to interact with human beings, Ellen turned her attention to the wall of closets.

The obelisks that had probably arrived flat-packed many years ago now stood like wonky soldiers guarding her dead friend's secrets. Ellen wasn't sure where Nigel had bought the furniture, or how it had been constructed and installed. By the way it stood she suspected that Nigel had been the architect and the builder for this project. If that was the case, then he had probably made the right career choice, choosing history over construction.

She pulled the first door. It squeaked in the early part of its travel, the squeak mutating into more of a grinding sound from the midpoint in its arc. Ellen pushed the door and reopened it. It made the same noise on closing and on reopening. She thought back to the kitchen—there hadn't been any oil, not even cooking oil that she could put on the hinges.

From the top to the bottom were filing boxes, each about twelve inches high, four inches wide, and, by the look, deep enough to hold a full-sized sheet of paper in a folder. Ellen read the end notes on each box: Research Papers 1998 Box 1, Research Papers 1998 Box 2, Research Papers 1998 Box 3. There was nothing from this century and no hints as to what could be in each box beyond research papers.

She closed the door and opened the next closet, finding herself taken aback to see clothes. On the top rail there were some jackets: his sand-colored corduroy jacket with the arm patches, his blue corduroy jacket with the arm patches, his brown jacket...with the arm patches, and a selection of dull-colored pants hanging from the rail with a few belts hooked over the hangers.

On the rail below was Nigel's shirt collection, a mess of indistinct colors and old fabrics. Ellen would have thought she was in a secondhand shop if she hadn't been so acutely aware that she was standing in her dead friend's bedroom, trying to understand why he was dead, and hoping for any clues as to why the TV news had said she was dead.

She opened the next closet and felt her heart sink: If Nigel had any secrets, this was where they were buried. If there was going to be any porn, any fetish gear, any toys or signs of sexual deviance, or something that was so sexually repellent that she had managed to mentally block out its possibility, this closet was it.

The top half had shelves of sweaters. Nigel didn't wear sweaters very often, but he had a wide collection, in a range of textures and in varying primary colors. She flicked through the accumulation, pushing her hands into the gaps between each garment, looking for anything hidden between or behind.

There was nothing.

She took a deep breath, steeling herself before looking at the lower half of the closet, then opened the top drawer.

She exhaled deeply, with relief, realizing that she had been holding her breath. Socks. She quickly rifled through the socks, again looking for anything that had been hidden.

She held her breath again and opened the next drawer. Yuck. Underwear. Woman-repelling underwear at that. This was the epicenter of possible hiding places. Ellen gingerly moved the first item, getting bolder and moving more earnestly through the contents of the drawer. Finding nothing, she closed it.

If there were no horrors in the first two drawers, then logically, anything that Nigel didn't want to be found would be in the bottom drawer. Ellen sat on the floor and pulled the last one, finding that it opened far more easily than expected. She looked down: empty.

She let out another sigh of relief and stood, kicking the drawer shut and closing the closet door.

The computer beeped and whirred, drawing attention to the desktop image: Hampton Court Palace. Nigel was a man obsessed and possessed.

She fired up his word processor and opened his most recent documents.

The first was a shopping list.

The second was his to-do list. Nothing about any big secret there.

The third was his draft speech that, as far as she knew, he gave tonight at the launch of *The Murder of Henry VIII*. She had spoken to Nigel about it—Boniface had given him strict instructions to make sure he kept it to three minutes, including pauses. Sure enough, Nigel had even put the pauses for breath, and in a few places he had marked "hold for laughter." So he did pay attention occasionally... Ellen scanned the note; there was nothing new.

The fourth and last document was Nigel's conspiracy theory explaining why Henry had been murdered. This looked like the points she had heard him expound many times, but she still skimmed the points:

- ```
  Wolsey was Henry's lord chancellor, chief
  executive, and general go-to guy
  ```

Urrggh. It was loathsome when Nigel tried to use Americanisms to sound cool. Somehow it didn't work for the Brits.

- ```
  Wolsey was resentful of the King. His
  extravagance. His irresponsibility. And
  most of all, his taking Hampton Court
  Palace.
  ```

- ```
  In 1530, Henry VIII and Wolsey argued.
  Wolsey had failed to secure Henry's divorce
  from Catherine of Aragon. [question:
  was this failure intentional in order
  to bolster Wolsey's standing with the
  Pope—the only source of power that could
  balance Henry?]
  ```

Always good to see questions. He was the leading expert on Henry and Wolsey, but he was humble enough to know that he couldn't second-guess Wolsey's true intentions.

- ```
  Wolsey was stripped of his position within
  government and sent to be Archbishop of
  York.
  ```

- ```
  Wolsey was charged with treason and
  summoned to return from York. On the
  return journey he "died" and was "buried"
  in Leicester. However, there is no marked
  grave.
  ```

- ```
  In reality, this was a fiction, created
  by Wolsey to cover his next move plotted
  with Anne Boleyn.
  ```

There was nothing new here. It was Nigel's standard argument and the basic outline of his book. She scrolled down a few more lines, continuing to read. "Alright, that's interesting."

She continued nodding and talking to herself as she finished the last few bullet points, then closed the word processor and opened his internet browser, clicking the history button.

His viewing over the last few days was what she expected: Boniface's website, articles by Boniface, articles about Boniface, links to Nigel's book on Amazon and a few other large bookstores, publicity about his book. In short, lots to do with his book, and thankfully no porn.

Then something caught her eye. She had missed today's entries. She clicked, and a long list unfolded. These must have been the articles Nigel looked at after he left the police station and before he went to his book launch at Hampton Court.

She looked at each in turn. It didn't take long for a theme come out: Sherborne, Sherborne's relationship with Princess Heidemarie, Princess Heidemarie's suspected illegitimate child, speculation about the father, and so it continued.

Ellen froze. She could hear someone trying the front door lock.

twenty-two

Mikhail Turgenev sat in his office reading the news ticker on the silent television screen. Breaking news: Professor Ellen Armstrong had been shot dead outside her home.

He was now another step closer to independence.

The phone rang. His private line. The number ID was a cell phone, but he couldn't recognize the number. Hearing the voice at the other end he relaxed, leaning back and throwing his feet onto his desk. "You have done well tonight. It is all over the news." He beamed like a proud parent. "So why are you calling, my friend?"

The humor fell from his face as he dropped his feet to the floor and sat upright. "Shot him? *Him*?"

There would be a time to be incredulous. There would be a time to be angry. This was not that time. For the moment, there were practical issues to be addressed, such as the lack of death of Professor Armstrong—at least the lack of death of the professor at the hands of the man he had sent to kill her—and ensuring that Kuznetsov did not learn about whatever had already gone wrong that evening.

"You say you shot a man. Professor Armstrong is a woman." He waited for the realization to hit, and for the excuses. "I don't care if he said 'da.' Da! An Englishman trying to speak Russian, and you shot him for that."

He cursed and started punching buttons on his keyboard, then clicked violently with the mouse. "This is all wrong. Where are you?" He picked up his keyboard, blew into it, turned it over, banged it on his desk, placed it the right way up, and started typing, his fingers hammering the keys.

"Surbiton? How the...?" He looked at his screen. "The map is right. I couldn't believe you would be that stupid and that far wrong." He zoomed out of the map and looked at the escape route he had planned. "So what went wrong? Go straight, at the railway, turn right, go over the bridge, drop the gun. Easy."

He pointed to the map on the screen. "Look. There. There. There. There," and then threw himself back in his chair in frustration, looking at the map.

"So where..." The caller had been expecting the question. "Burned it." The next excuse took him by surprise. "Pages missing?" He looked into his trashcan. The latex gloves were on top, underneath were the loose pages he had dropped in earlier in the afternoon. He picked them up and looked at them, raising his eyebrows. "So you're in Surbiton, you say?"

Turgenev threw the loose pages back into the trash and returned to his computer, opening the newspaper's database. He looked at the summary and clicked a link, which opened a web page. As the page loaded, a broad grin spread across his face. "I love it when other people tell you where they are," he muttered under his breath.

"We're on to a new plan. Are you listening?" Turgenev looked intently at the map on his screen and explained the directions. He waited while the man with the scar repeated the instructions back to him. "You're going into a place called Thames Ditton. I'll spell it for you, it's T-H-A-M-E-S D-I-T-T-O-N. Go up Saint Leonard's Road, and when you reach a roundabout, turn right. Follow that road for a short distance, and the road will kick to the left. This is where you want to be; you should be able to get down to the river at that bend. More to the point, you should be able to see Thames Ditton Island, and on Thames Ditton Island you will find...?"

Turgenev waited for the reply. "Yes, that's correct. Professor Ellen Armstrong, who is a girl, not a boy."

He flipped the map on his screen from street view to the satellite view. "There's a bridge going over the river, and that bridge starts where the road kinks. As far as I can see, Professor Armstrong is in the middle of the island. The best way to find her is to call her—listen for the ring of her phone; then you'll know where she is."

He dictated the phone number, listening to the man with the scar as he repeated the number. "Get there and check out the place. It's an island—all you have to do is make sure she doesn't leave."

twenty-three

After his call with Richard Sherborne, Peter Winckley, or Pete the Winkle to his mates—a nickname reinforced by his slight stature and his squirming personality—was mentally counting out the cash he was about to be paid.

It was a shame that the police had kept the documents he had liberated, documents that had not been seen in 500 years. But it was only a problem of timing: The documents wouldn't be listed anywhere in the Hampton Court archives, so when the police couldn't prove they were stolen, he could claim ownership.

But more to the point, he knew where they had come from and was slim enough to get back there again. The documents had been there for 500 years, and it didn't seem like anyone else had been in a hurry to get in there—and if someone *did* want to get there, they would need to be smaller than him to fit through the gap. Added to which, he had told everyone he was hiding in the gap, not that the gap led somewhere, so there was little chance of anyone nosing around. And he could be confident that they wouldn't fill the gap, because that would affect the fabric of the building, and the Palace was a protected historic monument, so it would take years of planning even to block the small cavity with a plank of wood.

Having the professor authenticate the documents was a huge bonus. It was a shame that he was now dead; he had seemed genuinely interested in the find and had, albeit inadvertently, alerted Pete to the value of the papers as well as confirmed their historical significance.

But as one door closes, another one opens. If the prof was dead, then that was an opportunity for Pete. The prof wouldn't mind him having a quick look around his house—he had obviously been proud of it; otherwise, why would he have kept talking about it? And in a police station? A place where you know you're going to find criminals.

Pete stepped off the bus and shook his hair loose. Within five minutes he reached the High Street and followed it to the two parking lots next to the bridge crossing the river to Thames Ditton Island. Two wooden steps led up onto the steep curve of the bridge, and in the middle he reached the gate with barbed wire and spikes protruding in an arc around its outside.

The keypad to the right of the gate gave Pete a moment of nostalgia. He remembered when people actually thought these things were secure; now these old models were as much use as having a "please do not steal" sign on a car with the keys in the ignition.

He guessed that each resident would have their own code. But there would be a separate override code for the engineers, so his only question was four digits or six. He guessed six and punched 9-9-9-9-9-9. There was a buzz, and the lock clicked open. Pete pulled the gate and walked through, listening to the squeal followed by the solid clunk, with a vibration echo that he felt through his feet as the gate slammed behind him.

He took the two steps off the end of the bridge and onto the island. To the right was a small fenced area with a few trash and recycling bins together with a junction box fed from some cables that appeared to be suspended under the bridge. To his left was a central path through the island, gently illuminated by the light seeping out of the homes on each side.

Some of the newer buildings were sturdier brick buildings; others were wood-framed beach huts on stilts, which looked as if they would bend in the wind. None had a big sign over the top saying, "Hey Pete, this is the professor's home." None even seemed to give a subtle hint.

He walked down the central path looking to his left and right, hoping for anything that might tell him which house belonged to the professor.

About 50 yards up, he saw it: a mock-Tudor beach hut with brick pillars to the left and right of the front door. On the left pillar stood a lion, and on the right pillar a unicorn: a miniature re-creation of the outer gate at Hampton Court. Maybe it wasn't a big sign hanging in the sky, but it was enough of a sign for Pete.

The prof had clearly been here since he left the police station—he had left a light on, which he would only have done in the evening.

Pete knelt as if to tie his shoelaces and worked a straightened paperclip out of the hem of his jeans. Having taken a quick look around, he stood and went straight to the front door. For the second time in 90 seconds, he found it hard to believe how little people cared about security in the twenty-first century. First there was the security code at the gate, and now there was a pin-tumbler lock on the door. Clearly the prof had too much confidence in the security gate and the river acting as a moat.

He bent the paperclip back on itself and jiggled it into the lock, feeling each pin in the tumbler. He turned it slowly, felt some resistance, jiggled a bit more, tried again, still felt some resistance, and pulled out the clip. Holding it gently between the thumb and middle finger of each hand, he made a few delicate bends and then returned the clip to the lock. He jiggled, turned, jiggled, turned, and mouthed a silent "yay" as the lock yielded to his most delicate request and opened.

The door banged behind him, and he stepped into the room. Before he could look around, he heard a noise from the second door on the right, and a short blond woman dressed in a blue suit and kitten heels appeared.

Not expected.

Not part of the plan.

He held out his hand. "Hi. I'm Pete. Is the professor here?"

He gauged the blond woman's reaction. His brazen approach was working so far; she wasn't screaming. His guess was she was stunned, but there seemed to be some upset, maybe some anger there too, and there was a serious amount of apprehension, which wasn't unreasonable for a woman who, until a moment ago, appeared to have been on her own.

Slowly she held out her hand. "Ellen. Professor Ellen Armstrong." Pete took her hand, careful to grip it firmly enough that it wouldn't feel like he had a limp handshake, but not so tightly that it would hurt. The woman continued, "I'm sorry. I don't recall Nigel mentioning your name. Are you a student of his?"

"No. No. I'm not a student." Pete gave his best reassuring look. "I've only met the prof recently. I'm what you might call an archaeological specialist. I deal with the practicalities of buildings rather than the intellectual study of them. I like to use a hands-on approach instead of looking at blueprints. We were working on some previously undiscovered documents in Hampton Court, and he suggested I stop by this evening."

"Oh," said Ellen, looking both reassured and slightly shocked. "Then you had better sit down. And perhaps you'd like a cup of tea?"

twenty-four

The swarm around Surbiton station soon thinned as the man with the scar on his face drove down the hill, following the instructions from Turgenev.

Within five minutes he reached the sharp left-hand bend in Thames Ditton and looked ahead: two parking areas; the one on the left seemed to be attached to the pub. The other, on the right, seemed to have no particular allegiance and no lighting.

Quietly slipping into the irregular parking lot on the right, he brought the small red car to rest between a beat-up Land Rover and a convertible. As he got out, he noticed that the lot seemed to double as a slipway into the river.

He turned to look at the pub. It was an English style he recognized: brickwork painted white with black woodwork around the windows and doors. The S-shaped ends of tie-rods—steel rods inserted into the building to hold together the bowing walls—suggested that the two-story building was old. The sagging of the bay windows on the upper floor suggested very old. He looked at the roof: a nasty mixture of clay tiles and slates. Old, probably very old, but people had messed with it over the years and had repaired it cheaply; instead of a quaint pub, the building was a brightly lit white lump that vibrated with the noise inside.

From the parking lot behind the pub, an arched bridge reached to the island in the river. He looked up and down—this was probably the island that Turgenev meant. There were two other islands downstream, but those both seemed small, not linked by a bridge, and he couldn't see any houses on either, whereas there were houses around the outside of this largest island.

The first task, before he did anything else, was to reconnoiter the area. Instinctively, he felt for the gun in his pocket as he walked back to the road and looked left and right. An unimpressive stretch of asphalt, the most noticeable features being its narrowness and the sharp bend on the corner where he was standing. He waited for a minute or two to check the traffic. One car passed—there probably wouldn't be much congestion when he left.

Cautiously, he walked into the next parking lot, noticing the two steps up to the steep slope of the bridge as he went around the back of the pub. Like the parking lot next to it, this one ended at the river. Unlike its neighbor, this didn't act as a slipway; instead, there was a wooden landing stage running along the edge of the river, with a ragtag collection of boats moored next to it. Some stacked two deep, others three deep.

He followed the landing stage as it went behind the pub, running up the river and parallel to the island. Before he went over the bridge, he wanted to cast a soldier's eye over his target to assess its access points, its escape routes, and its terrain, although to be frank it looked like a fairly flat lump of land.

He counted twenty-three houses on the closest side of the island, which suggested there might be around fifty properties in total. Each building was a single story with a piece of grass leading down to a continuous landing stage circling the island, with one or two boats for each property.

The island was longer than he expected. He estimated around 200 yards; he couldn't be sure of the width until he saw the island from the other side, and he wasn't about to steal a boat to check his precision.

The pub landing stage ended before the end of the island. He looked farther up the bank of the river. There were small boats moored at the ends of private houses. He contemplated crossing the ends of the backyards but decided against it. All he needed to do was to trip a security light, and someone might call the police. And if the police were sniffing around, then he couldn't get to the professor.

Turning back along the landing stage, he followed the passageway that passed to the other side of the pub. If it was in better condition and if there was more space to turn in from the narrow road at the front, then you could probably get a car down there. He didn't have time to put his car there, but for the man with a scar, it was another useful possible exit route.

At the road he turned right, walking away from the parking lots. He followed the asphalt for a few minutes, and when he was satisfied that there were no other access routes to the river, he crossed and headed back toward the pub.

As he came up on the inside of the bend, he saw a figure ahead of him. The man turned his head to check the road before crossing, then walked into the pub parking lot, heading in the direction of the bridge.

The other man hadn't made eye contact, but his face was familiar. The man with the scar had seen him recently. He had seen him this afternoon in the Silver Spike. He was the man who'd had a meeting with the big boss in the Observatory.

twenty–five

The man on the phone seemed calmer. Turgenev wasn't sure whether it was fear or anger at himself.

He'd find out soon enough. "I'm going to get on my bike and come down and help you. Together we can make sure that all the loose ends are tied up, and then I'll give you your own motorcycle escort to Heathrow." He kept smiling while he lowered the phone into its cradle. His face fell as he released the handset.

Turgenev lifted down his black leather jacket that hung on the back of his office door and slipped it on.

How could he get simple instructions so wrong? All he had to do was find Professor Armstrong, walk up to her, confirm her identity, shoot her, and leave. What was so difficult about that?

Instead, he had shot someone—someone whose identity was a mystery to both of them—and had then become lost on his way to the airport. He was meant to be a soldier, but what sort of a soldier can't find his way around a traffic diversion?

Turgenev looked at his computer. Professor Armstrong still seemed to be on Thames Ditton Island, where she had been while he talked to the man with the scar, and the man with the scar seemed to be on the bank near the island. Hopefully that meant he was checking out the area as he said he would.

Turgenev pulled out his phone and tapped the screen to open a map—with a few button presses he had two red dots: Professor Armstrong and her hunter. With a few more presses he had a map showing his route. It estimated a travel time at forty-six minutes. He laughed to himself. Forty-six minutes if you keep to the speed limit translated into 20 minutes on a bike, and with the way he rode, maybe 10 if he was lucky.

He went to retrieve a gun, but turned before reaching the safe and sat down again, pondering whether a plausible excuse could be found for carrying a gun in a country where firearms were largely illegal. It wasn't a problem for him, but it would be embarrassing for Kuznetsov if his staff were found with illegal weapons, and there was already a gun that should be at the bottom of the river by now.

Finding no reason, he stood, picked up his helmet, and headed for the elevator. "I'll be back soon. Probably in about an hour," he said to the swarthy man behind the desk without waiting for a response.

In the bowels of the building, he walked past the parked cars to his bike. The machine was perfect. A Russian Ural Wolf. Pure Russian engineering, and this model had a heritage dating back to Stalin's time, having been built in a former state-run factory 1,300 miles east of Moscow in the Ural Mountains. Turgenev knew this firsthand; he had visited the factory to specify his custom modifications and later to pick up the machine before he rode it back to Moscow.

The factory had told him that his was the only completely black model they had ever built. Every piece of paint was black; every bit of chrome was replaced with a hard-wearing black powder-coating. Every nut, bolt, and screw was black. The only pieces that weren't completely black were the mirrors, which were tinted, and the lights, which had been darkened.

It was a black Wolf, ridden by a black wolf.

Turgenev threw his leg over, clipped the phone with the map onto the handlebars, and then kicked the bike into life, feeling the solid rumble and hearing the throaty purr as it idled, roaring on the twist of his wrist. He slipped on his helmet and followed the underground parking to the exit ramp. Through the barrier, he turned onto St Giles's Circus, pointed the bike toward southwest London, and opened the throttle.

twenty–six

Boniface was still trying to get the smell of vomit and cheap Z-list-celebrity-endorsed perfume out of his nostrils. He hadn't enjoyed waiting in line for a cab, but after walking around for fifteen minutes it seemed the only place to get one was outside one of the nightclubs in Kingston, so reluctantly he joined the queue with the lightweight party-goers who couldn't hold their drink and were already going home.

He had contemplated going home, going to the office...going anywhere, but Boniface knew that it was only a matter of time before the police would search Nigel's home. Since his house wasn't the immediate crime scene, the cops wouldn't be able to access the property without a warrant or permission from the owner, and as the owner was dead, Boniface had a few hours, if he was lucky.

The journey had been swift, and the cabbie dropped him by the roundabout halfway up the High Street. As he walked to the end of the road, he found that he could begin to breathe through his nose again. By the time he got to the pub by the river, he was pleased for the refreshing breeze coming off the water. He crossed the road, went through the parking lot, up the two steps, and onto the curved bridge leading to the island.

When he reached the gate at the apex of the bridge, a well-padded middle-aged woman was coming out. "Let me hold that for you," said Boniface, opening the gate she was struggling to push.

Stepping off the bridge, he followed the central path, unsure which house was Nigel's. About fifty yards up, he saw a mock-Tudor beach hut with brick pillars to the left and right of the front door. On the left pillar stood a lion, and on the right pillar a unicorn. Boniface tried not to sneer.

He had spent the evening with an historian. If history teaches us anything, it teaches us that people forget, mislay, misplace, and lose their keys. So any smart historian without many friends would hide a key somewhere near his house.

Walking up the path, Boniface looked at the two figures, each standing on top of a four-foot brick pillar. He looked to the left, then to the right, and back to the left. Deciding on the lion, he grabbed it with both hands and lifted, resting its weight on the edge of the plinth on the top of the pillar. In the gunk accumulated under the lion was a key; he picked it up and returned the lion to its place.

After wiping it with his fingers, then surreptitiously wiping his fingers on the plinth under the lion, the key slid into the lock and turned effortlessly. As Boniface stepped in, he noticed the light was on, which wasn't surprising, and that the kettle was boiling, which, while it was welcome, was not expected.

Two chairs in the middle of the room pointed away from the door—and from the chairs two faces swung around to look at him. In the left chair sat a scrawny man of around fifty with long hair; a small blond woman wearing a blue jacket was on the right. She stood up. "Mister Boniface." She corrected herself "Sorry, just Boniface. You're in time for tea."

"Ellen?" Boniface wasn't sure whether this was Professor Armstrong—he had never met her—but she certainly looked like the woman who regularly appeared on TV. However, it was surprising that she was there, if she was Ellen. When he had spoken to the police, they had told him that she was in her neighbor's house and was too upset to talk.

The woman looked as if she had been crying, but the prime emotion she now seemed to be displaying was relief. Could it be that she was relieved he was here? It was almost as if she felt intimidated by the man who was sitting in the other chair.

And who was this guy, anyway?

"Yes, I'm Ellen. I'm so pleased to meet you. Nigel was always talking about you...he was in awe of you." Boniface blushed. "'Boniface,' he loved to say, 'my PR guru.' When you were first hired, he spent hours checking you out on the internet. He thought the stories of your exploits while you were a journalist made you cool. And then the time with the government sealed your reputation in his eyes."

"You make it sound like I was James Bond. I was once the press officer for the Minister of the Environment. I was hardly out there shooting baddies with a laser hidden in my pen."

Ellen's voice was soft. "But you impressed Nigel. He always liked the cliché that you don't know where the edge is until you go over it. You went over the edge, and he figured that made you a rock star among PR guys." Her smile was almost apologetic. "He also liked the stuff you wrote and thought you were working hard to make his book a success, as well as having some really smart insights."

Boniface's face cracked, and he let out a gentle laugh at the memory of Nigel. He could picture the professor's enthusiasm and how he would have loved the notion of this idealized figure working with him. It was a shame that the reality was far more mundane, and finding the edge, as Nigel put it, had, with Richard Sherborne's help, destroyed the tattered remnants of Boniface's career, pushing him to the edge of bankruptcy and necessitating a few loans that he now needed to repay as a matter of urgency, rather than making him some sort of rock star.

But it's always fun to know how other people think of you. Boniface thought of himself as an alcoholic who hadn't had a drink for a while.

Someone who was doing the only thing he could, having closed down every other avenue and alienated most of polite society during his apparent rock-star years. Strange how a moody photo on a website and a well-crafted bit of copy could change people's perceptions.

"I'm not sure how to respond to that," said Boniface, "but it's a pleasure to meet you, and I'm sorry for your loss. Nigel thought a lot of you, and I'm sure you'll miss him."

The electric kettle clicked off as Ellen turned away, seemingly hiding her tears. "Tea for everyone?" she asked, her voice unsteady, as if she was holding back the sobs.

"You've clearly been in England long enough to realize that we live on the stuff," said Boniface. "And I'd love a cup, please."

"Me too," said the long-haired man, rising from his chair.

"I'm sorry, I don't think we've met," said Boniface, offering his hand. "As you can tell, I'm Boniface. I am—or rather, I *was*—Nigel's PR adviser for the launch of his book." He reached into his top jacket pocket, pulled out one of the few remaining cards he hadn't passed out earlier in the evening, and handed it to the stranger.

The other man inspected the card. "Pete. Peter Winckley. As I was telling Professor Armstrong, I'm what you might call an archaeological specialist. I deal with the practicalities of buildings rather than the intellectual study of them. I like to use a hands-on approach instead of looking at blueprints. Nigel and I were working on some previously undiscovered documents in Hampton Court, and he suggested I stop by this evening. Obviously that was before…"

Boniface gave his best interested-to-hear-what-you've-got-to-say smile. "Really," he said reassuringly. "So you were working with him recently?"

"I was." The man stood straighter, as if trying to raise his status. The look of a scrawny, unkempt man with long, unwashed hair, grubby jeans that seemed to have cobwebs on them, and a fraying sweater over a dirty T-shirt didn't quite fit with Boniface's preconceived notions of one of Nigel's colleagues.

"There's your tea," said Ellen indicating the two cups on the counter. "The sugar's there if you want." She tilted her head toward the sugar as she picked up her cup and returned to her chair.

"Thank you," said Boniface, turning back to Pete. "So you were the specialist he was dealing with this week?" It was Boniface's best earnest and impressed look.

"Yes," said Pete, apparently pleased to be acknowledged.

"You're the guy who got stuck in a hole?" Pete's blush answered in full. "So is there any good reason we shouldn't call the police now?" asked Boniface quietly.

The grubby man turned to the counter, put two large spoonfuls of sugar in his tea, and took a sip. "Good tea." He walked between the two chairs, placed his cup on the table, and then returned to stand by the fridge.

"Let me make an observation," said Pete in a rough but unsettlingly high-pitched voice. "I think it's interesting that I am someone who has opened the lock with a paperclip; someone who you have just figured out was arrested today; someone who has done time inside, as Professor Nigel found out; and yet you're both talking to me." Boniface caught Ellen's eye. "You see...most people's immediate reaction would be to call the police, not to engage in conversation. And the phone is there." He pointed to the phone on the kitchen counter. "So that leads me to wonder..."

The intruder let the end of his sentence trail into an uncomfortable silence, which settled over the room as he stood smirking. Ellen looked up from her seat. "Well...I..."

Boniface caught her glance and softly shook his head. "I'm looking after my client." The other man frowned. "Whitefoot Thorpe Publishing, Nigel's publishers, is my client. I'm here for them, in case there's anything I should know."

The intruder acknowledged this and stepped to the table to take a sip of his tea before sitting in the chair he had been occupying when Boniface had entered. Boniface looked to Ellen, shrugging and giving an I-don't-know-what-the-heck-I-should-say look.

"And Professor Armstrong is here as Nigel's friend." Ellen nodded, sniffing.

Boniface felt more confident. "And for you, it's lucky to have us both here, as we can help you with whatever you've found. Remember, in this room, you've got a PR guru, as Nigel apparently liked to call me, and one of the leading experts on the English constitution, and quite a historian herself." Boniface gestured toward Ellen, who bowed her head, apparently uncomfortably self-conscious about the compliment.

Boniface put a teaspoon of sugar into the last cup, stirred it, and took a sip. "Good tea. Thank you." He walked behind Ellen's chair to the other side of the coffee table, placed the cup on a coaster, and stood up straight again, facing the other two.

The small man looked at Boniface. "Now please don't misunderstand me. I'm not ungrateful for your offer, but I've found something that has been hidden for the last five hundred years, and without me, it will probably remain hidden for the next five hundred years. And this is good stuff...Nigel was very excited about the few samples I took with me. He was very keen to take photos but was a bit annoyed that he only had the camera on his phone. I think he wanted to take the documents to be professionally photographed."

"He would," said Ellen. "He's got someone who will do that sort of thing, making sure the documents aren't touched, exposed to harsh lights, or any processes that could damage them. We can put you in touch with that photographer if you want."

A slight sneer crossed the man's face. "These are kind offers, but I don't think you quite understand. I've already got enough interest; I've got a buyer who wants the documents, and I'm sure this buyer will be interested in everything else I can bring to him."

Ellen slumped back in her chair and looked up at Boniface, who took the cue and proceeded. "Look, can I summarize the situation?" The thief took another sip of his tea, returning his cup to the low table. "You have found some documents of value. I presume Nigel saw them and agreed there is value."

The longhaired man nodded.

"So you have some documents, and you have a buyer."

The man nodded.

"Out of interest, who is the buyer?"

"Nice try, Mister Boniface, but no."

"Please, just Boniface, no mister." He gave a reassuring tilt of his head. "Seriously, who? There's a good chance that one or both of us knows him."

"Or her," said the intruder.

"No, this is a him," said Boniface. "And as we are likely to know *him*," he stressed the gender and continued when the smaller man nodded his surrender, "then we can help you with the historical context and veracity of the documents, and also with the negotiation. Think about it—do you *really* know what those documents are worth?"

He softened his voice and pointed at Ellen. "She does. And while I'm sure that you're going to tell me that only you know where the documents were found in Hampton Court, there's a good chance that at some point the location will be found, especially when you have a leading historian," he gestured toward Ellen again, "on the case. Now that we know there's something to look for, other historians can go looking. And when—not if, *when*—we find those other documents and whatever else is there, the scarcity value of what you have will fall quite considerably. So get us on board, and we'll get you a deal at the earliest opportunity."

The intruder subtly bowed his head as Boniface pushed on. "And without wishing to sound too pissy about it, there's also the fundamental issue that you came here for a reason. If you had everything you needed, then you would be off selling whatever it is you've got and taking the cash to buy your yacht. But instead, you've broken into the home of a dead professor."

"Sure. I hear you," said the scruffy man. "But remember, at the moment I'm holding the cards, and you don't know what I know." His face cracked a thin smirk. "And without wishing to get too pissy about it, you don't know much at the moment."

twenty-seven

The man with the scar on his face retreated farther into the shadows on the inside of the bend as he watched the man he had seen at the Silver Spike disappear, heading into the parking lot and toward the bridge to the island.

Swiftly and noiselessly, he crossed back to the slipway and crouched behind the wall separating the two parking lots, looking up at the bridge as the other man neared the gate halfway across. There was a creak as the gate moved, and then a squeal as the gate opened more quickly. "Let me hold that for you." It was the man speaking. He stood back, and a fat woman waddled out. There was another squeal and the gate slammed shut, leaving the earth under his feet shuddering.

The man with the scar watched as the fat woman came down from the bridge. With each step she got closer and the ground shook more. Gracelessly, she took the two steps down from the bridge and caught sight of where he was standing. "Oh yuck. Don't piss there! Go in the pub if you really can't hold it in."

"Sorry," he said and turned, crossing behind her as she walked through the sloping lot to a small silver car. The car's suspension groaned as she got in, and he was certain it was leaning dangerously to her side as she drove out, leaving a gap next to one of those old French peasant cars.

He scanned the parking lots as he mounted the bridge and walked up to the gate. He tried it. It was locked, and the keypad to the right suggested it wouldn't be easy to get open quietly. It would be far simpler to climb around when all he had to deal with were a few spikes and a bit of barbed wire. Nothing difficult—it wasn't as if there were guns shooting at him.

The spikes were each about two feet long and arranged as an arch over the gate, which then continued to the level of the bridge floor. He turned to the shadows on the right, away from the glare of the pub on his left, and eased himself over the handrail, letting his feet down until they reached the lip of the bridge floor.

Silently, he moved up to the spikes and, holding the handrail in his right hand, crossed his left hand to grab the outer fitting, which held the spikes in position. A firm tug told him it was solid. He crossed his left foot onto one of the lower spikes, which jutted out horizontally; and with his left foot secure, he released his right hand and swung around the spikes, grabbing the rail on the other side. In one continuous and silent movement, he was over the handrail and back on the bridge, walking as if he had stepped through the gate.

As he took the two steps off the end of the bridge and onto the island, there was a small area to his right with a few trash and recycling bins that had been fenced off, and a neat junction box fed by some cables suspended under the bridge.

Turning away from the fenced area, he looked toward the central path with the single-story buildings to the left and right. Each dwelling was different in its own way, but none had any distinguishing features. He walked to the far end of the path, acting like a lost visitor, and returned to the fenced area at the end.

The junction box gave him an idea. If the fat woman he had seen earlier was any indication of the residents, then it should be easy to get them to move off. Hopefully the professor had other reasons for being here and would stay, and it couldn't be coincidental that the man in a suit was here, could it?

After looking around the bins for a moment or two, he found a length of rusted pipe and levered the padlock off the junction box to reveal a tangle of wires. He turned back to the trash and looked until he found a discarded plastic container. It was three steps down to the river to fill it. He returned and emptied the water over the electrical tangle.

There was a crackle followed by a low-frequency *pffft*, and the island went dark.

He moved in behind the bins and waited. A few residents came out of their front doors and looked around, and then, at a house about fifty yards up on the right, the man he had seen in the office took a few steps out and looked around.

Now all he had to do was wait.

Slowly, starting with one or two people, but increasing in number, the residents began to leave their homes. They all seemed to mutter and complain; the only clear word he could make out as they passed was "pub."

He counted 82 people leaving and then waited. There had been five minutes of complete stillness when he stepped out. Without the glow from the houses, the central path was much darker. There were three houses with a flicker of light—at a guess, one was kerosene and two were candlelit. His target, where he had seen the man who had been in the office come out, was the second candlelit house.

Slowly he moved into position to look through the window, staying far enough away that he could reach cover if anyone looked out. In the flickering candlelight, he could see two people standing. At the far end of the room was the man he had seen. He was talking quite intently to the other person, whose back was to him. Long hair: This must be Professor Armstrong.

He moved closer, taking out his gun and phone. He dialed the number that Turgenev had dictated to him: the professor's number. It took about ten seconds until he faintly heard a phone start to ring in the house in front of him, signaling that he should pull the trigger.

He didn't need much light to see the side of a head explode, and when he saw splatter like that, he knew his job was done. He ended the call before the phone was answered and slipped back into the shadows, ready to leave the island.

In the distance he could hear the distinctive throatiness of the Ural Wolf. Even this far away the sound was reassuring, like picking out your hometown accent in a foreign bar. Turgenev was close, and now he had something positive to report.

Now he had corrected his earlier failure: The professor was dead.

twenty-eight

Boniface had several images flashing in his consciousness and was trying to arrange their sequence in chronological order.

He had been talking to the guy with long hair, and he thought he was close to convincing him that he and Ellen could help. But then a phone had rung, there had been a noise outside, the front window had broken, something semi-liquid but perhaps containing solid particles had splattered across the wall, and the long-haired man had fallen down, hitting the chair as he fell.

Then Ellen shrieked.

A short shriek, but now she was still.

He looked at Ellen sitting in her high-backed chair, illuminated in the gloom by two flickering candles. She had drawn her legs up and was sitting in the fetal position, staring at the splatter of what he guessed was brain, blood, and bone across the wall, with her lower jaw trembling. "He's been shot." Her voice a whisper. "That wall looks like the front of my house where..." Her voice trailed to silence, but her mouth kept moving.

Boniface remained paralyzed. As his website announced, one of the services he offered was crisis management. This seemed like something of a crisis, and for the second time that evening he felt unable to think, to function, or to move. He was aware that he was breathing. From the pounding in his ears he was conscious that blood was pumping through his body, but apart from that he wasn't sure what time it was, what day it was, or what he was doing there.

"Boniface." It was Ellen, now standing near to the French doors but with her stare still fixed on the wall. "He's been shot. We need to get out of here."

"Huh?" Boniface moved toward the front door, his gaze still draw to the spatter on the wall, visible in the candlelight.

"Where are you going?"

"To have a look..."

"Not that way. Man with gun..."

The last comment shocked Boniface, and he turned to stare at Ellen. He held her glance for several seconds and then broke, snapping out of the gaze and coming out of his trance. "What the fuck just happened?"

"A bullet came through the window and hit him." She was fixated again on the splatter across the wall, her voice small and trembling, her face cracking as tears started to flow. "Is he dead?"

Boniface craned his neck to look, unsure about stepping closer. "If he's not dead, he should be. He would want to be."

"So what are we going to do? You're meant to be the expert in this situation." Ellen's voice was started to crack.

"You don't happen to know where Nigel's car is, do you?"

"The parking lot on the other side of the bridge."

"And the keys?"

"Third drawer, I think," said Ellen, pointing to the drawers under the kitchen counter. "You'll also find some other keys in there. One set must fit this door." She softly tossed her head toward the French doors behind her.

Boniface walked to the drawers. "So who were they after? You, me, him...what was his name?"

"Pete, I think he said, but I'm not sure."

Boniface retrieved a handful of keys and walked over to Ellen. "Can you drive?"

"Yes."

"Good. Here's the key." Boniface passed an old key with a battered Citroën logo on a keychain with Nigel's work identification attached. "Now, which key opens this?" He gestured to the doors and held several bunches of keys in his hands.

Ellen looked at the keys, sizing each one, as if visually imagining whether it would fit the lock. "This one." She picked a brass key on a ring with several others, placed it on the lock, and twisted. "Can we get out of here now?" She pushed, and the door swung open.

"One thing," said Boniface returning to the open drawer and dropping in the remaining keys. Ellen looked at him quizzically. He picked up the phone and dialed three digits, waiting for it to be answered. "Police. Murder." He laid the receiver on the counter and walked toward the door, raising his eyebrows to point Ellen outside.

The stillness of the night was broken by the throbbing sound of a motorcycle approaching from a distance. "Here come the filth hounds of Hades," said Boniface. "They're close. Probably going to the pub."

The stretch of grass between Nigel's house and the river was damp in the evening dew. As they got to the end of the lawn, they looked down to the wooden landing stage surrounding the edge of the island. Boniface jumped down and looked back at Ellen. "Neither of us is really dressed for this, are we?" He held out a hand for Ellen to steady herself as she cautiously stepped down, using a heel to stop her slip.

The motorcycle cut out, leaving the sound of boats clinking with the constant movement of the flowing river.

Boniface looked up and down the slim wooden platform, flanked along its length by boats. There were small cruisers, boats that would normally be powered by outboard motors, a rowboat, and lying on the stage were several nasty plastic kayaks. About twenty yards up, Boniface spotted what he was looking for. "That's the one for us." He led Ellen to a battered plastic boat, largely rectangular but with rounded corners.

Ellen stared at Boniface. He ignored the question implicit in her incredulous stare and looked around as if searching for something he had misplaced, then raised his eyes, purposefully strode out, and returned holding a single paddle with a hand grip at the end.

"We need to get out of here, Boniface," said Ellen, her voice finding an urgency that hadn't been present moment ago.

"On the other side of that house there's a man with a gun, so our options are kind of limited: It's a case of swim or get in a boat. That's a nice suit, and those are great shoes you've got there, but you're not dressed for swimming, and I'm a physical coward. This"—he held up the paddle—"seems the best thing to use to try to steer this boat."

Ellen shrugged with little commitment, continuing to stare at the small vessel.

Boniface knelt by the side of the boat, holding it with one hand and offering his other to Ellen. "This boat seems to be the easiest to get into and out of." Ellen took his hand and cautiously lowered a foot into the boat. "Most of the other boats are narrower, so they would probably wobble, and they have a point at the front."

Boniface released his hand as the professor sat in the bow of the boat, the front edge straight, stretching the full width of the vessel. "Now, notice the floor of the boat," said Boniface. "I'm sure there's a nautical term for the floor, but you know what I'm talking about. See how it rises to meet the top rim of the boat? I figure that when we reach the bank, we need to run aground and we can get out. If there was a point, well, we might need to jump."

"It sounds like a good plan." The academic spoke slowly.

"I knew you'd see it that way. Hold this." Boniface passed the handle of the paddle to Ellen and proceeded to untie the boat, throwing the two ropes into the vessel. The professor gave a slight look of horror as the boat moved freely without Boniface having hold. Her face relaxed when he sat on the landing stage, dangling his legs into the craft. "Hold tight," he said and moved into the stern of the boat, rocking it from side to side as he shifted his weight.

As the boat found its new equilibrium, Boniface asked, "Have you even been in a boat like this?" Ellen shook her head, her blond curls flicking with each twist. "May I make a suggestion then?"

She inclined her head slightly.

"The river seems to be moving quite quickly."

Ellen looked at the river. "You're right. That's fast. Are you sure...?"

Boniface cut off her question. "Nigel's car is by the bridge?" Ellen nodded. "All we have to do is drift downstream"—Boniface made it sound like a romantic afternoon on the Thames—"but instead of paddling, we'll hold on to the moored boats as we go. Once we can see around the end of the island, then as long as there's no one there with a gun, we'll try and use that paddle thing to get across to the car."

Ellen made an unconvincing sound of acknowledgement, gripping the landing stage more tightly.

"And if that fails, we'll duck down and keep drifting until we run aground somewhere." Boniface grinned.

Ellen's eyes darted around. "Couldn't we...no...perhaps...?"

"What, go the other way? Go upstream?" Ellen opened her eyes widely, questioning without articulating. "Too much fuss, too much noise, too hard to paddle against the current. This way we can stay pretty silent, and all we need to do is wait until whoever is around the corner has gone. Now that there's no light from the island, we should be able to stay in shadow, as long as we stay out of any light streaming from the pub."

Ellen shrugged. Boniface kept his gaze fixed on her. She shrugged again. "Okay. Let's do it."

"Then put the paddle down," said Boniface. "We don't need it yet. For the moment, let's get past these boats here. Hang on to them, and we'll do the hand-to-hand thing to move along the edge of the island."

Ellen laid down the paddle. "So how do we do this?"

"Push your end out... I'll keep hold of the landing stage but will move us along. When you can reach that boat, there," Boniface pointed to the small cruiser immediately downstream of them, "grab the rope around the outside, then I'll let go, and we should be one step closer to getting out of here."

"Or one step closer to drowning."

"Or one step closer to drowning," Boniface muttered cheerily.

They moved past the small cruiser and a nearly duplicate boat next to it, past a rowboat at the end of Nigel's property, and past several other craft. It took a while to get the rhythm and longer to build up the confidence in the direction that the boat was drifting. When they were sure that the general trend of the current was toward the bank, they became less concerned about drifting and focused their efforts on moving toward the end of the island.

Ellen broke the silence. "You were going to do a deal with him, weren't you?"

"Who?"

"Mister Longhair...the architectural specialist."

"No. I didn't come here to do a deal with a thief."

"So why are you here, Boniface?"

"Because..." He sighed. "It was something Nigel said."

"It sounded like you were going to do a deal."

"Of course it did. He was obviously after something, and by talking to him we found out that he's got a buyer." Boniface felt the impatience in his tone. "But I wasn't going to do a deal."

"So if you weren't going to do a deal, why did it sound like you were ready to?"

"Because he had a point. We don't know anything." He stared directly at Ellen. "I didn't want to do a deal; I just wanted to know what he knew and how he got stuck in the hole. Nigel didn't explain that to me." Ellen looked confused. "It's a whole long stuck-in-a-hole-at-Hampton-Court story; he got stuck, then arrested, the police called Nigel... Anyway, I figured if he thought that we could do something to get him some cash quickly, then we could get the information out of him, and we might get a step closer to figuring out who killed Nigel and why he was killed." He paused. "You don't happen to know why Nigel was killed, do you?"

Boniface watched as Ellen processed his logic. "But you do know something, don't you, Ellen?" She tilted her head slightly. "If there wasn't something to find out, you wouldn't have come here, would you?"

"Hold on. You haven't finished yet, Boniface. If you weren't going to do a deal, then why are you here?"

"What's this?" said Boniface. "I'll show you my motivation if you'll..." Ellen pushed out her bottom lip. "I told you, it was something Nigel said this evening. I came here to see what Nigel had left around. There was a loose end."

Ellen looked at him quizzically. "Loose end?"

"Given what has transpired, it's probably nothing," said Boniface, turning away to hide his blush. "You understand it's bad for business when a client gets killed. I take it personally." He watched, waiting as Ellen blinked her acknowledgment. "Now, I think it's time for some reciprocity."

"No, not yet. What did Nigel tell you?"

Boniface raised his eyebrows. "Not much. I stopped him talking at the book launch about whatever it was he found. It's not good to tell people why the book you're launching is out of date before it's in the shops."

Ellen smiled softly. "That's Nigel."

"Then, in the cab on the way to Kingston, he seemed to spend the whole time dicking about with his phone. I wasn't listening to what he said, something about it being too slow."

"So what was he doing with the phone?"

"I don't know. Something with photos? Perhaps the photos he took of the papers Mister Longhair stole?" Boniface exhaled. "I don't know, I'm guessing. Longhair said Nigel took pictures with his phone, right?"

They were approaching the end of the island, and the boats were thinning. "See that mooring post." Boniface pointed at a post past the end of the island, maybe twenty or thirty yards away. "If we drift, we should be able to grab that post. In fact, if we drift from here, we'll probably hit it. When we reach it, we can tie up." Boniface scrambled for the rope lying in the bottom of the boat, which had one end tied to the stern of the plastic craft. "Once we're stationary, we can sit and wait for a few minutes to make sure there are no nasty men with guns before we do our bit of paddling."

"You reckon we'll reach the post and won't drift past." Ellen let go of the boat they were passing and turned to face Boniface.

"I do." Boniface pushed away, letting their craft drift toward the mooring post. "And when we're tied up, you can tell me what you found."

twenty-nine

Fourteen minutes door-to-door.

Mikhail Turgenev rolled his Ural Wolf into the parking lot, pulling into a space beside an old Citroën 2CV, and killed the engine. He took off his helmet, yanked the phone off the cradle on his handlebars, and zoomed in, straining at the screen. It was too small; all he could see were two overlapping dots, suggesting Ellen Armstrong and the man with the scar on his face were both on the island.

All he had to do was find the man with the scar, tie up the loose ends, and get back to the office before anyone noticed things had gone wrong. And when the problem caused by the other man became apparent, neither of them would be implicated.

The Russian jumped off his bike and looked around. There was a brightly lit white pub and, to its right, the bridge connecting the island. The island seemed to be in darkness. He had expected that there would be more signs of life; otherwise, what was Professor Armstrong doing there?

The parking area didn't seem very well organized. It was an irregular shape on a piece of sloping, twisting land, and each car seemed to have parked without a thought for other drivers. The slope seemed strange; he was surprised that the ground hadn't been leveled. His eyes followed the slope, reaching the river, and it made sense. It wasn't a parking lot; it was a slipway where cars happened to be left.

His eyes followed the slope into the river, and he watched the swift current, becoming aware of the clink of the boats moored along the bank and around the island, mixed with the gentle hum from the pub. His musing was interrupted by someone coming out of the pub. He looked. Big mistake. With the background light spilling out of the pub, he lost some of his night vision.

It was disorienting. He thought he heard a phone ring out on the river; by instinct he would have placed it around the end of the island, but when he looked he couldn't see anyone there—not that he could see so well having looked toward the light. By the pub door there was a man on his phone, but the ring didn't seem to have come from where he was standing. Even with bouncing echoes, something still didn't seem right. Turgenev looked out again onto the river. It was as if he could hear whispers. But however hard he looked, he couldn't see anything; it was too dark, and his night sight was still shot to pieces.

Someone was coming over the bridge; he couldn't make out anything beyond a shape. Whoever it was seemed to be looking in his direction. He casually took some cover behind the wall separating the two parking lots and maintained his surveillance.

The shape reached a gate in the middle of the bridge. There was an electronic clunk and a squeal as the gate opened, followed by a squeal as the gate closed and a solid slam with vibrations he could feel through his feet. He watched the shape maintain its progress; he was still looking at him when the shape raised his hand in acknowledgement.

Turgenev stepped into the open. The man with the scar took the two steps down from the bridge and rounded the corner into the second parking lot. The men embraced, slapping each other on the back.

"It is good to see you, my friend," said Turgenev. "Have you found the woman?"

"Mikhail Igorovich Turgenev," said the man with the scar. "I have done more than that. I have fixed the error I made. The woman is now dead. I shot her; I saw her head explode."

Turgenev felt an overwhelming wave of relief. "That is good, very good. Tell me what happened."

The man with the scar explained how he had checked out the area, made his way over the bridge, knocked out the junction box, and then located the house. "In the candlelight I could see the woman with the long hair through the window; I called the phone number you gave me so I was sure I had the right house, and when I heard the phone, I pulled the trigger. Her head exploded. There is no doubt that she is dead."

Turgenev felt his head involuntarily rock forward and back, keeping sync with his slowing breathing. "This woman had long hair."

"Yes. Long, dark, straight hair."

Turgenev recalled the image of Professor Armstrong he had seen on the television in Kuznetsov's office. You could argue about whether her hair was short or shoulder length. What was beyond doubt was that it was blond with curl. Not long, dark, and straight.

"You have done well, my friend. Very well."

He flinched, bending his knees to reduce his size, slightly hunching, and looked to the left, pointing with his eyes. The man with the scar picked up on the danger sign and turned to look in the direction indicated by Turgenev. As he did, Turgenev exploded, his bent knees straightening to increase the force of the single blow from the outside of his right hand, which landed on the other man's windpipe.

The man with the scar on his face fell to the ground.

Turgenev went through his pockets, removing the gun, the phone, his passport, and the car keys before dragging the body along the slipway into the river, stepping into the water to hold the man's head under. When no more air bubbles came from the man's nose and mouth and Turgenev could feel no pulse, he rolled the inert lump in the water until it was face down, and then pushed it into the current.

Somewhere in the distance he could hear sirens.

thirty

The boat drifted, aiming squarely at the mooring. Boniface leaned over Ellen to wrap the rope around the post, then tangled the end in a vain attempt to make a knot that would hold. He tugged the rope, felt the tension, and guided the boat away from the post before sitting to wait for the drift to pull the line tight.

They jerked to a stop and the line stretched, holding the boat stationary in the current. There was quiet, apart from the distant sounds of the moored boats banging and clinking, and the rushing sound of water passing the flat, square stern of their boat. Across the river the white pub glowed like a beacon, and a gentle burble of noise echoed.

Ellen and Boniface sat looking toward the bank, neither breaking the hypnotic stillness.

"So," said Boniface, his voice gentle. "Tell."

The still was shattered by Boniface's phone. By the second ring he had muted the noise, leaving the sound to echo around them and diffuse into the rumble of someone coming out of the pub, talking loudly on his phone.

Ellen pointed to the bank.

Boniface frowned.

Ellen pointed again, but with more emphasis. Boniface re-scanned the bank and saw a solitary figure in the lower of the two parking lots. From a distance he looked to be wearing a black jacket, but all cats are gray in the dark, right?

Boniface looked back to Ellen with wide eyes. A look passed between them, and they returned their gaze to the lone man. Without breaking his attention, Boniface whispered, "So what did you find?"

"Quite a lot, but not enough." Ellen lowered her voice, taking out some of the harshness in her tone. "I went through his closets."

"And?"

"And nothing. I thought it would be stacked with porn, but it wasn't. I was looking through his computer when Mister Longhair came in, then you arrived, and the power went out."

"So what did you find?" Boniface had not been a patient child, and he hadn't grown up to be a patient adult. "What did you look at on his computer?"

"I looked at his word processor documents and had just finished checking his internet history when I was interrupted."

"Wrong order. Always start with the email, then the calendar."

"Thanks. Next time you get there first and do the digging." Boniface could hear the edge of annoyance in Ellen's voice.

"Sorry," he mouthed. "So what did you find?"

"A lot of it was standard Nigel conspiracy stuff. You know, Henry didn't break with Rome, Wolsey did. Wolsey never failed at anything, so the failure to achieve a divorce for Henry must have been for a reason, perhaps so he wouldn't have to deal with people in the church who would recognize him after he took power."

"Really?" said Boniface.

"Perhaps. Maybe part of it was Wolsey's anger at his mistreatment by Henry. If someone took Hampton Court away from you, wouldn't you be pissed? Perhaps he wanted all the power for himself. Maybe he felt that Henry didn't fight hard enough for him to become Pope, which would have effectively made him King of the Vatican, so he became King of England in the old-fashioned, violent way."

"But this isn't new." Boniface wanted to scream, but while floating in a small boat when someone with a gun may be after you is neither the time nor the place.

"No, it's not new. But Nigel's view was that Wolsey was Lord High Master of the Paperclip: He kept every document, every bit of paper, anything written down. It was a good job there wasn't toilet tissue in Tudor times, because he would have filed that, too."

Boniface grimaced.

"Nigel's logic was that there must be a piece of paper somehow confirming that Wolsey murdered Henry. Nigel was convinced that when he found the proof that Wolsey had murdered Henry, he would also find how he achieved the cover-up."

"Was Wolsey that much of a paper-pusher, or is this just a wacky theory of Nigel's that seemed interesting to him but had little validity?" Boniface struggled to keep his voice quiet. "I mean, I thought this was just an interesting idea and that he got the book deal because it supported the notion that the monarchy was a busted flush in the sixteenth century and therefore had even less of a place in the twenty-first century."

"No, no. Nigel was serious about this. Even to the point of chasing down any facts that could undermine his theory—like look at Wolsey's death. Conventionally, Wolsey is believed to be buried in Leicester Abbey. To Nigel's way of thinking, that lack of certainty is one possibility why Wolsey could have died in 1530 when the accepted history suggests he did."

A breeze came across the river, and Ellen pulled her jacket tighter, crossing her arms across her chest. "Nigel was always of the opinion that Wolsey would have ensured that there was a grave, even a very simple grave, to give definitive evidence of his own—albeit faked—death. In other words, if he had murdered the King so that he could replace him, then he would have done everything necessary to prove and authenticate his own death. But that lack of grave was one angle Nigel could never resolve."

Ellen fell silent and pointed to a figure on the bridge. Boniface looked and returned his view to Ellen. Ellen shrugged at Boniface, who exaggerated a shrug in return. "Not a clue," whispered Boniface. "Our shooter?" Ellen's head moved slowly, bobbing like a twig on the river before she pointed to the man on the bridge followed by a man on the bank. Boniface pushed out his bottom lip, exhaling.

The man reached the middle of the bridge, opened the gate, and let it slam behind him. As he continued, he made a small gesture with his hand. Coming off the bridge, he spun into the lower parking lot, embracing the man who had been in the shadows.

There was a low rumble of sound as they talked. Boniface strained but could not hear what they said.

His concentration was broken when they both appeared to be startled and looked toward the pub. Boniface could see nothing in the direction they were looking. Another swift move, the sound of flesh hitting flesh, and one of the men was on the ground with the other over him. Then the man still standing dragged the other man into the river and squatted, holding his head under water.

"Shit!" spat Boniface under his breath, looking at the shaved head of the man in black who was holding the other man underwater. "We're fucked. It's Turgenev."

When she spoke, there was grit in Ellen's voice. "What? At a time like this you're making up names that sound scary to amuse me. Is this your idea of a joke?"

"No. We're in deep shit. That's Kuznetsov's head of security." With the words *head of security*, Boniface made quote marks with his fingers. "I don't know if he's after you or me, but he's not here to take the night air."

"So?"

Boniface sighed. "It's probably not a coincidence that he's near where there's been a shooting, and my guess is that if he finds us, we're both dead. And it won't be a nice death: He's got his own special version of the Kama Sutra with his own special ways to fuck you. He'll fuck us any and every way he can, and then kill us."

They sat in silence, watching Turgenev turn the man over and push him along the river. The body started to move with the current, sinking below the surface. Turgenev stood, fixated on the spot where the body had disappeared, before turning and heading onto the bridge. He stopped at the gate, the light from the pub bouncing off his shiny head.

He tried the gate, and a frustrated rattle drifted over the Thames as the lock refused to open. He looked over the left side of the gate, and his head followed the outline of the spikes up, over the arch, and down onto the right side before he eased himself over the handrail and clumsily clambered around the spikes, giving a low grunt as he caught his leg.

"That's a man on a mission. That's a man on a mission who's in a hurry. We need to move. We need to be gone, now." Boniface pulled on the rope tying the boat to the mooring post and started picking at the tangle, swearing under his breath. "Are you any good with knots?"

"That's what you're calling it now, a knot?" Ellen's tone was flat. "Why don't you untie the other end? The nice, easy, dry knot that someone else tied to the boat. It's not as if we're going to need that rope once we get to the car."

Boniface reached for the other end of the rope, fiddled with it, and cast off the line, leaving the boat to start floating with the current. "And for that, you get the privilege of being first to paddle," said Ellen, handing Boniface the oar.

Somewhere in the distance a siren was wailing. Ellen looked at Boniface. "Paddle faster."

thirty–one

As he took the two steps down from the bridge, Turgenev felt a twinge in his calf where he had caught his leg on a spike as he negotiated his way around the gate.

It might be unrelated—there didn't seem to be anyone around who might have called the police—but the sirens were unlikely to be coincidental. Whatever the case, he needed to find out what had happened and get out.

Quickly.

The first challenge was to find the house. To the left, along the spine of the island, was a pathway with houses on either side. Most houses were dark, but there were lights from three of them. One seemed to be lit by a kerosene or gas lantern; the other two seemed to be candlelit. The man with the scar on his face had said he shot a longhaired woman in a house with candlelight, giving Turgenev a choice of two.

Silently he moved along the path, sharpening his senses to notice any change around him.

The front window of the second candlelit house was spider-webbed with a hole in the middle. From his place in the shadows, Turgenev became aware of the sirens being drowned out by the sound of a car trying to start. Or at least he presumed it was a car. If it hadn't been nighttime in suburban south London, he would have assumed it was a lawnmower or an agricultural vehicle starting.

He paused for a moment, watching for any sign of movement in the house, then walked up the path. There were two pillars; each seemed to have a separate animal on top. Perhaps it would be clearer with some light, but in the gloom they just looked ridiculous.

The car, or agricultural machinery, or whatever it was that was trying to start, took a break, and the sound of the sirens became clearer. After a cursory glance through the cracked window, Turgenev pushed the front door. It didn't move. Turning his back to the house, he waited; as the car tried to start again, he back-kicked the door, which swung open, slamming into the side wall.

On the third attempt, the engine caught and the car chugged into life. Whatever it was, it had less power than his bike, and that revving wasn't going to impress anyone.

The sound of over-revving and grinding of gears was joined by a third sound of squealing brakes and skidding. It sounded like someone had left the pub and was now trying to move a car around the parking lot. He turned, stepped into the room, and wasn't sure where to look first: at the body or at the spatter on the wall. Instinctively, he went to close the door behind him, but it wouldn't shut properly with a broken jamb.

There were two doors to the right. In the first he could see a bathroom, and he guessed the second would be a bedroom. The rest of the house seemed to be made up of the open plan room where he was standing.

At the front was a kitchen area with a burning candle standing on the counter next to the stove. The room was divided by two high-backed chairs with their backs to the kitchen area. Behind the left-hand chair—which had a blood smear down the back—and in front of the fridge was the body. Up close it didn't look very female, and even by candlelight the long hair clearly needed a wash and some serious hair-care products. The ladies of Sodom and Gomorrah could've offered him some advice.

In front of the chairs was a low table with some cups and two lit candles giving enough light to illuminate the blood, bone, brain, skin, and hair splattered across the left wall. Turgenev cursed under his breath: How could someone who could kill so perfectly fuck up so completely in identifying his target?

Twice?

He knelt to look at the body, moving the hair away from the face. Definitely not female. Probably around 50. Not a clue who he was or what he was doing here. Turgenev quickly patted the man's pockets, pulling out the contents where he felt a bulge. A phone, some change, a few tissues, and nothing more.

From his kneeling position he looked around. At his eye level, hanging in the lock of the French doors, was a set of keys. He walked around the table and tried the door, which opened onto a small area of grass. Quietly he jumped from the grass onto the landing stage to look up and down the wooden jetty skirting the island. Lots of boats, but whoever had gone out through the back door wasn't there now.

He walked back into the house. The different perspective made him reconsider the table. Something was wrong. Three cups. He reached over and felt them individually. They were all still warm, and by the look of them contained tea. How English.

Three cups? Three people. The guy with long hair and two other people, and the two other people—two witnesses, the professor, probably, and someone else—had most likely gone out the back as he came in the front.

He pulled out his phone and called up the map. The two dots had separated. One was where he was standing, which was to be expected as the phone he had taken from the man with the scar was now in his pocket. The other, Professor Armstrong's, was now on the riverbank, on the road running parallel to the river, going away from the High Street. The dot wasn't moving quickly, but it was moving.

Was that the car he'd heard?

Turgenev ran out the front door. The sirens had stopped, to be replaced by the oblique reflection of blue flashing lights. At a guess, they were in the parking lot by the bridge.

He went back inside and hefted the front door closed, applying his boot to make sure it would at least look locked from the outside, then slipped on the security chain and turned to blow the candle on the counter before walking around to the coffee table and extinguishing the last two candles. He took the keys out of the French door, locked it behind him, and walked down to the landing stage.

thirty-two

On the fifth attempt Ellen managed to get Nigel's 2CV started and jerked it round in the parking lot, pulling to the top of the slope. "Which way?"

Boniface sat uncomfortably in the passenger seat. "Flashing blue lights and nasty sirens in that direction; let's go right."

The car kangaroo-hopped onto the road, finally finding some equilibrium, but with the engine straining. "Where's second gear?"

"I dunno. Where was first?" Boniface fiddled under his seat, looking for some way to adjust the medieval form of torture he was strapped into. "Find first gear, then move the knob in the opposite direction."

"I don't know if I'm in first; I pulled the lever and the car moved. I don't do stick shifts, and as for clutches..." Two police cars drifted behind them, their sirens silenced but the blue lights on each roof still flashing as they entered the parking lot. "And why am I driving, Boniface, instead of you? You know where we're going."

"I can't drive."

"Can't or won't?"

"Can't. Rather a hangover from that rock-star behavior. Her Majesty's justices felt it would be best if I didn't take to the wheel for a while."

"Oh." Ellen stepped on the clutch, slid the gearshift, and released the pedal. The high-pitched squealing was almost drowned out by the graunching sound of the gears, neither of which could distract from the violent shaking as the car came to a halt with the engine dead. "I told you I don't do stick shifts."

Boniface understood when blame was being ascribed. The silence seemed to agree that Ellen might have a point, so Boniface changed the subject. "You still haven't told me what you found on Nigel's computer."

Ellen narrowed her eyes and turned her head to face Boniface. "Aren't there more pressing matters? We just saw someone get shot. There's a homicidal maniac about fifty feet away over there." She pointed through the buildings separating the road from the river, in the direction of the island. "There's a dead body in a room that has both of our fingerprints all over it, and we've run away from the scene where the police have just arrived. And to make matters worse, I can't drive this horrible car, and we're sitting in the middle of the road looking really conspicuous." Her eyes filled with tears. "That's before we talk about my friend who was killed tonight."

Boniface pondered. Go for glib. Go for sympathetic. Go for practical. Go for angry. Go for indignation. In the end, he decided to leave the car seat alone and go for silence. A car came up behind them and angrily flashed its lights, the driver gesticulating as he passed the badly parked 2CV.

Ellen bowed her head to wipe her tears with her sleeve. "I'm sorry, Boniface." She lifted her head to look up at him.

"It's alright," he mouthed silently. Ellen smiled cautiously, like a child looking for reassurance. "Really, I get it. Well, I get some of it... I was only there for the second shooting...and the first drowning." He watched tentatively, trying to judge the reaction. "This French peasant-wagon can have a real emotional effect on people, can't it?"

Ellen laughed guiltily. "He loved this car, you know."

"Unfortunately, I do," said Boniface. "Nigel told me all about it this evening. Now, shall we get moving? I feel you're right that we're probably a bit too close to danger."

"Where are we going?" sniffed Ellen.

"Hampton Court," said Boniface confidently.

"Why there?"

"Got any better ideas?"

"No."

"Me neither. And as it's the only idea we've got, we'll start there."

"Let me try and figure out where the gears are." Ellen jiggled the gearshift up and down. The only sounds: the lever squeaking through its hole in the dashboard and the movement of machinery in the engine block, with an occasional low squeak as she pressed the foot pedal. "It's not going to be perfect. Nothing with a clutch is going to be anything near good for me, but I'll try." She inhaled, seemingly finding new resolve. "Hampton Court?"

"Hampton Court, please, Driver, and you can tell me what you saw on the computer as we drive." Ellen turned to scowl at Boniface, who was giving his cheesiest grin. "Before you forget, of course."

"Let's get the car started first," said Ellen. She stomped on the clutch and turned the key. Slowly and painfully, the engine spluttered to life, the car's body rising by two or three inches as the suspension filled. "That always freaks the hell out of me."

"But that's how the peasants could drive across fields," said Boniface, glancing over his shoulder at the blue flashing lights reflecting off the windows of the buildings along the street.

Ellen dropped the gearshift into place with minimal grinding and lifted the clutch. The car jerked, finding how to combine forward movement with some smoothness. "Ready?" said Ellen.

"Huh?"

"Second gear." She hit the clutch, slid the lever out of gear and jiggled it, all the time the car slowing. "There," she said, pushing the gearshift forward. The car jerked again as she lifted the clutch and strained to accelerate. "This really is a pile of shit, Boniface."

"Don't judge it yet. We haven't done corners, and by the way, you want to take the next left."

"Left?" said Ellen. "Don't we want to go straight and then turn right?"

"We do," said Boniface, "but you can't turn right at the end, so we'll follow the back-doubles and come out farther up the road."

"Whatever you say," said Ellen, easing the car into the left-hand bend, her hands tightening on the wheel while Boniface looked for something to grip.

"It feels like we're at about forty-five degrees."

"More," said Ellen, straightening the wheel. The car slowly returned to the vertical, bouncing from left to right and up and down until it sta-bilized. "And you bring us the route with road humps," she said hitting the first bump.

The car stayed perfectly level, its suspension effortlessly absorbing the traffic-calming measure.

Ellen and Boniface looked at each other in open-eyed amazement. "So this horrible little peasant car, which is impossible to control and has all the power of a sewing machine, the aerodynamics of a sewing machine, the road-holding of a sewing machine, the grace and comfort of a sewing machine, is actually the best vehicle ever when going over humps," muttered Boniface. "I'm stunned. Put the pedal to the metal, and let's go."

"My foot's flat," said Ellen. "This is the top speed, unless I change gear again."

"Well, don't go wild," said Boniface. "There's a junction coming up, and I guess it's not going to be graceful."

"So what's the strategy when we get to Hampton Court?"

"First..."

Ellen smirked, not meeting Boniface's gaze. "Well, for all the buildup, there's not much to tell. As I said, the documents were all as you would expect. There was Nigel's speech for tonight."

"He really did write it down and memorize it?" Ellen made a noise that might have been acknowledgement. "I'm impressed."

She pulled the car through the right bend. "Is it meant to lean like this?"

"Probably not." Boniface grimaced.

"So how was his little chat?"

"It was quite good, actually. I shouldn't say I was surprised, but I was. Anyway, please continue—your search of Nigel's computer."

"There was his standard conspiracy-theory piece, you know—it was Anne Boleyn and family aided by Wolsey, and once Wolsey had power, he started to wipe out anyone who could possibly blackmail him, in particular, Anne. She was probably his first significant victim, but he decided to leave the kids, at least initially."

"Kids? Plural? As in more than one child?" Ellen nodded as Boniface continued. "But wasn't there only one child when Henry was done in?"

"Nope," said Ellen with a small grin pushing her cheeks. "Not at this point."

"I thought Elizabeth came later," said Boniface, hearing the bewilderment in his voice. "I thought she was fruit of the unpleasant union between Anne and Wolsey, after he started playing Kings and Queens."

"In Nigel's view, Elizabeth's father could be either man, although it probably was Wolsey. But you're still missing Henry's second child: his son."

"Now I'm confused," whined Boniface. "I thought that Edward came later, when Henry—or Wolsey acting as Henry; it all gets very confusing—married Jane Seymour."

"He's child number four," said Ellen. "You're missing child number two: Henry FitzRoy."

Boniface looked ahead at the road. "At the roundabout, you want to turn right…"

"Gotcha." Ellen's view remained fixed on the road.

"Forgive my ignorance, but who was Henry FitzRoy?"

"Short version?"

"Mmm."

"He was Henry's illegitimate son by his teenage mistress, Elizabeth Blount, who became Lady Clinton in later life. An interesting name for an adulterer, don't you think?"

Boniface sighed sardonically. "So the short version."

"Henry FitzRoy was born around 1519 or 1520, when Henry's marriage to Catherine was on the rocks because she couldn't produce a son, let alone any other child. So FitzRoy was born after Mary, but before Anne came on the scene. And you get bonus points if you can guess who FitzRoy's godfather was."

"What do I win?"

"A smooth journey round the roundabout." Ellen threw the car into the roundabout, the wheels barely maintaining grip with the surface as it leaned precariously through the three-quarter circuit.

"I choose death; it's less scary," said Boniface, feeling the car rocking from side to side as it righted itself while it pulled off the roundabout.

"Go on, guess," said Ellen.

"I don't know. Keep going straight here; you know where you are."

"Stop changing the subject and guess."

"Thomas Cranmer."

"Have you been paying attention? Wolsey. Wolsey was the godfather to Henry's illegitimate first-born male child. Henry's first-born male child who was considered as a potential heir but who died at the age of seventeen, sometime around 1536, in other words..."

"Not that long after Wolsey would have become King," said Boniface triumphantly. "And if he had become King, and had become King by murder, then it's not unreasonable to assume that FitzRoy was ultimately murdered so that there were no male heirs if the death of Henry became public knowledge, or perhaps FitzRoy was putting the squeeze on Wolsey."

"Precisely."

"See, I did pay attention to Nigel," said Boniface, pondering the significance. "But none of this is new information, is it? None of this relates to what he might have seen at the police station." Ellen shook her head as Boniface returned to his questioning. "So what else did you see? You mentioned websites."

"He was a big fan of yours, Boniface. He spent a lot of time looking at your website and Googling articles by you and about you." Boniface groaned as Ellen smirked. "He was smitten with you."

"But there must have been more," said Boniface.

"Obviously there was a lot of stuff about the book. He had Googled pretty much every online retailer, and read every review..."

"I feel there's a *just one thing* in here," said Boniface, desperate to tease out any last detail.

"There is. Do you know my publisher, Richard Sherborne? He owns..."

"Know him?" Boniface felt his throat go dry as he tried to keep the incredulity at the question out of his voice. "Do I know dear old Dickie S? He's the reason I'm virtually unemployable. He's the reason I've had to set up my own business instead of getting a proper job."

"I'm sorry, I didn't realize," said Ellen, flinching. "Then I'm not sure whether it's good news or bad news, but from this afternoon's browser history, Nigel seemed to be looking at a bunch of websites that talk about Sherborne, his relationship with Princess Heidemarie, Princess Heidemarie's son, and speculation about the father of the child. You get the idea."

Boniface laughed out loud. "Nigel's last internet search...and he was looking for gossip about Sherborne... Shit... He could have asked me. I've got a lifetime of dirt on that unctuous little—sorry unctuous *big*—corpulent creep. I would have told him." Boniface sneered. "I would have given him archives and research to last until doomsday."

"Well, you were one step ahead of Nigel without knowing it, and now I've told you everything. So it's my turn for a question, and all I want to know is, what's our plan?"

Boniface smirked. "Don't get dead." Ellen flashed a look of disappointment. "Seriously. Stay alive."

"Nigel thought you were a strategic genius, and all you can come up with is don't get killed?"

"Yup." Boniface was resolute. "But the key issue is how we don't get killed. How we stay alive."

"You have a ready audience here, Boniface. Tell me, how do we stay alive?"

He relaxed into his seat, which hadn't become any more comfortable with time. "Well, the strategy is easy. The implementation may be tougher; but the strategy is easy. First, we find out who wants us dead: We need to know who they are so that we know who to run away from."

"But isn't that easy?" Ellen asked impatiently. "It's that man with the shaved head. The one who was in the parking lot and who climbed over the bridge."

"Perhaps," said Boniface. "But we don't know who gave him his orders. If there's someone else pulling strings, we need to find them; otherwise, they'll send someone else with a gun, and because we won't know what they look like we won't know to run away from them. If it's Kuznetsov sending people, we've got a problem—he's got a whole army of ex-Spetsnaz guys."

Ellen remained focused on the stretch of comparatively straight asphalt ahead. "Don't we need to know why they want us dead?"

"That's tomorrow's problem," said Boniface. "For today, let's focus on the *who* issue and the second part of the strategy: We make sure we're more valuable alive than dead."

"That's it?"

"It's simple. If someone believes they've got more to gain by keeping us alive, then they won't kill us."

"That's the big strategy?"

"Yup. And until we find something better, we need to find something so that whoever finds us thinks they will lose something by killing us."

"Someone? Something? You think this is going to work? Or perhaps we should try something a bit more vague?"

Boniface grinned. "I'm open to ideas if you want to suggest anything better." He looked at Ellen, who remained silent with her eyes on the road ahead.

thirty–three

Turgenev stood on the landing stage that ran around the perimeter of Thames Ditton Island, looking at the blue flashing light reflecting off the downstream river.

He felt in his pocket for the gun he had taken from the man with the scar on his face. Pulling it free and weighing it in his hand, he contemplated his options and then tossed it. The gun hit the river, disappearing, the disturbance immediately lost in the fast-flowing current. He looked at the keys from Nigel's back door, raised his eyebrows, and dropped them in the river, too. The phone he had retrieved ended in the river as he started to walk up the landing stage.

The boats bobbed and clinked; there wasn't one that he would want to choose. The rowboats looked old and heavy. The small cruisers, assuming he could start one of them, would be slow and noisy, and the small boats without their outboards were pointless.

Two yellow kayaks lying on the landing stage looked old but were probably the best option. On the fourth house he passed, he saw what he was looking for: a double-ended paddle resting against the back wall. He took the paddle and returned to the kayaks, lowering the larger onto the water.

The Russian sat on the landing stage with his feet bracing the kayak against the current and pulled out his phone to look at the single dot marking Professor Armstrong's location. According to the map she was on the road that ran parallel to the river, roughly level with the top end of the island.

And was stationary.

He looked downstream at the flashes of blue that pulsed regularly on the water. An occasional voice could be heard, probably shouts from the police. Somewhere he heard a car start and gears grind.

There were two choices: Go and get his bike so he would be mobile, or try to move upstream and get onto the bank, where he could find the professor while she was still close.

He moved into the kayak. When he was satisfied that the craft would hold him, he checked his phone again: The professor's dot had moved—not far, but it had moved. That was enough to make the decision: He needed to be mobile; he needed the Wolf. He slipped the phone into his pocket, grabbed the paddle, and pushed off from the landing stage, letting the flow of the river take him downstream.

He took a stroke or two, feeling how the kayak maneuvered, and then took a few backstrokes to slow himself as he drifted. Past the end of the island there was a mooring post; Turgenev held his paddle in the river, guiding and slowing the craft, and as he reached the post he stopped the boat with his arm, holding onto a piece of rope tangled around the post while he looked back at his bike.

The river was moving faster than he had expected, and the sound of water rushing past the boat was distracting, drowning out the fragments of conversation from the police standing in the parking lot.

In the flashing blue lights he could see six officers and two cars, one parked in each of the two lots. The one in the lower lot had reversed into a space next to his bike, and two officers were admiring the machine.

Scratch plan A, on to plan B.

He pulled out the phone and called up the map. Professor Armstrong had moved. By the look of the map, she had gone up the road and turned left.

With the phone securely returned to his pocket, he let go of the rope. The kayak drifted while he held the paddle in the river to pivot 180 degrees, and then he began paddling, careful not to draw attention as he began to move against the flow of the Thames.

Having pulled past the end of the island and out of sight of the police, he paddled harder, applying additional power each time the blade cut into the water. Slowly, he felt himself gain additional momentum, and the boat moved upstream.

About a quarter of a mile up from the island, he saw what looked to be some sort of boating club with a large landing stage on the side of the river where the professor had passed. Grabbing the stage with one hand, he retrieved the phone with his other. The map showed a road running perpendicular to the river, about half a mile up from where he was. Professor Armstrong's dot was slowly moving along the road from left to right.

The Russian looked ahead: On her current course, the professor would pass over the bridge crossing the river. After that, the road split. One road continued away from him, running parallel to the river. The other went along the edge of the area marked as Hampton Court Palace Golf Club.

The kayak wasn't going to be fast enough. He checked his side of the river: There was a railway line and another river joining the Thames—both inconvenient hazards to cross, both made the decision easier. He returned the phone to his pocket, pushed off, and paddled furiously for the other bank.

It took a few moments to find somewhere to get out, and as he scrambled up the bank, the kayak began to drift. Professor Armstrong's red dot was still moving, as he started jogging in the direction she was heading.

thirty-four

"So why is Nigel dead?"

"Dunno."

"Why is Mister Longhair dead?" Ellen seemed to be keeping the car moving as fast as it would go, passing Hampton Court train station and heading toward the bridge over the River Thames.

"Dunno... Lack of attention to personal grooming?"

Ellen smirked. "You don't know much, do you, Boniface?"

"Nope. But I do know this roundabout isn't going to be pleasant."

Boniface looked at the view of the main entrance to Hampton Court Palace for the second time that day while Ellen drove over Hampton Court Bridge. As the car descended from the apex of the bridge, she let it coast, losing speed before the 360-degree spin around the roundabout.

"I feel seasick," said Boniface as the car righted itself and Ellen turned into the outside gate. He tilted his head toward the lion and the unicorn on top of the pillars. "Look, they've stolen Nigel's idea."

Ellen jerked the car to an undignified stop as the guard came out of his hut behind the gate. Boniface recognized a familiar face and scrabbled around, looking for the door handle. "Leave it with me," he said to Ellen, who seemed to be feeling for the window crank.

Boniface found the handle and stepped out; walking around the front of the car, he offered his hand to the guard. "Good to see you again. I had hoped to see you someday, but I wasn't expecting it to be quite this soon."

"Mister Boniface." The guard seemed pleased to be remembered. "It's a pleasure to see you, too."

Boniface saw Ellen give up her search for the window crank and look at the side window, scanning the horizontal split halfway up the pane. Her raised eyebrows seemed to say "aha" as she saw a catch at the bottom of the glass. Her hands went to the catch, and the lower pane flipped up from the hinge in the middle of the window.

She twisted her head to look out the opening. "Y'all know I've got to be at the airport at sunup, and I need ma phone."

Boniface was momentarily stunned to hear a Southern accent that hadn't been apparent while he was in the car, but he took the cue. "Yes. My friend left her phone in the Great Hall. Could we dash back and pick it up. As she says, she's flying out first thing in the morning, so we can't come back tomorrow." Boniface grimaced his apologies, holding out his hands in a what-are-you-going-to-do gesture.

The guard looked at his watch. "We're running a bit late tonight, what with your bash and some of the cleaning crew being sick, but if you hurry." He turned to Ellen. "You know where you left it?"

"Sure do, sir."

"Be quick. The guys will probably be around at about half past eleven, so you need to find it before then." He turned to Boniface. "And you remember where to park?"

"I do. Thank you for your help." Boniface shook his hand again and jumped into the car.

As the car jerked, crunching gravel, Boniface turned to Ellen. "How long have you been channeling Scarlett O'Hara? I was in the car, sitting next to a woman from Richmond, Virginia—didn't Nigel say that's where you're from?—but now living in Richmond, London, and when I get out, the next thing I know there's some southern belle telling lies."

"I told the truth," said Ellen huffily. "I have got to be at the airport first thing tomorrow, but to pick up my sister. You lied when you constructed the notion that I was flying out. And as for Scarlett O'Hara, there's something deep in the English psyche that makes men go weak when they hear a Southern accent. I don't understand it either, but it always works. And we need to get in here, don't we?"

"We do." Boniface looked up at the building, looking as Cardinal Wolsey would have seen it, but with the addition of electric floodlighting pinpointing the Palace against a blanket of darkness. "It's magnificent, isn't it?"

"Stunning," said Ellen, twisting the steering wheel to keep some sort of control as the car wobbled up the grand drive. "If I don't crash this thing and kill us both, I should bring Montbretia here."

"Who?"

"Montbretia. My sister. Remember...we've just had that conversation—she arrives tomorrow, and I have to pick her up at the airport. I'll take her around the Maze and show her the rest of the Palace." She sighed lightly, her tone softening. "I wish we had Nigel here to give her the detail, but it'll be fun."

"Who will win the race to the center of the Maze?" Boniface regretted a question that didn't move the conversation away from Nigel.

"She will. She always wins anything competitive. But she's made me get this clever phone with GPS and all that sort of stuff. I don't understand it; it's all to do with my website. But anyway, maybe I can use the GPS in the Maze?"

"He wants us to park up over there." Boniface pointed to the right of the Great Gatehouse, managing to move the subject away from Nigel. Ellen slowed the car, following a large loop to bring it pointing in the direction from which they had come as she jerked them to a stop. Boniface pulled a quizzical face and asked gently, "Why?"

"If you can figure where reverse gear is, then we can go backwards.

Until then, we go forwards," said Ellen definitively. "I've done my bit of thinking, so tell me, oh great strategist, we're still alive and we've got past the gate. What's the plan now?"

They stepped out of the car and gazed up at the Great Gatehouse, which commanded their attention. Boniface started talking softly, almost absent-mindedly. "Now...? Now we go in. Look. See what we can see. Perhaps accidentally, very accidentally, get lost and see if we can figure where Mister Longhair found his papers. But whatever happens, get out quickly and get away from here before a tall, shaven-headed Russian figures that we're here."

Ellen remained entranced by the architecture.

"Let's start moving," said Boniface, indicating the bridge that led across the dry moat, the path then passing under the Great Gatehouse arch.

They walked through the gate, entering the courtyard with Anne Boleyn's Gate at the far end. "If I marry my Prince and then become a Queen, my King will definitely have to build me something like that," said Ellen wistfully, looking at the golden astrological clock illuminated like a sun over the courtyard, her kitten heels clip-clopping as they walked.

Reaching the far corner of the courtyard, Boniface indicated the door. "The Great Hall?" she asked.

Ellen led them through the entrance, immediately turning right, following the passage to the Great Hall. The main lighting had been extinguished, leaving the hammer-beam roof in darkness, its dulled timbers visible but the detailing of the master craftsmen lost in the gloom. Muted safety lights let off a gentle glow, enough to see the room but not enough to be a fire risk.

Boniface let out an expletive as he surveyed the mess of the room. "Useless people." Ellen paused, seemingly waiting for elaboration. "Look." Boniface pointed around the hall without identifying any particular object. "The caterer hasn't finished clearing up." He walked over to a tray of half-eaten food and looked down a row of several tables covered with the detritus of finger food. "In fact, hasn't started clearing up. Swan vol-au-vent? Probably with added salmonella by now, along with the other bacteria from people prodding and poking them."

Ellen looked at the tray of food and made a face. "Yuck. People ate that?"

"Not me," said Boniface, turning to look at the rest of the room. "Now that's just stupid. You get a stack of books printed, and then you leave them laying around after the event."

"It's a mess, but isn't that good for us?" Ellen turned to Boniface. "Doesn't that mean that whatever was here won't have been disturbed?" Ellen watched as Boniface looked back at her. "That's good, right? We can forgive the laziness and be thankful?"

Boniface nodded. At first, a small nod of the head, but then increasing the swing of his skull. "Well, get looking then," he said. "I've got a call to make."

thirty–five

Boniface moved to the side of the Great Hall, pulled out his phone, flicked his wrist to open it, then hit a speed-dial button. "Hey, it's your favorite ex-husband...only ex-husband, so I must be your favorite... How're you doing? Have you nailed Oscar yet? Got your big scoop to make Mister Kuznetsov proud?"

He watched as Ellen started to work her way around the room, systematically checking each and every object. She looked under tables; on, under, and behind chairs; under the detritus left on tables and on the floor; and she delicately peeked behind the tapestries hanging on the walls without touching them. Each time she satisfied herself that there was nothing to be found or that what she had found was of no interest, she moved on: a one-woman grid search applying cold, hard logic and pure persistence to a problem.

Boniface huddled around the phone, holding it tighter. "Look, I've got a problem. There are three dead bodies, and I think Turgenev is chasing me. What have you and Kuznetsov got me into?"

He listened, more attuned to how the response was delivered than the words that were being spoken. "I'm not sure you're taking this with the same seriousness that I am. Nigel is dead...he was shot. I watched some complete stranger get shot as he stood next to me, and then I saw Turgenev drown a man and float his body down the river."

He turned to look at Ellen continuing her progress around the room, then turned back, keen to shield her from the conversation. "Yes. Yes... Nigel was shot outside Professor Armstrong's house." He listened, understanding that the journalist instincts would be kicking in at the other end of the line.

"Apparently I was the emergency contact number programmed into his phone, so they called me first... Definitely outside Professor Armstrong's house... Well, there you are; there's your scoop. Now you know whose body that is. So when you ask Mister Kuznetsov why Mister Turgenev is following me, perhaps you could tell him about Nigel and say sorry, I didn't mean to get him killed."

He waited, walking in small circles, looking at his feet. He knew the game. A journalist had new information, and Veronica was more than a simple journalist; she was responsible for a whole newspaper, so she needed to get someone working on the story first. And it was to his advantage to let her clear her mind. That way, he could rely on her giving one-hundred percent focus to him.

Veronica came back on the line and Boniface listened. "No. Not dead... Very much alive... Why did you think she was...? I'm looking at her now, and she's very alive. Who was the source?" He looked up at Ellen, making sure she was occupied and not aware that she was the subject of conversation.

"My location? Let's just say London. You're not the only one to hold back information." A broad smile broke out across his face. "Right. You go find out why there are gentlemen with guns running around, and I'll go and see what the not-dead professor has found. Speak soon." With the well-practiced smoothness of a gunslinger, he flicked his wrist and returned his phone to his pocket in a single movement.

"Talking about me behind my back?" asked Ellen, her stern face giving way to a guilty grin.

He lifted the sides of his mouth weakly, wondering when she had started listening, becoming aware that the look of joy and expectation was not fading from her face and that she was standing with her hands behind her back. "What have you found?"

"*Ta-dah.*" Ellen held out a battered leather satchel briefcase. Boniface raised his eyebrows in a so-what motion. "Nigel's briefcase."

The cynicism dropped from Boniface's countenance, to be replaced by enthusiasm and his own version of childlike wonder. "Where was it?"

"The books at the end..." Ellen tilted her head in the direction of the table on the small stage at the end of the Great Hall, piled with hardback copies of *The Murder of Henry VIII*. "Under there."

"No," said Boniface. Ellen nodded as Boniface's astonished face morphed into a large grin. "I'm guessing we've got all that's worth finding here, so let's get moving." Ellen turned toward their exit. "But do you fancy accidentally taking the wrong turn on the way out? Perhaps we might see where Mister Longhair decided to get stuck in a hole. It may not tell us where the other documents are, but at least it's a start."

"Lead on," said Ellen, indicating the door.

"I was rather hoping you would lead," said Boniface. "After all, you are the historian."

"But..."

"But nothing." Boniface was resolute. Ellen moved toward the door, signaling her assent. "And while we walk, you can tell me what's in the briefcase."

Ellen gave a maybe-yes, maybe-no side-to-side tilt of her head, then returned to her excited grin as they turned out of the door, walking in the opposite direction from which they had arrived. "Okay, and then you can tell me what you said about me." Boniface opened his mouth to speak and found that words didn't come out.

"Shut your mouth, Boniface, and start walking. I don't know where we're going, and I'm making no guarantees that we'll find anything, but

I've got a few ideas. How long have we got?"

"Dunno. Not long, I guess."

"Alright then." Ellen started to stride out, Boniface trailing behind. "Some pieces of paper."

Boniface stared blankly at Ellen, trying to keep up with the pace but unsure where the conversation had gone.

"The briefcase. You wanted to know what's in the case, and the answer is, some pieces of paper. His speech, I think. A few handwritten notes, something that looks like a hand-drawn family tree... A few printed pages, some handwritten pages, and that's it. All of the paper is new, as in there are no historic documents. But it was too dark in there to really read it. I even tried snapping a few pages with the camera on my phone—trying to see whether the flash illuminated it enough—but it was no use, so can we go somewhere with enough light to see past the end of my nose."

Somewhere in the dark there was a shout and the sound of running boots. "You asked how long we had?" Ellen looked back at Boniface, waiting for him to answer his own question. "Well, I think our time's up."

thirty–six

Nigel's 2CV sped along the main drive as fast as its 602cc, 28-horsepower engine would let it move when loaded with two adults. It was going somewhat faster than jogging pace, but the zero-to-sixty time was more of an aspiration than something that was ever going to be achieved and measured scientifically.

"What was going on there?" asked Ellen, her foot flat and her eyes fixed ahead, hands twisting the steering wheel, continuously nudging the car in a straight line as it spat out the gravel along the drive.

"I don't know." Boniface looked behind him, searching for any clue. "There's a time to be brave, a time to stand up and be counted. And there's a time to run like hell." He smiled softly. "Call me a coward, but I'm a live coward, and I vote that we run."

The guard stepped out of his hut to face the approaching car. "Better say goodnight," said Boniface as Ellen started bringing the car to a jerky stop, skidding the last few feet on the loose gravel.

Boniface flipped up his window and twisted his head to face the guard, who was peering through the rear door at the back seat of the car before bending to look directly through Boniface's window. "Did your friend find you?" he asked.

"Friend?" Boniface couldn't keep the questioning tone out of his voice.

"Yes, the young lady's friend. He said he had your phone, and as I knew it's urgent with you flying out tomorrow, I sent him straight through."

"What did this man look like?" asked Boniface.

The guard frowned and took a step back. "Tall." He held out a hand to indicate his height. "Black leather jacket. Shaved head. Had an accent, Russian perhaps? Said he had run after you. He was sweating a bit but didn't seem out of breath—he looked fit, muscular. From his posture, I would say he's a soldier, or he's been a soldier."

Boniface was glad for the darkness hiding the pallor of his skin. "He's no friend of ours." His tone was flat and commanding. "Call the police. Now. Get ambulances; you have a serious emergency on your hands." The guard stood frozen. "Now," said Boniface, waving in the direction of the hut as the man started to move, suddenly galvanized by Boniface's instructions.

"What now?" asked Ellen.

"Go left." The car started to move away with its customary lack of decorum, the engine complaining as it got onto the main road before

Hampton Court Bridge. "Your phone?"

"My phone?" said Ellen.

"This clever stuff your sister set up?"

"Yes."

"Did she do anything to tag your location? You know, so your photos, tweets, posts, and whatever have some sort of location?"

"Of course," said Ellen. "This is the twenty-first...oh shit. I get it... Shit. Shit. Shit." She hit the brake. "Shit. Shit. Shit." The car pulled to a stop on the brow of the bridge, and she reached into her pocket, handing Boniface the phone. "Take it. Throw it in the river."

Boniface opened the door and got out of the car, then immediately got back in. "I've got a better idea. Drive."

Ellen eased the car forward. "Where to?"

"Over the bridge, then pull in to the station on the other side." Boniface pointed. "See up there?"

Ellen pulled into the station, and Boniface got out of the car. "Go and park up the other end; turn off the lights and kill the engine so you can't be seen. Then wait—I'll only be a minute." As Ellen moved off, he slammed the door and ran through the ticket office and along the concourse toward the platforms. "I'm sorry, sir. After the train has the signal to leave, we cannot let anyone board." The over-officious guard stood to protect the entrance to the platform.

Boniface kept running, dodging the man. "My wife's phone," he shouted, waving Ellen's phone at him. He passed the first two carriages and jumped into an open door on the third, surreptitiously slipped the phone onto the luggage rack above the seats as the doors started to beep, then turned, pushing his way through the sliding doors as they closed on him.

He walked back up the platform. Seeing the guard at the gate, he held his hands in an I-surrender pose. "I'm sorry. The wife scares me more than you do." The guard gave a knowing nod as Boniface walked past and back along the concourse.

He reached the exit from the ticket office and stood back from the door, looking across the drop-off area. Nothing seemed out of place as he edged forward, looking in the direction they had driven from. A few cars passed. A night bus. No man in black with a shaved head.

He turned left and jogged down the parking lot, looking for Ellen, and found the car backed into a concealed gap. "So you found reverse gear?"

"It's me they're after." As Boniface got into the car he could see the tears streaming down Ellen's face, her arms wrapped tightly clutching her stomach. "It's me, isn't it? It was my phone they tracked, and having that briefcase just makes me an even bigger target. Get rid of it. Now."

"I don't know," said Boniface, trying to work out the best lie to tell his driver. "But if you're right, we need to move. We need to get off the route your phone passed."

He waited, watching the academic shrivel, pushing herself back into her seat.

"Please." He kept his tone soft.

"You go." Her voice was strained. "It's me they're after, not you."

He leaned over, reaching to twist the key in the ignition. The engine turned over, then died, and the dull lights briefly illuminated the parking lot. "Well that didn't help," muttered Boniface. "If they didn't know where we were before, they will now." He sighed and stared at Ellen, who wouldn't meet his gaze. "Please. One-hundred yards up the road." He continued to stare at her, watching her eyes flick around the car but still not meet his. "Please."

thirty-seven

How did Henry VIII get anything done? He must have spent his whole time trying to find his way around the Palace. Or perhaps he had some flunky whose only job was to guide him around the buildings. He had somebody to do everything else for him—as every Russian schoolchild knew, he even had someone whose job it was to wipe his bum. And that person had the most prized job in court. Now that really was Western decadence...

He hadn't found Professor Armstrong, but he knew she had a man with her. It was kind of the guard to tell him. It was kind of the guard to be gullible enough to let him past just by waving a phone. But what was that he said? Something about needing it because she was leaving tomorrow? He hadn't been paying attention; he was running again by then.

If he had paid attention, he might have heard where the professor and her escort had gone. Instead, he tried to find his own way through the labyrinthine layout of Hampton Court and ran into the two guards. The first one tried to play the hero and ran at him, so he hit him. A younger man could have taken the blow, but this was an older man, and he fell on contact.

The other guard shouted, and that brought two more guards. They all had the look of old soldiers: upright posture, gleaming uniforms, slavish observance to detail, and fatally, a belief in immediate action. It's one thing to take action when you're a seventeen-year-old conscript being shot at from all sides. It's another when you're over seventy—in fact, probably closer to eighty—and the last time you saw active service was in Korea.

Of the final three, the first had come at him, his head bowed as he tried to overpower with his shoulder. In a single move, Turgenev had twisted his neck, feeling it crack as he dropped the lifeless body at his feet. The next two thought they had safety in numbers. They were wrong. They were even more wrong to think that the flashlights they carried were any sort of weapon.

It took two blows.

The first he hit squarely in the middle of his face with a flat hand. He felt the nose crumble and the old cheekbones crack. The Russian wasn't sure if the man had survived, but he stopped fighting after that one contact.

Turgenev then turned, stumbling over the body of the man with the broken neck, and, as he righted himself, he powered the butt of his hand up into the jaw of the last man. His neck snapped backwards. If that didn't kill him, then he would be in a wheelchair to the end of his sorrowful days.

The silence in the middle of the courtyard as he stood surrounded by four bodies was broken by a car starting. It sounded like the car he had heard while he was on the island, but this time it started on the first attempt and moved off immediately, with no crunching of gears.

Turgenev ran through an arch under what looked like a golden sundial suspended between two imposing octagonal pillars, entering another larger courtyard that he sprinted across, passing through another arch that took him outside the Palace building at the end of the drive from which he had entered. At the opposite end of the drive, he saw the taillights of a car pulling out, turning left onto the main road and passing onto the bridge.

He looked at the map on his phone: Professor Armstrong's red dot was moving over the bridge. He put the phone back and started to sprint up the gravel path to the main gate.

As he approached the gate, the guard who had let him in came out. "Hey you. Yes, you—I want to talk with you."

The Russian slowed to a walking pace and looked behind him. There was no one else; the guard was definitely addressing him. Turgenev smiled broadly, moving directly to comply with the instruction. "Certainly. How can I help you?" The guard stood firm, waiting for the man with the shaved head to reach him.

As he reached the hut, Turgenev gave a submissive bow of his head, gesturing inside the hut. "Please...how can I help you?"

The guard relaxed, turning toward the hut. "If you would just..."

Like the others, this guard needed one blow. This time, the side of his hand slammed into the old man's neck was sufficient. Turgenev grabbed the old man under his arms and dragged the inert body into the hut, looking for the darkest corner in the gloomy chamber to drop the corpse.

He flicked the light switch, extinguishing the glow as he exited the hut, closing the door behind him. As the door clicked, Turgenev became aware of sirens for the second time in less than an hour.

He jogged through the outer gate, turning left and heading over the bridge.

thirty-eight

The Citroën steadfastly refused to contemplate any speed in excess of 23 miles per hour, less as the car turned the gentle bend and headed into a light oncoming breeze.

"You were talking about me, Boniface." Ellen's voice was quiet but barbed. She hadn't asked a question, but the statement demanded a response. Seemingly, her fear—having concluded that she was the target of the Russian who was chasing them—had mutated into hostility toward Boniface.

He reflected on what his former wife had told him: Ellen's attitude during an interview that afternoon had upset Kuznetsov. It might be true, but it was a detail that Boniface was struggling to fit into the context of the last few hours, and in any event, Veronica was certain that Kuznetsov would not sanction the killing of an academic on a London street.

Blurting that she had annoyed someone she had probably never met was also likely to infuriate Ellen, and given her fragility, he didn't want to divert her from her present focus of driving them as far away as possible—and as quickly as possible—from the pursuer.

"It didn't start that way, but you came up in conversation." Boniface tried, and failed not to look sheepish.

"Elaborate," said Ellen, her tone calmer, more measured, but still expecting an answer.

Boniface softened, trying to sound reassuring. "I didn't know about the news reports saying you had been shot until I had that phone call. That's how you came up." He paused. "I'm sorry. It must have been awful for you."

"It's worse for Nigel," said Ellen, almost apologetic.

"But it's not pleasant." He gauged the minute reactions—a twitching ear, a tightened grip, a darkening of the skin—trying to collate the individual elements into an understanding about how his driver was feeling. "I didn't know about the story because the police called me and told me about Nigel. Apparently I was his emergency number."

Boniface watched as Ellen's bottom jaw tightened. Sensing he had been wrong to bring to her attention that she wasn't Nigel's first choice in case of an emergency, he elaborated. "Your apparent death was reported by the papers tonight. You know that, of course. But I don't know whether you know that the paper that broke the story is owned by Ivan Kuznetsov, as in the man who owns Whitefoot Thorpe Publishing, publisher of *The Murder of Henry VIII*."

Ellen nodded as Boniface kept talking. "The paper that made that first report is edited by Veronica Rutherford. Have you heard of her?"

"No. Well, I guess I've heard the name, but I couldn't pick her out in a lineup." Boniface couldn't read anything in Ellen's face as she kept her gaze on the road ahead.

"Sure. There's no reason you would know her, but I do." He waited a beat. "She's my former wife, and she is who I was talking to. About you."

"Oh."

"And while we're getting things into the open, it was my ex-wife who made the decision to publish the story about your death. She also works for Kuznetsov, and yes, that's the same Kuznetsov who employs the man with the shaved head who we saw drown the guy and then climb over the bridge to the island." Boniface watched Ellen nodding slowly. When he was sure she had taken in each separate fact, he continued. "My ex-wife also did me a favor by recommending me for the PR job representing Nigel's book. In other words, she's the hub from which most of the spokes radiate."

"Question, please," said Ellen.

"You want to know how they got the story?" Ellen stared at Boniface, her eyes wordlessly asking Boniface to explain. "They got a tip. Someone called in with very specific details."

Boniface watched as Ellen tried to form a question, her lips quivering as she seemed to try to make a "wh" shape.

"Whatever you want to ask next, I don't know the answer. I'm as mystified as you are as to why someone would report you as being murdered."

Ellen's mouth kept moving until she formed a question. "But why did they run the story if all they had was a tip from a phone call? Don't they try to verify these things?"

"They do." Boniface weighed how to explain the story Veronica had told him. "There was a lot of interest because you've been in the limelight recently with the campaign for the referendum."

"Really?"

"Yup. You are now officially a D-list celeb."

"You say that once more, Boniface, and I'll crash this heap of junk, killing us both."

Boniface smiled, noting his driver's attempt at humor but feeling she might not be entirely unserious. "Alright, I believe you. Back to the explanation: When the journalists started looking into your death, there was confusion. They asked the police, the police said there was a male body, the press said 'No, we're after the dead female,' the police said, 'There is no dead female,' and it all descended into chaos. No one cared who the dead man was, no one could find you, and anyone official either didn't know or denied everything. You get the idea, complete chaos."

"They could have called—I did have a phone. Then."

Boniface gave a resigned nod. "I'm sorry about your phone. Let me buy you a new one."

"I'm sorry, I didn't mean..." Ellen's voice trailed off as she flushed slightly.

"You're right, they could have called you—they could have called me, and I would have told them about Nigel. But they didn't and they had a deadline. They knew something had happened. They knew someone was dead. They printed your name. It was a mistake."

"Oops, sorry. We made a mistake." Ellen turned to face her passenger, her tone souring.

Boniface met her watery gaze and flicked his eyes forward, noting how the skin on her fingers was turning white as she returned her eyes to the road. When he recommenced, his voice was soft but resigned. "It happens."

Ellen let out a sigh of exasperation, slowly shaking her head. "This isn't helping, Boniface. This isn't getting us any further."

"But if..."

"No, Boniface. No." Ellen hit the brakes and fought with the steering wheel as the car slowed. A front wheel bumped over the curb at the side of the road, and eventually it came to a halt with the engine stalled, the weak headlights throwing their muted beam into the gutter.

She turned toward Boniface, tears streaming down her cheeks, banging her arms on the steering wheel as she shouted. "This isn't helping! I saw my friend's dead body tonight. I saw his brains splattered over my house. I might not look it, but I'm very upset about it, and if I had my way, I would be at home sobbing on my bed. But then someone said I had been murdered and that there was a man with a gun outside my house, so I got a bit windy and I ran. And then someone got shot in front of me, and that man was drowned, and the guy with the shaved head was chasing me at Hampton Court, so I'm really not having a good evening, and to be quite honest, suddenly finding that you're on their side makes me pretty scared."

The car vibrated with the aftershock of Ellen's outburst. Boniface sat and watched as she turned away, burying her head in her hands. Gradually the sobs became less frequent, and she started to wipe her eyes. Boniface wriggled uncomfortably to get his hand into his pocket and pulled out a handkerchief, offering it to Ellen. "It's clean."

She took it with a mumbled "thank you" and started to mop her eyes and wipe her dribbling nose. Boniface remained motionless in his uncomfortable seat, watching. "I'm sorry... I'm a mess... I'm not used to this sort of thing."

He waited. Ellen looked up, giving an embarrassed grimace. He tried to look reassuring. "This is tough..." He struggled, trying to sift through the usual platitudes and clichés that came to mind. "You've managed to avoid two bullets tonight; I think we should try to make sure there isn't a third."

"You mean they're…" Boniface could hear the rising panic in Ellen's voice.

"I mean, I don't know." Boniface kept his voice calm, trying to be reassuring. Hoping if he faked being in control of his emotions, it would come true.

"You don't know why they said I was dead. You don't know why the shaven-headed guy is chasing me. You don't know what Nigel found. You don't know what we're going to do next. Really, Boniface, you don't know much!"

The two sat, staring at each other, tears running down Ellen's face.

Boniface felt the edge of his mouth twitch and tried to suppress a smirk.

"I'm serious, Boniface."

"So am I," he replied, now making far less effort to hide his inability to stifle his grin as Ellen started to smile through her tears.

"I'm deadly…" He stopped himself. "I'm very serious." He exhaled. "But here's the thing—do you want to hang around and get answers? We're less than two miles from Hampton Court—do you want to go back and find Turgenev to ask him why he seems to be chasing you?"

Ellen raised her shoulders, giving an almost imperceptible shrug.

"There have already been two bullets near to you—they may have been meant for you. I don't know. They may have been meant for me. I don't know. But what I do know is that a moving target is much harder to hit, and that a target that is hidden from the shooter is almost impossible to hit. So I suggest we keep running and follow what few leads we've got until we find something we can bargain with." He tried to reassure. "Remember, we need to be worth more alive than dead, so let's get somewhere where we can have a proper look inside Nigel's briefcase."

Ellen's jaw fell open. "You didn't tell your wife about Nigel's briefcase?"

Boniface kept his voice soft. "I didn't know about the briefcase, so Ronnie certainly doesn't know about it. Ronnie doesn't know about our trip to Hampton Court. Ronnie doesn't know about Mister Longhair and what Mister Longhair might have found." He exhaled. "To be frank, Ronnie doesn't know much, apart from the fact that she needs to print a groveling apology to you."

"I still think we should get rid of the briefcase," muttered Ellen.

thirty-nine

By the time he had passed the brow of Hampton Court Bridge, Turgenev's head was gleaming like a disco ball. Out of sight of the main entrance to the Hampton Court grounds, he looked over the river as he pulled out his phone, then zoomed in on the map.

He watched the red dot as it moved away from him, keeping parallel to the road. "The road's there...not there," he said to the phone. The red dot moved in a straight line, keeping parallel with the map of the road. He watched the dot as it passed the point on the map where the road bent to the right, but still the dot carried on in a straight line.

He shook his head, catching sight of the building on the other side of the bridge. "Shit. A train." He slipped the phone back in his pocket as he started running, increasing his pace as he freed his hand.

He came off the bridge, sprinted the short distance to the station, passed through the ticket office, and turned right, crossing the concourse toward the gate. A man in uniform was pulling a latticed security grille across the entrance to the platforms. Turgenev slowed as the guard looked up. "I'm sorry, sir, you've just missed it." He threw his head in the direction of the train lines, and somewhere in the distance the red taillights twinkled."

"When's the next one?" asked Turgenev.

"Five fifty-four tomorrow morning, sir," replied the guard. "Someone else will be here for that."

"Thanks," said Turgenev, turning to walk away. He took a few steps and spun his head without breaking his step. "Where does that train go... the next stop?"

"Thames Ditton."

"And after that?"

"Surbiton." The second mention of Surbiton in one night. First the man with the scar on his face got lost and ended up there, and now the train carrying Professor Armstrong was heading there.

"Okay. Thank you. Is there a phone around here?" said Turgenev, picking up his pace.

"Big red box. Through the hall, turn right, and turn right again." Having closed the gate, the guard was now offering directions with his hands.

Turgenev held up a hand to acknowledge his thanks as he turned into the ticket office, then right out of the entrance, and right again at the end of the building. He pulled the heavy phone-booth door and stepped in.

The door closed slowly as he picked up the receiver and punched three buttons. "Police."

forty

The 2CV chugged with a bad temper along the tree-lined main road heading away from wherever Turgenev might be. Boniface broke the contemplation. "Waterloo."

Ellen kept her foot pressed hard to the floor. "Eighteen-fifteen. Napoleon surrendered. You English are rather proud of it. Still."

"No. Waterloo train station. Middle of London. South of the River Thames."

"I'm sorry, Boniface. You've lost me. I mean, yes, I know Waterloo station—who doesn't—but why are you telling me? Do you want me to drive there?"

Boniface chuckled. "No. That's where your phone has gone. I figured that if Turgenev is following your phone, we should at least try to send him in the wrong direction. And as the train keeps moving, he'll keep chasing it."

"That's priceless."

"And there's a chance you'll get your phone back. Call lost property tomorrow—someone's bound to have handed it in. Or better still, call your phone and see who answers."

Ellen kept her eyes on the road ahead. "So if we're not going to Waterloo, where are we going? Or do you want me to keep driving until we run out of gas?"

Boniface ignored the question. "Nigel's phone..."

"His second most prized possession, after this fine piece of automotive history," said Ellen, seemingly adding as much sarcastic sincerity as she could muster.

"It's the key to this, isn't it?"

"How so?"

Boniface sat back in the seat, winced, and twisted. "You didn't seem overly enthusiastic about the contents of the briefcase, but his phone has the photos he took in the police station. The documents or whatever they are that Mister Longhair recovered."

"Yes."

"And that phone is in the possession of the police." Boniface chewed his bottom lip. "So do you think...maybe we should...I don't know...what do you think?"

"What do I think about what?"

"Should we try to get it back?"

The contemplation was filled with the sound of the straining engine and Ellen crunching into third gear. "Why would we?"

Boniface tried to keep the exasperation out of his voice. "Won't the photos answer all our questions? Or at least all of our questions for which there is an answer."

"You're missing my point. Why would we try to get the phone when we're bound to fail and there's a faster way to get the pictures?"

Boniface turned his head as if his neck were spring-loaded. "What?"

"You said Nigel was messing with his phone."

"Mmm."

"Nigel uploaded everything."

"Uploaded? Uploaded where?" asked Boniface. "Nigel said something about the photos taking too long to upload, but I didn't understand what he meant by that, so I ignored him."

It was Ellen's turn to fail to stifle a sigh of exasperation. "He will have uploaded the photos to an online storage service."

"But how can you sound so certain about that?"

"Because Nigel kept all his files online." Boniface frowned and Ellen continued. "Nigel wanted his computer files to be accessible wherever he was."

"Couldn't he just use one of those thumb-drive things you plug into your computer like the rest of us?"

Ellen shook her head. "Not Nigel. He didn't trust those things—he thought they were always faulty—plus he didn't want to have to remember to copy specific files. He wanted everything available everywhere, and with online storage all he had to do was remember his password."

"Look, I've got a Stone Age phone, but you're saying he will have done this with pictures on his phone?"

"If the pictures mattered, then yes. That way he could share the photos, and they would be safe if the camera got lost... You know, like if someone put it on a train or something strange like that."

Boniface ignored the quip. "So how do we get at the pictures?"

"If I had my phone, I could tell you which service Nigel uses, but since it's on its way to Waterloo, then get me to a computer and I'll check my email to tell you. It was something like online-file-store-dot-net, but I can't be sure. Then all we need is his password, and we're in." Ellen gave a self-satisfied look.

"Go. Go fast. Well, go as relatively fast as we can go."

"I am. Look at my foot, it's flat." Boniface craned his neck to look, gave a brief nod, and slipped back into his seat, listening to Ellen. "So where's the nearest computer? We can't go round to Nigel's, and mine is probably not the best place to go to at the moment. Have you got a computer somewhere?"

Boniface pondered for a moment. "The office is too far. The closest I can think of is Surbiton."

"Surbiton?"

"Mmm. There's an internet café opposite the station. As far as I know it's open twenty-four seven. It'll probably be filled with students, but at least we can sit down, and we might also be able to look at Nigel's briefcase in something approaching a reasonable light."

forty-one

Turgenev opened the door of the red phone booth and stepped out with a schoolboy grin across his face. He pulled out his phone and called up the map for the route back to the parking lot by Thames Ditton Island: Head west, take the first road on the left—Summer Road—and follow it. It would only take a few minutes if he jogged.

As he got close to the island, he crossed to the path on the inside of the bend. About fifty yards away he stopped running, choosing instead to walk, but walk and make a lot of noise: He scuffed his feet, whistled loudly, and kicked stones and tin cans—anything that would alert people to his presence.

The two police cars were still in the lots and had been joined by other official-looking cars and a white van. The gate in the middle of the bridge had been propped open, and from the other side of the road, Turgenev could see a young police constable, no more than twenty-two or twenty-three years old, still very pink-cheeked and soft-skinned, standing guard a few feet from the bridge steps.

The Russian crossed the road, walking toward his bike. He stopped once he was sure the young officer was watching him, and looked around. "What's happened?"

"I'm afraid there's been an incident, sir," said the officer, with the gravitas of a young man trying desperately to bring all of his people-handling training into practice.

"An incident?" said Turgenev, raising his eyebrows. "It must be very serious with all of this." He loosely pointed to the official vehicles. The officer followed his direction, nodding as if acknowledging that he had heard the comment. Turgenev mirrored the young policeman, exaggerating the nod, and keeping up the momentum asked, "A murder?"

"I'm sorry, sir; I can only say that there has been an incident. As I'm sure you can understand, we can't prejudge the situation until we know more details."

"How shocking," said Turgenev, as if he hadn't heard the officer's reply. "You don't usually get crime like that around here."

"You don't, sir."

"Well, I'll pick up my bike and get out of your way." He moved toward the Wolf.

"Is that yours?" Turgenev had heard the question many times before. He nodded, waiting for the follow-up question. "What sort of bike is it?"

"A Ural Wolf," he said, lifting his helmet off the mirror. "I would offer you a ride, but"—he shrugged—"you don't have a helmet." The officer gave an envious look as Turgenev threw his leg over the beast. "Perhaps next time."

He didn't hear the reply under his helmet as he kicked the bike to life.

forty–two

The 2CV made a fuss about the slight incline in the road leading toward Surbiton station. "Park it around the corner," said Boniface, pointing to the road on the left. The car complained a bit more as it turned and vigorously expressed its displeasure as Ellen parked it.

The two got out, Boniface with Nigel's briefcase, Ellen with the key attached Nigel's work pass; both stretched as they released themselves from the unnatural position required to stay seated. "I wouldn't bother locking it," said Boniface under his breath. "We're going to be quick, and no self-respecting thief would be caught dead in one of those things."

As they reached the junction across from the station, one train was motionless and virtually deserted. Small clumps of people spilled from the station onto the streets, and on the platforms station staff wearing Day-Glo jackets were officiously bossing passengers. Some staff had managed to find megaphones and were using them with the relish of an army guard commanding concentration-camp arrivals, with the last few former passengers being heckled to disembark and evacuate the station.

"Any clue?" asked Ellen.

"Nope," said Boniface, twisting his head to exaggerate that he was listening to something in the distance. "Sirens. Again. I don't know about you, but I'm starting to twitch when I hear those things. Let's get in and out; I don't think we want to be hanging around here."

Ellen wrinkled her nose.

They pushed through the few people on the street who were starting to congregate and turned into the internet café, which seemed to have become the first point of refuge for the train evacuees. There was one spare computer terminal in the middle of a row of four. Boniface pointed. "Go."

With two steps Ellen was at the terminal and seated, the mouse in her hand. "Right. What am I looking for?" she asked as Boniface reached her, having pushed his way through the mass of late-night students and misplaced passengers, combined to form a morass of indecision.

"This online storage thing you mentioned? I don't know—you sounded like you knew what you were talking about."

"Sorry, mate." A student with dilated pupils knocked into Boniface and made his best effort to construct a sentence. "I...you know...it's crowded."

"It's okay," said Boniface, taking stock of the rising flood of humanity drowning the small room. He had no clue what the walls or the floor looked like. All he could see were people trapped under a suspended square lattice ceiling holding dirty tiles and the occasional banks of neon lights flicking and buzzing like some form of highly stylized torture imagined in a Hollywood movie.

Ellen tapped away at the terminal in front of her as Boniface lifted the briefcase, flipping the flap open and peering inside. Another drunken student, wearing a tie-dyed T-shirt with a peace sign, walked into him, spilling his can of lager. He looked at Boniface, Boniface stared at him, and the student turned, puking on three other students behind him.

For the second time that evening, Boniface's nostrils were filled with the smell of vomit. He snapped the case shut; whatever was in there would have to wait until he could find somewhere less crowded. He turned and bent over Ellen. "Any luck?"

"Nope. I can't get the pictures; I tried all the obvious passwords, but they don't work."

"Is there anything more you can do here?" Ellen shook her head. "Then let's get away from this stench." She stood and turned to the door. Boniface shook his head and pointed toward the back of the café, leaning to whisper in her ear, "Sirens, police. Maybe I'm being paranoid, but I'm sure there's a back exit."

The overwhelmed cashier stepped out from behind his counter with a mop and bucket, struggling to reach the location of the latest puke eruption. Checking that Ellen was behind him, Boniface pushed through the crowd and headed behind the counter, turning right through a doorway.

"It might smell of rotting food," said Boniface, wrinkling his nose and looking at the overflowing bins, "but it smells better than the puke and unwashed students in there." He closed what turned out to be the fire-exit door, cutting off their main source of light and muffling the sound of the internet café. "So did you find anything?"

"I found who he's with—it is online-file-store-dot-net—but, apart from that..." She sighed. "Nothing."

"Pity," said Boniface as he started making out shapes in what seemed, with his limited night vision, to be an alley behind the storefronts.

Ellen shivered in the breeze coming down the alley and pulled her jacket tighter. "So what do we do now?"

"I need to make a call." Ellen looked sternly at him. "I might be talking about you, but you can listen."

He took her softening look as agreement as he put his phone to his ear. "News?" His face remained impassive as he listened. "Okay. That's good... No, I haven't heard anything about the dear fellow—why would I? I was rather hoping you were going to tell me he died from a coronary after tonight's sting. Or is that me dreaming? Moving on: computer hackers. You must have a tame one somewhere."

Boniface registered a slight squeak—which might have been shock—from Ellen. "A bit of hacking into one of those online storage thingies... Must be good...deniable for both of us would be sensible...but primarily good and quick. Do you think you could get one of your contacts' contacts to find one?" He paused, waiting for the indecision at the other end of the phone to pass. "Great. I'll get back to you with the details in a couple of minutes. There's somewhere I need to be first." With a flick of his wrist, his phone was shut and re-pocketed.

"Hacking? Isn't that a bit extreme and—I don't know—against the law?" Ellen seemed concerned.

"Murder is against the law, but that didn't seem to slow any bullets tonight." Boniface was quite matter-of-fact. "In any case, we won't be doing the hacking, and you're focusing on the unimportant details." Ellen went to ask the next question, but Boniface kept talking. "Nigel's office?"

"Mmm."

"Do you know where it is?"

"Of course."

Boniface raised his eyebrows. "And would the university extend the courtesy of access to a visiting professor at this time of night?" He listened, unable to see her features clearly, but imagining her collecting every reason not to try, and carried on. "Before you say no... First, his office will be quiet, which..." he threw his head back toward the café, recalling the vomit that had started to flow across the floor, "will be a significant improvement, and second, isn't that the sort of place where he might have noted his password?"

"But isn't..." began Ellen.

"I take it his office is on the campus just up the road. That's less than a mile, so even our grumpy little car should be able to make it in under six hours."

Ellen gave a resigned nod. "So what else did your ex-wife have to say?"

"Two things. Let's start going back to the car." Boniface pointed somewhere in the general direction of where he guessed they had left the car as they started along the back alley. "First off, Kuznetsov definitely does not know what Turgenev is up to. Veronica said he seemed quite shocked. And he was sorry to hear about Nigel."

"So we're safe?" Ellen stopped walking and spun to look at Boniface, her face like a child on Christmas morning.

"Not quite." He kept walking, leaving Ellen to scramble to keep up in the poorly lit passage. "If Kuznetsov didn't order Turgenev to kill you, then we can't be certain about Turgenev's motives. So we can't be certain that you are the target. I might be the target, or it might be coincidence that he's following us." Ellen looked up, the hope draining from her eyes. "And the bigger problem is they can't find Turgenev, so they don't know where he is or what he's up to."

"And you didn't tell her that he's roaming around south London, drowning people for sport, because you don't want her to know where we are?"

"Yup. And I don't know about you, so just for the moment, I'd rather sit in a quiet little office that neither of us has a connection to and look through the papers in this briefcase, safe in the knowledge that Mister Turgenev will not be dropping by for a chat."

"So what else did she have to say?"

Boniface looked up; they were approaching the end of the alley. "Ronnie's other point is far less interesting. She was asking—being as I am with you, and given my history with your publisher, the delightful Mister Sherborne—whether I had heard anything about him."

"What? She wanted you to try to get information about Sherborne out of me?"

"No. Apparently he blipped on the radar tonight. Another tip. You'll understand they are a bit cautious of tips at the moment. She was wondering if I had heard anything, and because you have been at my side since we last spoke, you know that I haven't."

They reached the end of the narrow alley and joined the road where they had left the car. Several police cars seemed to have been abandoned in haste in front of the railway station, their engines off, doors open, and blue lights still flashing. An area around the front of the station was being cordoned off with crime-scene tape, and the police were trying to encourage the displaced passengers and rubberneckers to disperse.

"Maybe they're not after us, but it doesn't look like the place we want to be."

forty-three

It felt good to be back on the Wolf.

Turgenev had ridden slowly down Thames Ditton High Street while he knew the fresh-faced policeman would still be watching him, but he let rip as he turned out of sight. When he got to the main road, he held back the speed and kept his revs low. Everything to minimize his visibility as he followed, in reverse, the directions he had given the man with the scar on his face.

Motoring up the slight incline toward Surbiton station, he was pleased to see a lot of activity. It was amazing what you could do with one phone call.

About fifty yards short of the station, he parked and walked up the slope, passing an internet café, which seemed to be the only place still open besides the burger stand from which the owner had been evicted by the police. Glancing through the window, the internet café looked like an unpleasant mass of drunk and stoned students crammed into a very small room.

There were two police cars outside the station. From the angle at which they were parked and from the way the doors had been left open, he guessed they had arrived in a hurry. It wasn't clear where the police were, but one of their number—another fresh-faced young idealist—was busy fixing crime-scene tape around the outside of the station forecourt area in an attempt to create some sort of cordon.

Turgenev gave a wry grin as he saw the officer struggling to attach the tape, looking forlornly for the next sturdy object he could wrap his ribbon around while the guy from the burger stand berated him. Like that thin strip of plastic film would stop a bomb blast...

Not that there would be a bomb, but the police didn't know that. As far as they knew, the train from Hampton Court station had a bomb on board.

As far as Turgenev knew—and he did know more than the police; after all, he had called in the bomb threat—there was no bomb on board. However, it did seem a simple way to stop the train and get all of the passengers onto the street, where it would be easy to pick out Professor Armstrong and the man who was with her.

He walked around the perimeter, mimicking the behavior of the other rubberneckers, pretending he felt safer at a distance, but looking for somewhere from where he could watch for two specific people and not be obviously seen, either by any CCTV or by the two as they exited the station.

The main road from Surbiton to Kingston ran perpendicular to the station; it was the natural path for anyone to follow if they were looking for alternate means of public transport. Turgenev walked down the street, ducking into the shadow of a shop doorway to look back at the station.

The police and railway staff seemed to have cleared the station but were taking their time with the only train that was still standing at the platform. There seemed to be some confusion: Turgenev guessed they were trying to figure whether they were there to evacuate, to find the bomb, or to look for witnesses.

The red dot on his phone was stationary; he was almost close enough to be able to reach Professor Armstrong and snap her neck with the flick of his wrist. In a few minutes she would be evacuated from the train, and he would see her walking out of the station. All he had to do was to get her on her own, and then he could be back on his bike and back at the Silver Spike.

When he saw Professor Armstrong during her interview that so enraged Mister Kuznetsov, she had been wearing a blue jacket. There was a good chance she hadn't changed, but he couldn't be sure. He wasn't sure about her height—on the television she had been shorter than the other two interviewees, and she had also appeared to be shorter than the aggressive woman conducting the interview. All he could really be sure about was that she had shoulder-length curly blond hair and that he could track her phone.

He looked back at the map on his phone. The red dot wasn't moving, but there didn't seem to be any passengers still on the train. From where he was standing, it appeared the police were going through the train looking for any last stragglers and trying to locate anything that looked like it could be a bomb. He looked harder at the platform on the other side of the chain-link fence that separated the line from the drop-off area at the front of the station. The police seemed to be drawing a blank, which wasn't surprising.

The last few people who had come off the train were dispersing. Professor Armstrong had yet to appear. She definitely hadn't come out, which meant she was either hiding somewhere or she had stepped off at the last stop and left her phone behind. Turgenev stepped from the shadow of the doorway, cursing silently. If she had disembarked at the previous station, there was no way to know where she was.

He checked the dot again. Definitely stationary.

Most of the passengers had dispersed. Some were standing around making calls; others were walking with a purpose, heading for some other form of transport. The younger people seemed to have gravitated to the internet café.

There were even fewer people around the station as Turgenev started walking back toward his bike. As he looked to cross the road where he had been standing, he caught sight of two figures leaving a side alley: a taller man and a shorter blond woman. A shorter blond woman with curly blond hair, wearing a blue suit.

A broad grin spread across his face as he subtly changed direction, moving back into the shadow to watch them walking down the street.

They reached a battered car and got in: she in the driver's seat, he in the passenger's, both ignoring the comments from a group of students standing near the car. As the man opened the door, he looked behind him toward the station.

Turgenev felt a jolt of recognition and a spark of elation as he realized who he was looking at.

Now that he knew where Professor Armstrong was, he could complete his task. Not only that, he could also tell Mister Kuznetsov that the man he had met this afternoon was working with the professor. Working with Sherborne's woman. Sherborne had managed to get someone close to Mister Kuznetsov, but he, Mikhail Igorovich Turgenev, had used his initiative and had found the infiltrator.

If this didn't prove his value to Mister Kuznetsov, then nothing would.

The professor started up the car—Turgenev laughed out loud. That was the ridiculous sound he had heard from the island. They were making it so easy to follow them; he just had to use his ears.

He started jogging back to his bike.

forty-four

"Drunk but harmless," muttered Boniface under his breath as he and Ellen approached the car, where a group of students had gathered to laugh at the museum piece.

"D'you want a push, mate?" one asked, his friends laughing out loud as Boniface and Ellen got in.

"I can walk faster than that drives," offered another, frowning and looking around when his comment didn't generate the expected mirth from his comrades.

Ellen started the car on the first attempt. "Now please, little car, I know I've thought unpleasant things about you, but please, just this once, please move off without any drama." She slid the car into gear, there was a mechanical clunk as the gear reached home, and then the vehicle moved off slowly and without incident.

"I'm impressed," said Boniface, graciously waving at the students as the car chugged past.

"Now impress me, Boniface. Tell me what we're doing. Tell me what the plan is."

He picked up on the tension in Ellen's voice. "You're worried about this computer hacking thing," he said as another police car sped toward Surbiton station, its blue flashing light announcing its urgency.

"I can't say it's been one of my ambitions. So are you going to explain what we're doing?"

"There's not much to explain," said Boniface. "First we're going to Nigel's office to see if we can get into this online file storage thing while we don't have the pressure of people puking over us, and while we're there, we're going to have a look around. That's not too outrageous, is it?"

"I'm confused," said Ellen. "If we can access the photos from the university, then why do we need the hacker?"

"I hope we won't need a hacker, and anyway, it's a bloody dangerous strategy to get a stranger to open up files for you. I've asked Ronnie to find one in case we need it. That way we won't have a delay once we've exhausted our options." Boniface watched Ellen as she reasoned the proposition internally.

"This is where we need Montbretia to help us. She understands these things much better than I do. If we can wait until tomorrow morning, then she'd be ready to have a go." Ellen paused. "Tomorrow morning."

"Tomorrow morning?"

"Montbretia arrives—you remember, we had this conversation. I've got to pick her up at the airport. Now, apart from the fact that I haven't booked a cab..."

"Who needs a cab when you've got a car?" asked Boniface, holding his arms open and looking around the car.

"Yeah right. Even if I leave now, I won't make it in time, and not without doing serious and permanent damage to my skeleton. No, the problem is that she's going to call me as soon as she lands, and my phone is... I don't know, Boniface. Where is my phone at this precise moment?"

Boniface smiled. "It should be just outside Waterloo, being pursued by a shaven-headed man who likes to drown people."

"So that leaves the challenge as to how my sister and I communicate."

"Not a problem," said Boniface. "Tell her to call mine."

"Could I?" said Ellen. "Really?"

"Sure. Do you want to send her a text now to tell her to call this number?"

"Really?"

"I might not be the most technologically advanced, but I can just about manage to send one hundred and forty characters typed awkwardly on a phone keypad." Boniface pulled out his phone and flipped it open. "My price is that you explain why you got the conventional—very pleasant, but conventional—name and she got the wacky one."

"We both got...interesting names, but I use my middle name. And no, I'm not going to tell you."

"Is it a flower?"

"Our mother was a hippie. That's all I'm saying," said Ellen, blushing.

"So why didn't Montbretia change her name?" The urge to keep digging was starting to kick in.

"Because her middle name is Sylvia—which I never really liked—and after our mother died, I wouldn't let her change her name. Also, it shortens well to Monty, so it's not as bad as..."

"As?"

"Nice try, mister. Can we get on with the SMS? We can talk about weird names later, if that's alright with you, Alexander?"

"Touché. What's her number?" Slowly he input each figure, repeating as he went. "What do you want me to say?"

"Hi sis, really looking forward to seeing you, got lots to tell you..."

"One hundred and forty characters, not words."

"Sorry. Okay then, hi sis, lost my phone, call me on this number, love E. How's that?"

Boniface manipulated the tiny keypad, squinting at the screen. "Eighty-seven characters to spare. I've sent it."

"But I..."

"We can send another if you want," offered Boniface.

Ellen shook her head. "Later. Let's do what we need to do here first."

"So where's your sister coming in from?"

"Turkey. Istanbul."

"Very nice. Does she live there?"

"No, she's been doing some traveling. She did the whole mature day job for a few years, but she didn't enjoy it and so figured she would go wild for a while, before knuckling down and accepting that she had to be sensible and admit she was an adult."

"Like becoming a university professor and getting shot at?" Ellen remained impassive as Boniface continued. "Does she have a big plan, or is she going where her heart tells her until the money runs out?"

"Mostly the latter, but some of the former. She writes everything she does in this blog. It's a real hoot—some of the things she does are pretty risky. As you've probably guessed, I'm the quiet one, I'm the one who reads books; she's the more out-there sister."

"How out there?"

"Well, two days ago she was swimming across the Bosporus at midnight. That's nearly a mile: Europe to Asia. I mean, do it, but not at midnight in the freezing water with jellyfish, passing tankers, and I don't know what else floating in the water."

"So she hasn't inspired you to dash back to the Thames for a post-midnight dip when we're done?" Boniface let the question hang as they approached the front gate of the university.

"How do we play this?" asked Ellen. "There's a guard. He's going to ask some awkward questions, isn't he?"

"Act casual...act relaxed..." He sighed. "Nigel must have told everyone about his book—that was rather in his nature."

Ellen had a look of slight disappointment.

"And he's probably told everyone about one or both of us?"

More disappointed nodding.

"The one person who can't run away is a security guard. He probably had to listen about both of us: you the brilliant professor, always on television, me the maverick whatever I am. And he probably knows that Nigel's book launch was tonight. So the guard will know us, we've got Nigel's car and his pass on the key ring, and all we need to do is tell him that Nigel rather overdid things and we're here to collect some papers he needs for tomorrow morning. Look—we've even got his briefcase. What could be better proof?"

Ellen nodded in resignation as she turned into the university entrance.

"But don't embellish. Stick with the simple story. Don't go Scarlett O'Hara on me again."

forty-five

As he crossed in front of the station, Turgenev became increasingly aware of what he wasn't seeing.

The two police cars were still there, along with a third that had joined them—their unsynchronized lights continuing to bend and break—and the tape to cordon off the station forecourt was still in place, but for all this activity, there were few people.

The young, fresh-faced policeman who had diligently stretched the tape around the perimeter was not in sight, and the last two police officers who had turned up were on the platform, looking anxious and self-important, and badgering the train station staff.

The train was still in the station, with one officer seeming to want to have a final look for the bomb.

Turgenev paused, muttering under his breath: "Very clever, Professor Armstrong. You almost had me fooled." He smirked. "Perhaps you will thank me if I return your phone."

The route to the train meant going up the stairs that crossed the line, then down onto the platform that stood between the train lines—far too much chance of being stopped, especially when all he had to do was get over the chain-link fence topped with three rows of barbed wire.

He sprinted across the forecourt to the chain-link fence. Placing one hand between the barbs and the other on a concrete fence post, he levered himself over, landing on the stones beside the tracks. He jogged around the back of the train, then jumped onto the platform before ducking into the last door of the end car.

He pulled out his phone, smiled as he hit the call button, and started to walk up the central corridor of the train. As he walked through the connecting doors joining the next car, the call passed to voicemail. He hung up and redialed, continuing to walk up the central passage.

As he opened the door to the third car, there was a single ring. He stabbed his phone with his finger to redial. The parcel shelf by the door started ringing as the lone policeman checking the inside of the train came into the car. "Hey! There's a bomb. Get off the train."

Turgenev ran, grabbing the phone as he passed, sidestepped out the door, and accelerated up the stairs, not stopping until he reached his bike.

As he passed the place where the 2CV had been parked, a group of drunken students were milling around. At the sound of his Ural Wolf, all turned, some pointed, most mimicked *Easy Rider* poses.

A five-way junction marked the end of the straight road. The road he had followed behind him, a perpendicular main road going left and right, and two roads in front, splitting in a V-shape.

A junction, but no French car.

He killed the engine and slipped off his helmet. The acrid smell of a car burning oil filled his nose. The sound of the French car had lost none of its distinctiveness: It was on one of the roads in front of him. He leaned over, careful not to drop the bike, and looked down the left fork. No cars moving. The right fork curved away, obscuring anything around the bend.

He replaced his helmet, kicked the bike into life, and followed the curve of the right fork. As the road started to straighten, a junction at the end came into sight. A junction where an old, noisy French car was clumsily turning. He dropped the power, keeping his distance, and followed.

The car tracked the road through a right dog-leg and started to pass in front of a long three-story building. The building was, by English standards, comparatively new, probably late 1960s or early 1970s, and had then been built to a low budget and without any concern for aesthetics.

Reaching the end of the building, the car turned right into an entrance. Turgenev pulled up short and killed his engine. The car went across the front parking lot, pulling up to a barrier protecting a gap between two buildings. A short, scrawny man, seemingly prematurely aged by his unhealthiness, came out from the small hut next to the barrier and was met by the man he had seen in the Silver Spike, who got out of the car. After some discussion, the guard seemed to recognize the occupants and become far more relaxed with them, shaking hands before he walked back to raise the barrier, allowing the car to pass.

Turgenev kicked the bike back to life and moved. Drawing level with the barrier, he saw a gap between the buildings wide enough for cars to be parked on both sides. Professor Armstrong and the man Turgenev had now decided to call *the traitor* were getting out of their car and heading into the gloom next to the building on the right. He strained to see, but couldn't tell whether they had gone through a door or if they had followed some other passage behind the building.

He waited for a moment or two, then started to follow the perimeter. About fifty yards down, a minor road wound around the back of the site, passing buildings displaying a nasty mix of cheap construction and poor planning, coupled with no clear sense of space.

At the very back there was a large parking lot with no barrier and no guard. Turgenev carried on past the lot, following the perimeter road until it connected back to the main road, where he turned back on himself and headed to the rear lot.

He parked, pulling the Wolf into the darkest shadows, obscuring it from the road, and looked for any obvious road to drive through from the front of the site to the rear, but found none. Each new building seemed to have blocked off everything except a few narrow rat-runs for pedestrians. There was only one exit route for the French car.

He walked around the inner perimeter of the site, his eyes scanning like a bird of prey, and jumped over the low wall when he reached the front. Across the road, opposite the entrance, a brick-built Victorian hall with circular stone steps and a circular awning held up by four pillars provided an ideal place to sit and watch the sole exit.

He took stock. The guard had retreated to his hut. The car that Professor Armstrong and the traitor had arrived in was where he had seen it parked. The building to the right of the road behind the barrier was still in complete darkness. The building to the left was lit, and Turgenev could hear the thump of music being played. No one entered, no one left.

With his position staked out, he slipped out the phone he had retrieved from the train and started flicking through. It didn't make much sense, but it was interesting.

There was a text message with someone called Monty. The sentence "Perhaps he's found a pot of gold!?!" caught his eye. That alone bought Professor Armstrong five minutes longer to live while he extracted the details from her.

The photos were also interesting. Interesting in their dullness. No one took dull photos—what looked like photos of pieces of paper—if the photos didn't matter. He checked the timestamps: They were shot less than an hour ago.

It was going to be an interesting chat with the professor.

There was a sound from the hut. Turgenev jerked his head up to see the guard out of the hut and looking agitated. He had a phone in his hand, which he was clumsily dialing.

The shaven-headed Russian watched as the guard lifted the phone to his ear and started talking. The guard looked up, down, left, right, and several times at the 2CV. He pointed, gestured with his head, stood still, started to move again, nodded vigorously, and then put the phone in his pocket, remaining outside the hut like a small child desperate for the lavatory, nervously trying to control himself and stay strong.

After twitching for a while, he raised the barrier as if expecting someone to arrive, and stood in the middle of the road, waiting.

forty-six

Ellen led Boniface from the corridor into the office.

The very small office.

Against the wall separating the room from the corridor were three four-drawer filing cabinets, each a different color and showing a different manufacturer's logo, and all showing signs of wear with dents, scratches, rust, and paint patches. All had the customary two holes drilled above the lock to gain access when someone had lost their keys.

A small desk—at least Boniface guessed it was a desk under the stacks of papers and files—faced the door with its edge against the wall. One pile of papers was acting as a telephone stand for a gray phone with a knotted cord, and toward the wall sat an old computer, complete with 12-inch cathode-ray-tube monitor and circa-1983 clicky keyboard. A gap of about two feet was left to act as a passage between the desk and the filing cabinets, guiding the occupant to the chair behind the desk, which looked to have about as much comfort as one of Nigel's car seats.

"So how do we get from the secretary's office into Nigel's?" asked Boniface.

"Very funny."

"You're kidding." Boniface opened his eyes wide and let his jaw drop for emphasis. "This is it. This? This is Nigel's office. I was doing the press for a bloke who wasn't even worthy of a window? No wonder he was a bit nutty. I'd go like that if I had to spend all day in here."

Ellen followed the well-worn trail on the carpet and sat behind the desk, turning on the computer. "Clear off the top of the filing cabinets and lay the papers out there." She pointed with a sweeping motion to the tops of the three cabinets, which were covered with dying plants, dust, and more unspecified piles of papers, books, and files.

Boniface picked up the first flowerpot, finding it to be much lighter than he expected. "Nigel didn't have green fingers, did he?" Ellen drew her mouth tight and shook her head. He picked up the other plant, which was equally light, and placed the two in the corridor outside Nigel's office door; then proceeded to move the papers, stacking them in the free corner, finishing his edifice by lining the books along the wall.

He opened the case and rested it on one of the piles on the desk, removing the contents. The paper was new, but for Boniface it could have been historic archives. Careful to ensure no damage and that none of the papers had stuck together, he laid them out over the top of the cabinets, taking time to place each page and then reorder their positions until he was sure each page had been laid near to other pages with similar information.

"What am I looking for?" He turned to Ellen, who was transfixed in front of the computer screen, her head balanced on her hand, propped up by an arm resting on her knee.

"I don't know," said Ellen, her lower jaw remaining stationary on her hand, with the top of her head moving up and down as her mouth opened. "I guess that what he wrote in those notes was a combination of old information he was trying to link with the new material, so it would be good to know where one starts and the other finishes."

She sat up and started typing as Boniface tried to make sense of the contents of Nigel's briefcase. "No...not that...try something else..." Ellen had started to grumble, each grumble being followed by a burst of clicking.

The concentration was broken by Boniface's phone ringing. "It's for you," he said, opening the phone and passing it to Ellen.

"H...h...hello...? This is Ellen." Boniface returned to his papers, reading and reordering without finding any sense. "Monty!" In the short time he had known Ellen, he hadn't heard her so enthusiastic or excited. "No, I'm fine. It's been a bit of a long day. Shouldn't you be asleep? You haven't been watching the UK TV news? Good. No. Bit of a strange story...nothing to worry about... I'll explain it tomorrow, but if you see anything about me, ignore it... Yeah, big mistaken-identity thing."

Boniface looked over, catching Ellen's eye, and whispered, "Ask her about those storage things... Can she get in?"

Ellen mouthed "yes," and Boniface turned back to his conundrum, allowing Ellen to chat without being watched or overheard.

"I'll pick you up at Heathrow tomorrow morning. Yes, I'll be with Boniface." Boniface heard his name and spun to see Ellen staring straight at him, finishing her call. "Montbretia's looking forward to meeting you." She held out her hand to return the phone.

Boniface took it, his face registering confusion.

"She's heard the whole Nigel hero-worship take on you." Ellen grinned mischievously. "She wants to know if you're really that good."

"You seem to tell your sister a lot."

"We're close. We talk. It's not unusual, Boniface."

He pondered, carefully choosing his words. "No, but...now don't misinterpret this...and I know you've had a really bad night, but you seemed different talking with her. Your voice had some real enthusiasm, some real warmth." Ellen's eyebrows moved closer. "It's not a bad thing...quite the contrary. It's...I dunno...nice."

"We're close. We talk a lot. Well, talk, email, send text messages, whatever. We communicate a lot." Her face fell slightly, looking more serious. "We're sort of all each other has got."

The room was silent. Boniface waited, watching as Ellen connected with something deep in her subconscious.

"We've always been...it sounds pretentious, but I guess you would call it connected. Always. When mom died, we were the only ones who understood each other. But when dad died two years ago..."

"Jeez, I didn't know, I'm sorry."

"It's alright, we're... She's my sister." She sat straighter. "Anyway, apparently everyone uses these online storage things these days—thumb drives, hard drives, they're all for old fogies." She grimaced, slightly chagrined. "Tells me, doesn't it?"

"And me too," said Boniface, feeling mildly scolded and embarrassed by Nigel from the grave. "Once she finished telling you off, was she able to help?"

"I tried what she suggested, and it didn't work." She forced a weak smile. "Monty said that maybe we could get the password reset."

"Why don't we do that?" Boniface heard the enthusiasm in his voice.

"Because then they'd send a new password to Nigel's email address."

"What's the problem with...?" Boniface paused as the realization clicked. "And we don't have the password for Nigel's email."

"True." Ellen stood and walked to the cabinets, casting her eye over the papers. "So what have we got?"

"Not a clue. You're the historian," said Boniface. "As far as I can tell, there seem to be two family trees. One is the Henry and/or Wolsey tree, setting out the offspring attributed to Henry. Even if, after a certain point, Wolsey may have been Henry. It sort of seems to fit with what we know, as in he's looking at four children, including FitzRoy, the illegitimate one."

Boniface laid a finger on one of the papers and waited for Ellen's gaze to reach his finger.

"And while I'm in a pointing mood, this name," Boniface slapped his finger on another piece of paper, "seems to be coming up a lot tonight." Boniface moved his finger around as Ellen followed the references. "But I don't get the link. Or rather, I see the link; there's some guy called John Stephens who seems to have been alive, but young, during the reign of Henry and/or Wolsey, and this John Stephens has some descendants who are quite familiar to us." He stepped back, allowing Ellen to move closer to the cabinets. "You can see Nigel's drawn out the family tree."

She raised her eyebrows.

"So let me throw out a bit of idle speculation." Ellen frowned and looked toward Boniface. "Mister Longhair, may he rest in peace, implied that he had a buyer for his information."

"He did," said Ellen.

"Given the name that's on these pieces of paper, it would seem reasonable that he was a potential buyer, would it not? He has all the necessary qualifications to be a buyer: delusions of grandeur and stacks of cash."

"Perhaps." Ellen turned back to the papers, following the family trees with her finger.

"Have a look and tell me; I've got some hacking to get fixed. And maybe after that, we need to pay a visit?"

Boniface stepped back to carry on his conversation while resting against the doorframe. "Guess who?" He had connected before he heard the ringing tone. "I'm somewhere in London, but given that your boss's henchman has been chasing us around, you'll understand my caution while talking to you on your work-provided phone."

Boniface waited for the hurt feelings to subside before he continued. "I've got details of the online storage thing for you. Have you got someone lined up for us? All I need is for him to send me the password, and I'll take it from there."

He watched as Ellen studied the paper arrayed over the tops of the cabinets.

"So can he do it as soon as?" Boniface waited, listening. "Sure, I understand. Give me a call when he's on the case." Ellen swapped two sheet of paper. "By the way, any word on Mister Turgenev?" Ellen looked up, as if she had received a mild electrical shock. "No, we haven't seen him or heard from him for a while, but I'd rather not bump into him for a day or two... Okay... Thanks."

Boniface flipped his phone shut. "Have you found anything?"

"Nothing." She sounded disappointed. "I think we need to make the visit as you suggest."

"You've been there before. Will there be a computer there?"

Ellen grimaced. "Technically, I think it's called a computer, but what I saw last time was rather steam-powered."

"But it will connect to the internet?"

"I suppose." Ellen did not radiate confidence.

"And I'm presuming you can talk us past the front door. As you know, my relationship isn't exactly warm."

"There's little choice. I'll do what I can do." A door squeaked at the end of the corridor. "What was that?"

"The noise?"

"Mmm."

"We're not expecting visitors, are we?"

forty–seven

Turgenev became aware of a flickering light some way off accompanied by engines straining and wheels squealing: the sound of cars being driven at high speed.

He stopped looking through the professor's emails on her phone, slipping the device he had spent most of the evening chasing back into his pocket as the flickering soon turned into flashing blue lights, and the sound of speed turned into two silver BMW 5 Series with police markings turning through the main university entrance and heading toward the sick-looking guard, anxiously waiting by his raised barrier.

The guard bent down to talk to the passenger in the first car, pointing in the direction that Professor Armstrong and Boniface had gone. Slowly he returned to vertical, indicating their car, and then pointed to a few other points of interest, getting into his stride as a fellow member of the extended law-enforcement community. Finally, he stood back as the two cars accelerated through the gate.

Four officers got out, had a brief conversation, and then disappeared into the same dark hole where the occupants of the French car had gone.

The guard watched the police. As they disappeared, he closed the barrier and returned to his hut, walking with a swagger that hadn't been present a few minutes ago—in fact, probably had never been present in his life.

Turgenev waited for thirty seconds and then started walking toward the barrier. He feigned interest as he walked up to the security guard, who had boldly strutted out of his hut to greet the approaching stranger. "Busy night?"

"It is." The guard had the look of a man still feeling the pump of adrenalin and wanting someone to listen to his tale.

"What's going on?" asked Turgenev, looking around as he approached the guard, becoming aware of the pounding beat from the building behind the hut.

"You'll never believe who's just gone into the offices over there..." Turgenev raised his eyebrows. "She's the one on the news who murdered that..." said the guard, tucking in his stained shirt as the Russian stopped in front of him. Turgenev's right hand flashed forward, slamming the butt of his palm into the guard's solar plexus.

The guard crumpled like a pile of dirty laundry in front of Turgenev, who then crouched next to the body lying at his feet. Taking the guard's head, he twisted sharply, releasing as he felt a sharp crack. He looked around and fixed on a row of dumpsters at the far end of the parking lot. With a single movement he picked up the guard's corpse and carried it over his shoulder, as if it were no heavier than a backpack.

The Russian opened the lid to the first dumpster. Full. The second. Full. The third. Half full. The fourth. Empty. Perfect. He eased the body into the dumpster, closed the lid, and walked back to the guard's hut, placing his hand on the door handle.

There was a noise, shuffling of feet, voices, and laughter. "I am so wasted." Two guys, looking like students, stumbled out from the building behind the hut. "It's too loud in there, but I still need some…"

"Alcohol?" offered the other, turning to see Turgenev by the guard's hut. "Hey man…where's…?" He tapped his finger as if tapping an invisible horizontal bar, looking for Turgenev to supply the answers.

Turgenev raised his eyebrows. "He's gone to…"

"Have a piss," continued the first student. "That guy's never here. We're going to get some more alcohol, so you"—he pointed to Turgenev—"you are in charge until he gets back. And I want a full written report on my desk by the time I return." The two burst into laughter and started moving toward the outer gate.

The Russian waited until he was sure that their goldfish-like brains had forgotten him, then tried the handle.

The door opened, releasing the stale smell of cheap coffee, even cheaper cigarettes, and poor choices in personal hygiene. Turgenev wrinkled his nose in an attempt to block his nostrils as he let the foul air rush out, each individual molecule desperate to be gone from the fug. "There'll be no widow weeping beside your grave," he said as he stepped into the hut.

A small television showing 24-hour news flashed up Professor Armstrong's picture, followed by a live report from outside a small floodlit house surrounded by crime-scene tape. Next to the television sat a few chipped and dirty coffee cups, an overflowing ashtray, a small pile of newspapers, a few official-looking forms, and a battered clipboard listing people and vehicles who had come and gone. Collectively, the debris managed to hide the desk on which the clutter stood, which in turn obscured the filled trashcan sitting on a cheap piece of linoleum worn through in places, with tracks remembering the route into and out of the box, the position of the feet of the occupant as he sat watching TV, and the route of the casters on the chair as it moved in its tiny orbit. "Would it have hurt you to tidy up?" Turgenev asked under his breath. "After all, you're not that far from the dumpsters."

He turned off the television, flicked the switch to stop the buzzing strip light, and stepped out of the cabin. Sucking in clean air, he closed the door behind him and lifted the barrier.

forty-eight

Eric Whittaker quietly closed the car door as he tried to relax into the thinly padded seat after another fruitless attempt to find out what was happening with Richard Sherborne at Trumpeters' House.

He was still pissed about being excluded from whatever was going on tonight—someone said they had a sting set up to catch Oscar von Habsburg—but instead, he had been told to sit outside the fat man's house. The woman in the fuchsia jacket told him he had been chosen by the editor, Veronica Rutherford, but he could smell bull when he heard it.

He had lost count of how many loops he had made, but still he diligently recorded his notes from each reconnaissance. This last loop had been the outer circuit, the route he followed for every two inner loops that he completed. He preferred the outer loop: It was more scenic, and he could also complete it much more inconspicuously. It took him down Old Palace Lane where he had parked, and when the road ended at the River Thames, he would turn left along a broad stone path past a classical three-floor sandstone-block mini-mansion.

After a high wall, an iron fence separated Trumpeters' House and its long ornamental garden from the path. Beyond Trumpeters' House, there was another high wall shielding something that he couldn't see in the darkness but that he suspected was an apartment block, and finally there was a short row of three houses at the end of the path. He would then turn left from the river into Friars Lane—a wriggling back street with a mix of old terraced houses, a parking lot, a converted church, and some newly constructed houses built with old bricks—which led him back onto Richmond Green.

Around the edge of the Green were imposing three-story Georgian townhouses, brick-built with white plaster details, sash windows, imposing wooden front doors, and iron railings to the street. After the townhouses came another high wall; on this one, every brick looked about five hundred years old. This wall curved sharply to the left, going through ninety degrees before meeting the building behind it at an arched gateway over the road: The Wardrobe, a strange name for a road, but he couldn't change that.

The inner loop was riskier, and so the need for a disguise—to be changed for each loop—was greater. He looked to the pile of clothes thrown across the back seat: a gray, shapeless jacket, old combat pants, a nylon rainproof jacket, a flat cap, a fedora, and several different-colored baseball caps lay on the top of the heap. Each chosen, alone or in combination, to give him a different look when he stepped out from the shadows and onto the broad footpath that ran perpendicular to the road as he began his inner loop.

The wall on the left of the path offered him fresh shadow cover as he passed some newer—1970s, Eric guessed—houses. The next houses were set back from the path. These looked like a row of almshouses but were probably converted to executive homes by a smart developer whose mantra was location, location, location.

After this, the path ended abruptly, tossing him into Old Palace Yard: a teardrop of grass encircled by buildings.

In the corner was Trumpeters' House—Sherborne's home, and the place he was watching. Like the townhouses around Richmond Green, this was brick-built, with white plaster detailing in the central core and sash windows to the outer flanks. But this house was detached and much wider than the other houses.

Joining the other end of Old Palace Yard was The Wardrobe. Trumpeters' House was impressive, but the buildings along The Wardrobe were spectacular. A simple row of brick-built structures that looked to date from the Tudor period.

From Old Palace Yard he would walk the few steps to the Gatehouse arch and out of The Wardrobe onto Richmond Green to follow the same path as his outer loop. When the road around the perimeter of Richmond Green turned right to follow the outer edge, Eric took the left fork and followed the road as it snaked around into Old Palace Lane, straightening shortly before he reached his car.

It was during one of his inner loops, as he was leaving The Wardrobe, that he had to jump out of the way as the first car sped past, driving up to the gates of Trumpeters' House. A second car arrived not long after, and within a few minutes they had both left.

He couldn't tell how many people had arrived—four, he thought—with three leaving. As was expected of him, he had recorded their details and called them in. By now the owners of the cars would have been traced and every detail held about them on the oracle would have been sent to Veronica Rutherford.

He hadn't seen the next two cars arrive. If he had, he would have hung back and not stepped out from the passage and into the Old Palace Yard as he followed the inner loop. Once he was there he couldn't stop walking, but he had been able to hear the voice of the first man shouting to the second, who was getting into his car before driving away. The man who shouted was young and, from his accent, a Londoner. Eric didn't see what he looked like, but the other man who drove away was probably in his twenties, at least six feet tall, and well built. Eric had carried on with his circuit, calling in the plates and what he had seen before starting another swift circuit, where he had found the yard deserted.

That was an hour ago, and now he was bored and tired.

forty-nine

Turgenev stood, listening to the voices two floors above him. How had he missed finding the business card on the dead body? That was a mistake, but it was interesting to find that the dead man seemed to be a business associate of the traitor, Boniface. This was turning into an interesting story to tell Mister Kuznetsov.

The deeper voice continued. "Mister Boniface. With all your persuasive words, you seem to be forgetting that we have evidence of you having been at a murder scene. As well as finding your business card on the victim, you were identified crossing the bridge onto Thames Ditton Island shortly before the emergency call was made."

When the shaven-headed Russian had followed the route that Boniface, Professor Armstrong, and the four police had taken, he had found that instead of there simply being a dark abyss, around the corner and slightly set back from view there was an entrance. The foyer and stairs covered all three floors, and unlike the brick structure of the rest of the building, this was shielded from the weather by wired safety glass held in a flaking dark-stained wood frame.

The double doors on the ground floor led into a small lobby with vinyl floor tiles and white or beige—he couldn't tell in the gloom—painted plaster walls. Going away from him, the vinyl tiles led down an undistinguished corridor.

To the right, the staircase led to the next floors. The tiles followed the staircase on its slow progress, and the brown wooden handrail mirrored the dull wood in the window frames.

Turgenev stepped into the shadow of the corridor as the sound of Boniface and his escorts arrived at the top of the stairs, the incessant chattering from Boniface digging like a knife into his concentration.

The party began to descend. "What do health and safety say about this?" asked Boniface. "Surely we must be breaking all sorts of regulations? A man with his hands cuffed. I could have a dreadful accident and sue."

"Don't worry, sir. We'll catch you." The second voice was mirthless and insincere, characteristics that were probably finely honed over years of dealing with overly talkative criminals. Turgenev could imagine the look passing between the police at that moment—a wish, a hope, an aspiration, just once to be able to push and administer swift, unequivocal justice.

Without any hurry, the party came to the foot of the stairs. Boniface in the lead, his hands behind his back, two officers behind him—one to either side, going through the monotonous procedure of taking another fool into custody. Being required to hear, but not listen to, Boniface's continuous jabbering, which seem to be lulling the two into a trance.

As they came off the last step, turning toward the brown wood-framed door with its unpleasant wired safety glass, Turgenev silently stepped forward, sliding an arm around the neck of the closest officer and dropping him to the floor before crushing his windpipe under his boot.

Before the second officer could break out of his Boniface-induced coma, he was overpowered, Turgenev dropping his body next to the lifeless corpse of his recently deceased colleague.

"Thank God you're here, Mister Turgenev. You need to help us... I know Mister Kuznetsov's best interests would be well served if you could sort things out. Professor Armstrong is upstairs; she's been arrested too, and she's got the briefcase..."

Turgenev stared at Boniface, held up a single finger, and hissed "Shut up." Boniface went to talk. Turgenev shook his head in a small but decisive move. "Shut up, completely. I want silence." Boniface's body tensed and the bright cockiness in his eyes dulled. Turgenev jabbed his finger at him, like a shepherd telling his dog to stay. "And don't move." Boniface nodded once to affirm, the rest of his body motionless.

The two police radios crackled, breaking the still demanded by Turgenev. He reached down and pulled the first, then the second handset from their attaching wires, silencing them individually, and then searched the officers' pockets. Returning to his customary erect position, he looked at Boniface, murmured "not a move," and then dragged the first body into the shadow of the corridor, returning to remove the second.

He returned, looking through a set of keys, and pushed Boniface toward the door. "Move."

Boniface led as Turgenev directed him to the back of the closest police car. "In," said Turgenev, opening the trunk. Boniface went to speak as Turgenev pushed him, folding his head and legs into the cramped space before he closed the trunk.

As Turgenev reached the top of the stairs, he found the remaining two officers escorting Professor Armstrong, her hands also handcuffed behind her back.

Turgenev stared straight into Professor Armstrong's eyes and watched her quiver. "Good. You've got her," he looked to the first officer. "Did you retrieve the briefcase she stole?" The officer stared blankly. "The briefcase! The briefcase!"

Professor Armstrong relaxed as the two officers looked at each other in confusion. "I'm sorry, sir, we didn't see a case."

"Then come with me," said Turgenev. The officers exchanged a glance. "You come," he pointed to the first. "You stay," he pointed to the second.

"She's only a woman. She's in handcuffs—she's not going to do anything."

The first officer started moving back along the narrow corridor, speeding up as Turgenev got closer. They rounded into an office, and Turgenev saw a brown satchel-like briefcase lying on top of a pile of papers on the small desk facing the door. While the policeman still had his back to him, the Russian reached, putting one hand over the officer's mouth and the other over the back of his head; with a single jerk, he twisted.

As the body hit the floor, Turgenev went through his familiar routine: disabled the radio, frisked the body, found another set of car keys, then picked up the briefcase, looked inside it, dropped it, and left the room.

Reaching the other officer, Turgenev smiled broadly. "Your friend is coming. He said he's just checking..." He unleashed a single blow, striking the officer on the side of the head with the base of his hand.

The officer's neck twisted, giving an unnatural deep cracking sound as the rest of his body convulsed, compensating for the force needed to keep the head attached to the top of the neck. As his body moved, the officer stumbled, falling against the top of the banister, continuing to follow the inertia of his head. Turgenev gave a firm push to the officer's shoulder, and the momentum took the body over the rail, landing with a cluster of dull, soggy, impacts.

Turgenev turned to Professor Armstrong, who had tears starting to form in her eyes, and pointed toward the stairs. "I'm not going to have any trouble with you, am I?" She shook her head, taking her first steps.

As they reached the bottom of the stairs, Professor Armstrong delicately walked around the edge of the indistinct lump dressed in dark blue. Turgenev performed his customary procedure, then stood back, muttering to himself, "Why bother?"

He shoved her through the double doors and toward the car, opening the back door. "In."

Professor Armstrong gingerly put one foot inside the car, leaning to support herself while trying to reach with her hands still cuffed behind her back. "Faster," said Turgenev, pushing her as she fell in a heap in the rear foot well, before slamming the door with a kick.

He pulled out his phone and opened the map, waiting a few seconds for the data to download, then zoomed out until he saw the river. He moved the map, following the River Thames downstream, searching for a place to float two more bodies once he found out what they had to tell him. He flipped to the satellite view. It was perfect: a small, quiet access road, a discreet parking place by the river, no overlooking houses. What more could he ask for?

fifty

The road had changed.

There had been a very twisty-and-turny section—they had turned right out of the university, so Boniface guessed that was the Kingston one-way system—which then led to a fairly straight but lumpy road. At some point the car had turned off that road and had travelled more slowly on a road with a smoother, undulating surface.

The undulation gave way to an uneven road with potholes, which then seemed to be replaced by stony ground, with the car kicking up rocks under his head. After several twists, the car skidded to a halt, relieving Boniface's handcuffed body of the shakes and jolts of traveling.

Unaccustomed to the silence but becoming aware of the ringing in his ears, he listened and felt the movement of the vehicle. The driver got out, opened the rear door, and said something. Boniface couldn't make out what he said, but he guessed the passenger in the back was being invited to take some night air.

The car leaned. The passenger was probably being encouraged very strongly to stand up and come outside. As the car righted itself, he listened to the sound of footsteps on the stones. One set was sturdy, strong, and sure-footed. The other set of footsteps was lighter and uncertain, each step either a hesitant stumble or a move to correct a stumble.

After about ten steps, the sound of footsteps ended. This was probably where the stones ended, guessed Boniface. His conjecture was confirmed when he heard one set of feet—the heavy, sure-footed set—return.

The trunk lid opened, and Boniface took a few moments to allow his eyes to adjust to the light, even though it was only the ambient light from a few stars and a new moon. He became aware of Turgenev's presence as the Russian's arm came toward him, first pulling his feet over the lip, and then reaching back to lever the rest of his body out of the trunk. Flipping over the lip of the trunk, Boniface stumbled and fell, confirming for himself that the car was parked on some large and roughly cut stones.

"Get up," said Turgenev, slamming the trunk and pulling Boniface by his handcuffs, already in motion away from the car. Like a wild animal that is born as the herd migrates, Boniface had to walk or perish. By the third step he had found his balance.

After a few more steps, the stones ended, giving way to a grass verge, the junction demarcated by a row of vertical wooden fence posts, occasionally interspersed by large rocks. Boniface looked ahead: The man was obsessive; they were by the river again, and he remembered what he had seen the last time Turgenev was beside a river.

Boniface was jerked to the right and saw Ellen, kneeling, perhaps five feet away from the river, her hands also cuffed behind her back. Turgenev pushed Boniface next to her. "Kneel."

"Not really dressed for this, are you?" Boniface saw her eyes fill with a mixture of joy, hope, and then fear as she winced, watching Turgenev slap Boniface.

"Shut the fuck up, Mister Boniface. And if you can't be quiet, you can watch your girlfriend swim, and if she doesn't swim very well, then you can go in and help her."

"This isn't a good place to dump bodies," offered Boniface, forcing an air of joviality into his voice but watching Ellen's face register growing terror. Turgenev swung around, and Boniface flinched. "I'd prefer it if you don't hit me. But I am serious; look at the river." Turgenev raised his head and looked. "The river's tidal here, and you can see the tide is coming in; so if you dump us, we won't float away."

Turgenev's face registered a strange combination of anger and relief as the other man looked back to the silver BMW, pointing at it with his eyes. "But you have already decided to get rid of that, haven't you?"

The Russian cocked his head, an implied question without losing face by asking.

"By now they're going to have noticed a missing car..." said Boniface, as if to imply it was obvious, "and they'll be out looking. They'll be able to track it."

"Of course," said Turgenev, looking marginally surprised to be agreeing with Boniface.

"If you put it in the river, then that'll focus them on the car—they won't know which direction you went."

Boniface caught a change, as if Turgenev had recognized that he was trying to take control, and he continued less forcefully. "We'll stay here. You go and deal with the car." Turgenev looked to the car, then back to his two prisoners and back to the car. "Come on, we can't go anywhere. Look at her heels. She's not going to do any running in those, is she?"

Turgenev reluctantly started walking backward toward the car, keeping his body facing the two. He pulled the door open, looking puzzled.

Like a ventriloquist, Ellen murmured, "Why do you want him to dump the car?"

"Not a clue," said Boniface, his mouth equally fixed. "We need to slow down whatever happens next. I haven't really been in this sort of situation before."

"Silence!" There was no ambiguity in Turgenev's instruction, but he was now on the move, looking for something. He picked up one of the rocks around the edge of the parking area, walked back to the car, and sat in the driver's seat with the door open, the rock on his lap, and one leg trailing out of the door.

He started the engine and eased the car back from the wooden pickets around the lot; slipped the car into drive; stood up, keeping one foot on the brake with the other on firm ground; and dropped the rock onto the gas. As the engine picked up revs, he jumped back, releasing the brake to let the car leap forward, snapping the wooden barrier like a row of lollipop sticks.

The police BMW bounced over the grass verge between the parking lot and the river, losing momentum on the uneven ground but moving to the bank, which fell away to the river. As the front wheels passed the precipice, the car fell onto its belly, being pushed by the rear wheels, which increasingly lost their grip, starting to spin in the soft grass as the car slowed to a stop.

Progressively the wheels dug deeper, inching the car forward until eventually the silver vehicle started to tilt on the fulcrum of the edge of the bank. The nose dropped as the rear lifted, raising the wheels from the mud, which then splattered behind as the engine raced.

The car continued to overbalance and started to slide. As the front wheels reached the river, the underbelly slid and the rear drive wheels, spinning rapidly, made contact with the fulcrum, propelling the front of the car into the river and covering the engine and the driver's door. As the River Thames consumed the machinery, the engine started to splutter, the sound muffled by the water. Slowly, starved of oxygen and fed water, the engine moved from spluttering to occasional coughs and then, having taken its last gasp, fell into silence, its rear wheels shuddering to a halt.

Turgenev was back behind Ellen and Boniface, who were transfixed by the drowning car. "What sort of police force doesn't carry guns? It would be much easier and, to be honest, less painful in the long term for both of you, if I had a gun."

"We don't have a police force," corrected Boniface. "We have a police service. You are disparaging the Metropolitan Police Service. The Metropolitan Police Service whose car you have just dropped into the River Thames."

Turgenev lazily slapped him with the back of his hand. "Shut. Up."

Boniface instinctively moved to soothe the pain but found himself pulling on his handcuffs. Slowly he turned his head to face Turgenev. He couldn't make eye contact with the other man, but still he proceeded. "Look... We need to talk..."

Turgenev swung and Boniface flinched, relaxing when the blow didn't land. "We get it. For whatever reason you're not having a good day at the office." Some of the anger seemed to fall from Turgenev's scowl. "We don't care. Really. That's not something that worries us. It's just that we've found something that's kind of interesting, and we were working on it at the university, and we thought—thought—that what we found might be interesting to you."

Turgenev shook his head, menacingly revealing his teeth.

"I know this seems desperate. And believe me it is. Listen for a moment, please." Boniface tried to keep the tension he felt in his throat from reaching his voice, but only partially succeeded. "This whole thing started because of Mister Kuznetsov. Your boss…" Given that Veronica had told him that the Russian didn't seem to be responding to calls from Kuznetsov, Boniface wasn't sure whether to go with boss or former boss, but stuck with the positive.

Turgenev remained impassive.

"What we have found out in the last few hours will be important to your boss. If you can give him this information, then you'll be his hero." Boniface looked closely at Turgenev, noticing an involuntary flinch of excitement he had been hoping to elicit. "If we're dead, then that information dies with us."

He stopped and watched Turgenev, who seemed to be ready to listen but not willing to talk. "All I'm suggesting is that you listen to what we've got to say. Nothing more. Then decide."

"So talk," said Turgenev.

"Not here. How long until the police turn up? Five minutes? Perhaps ten? We need to be somewhere else. Anywhere else." He looked around. "Where are we, anyway?"

"Ham House," said Ellen.

"That's your neck of the woods, isn't it? Don't you live up the road? Can't we go round and have a cup of tea to talk things over?"

"Sure. It's about a mile or so back that way." She tossed her head behind her. "Why don't we all go? I'm sure we could have a very interesting conversation with the police who are bound to still be hanging around."

"Okay. Point taken," said Boniface. "I suggest we go down-river."

"Why?" Turgenev suddenly sounded cautious.

"Because that's where we've come from," said Boniface, pointing with his nose.

Turgenev jutted his chin, apparently accepting the simple logic. "To make sure we're clear, Mister Boniface, we walk in silence. If you feel the need to open your mouth for any reason—any reason—then you will find your mouth open in the river, with my foot on your throat. Clear?"

Boniface nodded, the last of the color in his face draining as Turgenev yanked him to his feet.

fifty-one

The path running parallel to the river was well worn, the embedded stones polished smooth by years of passing feet. To each side was a soft grass verge, onto which Boniface had fallen twice and Ellen once. At no point had Turgenev shown any sympathy, only frustration at the slow progress and apparent dumb insolence.

After about ten minutes of stumbling, Turgenev stopped the route march.

"Kneel."

Ellen and Boniface both complied, the dampness soaking into their knees as they sunk into the moist ground. "Decide now. Which one of you wants to be drowned first?" The anger in his voice was apparent, but the tone softened, becoming more sinister. "I like water. It's very cleansing. It removes so many forensic details. And we're far enough downstream that you won't float up to the car before the tide turns."

"But you haven't heard what we've got to say," said Boniface. "There was no point in letting us stay alive back there," he threw his head in the direction of the drowned car, "only to bring us here to kill us after we've scraped our knees a few times." Turgenev remained impassive. "But if you need to make a decision, then she goes first."

Ellen shook herself loose from her hypnotic trance. "What? You..."

Boniface laughed. "Kill her, and you lose everything. She is the most important person in your world at the moment."

"So I kill you?" asked Turgenev, his voice flat.

Boniface shook his head, softly tutting. "No. That would be an even worse strategy."

"So I kill Monty? Is that the answer?"

Ellen screamed, "No! Leave Montbretia alone. She's got nothing to do with this. She knows nothing. Leave her alone, and I'll give you whatever you want."

Turgenev stared at her, a big grin spreading across his face, as he reached into his pocket and pulled out a phone. "I believe this is yours."

"My..."

He turned to Boniface. "Your idea, I presume, the phone on the train. She's clever, but I'm guessing you're the cunning one."

"If I was that cunning, I wouldn't be in handcuffs, would I?"

"Enough." The Russian's tone was icy.

"One ques..."

Turgenev glared. "I ask the questions. You answer. That is the only time I need to hear from either of you."

Boniface blurted. "Why does Vanya think you're missing?"

"What?" All emotion had dropped from the Russian's voice.

Boniface talked hesitantly. "Vanya doesn't know where you are—you haven't been returning his calls. It's alright; I told him you were with me and the professor, so you don't need to worry about calling." Boniface relaxed, watching Turgenev's face, partially hidden by the darkness but clear enough to see that the certainty and the absolute resolve, so ever-present, had temporarily deserted him. "But you probably need to worry about keeping us alive, since he thinks that's what you've been doing."

"See, I said you were cunning. I didn't realize that you're a cunning liar."

"No lie." Boniface was almost casual. "I've told my friend Vanya where you've been tonight. I told him you came to Thames Ditton Island, then to Hampton Court, and then to Surbiton. You're not going to deny this, are you?" Boniface saw Turgenev stiffen. "So why did you send that other guy to shoot our friend here, Professor Armstrong?"

Boniface watched the twitches on Turgenev's face, a slight tightening around the eyes and mouth, a wrinkling on the bridge of his nose, perhaps the slightest frown, darting eyes that were just visible in the darkness, each showing as a small flash of light.

"So it was Professor Armstrong that you were after?"

"Why?" Boniface could hear the confused desperation in Ellen's voice, and watched as she asked herself questions, trying to understand the parameters of the enormity of being a murder target, while unprepared to react to such a situation, having spent a life spent in academia.

"It's okay," he whispered to her. He raised his eyebrows and smirked at Turgenev. "I'll explain." Softly he bit his lower lip, a mischievous smile slowing starting to break out. "Were you there when she annoyed Vanya? Did you see him watch that interview and decide to show him how you could sort his problems? A bit of proactivity in the workplace...but it didn't quite work out like you had hoped, did it?"

There was an unblinking refusal by the Russian to acknowledge. Ellen looked confused and muttered, "I've never met this Vanya. How could I have annoyed him?"

Boniface ignored the professor. "So that's it. You tried to play the big boy, but you don't know who got shot, do you?" He watched as Turgenev tried to keep an impassive face. "Boy, are you in the shit."

Boniface hung his head, trying to keep the glee out of his voice as he continued. "So the shooting outside Professor Armstrong's house. The shooter was your guy. Then you figured the wrong person had been shot, and you tracked her to Thames Ditton Island. I'm presuming it was the same guy who then took the shot through the window?"

He looked back at Turgenev and read the confirmation in his face. "And for the second time, you don't know who was shot. Do you?" He smirked. "Honesty is the best policy. Insanity is the best defense. But for you...I'd leg it. Do a runner, and make sure Mister Kuznetsov can never, ever, track you down."

Boniface looked at Turgenev; he wasn't sure whether he could see rage, confusion, or both, but he took a moment or two to collect his thoughts before he continued. "Your man shot Professor Trudgett. You know, the respected historian and Kuznetsov's golden boy who was going to prove the monarchy are usurping frauds, thereby triggering a nationwide demand for a referendum about replacing the monarchy with a president."

Boniface calibrated the tightening of the muscles in the other man's face. "So aren't you glad we're here to show you a way out of this mess you've created for yourself?"

Turgenev stiffened. "You're talking bollocks, Boniface. Do you think I care about you? I would shoot you here if I had a gun, but I don't so I'll break your neck." He placed one hand on each of Boniface's ears. "All I have to do is twist."

Boniface felt the heat in the hands burning against his ears, heavy exhaled breaths from the other man's nose on the top of his head.

The Russian twisted—his movement a blur of speed—but released the pressure enough so that his hands slipped with rough skin burning against Boniface's cheek and ripped at his ear.

Boniface reflexively sucked in air, and Turgenev returned his hands to their menacing position. "I'll tell Kuznetsov that I found you were working with the professor here. Sherborne's very own historian." He sneered at Ellen. "When I tell him that I have found and fixed his problem before he even knew about it, I'll be his hero."

Boniface felt his heart thumping and his breathing become shallower. He concentrated, trying to regain some calm. Turgenev remained impassive, his hands still in position to twist. "You misunderstand; Vanya already knows he's got a problem with you." He felt the grip on his head tighten. "Maybe you don't get it, which isn't that surprising since you seem much keener on snapping my neck than on listening to a route out."

Turgenev relaxed his grip slightly. "I don't listen because you talk too much. Your talking is giving me a headache."

"I'll be quick," said Boniface. "But could you let go of my head? What you're doing really isn't comfortable."

Turgenev stood up and walked in front of Boniface, facing him, and gave a small shrug, holding out his hands, his wrists exposed while he craned his head forward.

"Be quick and say less. Don't talk faster so that you can say more."

Boniface looked up at Turgenev's scowl and proceeded. "Trudgett was on to something and was about to tell Professor Armstrong when your man splattered his brains over her house. This was inconvenient, so the two of us…" he tilted his head toward Ellen, "the two of us went looking for details. Long story short, there was a loose end, and that loose end seems to be very significant. We were working on it at the university when the police came in…and then you…found us."

"So tell me about this loose end."

"Well, it's loose. We haven't been able to…" Boniface flinched, searching for the word, "tie it up yet."

Turgenev grabbed Boniface's hair, pulling him toward the river. Boniface fell forward, twisting and landing on his arm, which dug into the mud. "No, listen. This is the important point. This is how you get out of here alive."

He hadn't wanted to sound desperate, but he had failed. Turgenev released his hair, letting his head fall to the ground, then rested his boot on Boniface's windpipe. "Get. To. The. Point."

Boniface tried to speak, but found the weight on his throat too intense to create more than a faint hiss. He strained: "If you could release a bit of pressure, please." Turgenev relented, removing his boot, stamping it down in front of Boniface's nose.

"I know I'm not in much of a position to argue, but could we stop the histrionics?"

Turgenev frowned, then his boot connected with Boniface's stomach. "Next time, something will rupture."

"And if you kill either of us, you die." Boniface twisted in pain, gasping for breath. "But if we stay alive…" He waited for Turgenev's attention. "If we stay alive, well, that could be to your advantage. Wouldn't you like some information that Mister Kuznetsov would pay money for?" Turgenev focused on Boniface, his eyes boring into his skull. "Think what you could do. Trade it for cash. Trade it for your life. Trade it for both."

"A desperate gamble on your part, Mister Boniface." The Russian looked ready to strike again.

"Ask yourself one thing." Boniface heard the hint of confidence in his voice. "If Professor Armstrong and I weren't on to something, then why didn't we go to the police? Even a prison cell would be preferable to—and safer than—this."

"So what is this information?"

"If we knew that, do you think I'd be lying here? Don't you think I would've told you that before you tried to twist my head of?"

Turgenev went to kick him again but stopped before making contact, instead turning to watch the river. Boniface released the tension in his neck and laid his head on the wet grass, following Turgenev's movements with his eyes.

The Russian turned back to stare at Boniface. "So you're saying I shouldn't kill you because there's something important."

"Right," said Boniface.

"But you don't know what it is, and the person that did..." the Russian let his dull eyes fix on Boniface, "is dead." His eyes remained on the man lying in front of him. "This is not a compelling proposition, Mister Boniface. I don't see what I lose by your death."

"Again, you're contemplating decisions based on incomplete information." The Russian's face twitched, as it did with each implicit criticism by Boniface. "I don't know what there is—I'm not a historian—but I know there are documents. And I know what these documents show."

"You mean the documents photographed on this phone?" He pulled out Ellen's phone again and tapped the screen. *"Hi Monty, Nigel really excited. Perhaps he's found a pot of gold.* That's what you wrote and then you photographed some pieces of paper." He jabbed his head toward Ellen, who was still silently kneeling a few feet behind Boniface and starting to shiver.

"The documents in those photographs were written five hours ago," said Boniface. "I'm talking about documents created five hundred years ago."

The Russian went quiet. He looked down at the phone and then at Ellen. "So everything on this phone is worthless?"

"Not to me." Ellen's voice was pleading.

"Oops." The Russian lazily flicked his wrist. The phone spun in an arc, hitting the surface of the river about five feet from the bank before it disappeared. "Oh, I'm sorry about that. How clumsy of me." He turned to Boniface. "My patience is wearing thin. You're about to go and make a call on that phone if you don't convince me."

Boniface turned his head back to face Turgenev, rolling his nose through the mud. "There are two threads here—could you hold off with your boot until I've finished?"

The Russian said nothing as Boniface continued. "You saw the dead body on Thames Ditton Island—the guy with the long hair..."

Turgenev's face remained blank, his eyes holding Boniface motionless with their stare.

"He found the documents. He knew where there were more." Boniface watched the unchanging emotion of the other man. "He was talking to us about what he had found when a bullet... Well, you saw the mess."

"Shhhhit." Turgenev spat under his breath, turning away from his two captives.

"So, you understand, the two people who knew the most are now dead." Boniface kept his face blank. "But before he died, Professor Trudgett photographed some of the documents our long-haired friend found and uploaded them to an online storage service."

Something changed on the Russian's face.

"We've tried to access this storage thing but we can't, so we've got a hacker on the job, and we're waiting for him to call back. When he does, we need to be in front of a computer to access the documents."

"How is this hacker going to contact you?"

"He'll phone," offered Boniface.

"And your phone is where?"

"My jacket pocket." Boniface gestured downward with his head toward an internal jacket pocket. The Russian slipped his hand under the other man's jacket, then stepped back, examining his new acquisition.

"And this leads us to the second aspect." Boniface inhaled deeply. "In all our digging tonight, one name kept coming up, and we need to ask that person some questions about his connection."

"The name?"

Boniface tried to guess the likely reaction as he exhaled slowly. Then he braced himself. "Sherborne."

"Now you're fucking with me."

Boniface shut his eyes, bracing against the next kick. When it didn't come, he opened one eye and looked up to see Turgenev smirking at him. "I admire what you're trying to do, but do you think it's not obvious to me that you have been working for Sherborne all along? With that detail, I can explain everything."

"It would appear than you may again be laboring under a false apprehension, and in the interests of me not talking too much, can we just say there is some history, or if you would prefer, unrestrained animosity, between us. So when I say we need to see Sherborne, I'm not kidding." He grinned enthusiastically. "But if you don't like what Sherborne has got to say, then I'm quite happy if you want to kill him. His computer will still work even if he's dead."

"And how do we get to Sherborne?" Turgenev's voice was flat.

Boniface threw his head backward toward Ellen. "He's her publisher; she's been to his house." Turgenev grinned; Boniface corrected him. "She has been to receptions at his house. She couldn't tell you how his bedroom ceiling has been decorated."

Turgenev stopped sneering and looked at Ellen. "And where is this house?"

"About a mile in that direction." Ellen pointed downriver with her head.

"We're going to need a car," muttered Turgenev. "Can you get a car?" He looked back and forth between Boniface and Ellen, both shaking their heads, before grabbing Boniface's handcuffs and yanking him to his feet. He looked to Ellen. "Where's the nearest road?"

fifty-two

Walking on the path had been unpleasant in kitten heels and a fitted skirt, but it was manageable. Leaving the path had taken the experience to a new level of disagreeability.

Rather than follow the established track, Turgenev had taken them diagonally across the meadow at the bottom of Richmond Hill. Ellen lost count of how many times she had slipped or fallen, but now she had ripped her skirt as well as having mud everywhere. Everywhere. And it didn't taste good. Her shoe had become stuck in the mud, twice, and now her feet were encased with gritty mud, which was then wrapped tightly in her shoe. She had cut her knee and grazed her face, and worst of all, she had cow shit in her hair.

Did she say worst of all? No, worst of all—apart from being with a homicidal maniac and a man who seemed to get overly talkative under stress, which led to him trying to cut any sort of deal to stay alive—apart from that, the worst thing was the cow shit.

As they reached the far side of the meadow, there was a steep tree-lined slope, mostly mud, although a few ground plants tightly held onto the embankment between the tree roots, which lay in wait to trip the unwary.

"You." Turgenev directed Boniface to come closer to where he was standing. Boniface took the two steps toward him as Turgenev rummaged in his pockets. "Turn around." Boniface complied. The Russian grabbed the Englishman's handcuffs, lifting them and causing Boniface to bend forward. He tried the small key, which Ellen guessed he had removed from the dead policeman less than an hour earlier, and unlocked the cuffs.

Before Boniface could react, Turgenev jerked him backward, putting his back against a tree, and relocked the cuffs on the other wrist. He turned to Ellen. "It's up to you now. By your actions, you decide whether he lives or dies. And by the way, if he does die, he'll die here. He won't have a calm and relaxing death in the river. It will be slow and it will hurt. And once he's dead, then I'll have a lot a free time to go and find Monty—or what is it you called her, Montbretia?"

Ellen froze, staring straight at Turgenev, defiant but resigned, and with a mud streak across her face, covering a graze.

"Are you paying attention? This is quite simple. You do what I say, or he dies and then Montbretia dies." Ellen bobbed her head once. "Come here. Turn around." Turgenev removed Ellen's handcuffs, slipping them in his pocket. "Up that slope."

Ellen shot him a look of disbelief and was met with an unyielding stare.

"Now."

He shoved her, and she fell forward, beginning the slow ascent up the sharp slope, keeping at least three limbs in contact at all times and using her heels as climbing spikes. She reached the plateau with two shoes and only one kitten heel, puffing through the last few steps, slowly righting herself to find Turgenev waiting.

"We need a car, and you're going to get it." From the plateau, the ground leveled toward a small stone wall. On the other side a car sped past.

"But I don't have a car, and we left the last one at the university when you...when we came with you."

Turgenev looked at her with a mixture of disappointment and frustration. "The road." He pointed to the road the car had passed along. "Stop a car. Make the driver get out and bring them over here."

Ellen stared back.

"And make it convincing. You know what happens to your boyfriend and Montbretia if you mess about."

Ellen looked for any hint of humanity. Any softer side she could appeal to. Any rational logic she could deploy. She found none, just a single finger pointing toward the road.

Across the wall, on the other side there were some bushes and then the road. A few awkward steps—trying and failing to ignore the uneven heels and grit inside her shoes—and she reached the wall, where she sat, lifted her feet, and twisted, adding another rip to her skirt and another bruise on her leg. She then added a further rip as she pushed her way through the bushes to the side of the road.

A small, rusty, Korean-manufactured car headed away from Richmond. She watched it pass and then moved to the side of the road. A pair of headlights came up the hill and turned onto the road heading toward Richmond. Ellen took two steps forward and stood in the middle of the road. There was no need to fake the tears or the rest of her casualty look: The torn clothing, mud spattered everywhere, cuts, grazes, and bruises were authentic.

The headlights hit her squarely as she waved her arms and started to shout, "Stop! Stop! Please stop!"

The driver pulled up and jumped out of the dark blue sedan, leaving the engine running and his door open. A tall, slim man in his early thirties, dressed casually in jeans and a sweater, with wire-rimmed glasses. "What's up?"

"Please, you must help," said Ellen, tears running down her face and mud holding her hair in place. She grabbed his sleeve, bunching the wool in her hand, and pulled him toward the wall. As they passed through the bushes at the side of the road, there was a bright smacking sound—flesh on flesh, and Ellen felt the wool pulled out of her hand as the man fell to the ground.

"Congratulations," said Turgenev stepping out of the shadow. "This way." He pointed back to the car.

Reaching the vehicle, he opened the passenger door. "Please have a seat." Ellen got in and sat compliantly. "Your hands." Ellen looked confused and delicately offered her hands. Turgenev grabbed both arms, clamping them together with one hand, returning the handcuffs to her wrists with the connecting chain hooked over the passenger grab-handle.

And then Turgenev was gone. She saw him briefly look at the body of the man who owned the car, and then she looked away, focusing on the road.

She became aware that Turgenev had returned when the trunk opened: Someone was being stuffed into it. Whoever it was, they were being very compliant but seemed to be trying to engage the killer in conversation.

Turgenev shut the trunk before coming to sit in the driver's seat, closing the door behind him. He pulled out his phone and called up a map. "Show me. Where is Sherborne's house?"

Ellen looked to her hands, shackled around the grab rail, and back to Turgenev. "Could you... The cuffs are really digging into my wrists."

"No. Tell me. We are here." He pointed a dirty finger at the screen. "Where next?"

"To the town center. When you reach the junction with the bridge on the left, going over the river..." Turgenev scrolled the map with his finger, "then you keep going straight. The road goes downhill from there. At the bottom of the hill...look you can see...the road turns right, there's a big shop...well, at that point you want to take the left turn so you sort of go straight. Now pull the map a bit further."

Turgenev complied.

"That road leads onto Richmond Green. Halfway down on the left-hand side, there's a road that turns off."

Turgenev moved the map and zoomed in.

"That road is called The Wardrobe." Turgenev grunted as Ellen gave directions, each location appearing on his map. "As you follow The Wardrobe, you go under a gatehouse—it's a big brick arch. When you come out, Sherborne's house is in front of you."

"Here?" Turgenev pointed a dirty finger that seemed to cover most of Richmond.

"Move your finger back so I can see where you're pointing," said Ellen. Turgenev obeyed. "Yes. That's it."

"But that's impossible to approach without being seen."

"We agreed to take you there. You can't hold us responsible for the architecture. Anyway, I'm sure Boniface can help us get in. Where is he?" Turgenev pointed toward the back of the car with his thumb as he started to rev the engine.

fifty–three

"Here."

Turgenev took the left turn and followed the small side road lined with boutiques, restaurants, and bookstores, all closed. "This leads to the Green?" Professor Armstrong pointed with her eyes as Turgenev pulled to the side, looking at the map on his phone.

He grunted, took another look at the map, and slipped his phone back into his pocket. He edged the car forward, rolling it out of the feeder road at the bottom corner of Richmond Green. On reaching the perimeter road, he turned left. "Not here," said Professor Armstrong. "You turn farther down."

Turgenev checked the road sign: Friars Lane. He followed it, slowly, and as the map had told him, before the road turned to the left there was a public parking lot. He relaxed: lots of shadows.

He backed the car into the darkest corner of the empty lot and then jumped out, opened the professor's door, and leaned in to remove her cuffs. "Get out." As she stood, he bear-hugged her, returning the cuffs with her hands locked behind her back. "This way." He pushed her door shut and led her to the back of the car, flipping the trunk.

"Can I get out now?" Boniface was motionless apart from his head.

"Company for you." He turned to the professor. "Sit." He patted the sill of the trunk. She complied, and he put one hand behind her head while sweeping her feet with his other arm. There was a gentle rip of her skirt as he slid her into the trunk facing Boniface, who grunted as Turgenev pushed the professor fully into the trunk before slamming the lid and returning to the driver's seat.

Retracing his route along Friars Lane, he drove back and rejoined the perimeter road around the Green, slowing as he passed The Wardrobe. As Professor Armstrong had said, there was a brick gateway set back from the road, and although it was dark, he could make out that there were buildings on the other side. There was a slight movement—it might have been a figure coming from the other end of The Wardrobe; he couldn't be sure.

He continued following the perimeter road as it turned right at the corner of the Green, and then parked. As he turned to look back at the entrance to The Wardrobe, he saw a figure walking out from under the gate, wearing an incongruous mixture of a tweed jacket with a blue baseball cap.

The Russian kept the figure in view as it reached the perimeter road and turned left, following the road—behind his stolen car with the two passengers in the trunk—and taking the other fork in the road. According to the map on his phone, the road the man with the tweed jacket and blue baseball cap was following led to the river.

He sat and waited, looking at the road behind him in his mirrors. After about fifteen minutes another figure came out from The Wardrobe. This new figure had a similar height and build to the person who had passed earlier and seemed to have the same gait, walking as if he didn't want his feet to touch the ground. But unlike the previous individual, this one had a blue jacket and a flat cap.

Was this a setup, a fluke, security, or nosiness?

Turgenev waited patiently, focusing on the gate to The Wardrobe.

Nearly ten minutes later, a figure appeared, but this one hadn't come out of The Wardrobe; he seemed to have come from farther back, perhaps from Friars Lane. Turgenev watched, focusing on the details: the same blue jacket and flat cap, same height, same build, same gait, same apparent need to ensure his steps were silent.

Turgenev smiled. Same man. And not a soldier. Sure, he was cautious—to a certain extent—but he wasn't observant. If he had been, he would have noticed the parked car with Turgenev sitting in it, and he would have avoided it or investigated.

That left two options: bad security or press. Security wouldn't bother changing their clothes, so this man had to be press.

He waited for the figure to pass behind his car, take the road leading to the river, and disappear. Once the man was out of sight, Turgenev silently slipped out of the car, keeping low, and slunk, cat-like, following the probable journalist.

He turned into the narrow lane leading to the river and followed the road as it then bent to the left, straightening to point at the Thames. The properties on this side road were different. Where there had been large, grand Georgian townhouses set back from the road around the Green, the houses on this side of the road were more modern—or rather, less old—and were much closer to the road.

The first few were semidetached brick-built houses set over three floors. These gave way to two-story, white stucco-fronted terraces, and then to smaller cottages. Every step down the road was a step cheaper and a step less impressive. There were a few older houses on the left, but these ended shortly, being replaced with a high brick-built wall.

The road was wide enough to fit two cars. On the left was a row of parked cars, with the right side being left free for driving. As Turgenev came out of the bend, he heard a car door close quietly and he stopped, looking for any sign of movement.

The parked cars on the left all seemed to be empty. Some way down the road he thought he could see a light inside a car, or perhaps his eyes were playing tricks.

He ducked behind the row of parked vehicles and slowly moved forward, using the cars as cover while he worked his way up to the end car. There was a break and the next car was parked in shadow, but within that car he could see an outline of a person and a faint glow as if someone was illuminated by a phone. He looked around; there was no other cover and only one choice.

If he was right that this was a journalist, then he would be safe. If he was wrong or plain unlucky, then his next move could be fatal. He dropped to the ground and dragged himself along the asphalt under the last car, resting when he had a worm's-eye view of the probable journalist's car.

The glow was extinguished and the shape started to move, causing the car to jiggle slightly. A man got out, now wearing a khaki trench coat and a fedora. The new wardrobe additions didn't go well with his frayed blue jeans and sneakers.

Turgenev watched as the sneakers came toward him—each step silently placed—before turning to take a path to the right. The silent footsteps moved away; he tried to listen but couldn't hear them over the sound of his own heartbeat.

He pulled himself along the asphalt; rolled into the shadow at the side of the road; stood, wiping off the grit; and then cautiously walked to inspect the path where the journalist had just disappeared.

On the left-hand side of the path was a high wall. To the right were some houses, newer than those on the street where he had been lying. And in the middle, walking his quiet walk, the journalist. Turgenev followed, remaining silent and keeping in the shadows.

The Russian noted the houses on the right, which had given way to a set of smaller, more compact properties, set farther back from the path. He looked back to the journalist, who had disappeared.

Turgenev increased his pace, ducking slightly to lower his height. The path ended sooner than he was expecting, and he found himself in an area with buildings on all sides and a small tear-shaped green area enclosed by a low fence.

He looked at the biggest house and guessed it must be Sherborne's. To the left was the arched gate with a khaki trench coat disappearing underneath. He went to follow, then hesitated, turning to look at the largest building in the enclosure and the row of buildings on the far side, which looked old—perhaps as old as Hampton Court, but he couldn't be sure.

The large building stood in stark contrast to the old buildings. It was taller and a different style. Best of all, it had sash windows.

Turgenev returned swiftly along the path, back to the journalist's car, a faceless Ford with an indistinct color in the darkness and no identifying features. You could forget about it while you stared at it. The perfect car for a journalist.

He cast a swift glance at the terraced cottages on the other side of the road. All were painted a uniform white; the only distinguishing differences were in the small pieces of land between each house and the road. All were paved, but some had made more of an effort to create a courtyard garden.

Two doors up he saw what he was looking for: shrubs. Two shrubs opening into a broad-leafed canopy at a height of about four feet. Turgenev quickly hid and waited; if the journalist stuck to his routine, he would be returning to his car at any moment.

He didn't hear him; the footsteps were still silent, but he did see the flickering change of light as the journalist moved. Turgenev fixed on him like a bird of prey hovering, waiting for the journalist to enter the shadow by his car. As he saw him go for his keys, Turgenev moved, taking advantage of the distraction.

The Russian reached the journalist before the journalist noticed his approach. Placing one hand over the journalist's mouth, he grabbed the back of his neck with the other and twisted. He became aware of the sound of the journalist's neck reacting to the violence as he broke the fall of the lifeless body, at the same time looking around for signs that the noise had been heard by one of the residents of the street.

He took the car keys out of the journalist's dead hand and checked his pockets, pulling out a phone, a notepad, and some cash.

The body was heavier than he expected, but not so heavy as to slow Turgenev in stowing it under the canopy of the shrubs where he had waited a few moments earlier.

Cautiously, he laid the body on the ground, stood, and turned toward the river.

fifty-four

The trunk lid flipped open, and Boniface could see Turgenev's outline silhouetted against a streetlight.

"Okay, Mister Talkative. It's time for you to do your job. I don't care if you tell me he's not your friend—you're going to get us in to see Sherborne."

Turgenev stepped back, keeping his stare fixed on Boniface; Boniface remained silent, feeling Ellen's breath against his face, her breathing becoming shallow and faster.

"In case you don't understand, let me be clear..." Turgenev's eyes met his and locked. "You will get inside the house. At each step, you will give me"—he held up a phone that Boniface hadn't seen before—"a running commentary. If you fail, she dies. If I think you have failed, she dies. If you say anything unhelpful, she dies. If there is any period of silence, she dies. Clear?"

Boniface nodded.

"And please remember, not only is her life now in your hands, but also the manner of her death. If you make me angry, it will be a very unpleasant, lingering death, and you never know what could happen before she finally expires." He stared straight into Boniface's eyes, slowly rubbing his crotch. "And if she dies, then I'll go and find Montbretia."

Neither man moved.

"So are we clear?" Boniface nodded. "Do you understand?" Boniface nodded. "Is there any room for doubt? Any?"

"No, we're clear. I understand." Boniface's voice was soft, but he still couldn't hide the cracks. He looked at Ellen, trying to reach her through the fear in her eyes, and whispered, "It's gonna be okay. Really. It's gonna be okay." He turned to Turgenev. "What do I do when I'm in?"

"Keep talking. Make sure everyone focuses on you and Sherborne, and I'll send you a signal when I'm ready."

Turgenev reached into the trunk, rolled Boniface toward Ellen, and removed his handcuffs. Slowly and cautiously, Boniface began to lift himself out of the trunk, slipping and taking a few steps to regain his balance as he reached the road. As he stood up, he saw that the trunk had been closed behind him. "Come on. Make her comfortable."

"No."

"It will help me...focus." Boniface kept his gaze on Turgenev. "I understand my mission, but you need me to succeed. You don't want me to be distracted. And if you just say yes to this one thing, then I'll shut up and we can start."

Turgenev exhaled, laboring the breath, and flipped the trunk open. Boniface watched as the Russian rummaged inside the trunk and found an old tartan blanket, which he placed under Ellen's head. His raised eyebrows asked the question as he indicated the academic in the trunk. Boniface pulled his mouth tight, and Turgenev shut the trunk.

"Here's your new phone," said Turgenev, reaching into his pocket and pulling out the phone he had just shown to Boniface.

"That's not mine."

"It is for now. Don't worry; I'm still keeping your phone safe."

"You remember that we're expecting a call?"

"And you will remember that you're on your best behavior."

Turgenev reached into his jacket pocket and pulled out a small Bluetooth earpiece before dialing a number on the phone. He touched the earpiece, then slipped the phone into the breast pocket of Boniface's jacket. "Now say something."

"Testing, testing. One two," said Boniface flatly.

"Now walk and talk, and remember that I'm listening and you know what happens if you fail."

Boniface walked 50 yards around the edge of the Green, then crossed to follow The Wardrobe, soon passing under the arched gateway. "Right, I've just come under the arch, and I'm now in the...well, I guess you might call it the courtyard, there's sort of a bit of grass in the middle with a road around the outside."

He looked around, then recommenced, willing his voice loud enough that Turgenev could hear but not loud enough to draw attention. "Er... Well...I guess you know what's here, but given that silence on my part is bad, let me give you a commentary. I've come through the arch, but I've told you that already. In front of me is a teardrop-shaped piece of grass. On the left, some very old buildings; they look like they were built around the same time as Hampton Court, but I'd like to see them in daylight. To the right, there are some garages. I guess they're attached to the houses out there. There are also a few cottage-like houses on the right, facing onto the teardrop of grass."

Boniface took three steps. "I'm starting to move now; I hope you can still hear me. So, on the right, beyond the cottages, we've got a gap. I guess there's a path that leads out of here."

He continued walking. "In front of me, there's the house. Three floors...no two, I think what looks like the top floor might be the loft—there's only a window in the center block. More modern than the buildings on the left, but I'm still guessing it dates from around the 1700s. It's what I think is called English Baroque or maybe Queen Anne style. I'm sorry; I never was an architecture student. The roof slopes at a gentle angle, mock columns, rendered exterior in the center, brick wings outside that, sash windows. On the right, there's what looks like a separate stable block, but that could be something to do with the next set of houses. I don't know; it's too dark to see them from here, and I'm not going to have a look."

There was a white car parked with its nose against the gates. Rust was starting to show around each wheel arch, each door lock, and every joined seam—rust that was visible even in the poor light of the courtyard. "I'm at the gates now. There's a car parked up against them. It's old and showing signs of rust. If I were Sherborne, I'd call the police to come and move it, so I presume whoever drives it is inside." He laid his hand on the hood. "The engine feels warm. Not hot, but warm."

He looked up at the gates. "Okay. Gates. Tall, metal, iron I think, two of them. The one on the left is partially blocked by the car, and the one on the right has the knob to open it. Both seem to open inward, so the car shouldn't be a problem. Inside the gate you've got a few cobbles, then the door. Well, I say cobbles, more like stones set in concrete. I'm going to try the gate now." He twisted the knob, which had lost the definition of its decoration through layers of paint over the years, and pushed. The gate swung comparatively freely, making a smooth swishing sound from the hinges as they twisted.

"Gate opening." He gingerly stepped, his eyes scanning. "Gate closing, but I'm leaving it balanced on the lock, so all you have to do is push it open. I'm on the cobbles now." He took four paces before reaching the steps to the door. "Big door. I dunno, seven feet high, three feet wide perhaps. Maybe more. Probably more. Anyway, big, solid letter box, door knocker, no obvious windows in the door, but one over the door, and sash windows, two panes wide and full height, to either side of the door. Several locks visible from the outside. I can't see any sort of CCTV cameras. Nor can I see any other bell or buzzer, but it's pretty dark around here, and I can't see anything through the windows; it's dark in there." He grasped the knocker and banged twice. "Let's see what that does. We're going to replace the commentary with some whistling while I wait."

Before he could purse his lips, a light came on inside, and there was the sound of movement. "Right, I've got something. There's movement."

A few more lights came on, and finally the door opened. A tall, solid man in his late twenties answered. Boniface looked him up and down. The dark-blue blazer over a white shirt with a dark single-color tie and charcoal pants suggested his role. The severe haircut reinforced the assumption. "Evening, sir. How can I help you?"

"I didn't realize Mister Sherborne had taken on additional security. Are you alone, or are there more of you prowling the grounds?"

"Sir. Please."

"I'm sorry, I'm a bit shocked. I came round to see dear old Dickie and wasn't expecting to see a large chap like you. What are you six-three?"

"Sir." The guard was becoming insistent.

"Oh, I'm sorry," said Boniface, giving his best disarming smile. He offered his hand. "I'm Alexander Boniface, I need to see Richard as a matter of urgency. He's expecting me, and if he isn't, he should be. There may have been a few crossed wires in the communications tonight."

The guard remained impassive. Boniface took a step forward and was stopped by a large raised hand.

"Ask Dickie. He's expecting me."

"One moment, sir." The immovable object seemed unwilling to yield and pulled a radio from his outer jacket pocket, flexing awkwardly as he reached across while he kept his other hand holding Boniface in his place. "I've got a Mister Bon... I'm sorry, sir, your name?"

"Boniface. Alexander Boniface."

"Mister Boniface. Seems to think he's expected. Could you check?" There was static and a mumbled voice.

Boniface looked inside the jacket, under the arms as the poorly fitting garment twisted with the guard flexing. "So how long has Dickie had armed guards looking after him?" Boniface tried to sound casual.

The guard held his pose, seemingly listening to the static.

"It's a nice night to be out, but it's getting a bit chilly. Any chance I could step inside while I'm waiting?" The hand did not waver. "How many of you guys are there here? Is Dickie looking after you properly? Has Ada made you a cup of tea yet? If you were unannounced, then she probably died of embarrassment and started baking immediately."

The verbal war of attrition launched on the guard was broken by a voice at the other end of the radio. Boniface couldn't make out what it said. "Apparently you're not expected, sir."

"I think I am." Boniface was calm. "He had a telephone conversation with one of my associates earlier this evening. He may not have known I was involved, but he is expecting a visit. Check."

The guard's stare, pure cynicism, didn't waver.

Boniface met his gaze, locked on, and waited, calculating how long he could remain silent without Ellen being harmed.

The guard pulled up his radio. "Sorry, Harry. Could you check? The gentleman says an associate of his spoke to Mister Sherborne earlier this evening and that a visit is expected."

There was a static-filled pause followed by some more mumbling.

fifty–five

"Hey! This is an impressive entrance hall. I wasn't expecting it to be so grand. What is it...twenty feet wide and maybe thirty feet deep? Is that about it? And wow...that staircase going up the middle. That's impressive. It must be five feet wide, and the ceiling is, er, ten, maybe eleven feet. And that desk over there on the right..." Boniface leaned his head in the direction of a small, old but not antique, dark wood desk, its top empty apart from a small monitor screen and an out-of-place cheap telephone, its cord twisting over the floor, with a worn leather chair behind. "I didn't see the CCTV when I was outside—where are your cameras pointed?"

"Please sit down, sir," said the guard with an over-articulated accent, indicating the sofa in front of an empty fireplace. "Mister Sherborne will be with you in a moment."

"What? Sit on this dark-green leather scroll-armed Chesterfield-type sofa on the left, with all the greenery behind it?" said Boniface softly but swiftly. "Beside the fireplace, opposite this club chair. Do you ever light this fire? It must get quite cold, what with this marble floor."

Boniface sat as the guard turned, walking toward the desk. "As I said, Mister Sherborne will be with you in a moment."

The guard sat and Boniface stood. "Anyway. You haven't told me. How long have you been working for Dickie?" The guard's face was frozen in a look of interminable anguish. "And how many of you are there working tonight? Perhaps I should go and say 'hi' to your friend on the other end of the radio? And where is the indomitable Ada? I'm dying for a cup of tea."

The guard stood, knocking his chair, which rolled backward, hitting the wall. "That won't be necessary, sir. Please." He indicated the sofa. "Please have a seat." His jaw tightening. "Mister Sherborne will be with you very shortly."

Boniface sat on the green sofa.

There was a sound of activity on the next floor up. Slow, heavy, but irregular footsteps made their way to the top of the stairs and started to descend.

Boniface turned to see highly polished brown shoes appear from the ceiling, pausing at every step, with the same foot lowered each time. He watched as slowly and uncomfortably the obese figure of Richard Sherborne appeared: fatter, older, and closer to death than he remembered. In fact, on first look, it appeared that he could be reaching death at any moment.

With Sherborne creating a distraction, Boniface looked around the hall and hurriedly whispered a commentary. "As I said, large hall. Two suits of armor inside the door I came through. There's some other military hardware on the walls—pikes, spikes, and stuff like that. There are also a few muskets and other gun sorts of paraphernalia—Sherborne has always been interested in armaments. A few pictures, mostly maps and what look like treaties. I'm sure they're all part of the Sherborne family history and that Mister Sherborne will be more than happy to give you a guided tour."

As his host puffed his way to the bottom of the stairs, Boniface stood. Pausing for the first time since he had entered Trumpeters' House, he looked down at his own appearance. In the light he could see his suit was crumpled and muddy. He felt his top button undone with his tie loosened, his face streaked with mud mixed with a few cuts, and a glance at his reflection in one suit of armor told him his hair was styled by a subtle combination of mud, car-trunk fluff, and sweat.

"Well, this is a surprise. I was expecting someone else altogether." Sherborne looked Boniface up and down, sneering at his appearance. "I thought I had seen the last of you, Boniface." The two men faced each other, neither offering a hand.

"Come, come, Richard. Why would you have seen the last of me? You weren't that close to death last time we met."

"Ah, Boniface. Always the cutting tongue. Always a bit too quick with the jibes and too slow with the manners."

"Ah, Sherborne. Always the complete ass." Boniface sneered sarcastically. "You look like you need to sit down."

Sherborne pulled out a handkerchief from his top pocket to mop his brow and dry the moisture in the loose folds of skin around his chin as he waddled to the club chair. He turned and dropped, wedging himself into the seat.

Boniface returned to the green sofa. "So this is Trumpeters' House, where many a young lady has been invited to appreciate your horn performance. Or is that why you've got the guards now? To make sure they don't run away? How many guards have you got to keep those poor women from bolting?"

"Boniface, Boniface. You never could behave like a civilized human being. You always had to take it too far."

"I lack civility? Me?" Boniface couldn't keep the incredulity out of his voice. "You do remember why it is I..." He mentally searched for any word except hate. "Why I...have a problem with you? You do remember what you did to me?"

"And you do remember what you did to the rest of us, especially your poor wife?" Sherborne struck Boniface with a look of patrician disappointment.

A quiet fell over the room as the two men stared at each other, apparently content with the deadlock.

Boniface broke the still slowly and tentatively. "I remember. I remember and I regret. I hurt people—most of all I hurt Veronica—and I let people down. Any cliché going, that was me. And that's part of the reason I have to ask my few friends and old contacts to help me find scraps of work."

"You did more than hurt people, Boniface." Sherborne's look of disappointment remained. "You were always good at your job, but you didn't respect yourself for what you did. I'm guessing you're good at whatever it is you do now, but you still don't respect yourself. And if you don't respect your work, then your clients will think you don't respect them. You can't blame me for your situation."

"Can't blame you!" snapped Boniface. "I blame you for taking me from unemployed to unemployable. I know I was a mess, and I can't believe how many people didn't fire me—and I'm sure I kept several jobs only out of kindness to Ronnie—but once I was down, you didn't need to come in and give me such a good kicking."

"You deserved that for the way you treated Veronica."

Boniface hung his head, his eyes misting, his voice soft. "I did." He stared back at Sherborne. "But not from you. Not from you, Richard. All you did was to hurt Veronica by hurting me."

Sherborne winced. "How is darling Vron?"

"All the better for not working for you." Boniface paused, then carried on in a less strident tone. "But you will always look petty to her, and she blames you for the breakup of our marriage..." Boniface wasn't sure if it was true, but looking at Sherborne's reaction, he knew the comment stung.

A quiet fell across the room again. The guard moved in his chair, the creak of old leather breaking the trance as Boniface continued. "Anyway, I'm not here to talk about the failure of my marriage. I've come to Richmond Palace for a reason. This is Richmond Palace, isn't it? Richmond Palace, home for discarded Queens."

"Not quite, but close. Richmond Palace was..."

"History later, Richard. Let's talk about your newspapers." Boniface cut Sherborne's explanation short. "If I asked, I'm sure you would tell me you don't interfere in day-to-day editorial matters with your papers."

"And I don't," said Sherborne definitively, but somehow still managing to sound huffily defensive and confused about where Boniface was taking the conversation.

"But everyone knows you do, and I know that you will personally review any matter relating to the royal family." Boniface ignored the annoyance in Sherborne's face. "Some people, not me of course, but some people—you know those nasty, crude, gutter-inhabiting scumbags of the press—well, some of them might suggest this interest in the royals is due to your alleged friendship with Princess Heidemarie."

Boniface sat back squarely on the sofa so that he could look directly at Sherborne. "Some think that because of your *friendship*, you are keen to support the royals. Me, I'm the skeptical sort. I'm also the sort that likes a good rumor, especially a rumor about royalty and illegitimate children. And you know there's always been that rumor—the rumor that now gets regularly photographed falling out of all the nightclubs in London and occasionally playing polo. That's when he's not being caught by the newspapers trying to sell access to the royal side of his family."

"Oscar," said Sherborne gently. "He has a name, and it is Oscar."

"Oscar." Boniface looked conspiratorially around the room. "Now I wonder; is your motivation misunderstood?"

Sherborne frowned, like a bad actor without a speaking part, exaggerating the confusion he was intending to communicate in the hope of getting noticed by the director. "You're perplexing me, Boniface. We've had our differences—I know—and you've written some beastly things about me in the past..."

"Which were true, Richard."

The fat man grumbled under his breath. "That's a different conversation, Boniface. But what you have never done is behave like those—what did you call them—gutter-inhabiting types. Unlike many of your contemporaries, you never went after Oscar. Even when you were a drunken mess, losing jobs, and had a reason to disagree with some of my actions, you never took out your anger on Oscar." He softened his voice. "You have always been very principled in that way. Very honorable. And I respect that and hope you aren't about to change."

Boniface flushed and nodded his acknowledgement of the thanks before continuing. "And I'm still never going to go after Oscar as a way to attack you, but I do wonder with all this talk about a referendum whether you have a game plan that no one has twigged yet."

Boniface stood and looked down at Sherborne. "Kuznetsov's game is easy. He wants to become president as a power grab. For him it's pure greed—he thinks that if he achieves a referendum, then there will be a clamor for republicanism, and he will be best placed to stand as president. In truth, he wants to be a Tsar to legislate for his own benefit, primarily to take control of the banking system—or at least the regulation of the banking system."

Sherborne looked up.

"But for you, it's different. Theoretically, you've had power and influence for years. Whenever they publish a list of movers and shakers, you're there, Richard."

Sherborne grinned. "I don't move and shake any more. I'm more of a wobbler."

"Okay, so wobblers talking cobblers. But, if you've got the power—and I think it's fair to say that you do have some power by virtue of your publishing interests and not as a result of your royal connections—then there's only one reason that makes any sense for you to continue to support the royals in the way you have."

Sherborne's face kept his patrician concern. "You know there are many reasons to support the monarchy, Boniface."

"You might want everyone to think you're an old duffer, but you're smart, Richard. Really smart. Kuznetsov hates you. I understand that as a basic proposition—it saves the time getting to know you. But he doesn't understand how ruthless you are. I do. I've lost out to your ruthlessness. And there's only one reason you would play this game. You're not playing it for yourself. I mean, look…" Boniface took a step back and looked Sherborne up and down. "You're a coronary waiting to happen if your skeleton doesn't disintegrate under the mass of blubber first."

"You always did say the sweetest things, Boniface."

"Shhh. I haven't even started yet. I haven't told you where I think you're being clever, so pay attention."

Sherborne sighed, his mass sinking back into his chair.

"What I think is instructive, Richard, is the attitude of your paper. Kuznetsov calls for a referendum…and how do you react?" Boniface let the question hang, his voice echoing off the hard surfaces in the hall. "You don't say, 'Rubbish, we don't need one.' No, you say, 'Bring it on.' You're actively encouraging a referendum."

Boniface sat and leaned back in the sofa, relaxing. "Now to be clear, your newspaper has taken a very firm line, supporting the monarchy without question. It is a basic matter of principle that there should be a monarchy as far as the paper is concerned."

Sherborne looked squarely at Boniface. "And if you ask the British people, Boniface, the vast majority will support the monarchy. There's no shame in reflecting public opinion, as my readership is one-hundred percent monarchist."

"You're right, Richard. And by the way, just between us," Boniface dropped his voice, "I do agree about the outcome if there is a referendum. But you're smarter than that. You've finessed the proposition, and there seems only one reason for what you're doing."

fifty-six

Boniface had been mumbling since the moment he had started walking toward Trumpeters' House, and the commentary was becoming a persistent bee buzzing in Turgenev's left ear. Still, at least the commentary made Boniface focus on something, distracting him from the fact that he had been pushed into the wilderness to clear a path through any landmines.

And as far as Turgenev could tell, having to give a commentary also meant that Boniface hadn't figured that he was being followed. Turgenev was perhaps 30 feet behind, but presumably Boniface thought he was still back at the car, dreaming up new torments for the professor; and while that fear was etched into Boniface's brain, he would comply with Turgenev's instructions.

Turgenev watched Boniface hesitate inside the archway crossing The Wardrobe, and tried to ignore the Englishman's incessant over-description.

Boniface started moving and Turgenev mirrored, moving from shadow to shadow without being heard. He watched the other man stumble; clearly, he had never been a soldier. From the way he walked, he hadn't even been a Boy Scout.

Boniface turned and stood in front of the wrought-iron gate, twisted the knob, and pushed. From where he stood, Turgenev couldn't hear the gate opening; the only sound was the inane babbling. The Englishman proceeded across the cobbles, two cameras looking down on him, but somehow he hadn't seen them, according to his commentary.

He reached the front door and banged on it with the knocker. Never a sign of good security: Even if they don't stop you at the gate, they should be waiting by the time you get to the door. The Russian counted. How long would it take after knocking for there to be signs of life? One, two, three, four, five, six, seven...a light came on. So they don't pay attention, they're slow, and no one was near that door.

The door opened. Turgenev looked at the man who answered. He knew the type: He had probably once applied to join the army, maybe had been to some sort of activity day when he was a teenager, had perhaps spoken to a Marine or a Commando, but that was it. Not a soldier, but he definitely talked a good game at the gym, and if you didn't know any better, then you might be impressed. That is why the Russian Army would always be better than the British Army.

Turgenev smiled. This was a guard offering security for someone who didn't know better and who didn't know what real security meant. He chuckled; Boniface could be a pain in that guy's ass.

Boniface babbled as Turgenev edged around the outside of the courtyard and followed the path that led to the journalist's car near his impermanent resting place. He turned left off of the path; passed the car, instinctively checking his pocket to confirm the journalist's car key was still there; and followed the unlit narrow road down to the river, where he turned left again onto the broad path. It was a pleasure to be able to walk on a path by the river without Boniface constantly asking what the strategy was and without the professor in her heels slowing them both down.

He had first walked up this path after he had dealt with the journalist, and although his reconnaissance had been rushed, it had been long enough to get the lay of the land. He knew that up ahead was an iron fence, much like the wrought-iron gates that Boniface had passed through. When Turgenev had passed earlier, he had wondered about the security measures but had been unwilling to give them any real scrutiny for fear of tripping an alarm. Seeing how Boniface's approach had gone unnoticed, he was confident: There wouldn't be a trigger mechanism if he climbed the fence, there wouldn't be any alarms tripped as he went up the ornamental garden, there wouldn't be any guards outside, and if there were CCTV cameras, they would be attached to the house and would be static, so all that was necessary would be to walk around their field of view.

A quick look each way confirmed he was alone. He was over the fence in less than three seconds and able to follow the clean lines of the gardens funneling him toward the house. Even in the darkness he could tell that Sherborne had spent more on one day's gardening than he had on one year's security.

As he got close, he moved to the side, taking cover behind some rose bushes. Boniface was still talking; it sounded as if he was now inside and expecting Sherborne to appear at any moment. Turgenev smirked; from the few grunts that the phone could pick up, it also sounded as if the guard was ready to slap Boniface.

This rear elevation of the house seemed far more impressive than the entrance where Boniface had gone in, and it offered many opportunities for entry. On each side of the central door, there were six sash windows on each floor—twenty-five windows in total, including a central window above the door. The first two windows on each side sat under the huge portico supported by four Doric columns. The end windows were semi-circular, and the roof ridge above these windows was turned 90 degrees, pointing front to back, unlike the main roof ridges and each wing, which went left to right.

From where he crouched, the guttering along the edge of the roof was hidden, but it must be there, because something fed the four rain downpipes set between every other window.

The most obvious access point would be through one of the windows on ground level. All the windows were sash windows where the panes slid vertically; it was a case of flipping a lock with his knife. If any of the windows were going to be locked or alarmed, it would be the ground-floor windows. Given Sherborne's lack of attention to security, the upper floors were unlikely to have these distractions, and if Boniface and Sherborne were on the ground floor, the height of the upper floor would give him an advantage.

Light spilled out of several windows, making it harder to see the exterior of the building. The room to the far left on the lower floor was lit by an exposed bulb hanging from the ceiling. He guessed this was the guards' room, but was this the location of the other person who talked to the guard that allowed Boniface into the building?

Several of the other rooms downstairs had light spilling into them, probably from the hall where Boniface was now incessantly chattering to whoever would listen—and if they didn't listen, then he would probably talk with the suits of armor he had mentioned.

On the left of the upper floor, the first window at the end—the semi-circular window—was largely dark, but gave off a faint green/blue flicker, as if a television might be on. Windows two, three, and four on the left were lit, suggesting they were all part of a single room, and windows five and six emitted a dull glow, so again they were probably part of one room, and that room was probably getting some light from a passageway. The window over the central door was lit, but poorly.

He paused and listened to Boniface. There was another voice. Turgenev found it difficult to differentiate between English accents, but this had a different resonance. He seemed very full of himself. This was probably Sherborne, and if Sherborne was in the hall with Boniface, and Turgenev was right about the low-quality security, all eyes would be focused on guarding the principal. Looked at another way, it was now time for him to move.

The right wing of the house was in complete darkness. Turgenev ran to the second downpipe and tugged it. As he suspected, it was sturdy, cast iron, and securely attached to the wall. In other words, it was a near-perfect climbing aid. It took a moment to reach the upper floor, where he extended a leg and pivoted onto the brick windowsill. It took longer to open his knife than it took to open the window lock; it then required considerable force to slide the top window sash downward, breaking through years of bad maintenance and poor paint work, but once it did move, it created an opening that was large enough for him to get through without any effort.

fifty-seven

Boniface sat on the green leather Chesterfield sofa, camouflaged against the screen of plants behind it.

He had been angry at Sherborne and had not held back in expressing his ire at the way Sherborne had treated him in the past. But now, as the two men spoke, probably speaking frankly for the first time, he was starting to feel sorry for the older man.

Perhaps it was the result of a much too long day, perhaps it was seeing several people murdered in front of him, perhaps he had spent too long stuffed in the trunks of two cars, perhaps he had been handcuffed for too long, perhaps it was his concern for Ellen and her fear for Montbretia, perhaps for the first time he could see Sherborne's misguided motives, or perhaps it was his age leading him to get in touch with his feminine side.

Whatever the reason, it was undeniable; he had sympathy for the fat man.

He wondered if something had changed for Sherborne, too.

The man had always been fat—no, obese—but now he was starting to look close to death. The weight of his body and his enthusiasm for socializing were killing him, and he was dying in front of Boniface. The mass of his body compounded with the weight of his ambition—which was always so far reaching that it was doomed to remain unfulfilled—took their toll on his skeleton and organs. His heart had to work three times as hard as it should, his liver was always clearing gallons of alcohol, and all of his joints were worn down from years of carrying excessive bulk.

But beyond his morbid obesity, Boniface thought he could also see a man who was living on his nerves, having his worry fueled by paranoia. Where he had once seen the way Sherborne surrounded himself with women as pitiful—and it was true, he liked to have women around—he could now see that Sherborne had blanketed himself with people who would be kind to him, and to whom he could return the kindness without seeming weak.

While he was starting to feel sorry for the man, he still wasn't ready to trust him nor to give him a full explanation of the events of the last few hours. "So, as I say, that's the short version of the story... I've left out the really dull bits, but that's how I got to where I am. Nigel got shot, Ellen—who isn't dead—and I went looking for the papers, and everything has pointed to you."

"Quite an eventful evening you've had, Boniface. But you're sure that Ellen's alright—she must have had a dreadful shock, and with the loss of her friend..." His voice faded in a mixture of emotion and shortness of breath.

"She's as secure as she can be, given the circumstances," said Boniface, nodding cautiously.

"Good, good." The fat man muttered, wiping the sweat out of a fold that made its way down his cheek and ended in his third chin. "I'll call her in the morning to offer my condolences and see if there's any help I can offer."

Sherborne seemed distracted with his mopping as Boniface continued. "Now let me get back to the subject and tell you how I think you're being clever with the call for a referendum." He watched Sherborne twitch and wedge himself further into his club chair. "Oscar is a young man who doesn't seem to have a place in this world." Boniface hesitated, calibrating the other man's response. "I'm sorry, that sounds critical of Oscar. That is not my intent. Let me rephrase."

"You don't need to rephrase, Boniface. We don't need to change the subject. For once we're having a civilized conversation; it seems such a shame that you want to spoil it."

"I'm sorry, Richard, but after the night I've had..." Boniface exhaled, wearily, his voice resigned. "Let me at least express my comment in a way that is less critical of Oscar."

Sherborne snorted as Boniface carried on. "Oscar is in royal purgatory. He is neither within the inner circle of royalty—if you will, he's not at the top table of royalty—nor is he able to function with the freedom of a non-royal. Would you agree with this very broad proposition, Richard?"

"I don't know where you're going with this, Boniface." The fat man seemed to be annoyed.

"I'll take that as a yes," said Boniface, continuing without looking for agreement. "And while Oscar is in royal purgatory, he will never be happy. He will never have his place in the world, because he's neither one thing nor the other."

Sherborne remained quiet, apart from his labored breathing and the gentle mopping of his pooling sweat.

"Oscar can't cease to be royal. There's no mechanism to set him free from the burden of his birth—and you have realized that. Of course, it's worse because Princess Heidemarie always tells everyone that she's the most royal of the lot of them, what with the Habsburg connection. I mean, she even gave Oscar her maiden name because she thought she was more royal than the family she married into. Not to mention that she hadn't changed her name because they were still on their honeymoon at the time of the accident, and it didn't seem worth it after the husband died." Boniface smirked. "Or is the rumor true, Richard? She didn't give her son her husband's family name because her husband wasn't the father, and he wasn't the father because he had been in a coma for a year when the child was born after that skiing accident on their honeymoon? That would be one way of making Oscar un-royal."

Boniface paused, letting the old rumor swirl as he avoided making eye contact with Sherborne before continuing. "So the sole option for you—as a friend of the family, as a parent, as whatever—is to craft a place for Oscar within the inner circle and hope that with the weight of civic duty comes a degree of maturity, coupled with the royal machine to apply some level of control to those influences that may otherwise lead him into the tabloid headlines."

Sherborne remained impassive.

"Princess Heidi wouldn't be against the idea of Oscar having a greater role, would she? It would vindicate her position, and for her it would give Oscar something to do beyond getting drunk and using his allowance to pay off all those debauched hussies, as I guess you would call them." Boniface relaxed back into his sofa. "How am I doing, Richard?"

"It's all nonsense, Boniface. A great piece of fiction, but nonsense."

"No. It's a great strategy of yours. You're marshaling public support, and you know the monarchy will be supported, but at the same time you're planning a future for Oscar. That's brilliant!"

The room was hushed apart from the sound of Sherborne's labored breathing and the security guard fidgeting in his seat, each man looking at the other. "Well, I hate to disappoint you, Boniface, but I've got something far more interesting to think about at the moment." The fat man's tone was triumphal.

"Well, it would be interesting, Richard, but I hope you don't think my appearance here is coincidental."

fifty-eight

Turgenev slid up the top half of the sash window, returning it to the position it had been before he entered, and stepped back on the soft carpet, looking around the room. Two two-seater sofas, upholstered in flowery fabric, faced each other, both perpendicular to a fireplace. A few pieces of fragile, dark-wood furniture had been carefully placed around the room, and a three-cornered cabinet sat in the corner farthest from the door, which was shut. Above the fireplace, a row of silver-framed photos sat next to some porcelain figurines.

The door fitted tightly in its frame with no light coming in around the edges. The Russian lay on the floor, straining to see through a gap between the door and the carpet where he could make out light on the other side. He knelt and leaned forward, twisting his head to look through the keyhole. There was definitely light, but not a bright light.

He stood and put his ear to the door, listening. Delicately, he twisted the knob and pulled the door back, waiting for his eyes to adjust to the electric glow.

Cautiously, he edged into the corridor—lit by a single uncovered low-energy light bulb—which was featureless apart from the four other doors, all closed. The door to his right at the end of the corridor appeared to lead to the end room. He dropped to his knees and looked through the keyhole. Nothing. He crawled to the two rooms on the other side of the corridor, looking through each keyhole in turn, finishing with the keyhole in the door next to the room through which he had entered.

Nothing. All dark.

The end of the corridor led onto a landing that was poorly lit, but light floated up from the floor below, mingling with the sound of voices rising to the higher floor. By the sounds of things, Boniface was in full flow. He seemed to be getting into personal territory, talking about his drinking and his failed marriage. Turgenev sneered.

He put his ear to the door to the left of his entry room and pushed. It opened into gloom, the only illumination the ambient light coming through the window and the dull bulb in the corridor. He stepped in and looked around the room, a bedroom, but with an old-fashioned, stale, flowery smell. "Old woman's perfume," he muttered, scanning the room. Unable to pick out any distinguishing features in the dark, he closed the door as he left and tried the room opposite. Again a featureless bedroom, but without the smell. The room next to that was a bathroom with a bath, a sink, a toilet, and a small medicine cabinet. In the dark, the room was featureless.

He paused outside the room at the end, listening, then entered suddenly. It was narrower than he expected but ran from the front to the back of the house with windows at each end. He couldn't make out its main function, but he was drawn to the river end of the room, where a spiral staircase plunged into darkness on the floor below.

He left the end room, carefully shutting the door behind him, and moved silently along the corridor, pausing where it joined the landing. Boniface and Sherborne were engrossed in conversation and battering him from both sides—in his earpiece and with a momentary delay from downstairs. He couldn't tell whether they were enjoying the argument, trying to destroy each other, or both.

Grateful for the distraction the two created, he eased across the landing, past the top of the broad staircase, and, reaching the passageway on the other side, reflexively checked behind him before moving forward.

This corridor had four doors, and two of those were open. Turgenev weighed which door to choose first. The one at the end would be last: Given that he hadn't seen any signs of human habitation in the other corridor, if there was a guard upstairs, then he would likely be in the room that had given off the flickering glow Turgenev had seen from outside.

The first room on the left had its door open but no lights switched on. He stepped inside. Bookcases lined the walls to the left and right, and at the front of the room a scroll-armed sofa sprawled on the floor. Beyond the sofa was an imposing desk with a large leather chair behind it. A few papers lay on top of the desk along with two tumblers. A third tumbler, still half full, sat on a table next to the sofa.

He turned and, standing inside the room he had entered, faced across the passageway. Where there were two doors in the other wing, here there was only one. He stepped forward and knelt to check the light. Seeing nothing, he tried the door and slipped in, returning the door behind him to its previous position.

His eyes strained to see in the darkness, but this was a bedroom. Without his night vision he had to rely on his sense of smell, which was unfortunate. There was an indistinct bitter tang—he wasn't sure what it was, but he didn't feel the need to get a definitive answer. Adjacent to the farthest corner was a door into the next room. Turgenev took five paces to get to the door, at each step finding his feet impeded by soft objects on the floor—bedding, clothing perhaps? Hopefully.

He pushed the door, cringing at the low squeak of the hinge, until he could see enough to know that it was a bathroom. Guessing that there was no one in there, he returned to his exit. He stepped out, closing the door on the smell, and took a few silent strides to the next room on the other side.

The door was ajar, with light streaming around the gap. He listened, then opened the door without hesitation, keeping hold of the knob so that the wood didn't swing free. There was no one in sight as he stepped inside, returning the door to its previous position.

Like its neighbor, this room had bookcases filled with books along both walls. Unlike its neighbor, this room seemed more ordered. On the wall behind the door there was a long, thin, modern table with a light wood-effect top and a modern typist's chair facing it. The combination looked out of place, as did the computer and printer sitting on the table. The modernity was thrown into sharp contrast by the array of vintage flintlocks displayed on the wall above the desk. His soldier's interest in the craft of the gunsmith kicked in, and he had to shake himself loose, recommencing his survey of the room.

As he had seen from his external inspection, there were three windows. Against the two pillars between the windows, back-to-back bookcases stood, creating small bays. On the inside of the bays, a large, solidly constructed stand-up desk was placed so the reader could study while keeping his back to the windows. In front of the desk, with its back to the desk and facing the door, was another scroll-armed sofa.

The room at the end of the passageway was the only space unchecked.

Turgenev crouched at the door, trying to look through the keyhole. There was a blue/green light dancing around like the Northern Lights, but no obvious sound. He stood, flipped the earpiece out and placed his ear against the door, feeling with the tips of his fingers for any vibrations.

He took a deep breath and opened the door swiftly, looking around for any sign of movement. "So have you had enough of the old man yet? Is he still convinced we're going to be invaded at any moment by a gang of crack mercenaries?"

Turgenev turned to the voice. There was a man—wearing a white shirt with epaulets, sitting on a flimsy typist's chair in front of a computer screen—leaning forward as if trying to urgently pick up something on the floor with both hands. The Russian moved briskly; he could see the man's bare legs and dark pants around his ankles. On the table next to the screen lay a dark-blue blazer and an upturned cap with a gun and walkie-talkie nestled inside.

The Russian moved to stand behind the man and, without a word, placed one hand under his chin and the other just back from the crown of his head, then twisted. There was a dull cracking, and the body went limp, falling to the floor.

Turgenev remained motionless, staring at the computer screen, which was now visible and showing a woman, naked apart from her stockings and stilettos. Somehow she looked familiar. He read her name, Kristalle, and shrugged. It probably should mean something, but he wasn't sure why.

From the light given off by the image of Kristalle, he looked at the gun. The magazine dropped out easily; he checked it and returned it, then slipped the cold steel into his jacket pocket before he picked up the guard's blazer and checked the pockets. Nothing. He looked down at the body, naked between the waist and the ankles, and shook his head.

Across the landing, he walked to the room at the far end of the other corridor and entered, quietly shutting the door behind him before he descended the spiral staircase.

fifty-nine

Boniface sucked in air through his teeth, pausing as he tried to find a way to phrase his next question to Sherborne. There was a rustling in the greenery behind his back. Across the hallway, the security guard jerked his head to look toward the source of the sound without moving the rest of his body. "Hey!"

Boniface turned to look in the direction that the bullet traveled, realizing that he had instinctively flinched away from the blast behind his head. The guard had disappeared, being replaced in Boniface's line of sight by a spatter of blood, gravity starting its slow descent down the wall.

The reverberation seemed interminable, but as the silence began to assert its presence over the room, Boniface turned to look at the origin of the shot. "That was the signal, was it?" He sighed. "That's how you're going to tell me you're coming in?"

Turgenev stepped forward. Unlike the last time Boniface had seen him, he now had a gun in his hand, and a broad grin was spreading across his face. "I would have called, but I got all teary-eyed when you two girls kissed and made up. You know, I'm going to sell that story to Hollywood and retire on the earnings."

"Who are you?" bellowed Sherborne, remaining wedged in his club chair. "Boniface! Call the police."

Turgenev caught Boniface's eye. Boniface flopped back on his sofa as confirmation that he had heard, understood, and complied with the unspoken command.

"That won't be necessary, fat man." Turgenev kept moving, lifting his gun and transferring his gaze to Sherborne.

In three strides he was on the other side of the hall, crouching behind the body of the recently deceased guard but still facing the fireplace between Sherborne and Boniface. He checked the guard one-handed, the other hand keeping his gun trained on Sherborne.

As he stood, he slipped a newly liberated pistol into his pocket, then walked to the fat man and squatted beside him, positioning the gun that had just killed the guard an inch away from Sherborne's head, but sufficiently forward so that the fat man could see the end of the muzzle. He paused. Boniface watched as Sherborne's rate of breathing started to increase. He began to tremble visibly and sweat even more profusely than normal.

Turgenev began in a low, quiet voice, the sound barely traveling across the room. "Right, fat man. I've got a few questions."

"I...er...well...I..." Sherborne looked to Boniface.

"Just answer, Richard." Boniface felt the look of resignation crossing his visage. He continued, his voice was subdued. "He's serious."

"I...er...understand. W-w-w-what do you want to know?" Sherborne pulled his handkerchief from the top pocket of his jacket and started vigorously mopping the sweat from his face.

"It's very easy," said the Russian, his voice barely audible. "How many other people are in this house?" He let the barrel of the gun kiss Sherborne's temple; the fat man let out a muted scream. "It's a simple number. How many?"

"Three. Me and the two guards," blurted Sherborne. "There's one guard over there, and the other one is upstairs."

Turgenev looked at Boniface. Boniface closed his eyes momentarily; the Russian didn't react when he heard about the other guard.

"You and the two guards, you are certain?"

"Yes. Absolutely certain." His voice was higher and trembling.

"You're an Englishman. Don't you have a butler somewhere? I thought all Englishmen had butlers."

Sherborne simpered. "I don't have a butler. I have a housekeeper, Ada, who is staying with her sister tonight."

"Alright then, second question. Are you expecting any more visitors tonight?" Turgenev stood swiftly and moved in front of Sherborne, keeping the gun on him.

"No. Yes...yes, I am expecting one person. But I was expecting him hours ago, and I'm not sure where he is."

Boniface interrupted. "He's not coming, Richard. He's dead."

Turgenev spun and looked angrily at Boniface. "What are you talking about?"

"The guy Richard is expecting is the long-haired one who was shot in Trudgett's house." He tried to keep the disdain out of his voice but failed.

Turgenev swung the gun to point at him. "Is this another trick, Boniface, or is this something else you haven't told me?" Boniface shook his head. "How do you know he was coming here?"

Boniface contemplated the gun. "Remember, I met the guy; I spoke to him. I was speaking to him when..." Boniface imitated a gun firing with his hand. "He said he had someone ready to buy the information. Everything he told me fits with the details Richard has given me, and all roads lead to Rome, or is it Richmond?"

"You're guessing." Boniface could see Turgenev's grip around the gun's handle tightening.

"I like to think of it as making reasoned deductions. I would go and ask the guy to clarify, but you'll remember that someone put a bullet through his brain."

The room fell quiet again, apart from the sound of Sherborne's labored breathing while he mopped the sweat collecting in his jowls. "He's dead, Boniface? What else haven't you told me?

"Yeah. There's quite a lot I need to tell you, but now is not the time," said Boniface.

Sherborne wiped his face again as he maintained his questioning. "So what happened to the papers or documents or whatever it was that this chap found, Boniface? Did you get them before...?"

"No." He turned to face Turgenev. "No, we didn't get the papers or whatever it was he found. And that is why we need Professor Armstrong here, now, to help us."

Turgenev remained impassive as Boniface continued. "I've stuck to my side of the deal. I've given you the running commentary." He removed the journalist's phone and offered it to Turgenev, who snatched it. "Added to which, you need her to interpret whatever we can get hold of. She was the person who knew Professor Trudgett best and stands a chance of seeing what he was thinking. The sooner we can decode the documents when they come through, the sooner you can start your retirement."

Sherborne looked shocked. "I thought you said Ellen was safe."

Boniface sighed. "I lied, or rather, I allowed you to form the wrong impression." He looked sideways at the Russian. "Remember, I was being listened to."

Boniface felt the almost imperceptible movement of his head and watched the other man's confusion. "So where is she?" Sherborne seemed almost angry at the revelation.

"Locked in the back of a car outside," said Boniface, turning to Turgenev. "At least, she was when I last saw her." He stared at Turgenev.

Turgenev stared back, both men remaining silent.

Boniface cracked first. "Come on. We need her help, and it gets you out of here sooner."

"But why do we need her now? You haven't heard from that hacker yet." Turgenev took out Boniface's phone and waved it at him.

"But once we do, you don't want us wasting time while you go and get her." He turned to Sherborne. "We're going to need a computer, Richard. Have you got one of those in this museum? With an internet connection?"

"I've got one. I got a new one last month. It's quite a good one, they tell me. My secretary uses it. Not a clue how it works, but I do have one. It's upstairs in the library."

"Shall Richard and I go up to the library, and you can go and get the professor?"

Turgenev took a step, straightening his gun arm. "No."

sixty

It took nearly fifteen minutes for Sherborne to get out of his club chair and then reach the top of the stairs.

It felt longer to Boniface. Much longer.

"You know you can get gadgets to help? Things to lift your seat as you get out of a chair. Stair lifts so you can get up and down without difficulty."

"Thank you, Boniface. I'm not ready for the nursing home yet." Sherborne seemed to be annoyed at the reminder of his physical deterioration. "While I can stand, walk, wash myself, feed myself, pour my own drink, drink it, and most importantly wipe my own arse, I will not be fitting a stair lift, grab handles, or any other hideous contraptions in this fine, architecturally listed building," he snapped, ending the conversation.

Turgenev seemed to find the process of moving Sherborne beyond infuriating. Initially he appeared to think that Sherborne was bluffing and held a gun to his head. When he put a bullet through the ceiling, he found that Sherborne probably was being serious and did move even more slowly than one would expect a fat man like him to move.

Boniface felt compelled to help him out of his chair. The stairs, however, were pure frustration. Sherborne took one step, always with his right foot, and then stopped. Every third step, he took a longer break, and halfway up he behaved like a man with altitude sickness.

There was no elation when they reached the top, no planting of flags, no cracking of champagne. Just a fat, sweaty man, wheezing and looking as if he was about to have a heart attack. Then there was the slow, lumbering walk to the library.

"Sit." Turgenev indicated another dark-green scroll-arm sofa, this one in front of a stand-up desk constructed with what looked like oak tree trunks. "Your hands." He indicated the hands nearest each other as he moved behind their seated position to the other side of the desk. "This way." Sherborne and Boniface each held up a hand, looking slightly confused. "Toward me," said Turgenev, grabbing the hands when they were pushed backward without enthusiasm, one on each side of a substantial leg of the desk.

Turgenev grabbed Boniface's wrist first, returning the handcuffs that had been present until he was let out of the car, and attached the other end of the restraint to Sherborne's thick wrist. Moving around to the front of the sofa, he cuffed their ankles together, struggling to get the restraint around Sherborne's swollen leg.

The shaven-headed man stood back to admire his work before he turned to Boniface. "You remember our arrangement."

"I do." There was defeat in Boniface's tone.

"If I am in any doubt about what you are doing, Professor Armstrong..." He drew his finger slowly across his throat. "And she will die here, in front of you. You will watch her last hours but be unable to do anything to help. And if the fat man tries anything, it's the same story."

"I understand." He continued tentatively. "Will you leave my phone in case the hacker guy calls?"

Turgenev snorted. "You? With a phone?" He spun and left the room.

Sherborne and Boniface sat in the draft created by the vacuum of the Russian leaving, listening to the sound as he took the stairs three at a time and jogged across the marble hallway. The fat man broke the silence. "What the devil is going on, Boniface? Why are you working with this thug?"

Sherborne looked over at Boniface, who ignored the questions, and instead busied himself looking behind the sofa. "You don't happen to have a key?"

"What are you talking about, Boniface?"

"Handcuffs. Key. Get out. Call police. Get back before psychotic shaven-headed Russian comes back." Boniface tugged at his wrist and ankle, reminding Sherborne that they were manacled with a large desk preventing them from starting a three-legged race.

"Of course I haven't got any handcuff keys. I'm not into that sort of thing."

Boniface ended his visual reconnaissance and slumped back on the sofa, his right arm still behind him. "Well, you've got all those museum pieces." He waved his left hand at the flintlocks on the wall above the computer. "Why not a key?"

Sherborne frowned at the question as Boniface kept talking. "We don't have long. And I'm sorry about..." He exhaled. "I'm sorry about a lot of stuff. I don't have time to prove it nor to explain how sorry I am. But once this is over, perhaps we can have a cup of tea. Yes, tea, not booze for me anymore, and I can explain all the unpleasantness that has occurred tonight. But for the moment, the thing that's worrying me is Ellen. I want her here, with us, and not locked in the back of a car. If she's here, then she has a much better chance of staying alive."

"But who is he and what does he want?"

"This afternoon he was Kuznetsov's head of security, and when I met him, Kuznetsov seemed to trust him absolutely. Now? Now, I don't know. He seems to have left Kuznetsov's employment and gone freelance. He seems to have gone off the rails and spent the last couple of hours killing people or getting people killed. His man killed Trudgett—which mistake is enough to mean Kuznetsov wants him dead—and I'm guessing his man also killed our light-fingered document-acquirer."

"He's dead, Boniface? Really dead?"

"If we're talking about the same guy, then yes, he's very dead. His brains are spread all over Trudgett's living room wall."

Sherborne winced, picked his handkerchief from his top pocket with his free hand, and mopped his brow. "But you seem to have promised this chap that you will get him something on the computer. Or am I missing something?"

"No. You're right, Richard. That's what I've said I'm going to do."

"And what does he think you are going to give him?"

"Photographs of the documents that the guy who got shot was trying to sell to you."

Sherborne leaned forward, his eyes wide. "So they are real? These documents do exist?" The fat man's eyes were alive, boring into Boniface, eagerly questioning.

"Yes."

Sherborne's face lifted; a look of hope started to form but then fell from his face. "But if the documents are to be believed, based on what that chap told me on the phone, doesn't it rather undermine the campaign by my favorite Russian oligarch?" Boniface bowed his head slightly. "Won't that cause a problem for you with Kuznetsov?"

"At the moment we don't have any options, Richard. I've been playing for time for the last few hours, hoping something, anything, would turn up, but now I'm out of ideas." He paused, continuing softly. "I really hope I didn't get Ellen brought here just to die."

"So what's the idea? They always said you were good with strategy; that's probably why the Minister hired you."

"The strategy is that you, me, Ellen...we all play along with this and do whatever we can to give him what he wants. No heroics, no messing around, we just do what we can do."

"But shouldn't we..."

"No." Boniface turned to the fat man, using the handcuffs to exert enough discomfort until Sherborne looked directly at him. "Richard, listen. No heroics. This guy is a killing machine. He's probably killed half a dozen people with his bare hands this evening, and now he's got a gun, so don't try anything." Sherborne exhaled. "He's like an angry wasp. If you annoy him, he'll come back and sting one of us. And if he can't get one of us, well...he's scared the shit out of Ellen by telling her he'll go after her sister."

Boniface kept Sherborne in discomfort, waiting for his agreement. "Oh alright, Boniface. Whatever you say."

The room fell still apart from Sherborne's labored breathing. Boniface spoke first. "Oscar."

"Really, Boniface! This is neither the time nor the place." Sherborne's tone was sharp, but there was no energy behind his rebuke.

Boniface reinstated the pressure on the handcuffs and waited. "For pity's sake, don't be a stupid old man. This is your one opportunity to talk. Don't you get that there's a good chance we won't get out of here tonight? It's not as if you have a lot of leverage with our shaven-headed tormentor in this negotiation. You can be collateral damage, and the Russian won't care and neither will his former boss. In fact, I suspect Mister Kuznetsov might be secretly pleased if a stray bullet hits you."

"Well, if you release the pressure on my wrists, I might consider it."

Boniface held the tension, then relaxed. Sherborne shook his arm loose. "Jolly inconvenient. He could have chained us in a more comfortable position."

"Please hurry, Richard," whined Boniface. "Get to the point: Oscar is your son, isn't he?"

Boniface watched Sherborne deflate. "You have to understand, Boniface. Things are not always as black and white as you would like them to be. There's room for subtlety, nuance, understanding, and dare I say, compassion."

"I can do compassion," said Boniface in a gentle voice with a reassuring tilt of his head.

"Attitudes were different. My close friendship with Princess Heidemarie is well known and is fully accepted now, but when it first became clear that we were close, there was that awful business, of course."

"Awful business of you screwing a new bride when her husband was in a coma?"

"Boniface. We were friends, and she needed comfort—it was an awful time for her, and that bloody family did nothing to welcome her. They were all about stoical duty. And then she got pregnant. At that time it would have been incredibly uncomfortable for Heidi to admit that she had cheated on her husband to whom she had only been married for eight days before the accident, and she was my friend."

"And so you protected her." Boniface soothed.

"And so I protected her and denied any improper relationship. I always maintained that the boy's father was her husband. In fact, at one point, when the press started talking about the immaculate conception—there being no father who would stand up and claim responsibility—I even gave the impression that I was resentful that I hadn't had a fair crack at the whip, so to speak."

"I'm sure you cracked a whip like a good 'un, Richard."

Sherborne stared into the distance, as if looking at a far-off time.

"And not only did you crack the whip, but you fathered the child."

Sherborne nodded slowly. "Yes. I am Oscar's father. And for the record, he has always known I am his father, and I have tried to do the best I can for my son. I really am incredibly proud of him, Boniface. He is a gentle, sweet, thoughtful young man. Nothing like the loathsome hooray or borderline criminal that the tabloids paint him to be." He smiled. "And nothing like his father."

The room was quiet, neither man speaking. Boniface started, calmly. "So, if what the dead guy said is true, Princess Heidemarie, who has always claimed to be more royal than the present lot, may ironically have a child who genuinely has the better claim to the throne."

"It's almost Shakespearean." The fat man took on an exaggerated deep voice. "Thou shalt get kings, Sherborne, though thou be none."

sixty-one

A door—almost certainly the front door—slammed on the lower floor. From where Boniface and Sherborne sat, the sound wasn't loud, but the reverberations traveled through every beam in the structure of Trumpeters' House.

There were two sets of footsteps. One set dull, heavy, thumping. The other alternating between the sound of a small, sharp, loud heel and a soft shoe scraping on the marble; the alternation between the two sounds suggesting smaller, more frequent footsteps. The two distinct sets of footsteps gave way to the sound of people walking on the stairs, with neither set of feet being distinguishable, but the sound of a female voice, clearly in some discomfort, rising above.

At the top of the stairs the party started moving toward the library where Boniface and Sherborne were manacled.

When Boniface and Ellen had been arrested in Nigel's office, she had been exhausted but still fired up and excited about seeing her sister in a few hours. Sure, she wasn't quite as well presented as she had been on the television earlier in the day—her skirt had a small rip, the blouse was creased, her hair was windswept, and the green/black lines under her eyes were starting to show—but that was nothing that a bath and a good night's sleep wouldn't cure.

But now she looked different.

She still wore the same clothes, but instead of the well-tailored business suit, all Boniface could see were old bits of torn fabric loosely fashioned as garments, apparently held together by copious quantities of mud. Mud seemed to be quite a significant theme in the look Ellen was modeling. As well as holding her clothes together, mud was also acting as her makeup, to color her hair, and to keep her hair in place, which didn't seem to be the place Ellen had intended it to be the last time she had brushed it.

The mud also seemed to be acting as a first-aid supplement, covering her cuts and scratches, and soothing the bruises.

Ellen stood, shivering, her hands still cuffed behind her back. The remnants of her clothes still damp from falling into wet grass and mud, chilled further in the trunk as the temperature outside had continued to decline.

"Dear God. What happened to you?" Sherborne hollered, then lowered his voice as Boniface yanked his handcuff when he saw the shock on Ellen's face. "Are you alright, my dear?"

She flinched. Where a few hours earlier there had been passion in her eyes, now Boniface could see fear. Fear she had never known before. Fear that she didn't understand. Fear of physical violence that she was not equipped to deal with. Fear that the only person that mattered to her was being physically threatened. Fear that the only two people who could help her were an overweight, aging, would-be Lothario who could barely walk and a self-confessed physical coward whose mouth seemed to run wild when he was thinking. Fear that the two people who might help her seemed to be manacled together, unable to stand from the sofa on which they were sitting.

Boniface tried to communicate some form of reassurance. Any form of reassurance, but he failed with the subliminal messages. "It's good to see you." Her mouth moved as if she was trying to show human emotion but failed. He looked to Turgenev. "Could you at least let her wash her hands and face? Please."

"No." Turgenev was unyielding. "Sit." He turned to Ellen and placed a hand on each shoulder, twisting her so her back faced the sofa, and pushed. Ellen took two stumbling steps backward and fell, wedging herself between Boniface and the arm at the end of the green sofa, with her hands still behind her back.

"It's good to see you. I was so worried," whispered Boniface. Ellen blushed slightly.

"I've told you before. Shut up." There was no hint that Turgenev was taking a negotiating position. Boniface stiffened and complied.

A phone rang from inside Turgenev's jacket. "That's our man. Let me talk to him." Boniface held out his free left hand.

Turgenev remained impassive.

"We're not going to go through this shit again, are we? The only one that loses is you. The rest of us can go back to our day jobs tomorrow, but if you don't get the documents, then you're not going to have any leverage."

Turgenev stared at Boniface.

"Fine. Don't do anything. But if you're not going to do anything, then stop dicking about and let us go home."

Still no response.

"What's the calculation? Are we going to screw you?" Boniface saw a flash of recognition, a brief involuntary twitch above the eyes. "You're scared of us, and you don't know how to get out."

"No." Turgenev sounded defensive, his pride slightly pricked.

"Then give me the phone." Boniface was feeling argumentative.

The phone stopped.

"There goes your pension. Happy now?"

Turgenev moved forward, standing on Boniface's left foot. "Final warning. Shut. Up."

The phone rang again. Boniface remained motionless and fixed his face.

"Yes." Turgenev answered. He muttered a few words in Russian, then looked at Boniface. "Give me a credit card."

"Come on, Dickie. You're a man of money; you must have a card or two in the wallet that's always in your pocket." Boniface flashed a quick look at Ellen, raising his eyebrows. Ellen's mouth formed an "O" shape, half in surprise, half in acknowledged conspiracy.

"Well, I..." Sherborne began.

"Give. Now." The Russian held out his hand. Reluctantly, Sherborne reached into his inside jacket pocket with his free hand and pulled out a worn brown hide wallet. One-handed, he flipped it open and eased out a credit card with his thumb, grudgingly handing over the piece of plastic. Turgenev read the details, grunted, and flipped the phone closed, dropping the card on the floor.

He stood, staring at the phone in the palm of his hand. After 30 seconds it beeped. He opened it and read the message. "This is goodbye."

Boniface looked up to see the pistol pointing at him. He raised his eyebrows, questioning, but remained silent.

"Why so quiet, Mister Boniface?" Turgenev pulled his mouth tight, articulating each word individually.

Boniface waited, moving his head from one side to the other as if holding a conversation inside his skull. "Because I don't get it. You've really confused me this time."

The Russian cocked his head and opened his eyes more widely.

"You've got the password now, so you can get into Professor Trudgett's file storage account or whatever it is. You can look at the photos... assuming they're there."

The Russian stared at Boniface. A look practiced over years.

"But what are you going to do next?"

The Russian frowned.

"You haven't got a clue what's there, have you? More to the point, you won't know what's important and what isn't, so you're going to need somebody to help you. By the time you find someone who knows their way around this stuff, it's not going to be worth half what it's worth now, and somewhere, while you're trying to find someone who can help you, you're going to get ripped off. What are you going to do if someone simply publishes the documents you send them?" He paused. "Shouldn't we take a look for you? We do know something about the subject."

The Russian pondered. It was his turn to appear to have a conversation inside his head. "Remember who's got the gun." He tossed the phone to Boniface, who reached out his left hand, catching it as it spun toward him.

"And now if you would be so kind..." Boniface tugged on his right wrist and right ankle, jerking Sherborne.

Turgenev walked behind the stand-up desk and released Sherborne's left wrist, leaving the handcuff on Boniface's right. Both men shook their arms to reinvigorate the circulation. "That feels better," muttered Sherborne as the Russian moved in front of Boniface, taking the cuff he had just removed from Sherborne and attaching it to Boniface's free wrist.

Boniface held his manacled wrists up to the Russian, who looked at him and shrugged. "You can still use a computer."

Turgenev squatted to remove the restraint shackling the two Englishmen at their ankles, and pointed the younger man to the computer. "Computer... Password on the phone. Go." He looked to Sherborne. "I don't need to tell you not to move, do I, fat man? But just in case." He squatted and attached the loose cuff to Sherborne's other ankle.

Boniface got to his feet awkwardly, pushing on his knees with his handcuffed hands to give himself enough leverage from the low seat; walked to the computer; and delicately positioned the typist's chair, which spun wildly at his slightest touch. "I'm going to need her help."

Turgenev jerked the muzzle of the gun to indicate Ellen to join him.

"She'll need a chair, too," said Boniface.

Turgenev stepped back out of the library. There was a sound of a door opening, some banging, a door closing, and the Russian returned with a typist's chair. "There." He pushed the chair to Ellen, who was now standing.

"She'll need to use her hands," said Boniface, turning back to the computer and starting to type. Several screens came up before he flipped open his phone and entered the details that the hacker had sent.

Ellen turned and leaned to push her hands toward Turgenev. He unlocked one bracelet, leaving the cuffs hanging from her other wrist, and pointed to Boniface. "Help him."

The academic wheeled the chair next to Boniface and sat. "What have we got?" she asked huskily.

"Nine photos. Not sure what, but they're downloading now—either the photos are huge or this connection is slow." He turned to Turgenev, who was standing a few paces back, keeping the three within a tight firing arc. "It's going to take a minute or two, but there is something here." Turgenev snarled, allowing the room to fall silent apart from the quiet hum of the computer and the occasional squeaks from the typists' chairs.

The first image finished downloading, and Boniface hit the print button. The printer shook itself into action, vibrating, squealing, and rumbling, outputting the page millimeter-by-millimeter. As it finally spat out the paper, Boniface passed the page to Ellen.

She read in silence, then looked up, expectation on her face. "This is it. Well, not everything." She pointed to the printer. "Hurry up, next page...but this is it." Boniface hit the print button for the next page, and the printer began shaking itself into a frenzy again. "This is the proof we need; we now know where Henry is buried, which leads to the logical conclusion that it was murder." She held up the page.

Boniface read it slowly. "You mean...? That its only function is to cover up the...?" His sentence trailed off with the realization of what he was reading.

A large smile had broken out across Ellen's face. "What Nigel always believed after those TV people visited; here's the instruction." She picked up the next page coming out of the printer. "And look at this," she whispered. "FitzRoy."

Boniface turned to Turgenev. "This is going to take perhaps five or ten minutes, so why don't you sit down? What we'll do is put all the images together in a single file along with a few words giving an explanation of what you've got here, so you don't need to read everything now. It will all be together in one file."

Turgenev grunted dismissively and moved to the sofa, sitting on the arm farthest away with his feet on the seat. As the documents printed, Boniface and Ellen quietly muttered between themselves with Ellen dictating and Boniface typing. After some minutes, Boniface turned to Turgenev. "We're nearly done. Get a thumb drive or something, and we'll transfer the file for you."

"Why?" asked Turgenev.

"You need to get the files off this machine," Boniface slapped the computer on the desk, "and you don't want to leave the details on Nigel's storage account, which has been accessed by a hacker." He waited as if to emphasize the point. "Do you want to rely on a system that you know has been compromised? By someone you can't go and threaten with a gun?"

The Russian grunted.

"You must have some thumb drives sitting around somewhere, Richard. You know, the things people send to you that you give to the secretary and she plugs into the computer?"

"Oh, those. Yes. I've got some; they're in my desk." Turgenev stared at Sherborne. "My desk in the next room. Do you want me to go and get one?" The Russian removed one cuff from around Sherborne's ankles, returning to his position on the arm.

"Get two," called Boniface, now facing the screen again, typing rapidly. "One's always bound to be faulty."

Sherborne slid forward on the sofa, twisting as he went, landing on his knees and facing the sofa. He lifted one leg, placing his foot flat on the floor, and then levered himself up using the arm of the sofa. Straining to breathe, he eventually reached vertical. "I'll go and get those thingummies."

Turgenev watched him moving—glacially—toward the door. "Is there a phone in that room?"

"Of course," said Sherborne, seeming to lose his breath with the exertion of talking and standing simultaneously.

"Then I'm coming with you." He jumped off the sofa; in two paces he was behind Boniface and reached to pick up his phone. "Don't want you making calls while I'm out of the room, do we, Mister Boniface? And remember, I'm going to be standing in the corridor you need to come along to get out." He held the gun up, lowering it when Boniface nodded his acknowledgement.

sixty-two

"You understand that there's a lot I want to say—need to say—but at the moment, my focus is on getting all three of us out of here alive?"

Ellen nodded, her muddy hair following the movement of her head but not showing any bounce as her head came to rest. "I don't care about anything apart from doing whatever he says so that Montbretia stays safe."

Boniface reached to touch Ellen's hand. "Richard moves so slowly that we've got a minute or two and before we do anything else, I need something I can lob. It needs to be small and light, but with enough weight that it will carry."

"Small?" asked Ellen, pushing her chair back as she stood, turning to the bookshelves behind her.

"About the size of a thumb drive. About the weight of a thumb drive. Makes the sound of a thumb drive if you drop it."

Ellen scanned the shelves. "And you. What are you doing?"

"Me. I'm trying to make sure that whatever goes onto the thumb drive that we give to Turgenev looks like the real thing but has no value and can't do any damage to Mister Kuznetsov. I'm playing with fire if I leave Kuznetsov open to blackmail. These words you've dictated say a lot, but I've made a few edits, and as for what I've done with the photos..." He trailed off.

"No, Boniface. It's too dangerous." Ellen turned to face him, her lower jaw trembling as she tried to speak. Her voice was quiet but insistent. "Give him what he wants. I'm not going to put my sister at risk by lying."

"He won't realize—he won't have seen the original, so he won't know that the quality of the images has been degraded—he'll think Nigel took bad shots with his phone." Boniface kept eye contact.

"No, Boniface. It's too dangerous. You're putting my sister's life at risk."

"All of our lives—including Montbretia's—are already at risk. That risk magnifies if we cross Kuznetsov." He held her gaze. "If there was another option, I wouldn't be doing this."

"You're sure?" Boniface tried to seem relaxed. "Promise me, Boniface. Promise that you're really sure this will work."

"I promise," said Boniface.

Ellen held his gaze and then returned to her investigation of the bookcases. He watched as she pushed the third one, rocking it toward the wall, and flicked something loose with her foot. "I've got three choices for you. A wooden figure."

"An unpleasant wooden figure," said Boniface, rotating the object Ellen had passed him. "What is it?"

"A caveman? A tiger? I don't know... No, look, it's a walrus. And to go with that walrus, here's a one-pound coin and a small wooden wedge. By the way, that third bookcase is a bit wobbly. Someone removed the wooden wedge that was keeping it level, so don't try climbing it."

She passed the other two objects to Boniface, who inspected each in turn, looking at it, feeling its weight in his hand, and dropping it on the table, listening to the sound as it fell. After contemplating the three items, he pushed them to the back of the table and returned to the computer.

Ellen sat on the edge of the desk, looking through the papers Boniface had printed. "So if you're going to give our shaven-headed tormentor something with no value, by accident, of course, what are you going to do with the real version? Email it to yourself?"

"Not enough time—this connection is too slow. Turgenev will catch us." Boniface looked at Ellen; she didn't seem to share his conviction in the plan. "If you want me to email it to you, I'm more than happy to as soon as I've got a fast connection and no Russian with a gun."

Ellen's face remained fixed, then softened. "No, you're right. It's too risky. How are you..."

Boniface cut her off. "No time. Just go with it. What about the documents? What else have you seen?"

"Not much more, certainly nothing revelatory," said Ellen with a slight note of caution in her voice. "Several references to John Stephens—remember, the name on the family trees in Nigel's case—and now..." she held up one of the sheets of paper Boniface had printed, "we know how he fits in." Ellen pointed at two of the sheets on the desk.

sixty–three

"So the documents show Richard is the heir."

Boniface leaned back in the typist's chair, contemplating. "But there's a more immediate issue for him."

A silence hung. "Tell me, Boniface," snapped Ellen.

"Oscar." Boniface looked around furtively as Ellen leaned forward conspiratorially. "Dickie *is* the daddy."

"Does Richard know?"

"Does he know that he shagged Heidemarie? I guess he'd remember a night of passion with someone claiming to be the most royal person in Europe."

Ellen was getting impatient. "Does he know that he's the heir to Henry and so Oscar will inherit the claim?"

Boniface sighed, releasing a stream of air through his nose. "He found out something. Mister Longhair called him, trying to get some cash. But he doesn't know *how* the family connections link him to Henry, and without these documents, he has no proof to substantiate the claim." Boniface turned back to the computer screen, awkwardly trying to type and simultaneously use the mouse with his wrists handcuffed in front of him while he kept talking with Ellen.

"So Longhair tried to sell him the documents that are still in some police station somewhere."

Boniface chuckled softly. "Yeah. Our architectural-whatever-he-was was trying to scam Sherborne until he could find his way back into Hampton Court."

A noise came from the corridor. Not so much a single noise, but a collection of noises: the sound of Sherborne's labored breathing and of his shuffling walk, the sound of Turgenev's military footsteps expressing frustration at Sherborne's slowness, the sound of Turgenev moving to check his surroundings, although Boniface suspected that anyone who might be watching him was probably already dead. "And for the moment," Boniface dropped his voice, speaking rapidly, "to preserve Richard's failing health, I don't think we should highlight his claim to our Russian friend."

The two men entered the room, Sherborne first with Turgenev following, casting a final paranoid glance down the short corridor. Ellen stood up and took two small paces away from the desk as Sherborne staggered the last few steps like a man who was only moving forward in order to ensure that he didn't lose his balance. At the last moment he turned and sat on the computer table with his back to his collection of antique flintlock pistols. The table quaked as his weight made contact with the horizontal surface, then groaned as it accepted his weight. He wheezed, still gasping for air from the exertion of having walked from the next room, and took out his handkerchief to mop his brow and between the folds of skin around his jowls, which were acting as gutters for his sweat.

"Did you get the drives?" asked Boniface.

Sherborne tried to speak but instead wheezed, pointing to Turgenev.

"Sit over there, fat man." Turgenev waved his pistol in the direction of the sofa. Sherborne wheezed and nodded vigorously, patting his upper chest as if to communicate some sort of excuse to the Russian. "Now."

"Let me get my breath," rasped Sherborne.

"While you two are sorting out the seating arrangements, could I have the drives, please?" asked Boniface, holding up his manacled wrists with his hands cupped in the expectation of delivery.

Turgenev reached into his pocket and dropped the two drives into Boniface's hands, then stepped back, sweeping his weapon through the narrow arc covering his three possible victims.

Boniface pushed the first thumb drive into a port on the front of the computer and restarted his clumsy ritual of trying to operate the keyboard and mouse with his hands chained, but now with the fat man overwhelming the desk space. He watched the screen and waited while a file transferred, then yanked the drive out of the computer. "See. I told you: This drive is crap."

Three sets of eyes followed the flight of the unidentifiable small object Boniface launched; the pound coin and the figure of the walrus remained on the desk.

With the eyes distracted, as the wooden wedge hit the far wall and fell out of sight, Boniface twisted awkwardly, slipping the first thumb drive into his pocket. "They always go wrong; that's why I told you to get two," he said, pushing the second drive into the port on the front of the computer and dragging the file he had hastily doctored onto the drive.

The file transfer completed, and he turned to Turgenev. "Let me show you what you've got here."

Boniface opened the file as the Russian moved to get a better angle on the screen while keeping the gun trained on the three. "As you can see, there is a single file with all the photos of the documents. Here's the list of documents that Professor Armstrong has prepared, with a brief summary of each. Here's the first document from five hundred years ago, the second, and so on, until the last." Boniface flicked through the images in a blur, coming to rest on the final photograph taken by Nigel in the police station.

"Happy?" Before Turgenev could answer, Boniface yanked the drive out of the port and held it for the Russian, who grabbed it and stepped backward.

"So explain to me what I've got here."

"Really?" said Boniface. "You've spent the whole evening telling me I talk too much, and it's a really long story."

"Give me the short version. As you said, having a bunch of documents isn't much use. It's like having a gun without knowing where the trigger is."

"Okay," said Boniface starting to stand. "But let me sit over here." He stood and moved to the scroll-armed sofa, falling backward to sit.

Ellen moved to the space vacated on the desk and sat next to Sherborne. She turned to him, placing one hand on his shoulder and the other on his back, and in a soft voice asked, "Are you alright? Can I do anything for you?"

"I'm fine, my dear." The fat man's wheezing slowed. "I'm quite looking forward to this story."

"You two. Shut up. You." Turgenev turned to Boniface. "Explain."

"Well... Where to begin with the story of Henry VIII? At the beginning, I suppose... Henry was married to Catherine of Aragon. She gave him a daughter, Mary. Catherine got pregnant on several other occasions, but none of those pregnancies led to a live birth of a baby that survived. Henry had affairs, and there were probably lots of bastards; however, the one that he acknowledged was Henry FitzRoy, the fruit of his union with his teenage lover, Elizabeth Blount." Boniface snorted. "And they say unmarried teenage mothers are a post-war phenomenon... The infant's godfather was Wolsey."

"Everyone knows that, Boniface," blustered Sherborne.

"Maybe. Maybe not. But for our friend here," he tilted his head toward the Russian pointing a gun at him, "I'm keen to include all the details."

Turgenev grunted. "Continue. But get to the point quickly."

"Professor Trudgett put forward his theory that Henry was murdered by Wolsey, probably with help from Anne Boleyn, or at least the Boleyn family, sometime around 1532, give or take. Wolsey assumed Henry's identity, continuing to act as King, and proceeded to systematically eliminate anyone who didn't accept him as King. Many courtiers and nobles accepted the situation and survived. Those that didn't...died."

"This was the basis of Nigel's book," said Ellen. The Russian stared at her; she blushed and fell silent.

Boniface directed his story to Sherborne. "But Wolsey's cover story is brilliant. It's so good that it's still an intrinsic part of English history." Sherborne frowned. "Henry was a slim man when he became King. But Henry, or as we now know, Wolsey, was morbidly obese when he died. We all know the story, but have we ever seen the transition? Have you ever seen an in-between Henry? Is there a slightly overweight Henry?"

Boniface looked at Sherborne, who was pondering the question.

"No." The fat man shook his head slowly. "No, I have never seen a picture of a slightly overweight Henry, or a fat but not obese Henry."

"But you know the stated reason for the obesity?"

Sherborne straightened. Boniface was sure the fat man sucked in his stomach before he started talking. "Of course. Everyone knows this. It was a jousting accident. Henry was unconscious for two hours, but after that he never regained his fitness, and instead put on weight."

"The man was brilliant, wasn't he?" Boniface shook his head in disbelief. "That was Wolsey's cover story to explain how a thin man became fat, effectively overnight. And look at the detail: We all know he was out cold for two hours. No story with so much detail could be a fake, could it?"

"But that must have taken..."

"This process of inserting himself as King took years. Well, in many ways, it took the rest of his life—he just killed everyone who he thought could be a threat."

Sherborne shook his head in wonderment. "All that was a story concocted by Wolsey?" He laughed, a deep throaty laugh, which turned into a cough. He rocked with the rhythm of the cough and started to try to stand.

"Can I get you a glass of water or something, Richard?" Ellen's face showed concern. "Anything."

The fat man continued to try to stand. He lifted his weight, wobbled, and threw his hand forward for balance. "Sit." The command from the shaven-headed Russian was free from ambiguity.

Slowly Sherborne toppled backward, thrusting his other hand toward the wall where his flintlock collection was mounted, and with an uncharacteristically swift move he grabbed the nearest pistol, swinging it round to point at the Russian.

"Richard, no!" Ellen stepped in front of the antique gun, holding her hands in front of her in a mini I-surrender pose. "Richard! It's too dangerous. If he doesn't get what he wants, he's going to hurt other people. He's going to hurt..."

"Drop your gun now," said Sherborne, ignoring Ellen's protestations and pushing her to the side with the flintlock so that it pointed at Turgenev. "This gun might be old, but it's deadly, and I'm close enough to death not to need to worry about the consequences of killing you."

"No, Richard! No. We need to do what he says. My sister..." She laid a hand on the flintlock.

There was a thunderous crack. Ellen screamed and fell to the floor. Boniface looked to where she had been standing and saw a cloud of black smoke and Sherborne spattered with blood. He rolled forward on the sofa and started to lift himself but was knocked to the floor by the Russian approaching Sherborne.

Turgenev grabbed the flintlock from the fat man's loose grip and threw the gun across the room. It hit the bookcases on the far side at the same time as he landed a single punch in Sherborne's solar plexus. Boniface got to his feet, moving toward the heap of humanity as the man he blamed for so much doubled over and fell to the ground next to Ellen.

The academic lay silently, the smallest motion confirming she was breathing. Boniface knelt beside her, looking at her face and torso, a mixture of soot, blood, burned flesh, cuts, and shredded clothing. He reached out his manacled hands.

"Time's up," said Turgenev, yanking Boniface by the hair to a standing position and pushing him out of the door before he could gain a sure footing. In the corridor, he kept Boniface in front of him, holding the back of his collar and locating the barrel of his pistol in the small of Boniface's back.

The two moved slowly, the Russian accelerating with the gun and braking with Boniface's collar. As the corridor gave way to the landing, they paused before moving to the stairs, where they gracelessly descended to the marble-floored lobby, each step echoing around them.

"I just need to do one thing," said Boniface.

"No."

"One thing."

"No."

"One thing, and that's me done with arguing. You've got a gun in my back—and I know I'm only alive because you've decided I should be—so I'm not going to be stupid." Boniface pulled Turgenev toward the guard's desk. The guard's lifeless corpse lay where he had fallen, with a pool of blood now congealing.

Boniface stood by the old phone, picked up the receiver with his shackled hand, and dialed three numbers before lifting the receiver to his ear. He felt the cold steel as the Russian pressed the gun into his temple. The phone was answered and he uttered one word—"Ambulance"— before placing the handset on the desk, leaving the line open as he started moving toward the front door, pulling Turgenev with him.

The shaven-headed Russian reached around him to open the door onto Old Palace Yard, Boniface feeling the other man's sour breath on his neck as he looked out, keeping Boniface as a shield as he pushed the Englishman until they were both outside.

The first light of the morning had cracked the cover of night. There was no sign of the sun, but the sky had turned from black to a deep blue, mottled by the passing clouds. The birds were equally unwilling to face the day, but some of their braver number were tuning up for the dawn chorus with all the grace of an orchestra warming up.

The two men stood, expelling the odor of burned gunpowder and scorched flesh as they felt the morning breeze being blown from the river.

Turgenev broke the trance first, pushing Boniface down the path in the opposite direction of the gatehouse. They reached an indistinct Ford, and Turgenev flipped the trunk. "You know the drill."

sixty-four

Once in the trunk with the lid shut, plunging him into complete darkness, Boniface lost any sense of direction. Logically, the car would have returned to Richmond Green, but even then he couldn't sure, and the route after that was a complete mystery. By the stop/start nature of the driving, at times the route might have been a mystery to Turgenev as well, assuming he was still driving.

At first, the driver seemed to have a destination in mind. The car was driven hard and then parked for a few minutes before returning to its journey. After a second stop, something was loaded onto the back seat.

Following the second stop, there was some fast driving over poorly maintained streets. After that the driver seemed settled on his route, with one or two stops, until he got near to the end, when again the route became more erratic.

It had been a couple of minutes since the driver had killed the engine, although for Boniface, in the chill of the morning and having had his body pummeled throughout the journey, it felt like hours. In the front of the car he could hear Turgenev talking, probably on the phone—he didn't think anyone else had got into the car during any of the stops.

He didn't know where they were, but there seemed one logical destination. From the trunk he could hear planes flying over—they were low and, he guessed, passing at the rate of about one every minute—and the only place Boniface knew where you got that many planes at that height was Heathrow. Added to which, the shitty, twisty, poorly designed road layout suggested the airport, and the confusion over which direction they were going when they got close told Boniface that Turgenev had—like everyone else—been confused by the roundabout at Hatton Cross. Who designs a big roundabout with little roundabouts around the edges and then tells traffic to go both ways around the big roundabout but only one way around the small ones?

Someone who hates humanity. Even Turgenev wouldn't design that roundabout as torture for his worst enemy.

The talking stopped, and one of the car doors opened. Then shut. Another door opened, then shut, and Boniface could hear the sound of heavy footsteps, Turgenev footsteps, behind the car. The trunk flipped open, and Boniface blinked into the half-light. It was still early and the sun wasn't visible, but there was more light outside than in the pitch-black trunk.

He shivered. It had been cold in his prison, but he had built up some comparative warmth, which was now spilling out into the cold English spring morning. In place of his own personal fug, the unmistakable, irritating smell of aviation fuel was pouring. Another plane flew over with its undercarriage positioned ready for landing. If planes were landing, then Boniface knew it was after 6 AM, but from the light and temperature, not much after.

He remained motionless as Turgenev stood over him, looking around the trunk. "Your hands, please." He pulled his hands from under his head and held them toward the Russian, who snapped another handcuff around the chain connecting Boniface's hands, pushed his hands back over his shoulder, and attached the other end of the restraint to the small metal child-seat hook at the back of the seat forming the rear wall of the trunk. "I love your European safety standards. They keep small children very safe and make it so much easier to make sure people stay where I leave them."

Boniface groaned, trying to roll onto his back to relieve some of the tension on his wrists.

The Russian stared at him, indifferent to his discomfort. "You are staying alive for one reason." Boniface suddenly became alert. "You are staying alive to pass a message to Kuznetsov." Boniface nodded. "It is a simple message. You know the information I have." Boniface nodded again. "Mister Kuznetsov can be assured of my silence; that information will not go any further than me, and I will never approach him again, provided I am left alone." Boniface nodded more confidently. "You understand. I am not a problem for Mister Kuznetsov, and I will not be a threat to him, provided I am left alone."

"Got it," said Boniface.

"Good. Because if he doesn't understand the message, then I'm going to come after you first to make sure he understands how serious I am." Boniface flinched as the Russian's stare bored into him. "Make sure Mister Kuznetsov understands that I will destroy him if I even suspect that I am not being left alone."

"I will," said Boniface. "Now, can you undo these cuffs, and I'll go and tell him?" He tugged at the cuffs and found no slack.

Turgenev had the bored look of a schoolteacher who would rather be having a drink than dealing with a child who didn't understand some sort of rudimentary natural law.

"How long will you leave me here? I need to get out if I'm going to pass on your message. Will you call the police when you're about to board your plane?"

Turgenev laughed. "Who says I'm flying? This might be a convenient place to change cars." His face showed no emotion. "Don't worry, they'll find you soon enough. You might be here for a few hours. Maybe days. But they'll figure out soon enough that this is a stolen car...that is, once whoever owns it figures it's missing."

Boniface sighed.

"But to show you how much I care, I've got some presents for you." His tone was sarcastic. His face a confusion of staring eyes and a forced smile. "Yes, you, Mister Boniface. Some presents just for you."

He reached into his pocket and pulled out a key ring. "The policemen at the university gave this to me." He flicked through the keys and held one up. "Here's the key to undo your handcuffs." He laid the key ring about 12 inches in front of Boniface's nose with one key separated.

Boniface tugged at his restraints.

"I know you're enthusiastic to get to your present, but you're going to have to be patient. And anyway, you haven't seen what else I've got for you."

He took the car key and laid it next to the handcuff key. "Now I've heard that you don't drive, what with..." he mimed drinking from a bottle, "but once you're out of here, perhaps you can find someone else to take you home. And lastly." He laid a parking ticket next to the car key. "Your ticket out of here. I'm sure you can charge that expense back to Mister Kuznetsov."

The Russian stepped back and checked his pockets, dumping the detritus he found into the trunk. "One last thought for you. Don't bother shouting: You're parked in a distant corner of the parking lot, so no one will hear you, and no one is going to be passing because there are no empty parking spaces." He slammed the lid, leaving Boniface in darkness, trapped with the smell of aviation fuel and cold air.

The trunk flipped open again. "Silly me. I almost forgot." Turgenev held out Boniface's phone. "In case you need to make any calls. Here you go." The Russian slid the phone into Boniface's inside jacket pocket, patting it in position.

He slammed the lid again. Boniface listened as the steps became softer, then louder.

The trunk flipped open for a third time. "There's one thing that's nagging at me—you seemed too ready to give me that thumb drive."

"You had a gun," said Boniface without emotion.

"But still, taking the time to make sure I had a working thumb drive and throwing that broken one away..." The Russian leaned into the trunk, thrusting his hands into Boniface's jacket pockets, then into his trouser pockets.

He stepped back, grinning and holding the second thumb drive for Boniface to see.

sixty–five

Sergey Krylov felt a buzz in his crotch.

The music was pounding—Def Leppard's "Pour Some Sugar on Me"—and the dancers were working, each throwing the same shapes as the others, each thrashing in a way they thought was sexy, and if not sexy, well, they were doing what they knew would generate tips. The Russian relaxed as he felt the pleasure of the buzz, then jolted and reached into his jeans.

His pleasure prematurely interrupted, he yanked his phone out of his pocket and looked at the screen. He didn't recognize the caller, but from the number it was someone inside the Silver Spike. He hit the answer button, pulled the phone close, and shouted, "Wait while I go somewhere quiet!"

He stood, pushed his way through a few drunk businessmen—their ties at half mast, their suits crumpled and stained—groping any female flesh they could reach as the bouncers encouraged them toward the rear exit and the privacy offered by the back alley, where Krylov knew the CCTV cameras always seemed to be in need of repair.

The barman stood aside as the Russian walked behind the bar, leaving the flashing lights and stepping through a door into a concrete corridor, lit by a single flickering strip light suspended from thin chains. The door moved slowly behind him as the spring closer narrowed the gap to about four inches, then slammed the heavy door shut, muffling the sound outside.

"This is Krylov." He straightened and put his finger in his ear away from the phone, and pushed the phone closer to his head. He nodded, hung up, then called another number. "Grigorii. Get a car and meet me outside the club." He paused. "Now."

The rotating spotlight caught his line of sight as he pulled the door and headed back to his seat. Putting on his leather jacket, he headed for the exit, taking the wide spiral steps up to the ground level—with each step, feeling the transition from the desert-dry air conditioning to the gentle damp of a breaking English morning in spring.

As he stepped into the early morning light he took a deep breath, substituting the odor of other people with pure air. From the service road running down the side of the club, two men in suits walked unsteadily. Krylov smirked; when he had last seen them, they had been far friskier with their hands, and they didn't have the red scuffmarks on their faces nor the blood on their shirts, and their suits were only crumpled, not ripped.

He straightened his jeans, slipped off his jacket, and pulled his T-shirt straight as the gunmetal grey Vauxhall Insignia pulled up, skidding the last few feet as the driver leaned over to push the door, which Krylov slammed behind him. "Drive. The boss has a job for us."

"What does Turgenev want us to do?"

"Not him, *the* boss. And I don't know—all I know is he wants us to get to Heathrow airport. He's going to call, so drive." He pointed, indicating to then turn left, and fell back in his seat as the car tires squealed and dug into the road.

Krylov pulled down the sun visor in front of him and looked at his visage in the mirror: dull, pockmarked skin, sunken on his skull, and maybe ten days' growth of hair on the top of his head. He slapped his cheeks, but failing to encourage any signs of life, he turned to compare his complexion with his driver's. "Did you shave this morning?"

"An hour ago," said the driver, feeling the smoothness of his chin. "My father was Greek—at least, the man my mother thinks was my father was Greek—and so I spend my whole life looking like I need to take a blade to my face."

The older man grunted, fixing on the crescent-shaped scar behind the swarthy man's ear.

"So why are we getting instructions from Mister Kuznetsov? Why is he getting up early to talk to us?" asked the driver.

"I don't know; I spoke to his secretary, who told me he needs us at Heathrow. And as far as he's concerned, this isn't early. He gets up at five every morning and then spends at least an hour with his trainer."

The driver snorted. "Pretty girl in Lycra, big butt, big..."

Krylov cut him off. "You remember when you were first assigned to the unit and joined the training battalion?" The driver grunted. "You remember those trainers—sergeants who did anything they could to break you?"

The driver talked quietly, as if trying to force grit out of his throat without scratching. "Bastards. They treated you like a dog, pushed you beyond your limits, made you want to kill them, and if you didn't kill them, you wanted to kill yourself. In the end, they left you filled with rage. You go to war because it's preferable to the training camp and less violent."

The older man mirrored the driver, slowly nodding. "That's who trains Mister Kuznetsov. One of the training battalion sergeants." The driver turned to face Krylov, who remained impassive and pointed back to the road. "Focus. He needs us alive."

sixty–six

Each time his phone rang, Boniface pulled at the cuffs chained behind his head, giving up the struggle in the dark when the pain around his wrists won the battle.

Reflexively, he reached for his phone to check the time and winced as the cuffs again bit into his raw flesh. With the pain subsiding, he tried to estimate the number of planes that had arrived since Turgenev had left him. Best guess? Perhaps one hundred and fifty? If there was a plane landing every forty-five seconds, perhaps every minute, it might be around two hours since the Russian had departed. Two hours, which—assuming there was a convenient flight—was enough time for the shaven-headed thug to buy a ticket, get on a plane, and leave. And after that, if the plane had a phone and Turgenev used it, then Boniface would be free. If not, he didn't know how many hours, or days, he would be waiting in the dark.

The sound of the planes passing a few feet overhead masked other sounds, and several times he became aware that someone had been close but that he hadn't heard them until it was too late. Perhaps there was a car door closing in the distance, or some footsteps that were sharp enough that they couldn't be too far away, or maybe a car passing.

As a door slammed, he became aware that someone had closed the door of the car next to him. He shouted. The response was the engine coming to life with the driver revving until the engine gained some rhythm. And in case Boniface could be heard, the driver made sure his CD—some misguided 1990s dance music—was loud enough to induce permanent hearing loss.

Boniface lost heart as he heard the driver grinding the car into gear and pushing the engine. The motor roared, and suddenly his prison was jolted sideways—the violent lurch accompanied by the sound of metal fighting metal.

The noise of torture ended, and Boniface felt his car rock back to the level. The engine of the other car stalled, the music stopped, and a door opened. Footsteps. "Ah shit!" A slurred, angry voice.

Boniface opened his throat and screamed; a deep, throaty roar, partly in fear, partly in desperation, until the trunk flipped open, blinding him with the light of a bright spring morning.

He fell silent and looked up. Where previously there had been a shaven-headed Russian, now a man of average height stood, a bit pudgy around the edges from too many expensed dinners, a decent but crumpled suit, unshaven with dark rings under his eyes, and in need of a few hours' work on his hair. "Jesus Christ, man. What the hell happened to you?"

Boniface exhaled slowly. "Long story. See that key there…" He pointed to the handcuff key with his nose. "It undoes these handcuffs, if you would be so kind." He threw his head backward, indicating his cuffed hands.

The man stood with his mouth open, looking around Boniface's prison.

"Please," said Boniface. "It's not the most comfortable position I've ever been in."

"Sorry," said the man, still staring at Boniface as he picked up the key before he leaned into the gaping hole. Boniface recognized the smell of whisky. If he hadn't been so desperate, he would have sneered at someone who could drink the swill they hand out for free on airplanes; this guy was a drinker, not a connoisseur.

"Just got off a plane?" asked Boniface.

"For my sins they put me on the red-eye," said the man, fiddling to remove the cuffs that locked Boniface to the child-seat hook. "There," he said triumphantly as Boniface flopped his arms flat in front of himself.

"That feels good. Thank you. Now if you could help me get out of here, then perhaps you can get these cuffs off my wrists. It'll be much easier for you when I'm out."

Boniface rolled over, pushing himself up to a kneeling position. "That hurts."

The disheveled man offered Boniface a hand and put his other behind his head. "Careful. You don't want to knock yourself."

Boniface leaned on the man while half standing in the back of the car and jumped, landing gracelessly but finding his feet. He held out his hands, and the other man removed the restraint, standing back as Boniface started to vigorously shake his arms and stamp his feet, slowly rotating on the spot.

As he completed a full rotation he stopped, took a deep breath, closed his eyes, and exhaled, bowing his head. The other man remained silent. Boniface raised his face, opened his eyes, smiled broadly, and held out his hand. "Pleased to meet you, savior. I'm Boniface, Alexander Boniface, but please call me Boniface."

The other man looked befuddled as he shook hands. "Clive Barratt. Slightly shocked, but very pleased to meet you…Boniface."

"Really good to meet you, Clive," said Boniface, reaching into the car to grab his phone and check the time. "It's a really long story, and I'd love to explain, and I *will* explain, but first, could you drive me to the terminals—terminal three, I think."

"Shouldn't we call someone?"

Boniface shook his head slowly. "The guy that did this has probably already left the country. But if he hasn't, then there's someone else who might be in danger, and I need to get to her."

Barratt remained motionless, his eyes growing larger.

"Please." Boniface pursed his lips and cocked his head, waiting.

"Oh, of course. Of course. Get in." Barratt turned and walked toward his door, allowing Boniface a view of his car, a four-door black Mercedes—one of the lower-priced models—gouged down its length. Boniface turned to the Ford he had traveled in, looking at the crumpled rear quarter with scrapings of black paint flaking off, grabbed the car key that had been left in front of him in the trunk, slammed the lid, and walked to the passenger door of the Mercedes.

As Boniface enjoyed the feeling of being softly held in a car seat rather than thrown in the trunk, he turned to his driver. "Please don't think I'm being rude, but I've got a call I really need to make. As you saw, I've been a bit tied up."

"Sure," said Barratt, firing up the engine. Nineties dance music bombarded them from all directions. He smacked the off button. "Sorry about that." His cheeks went slightly red. "The kids love it." Boniface nodded, unconvinced, and pulled out his phone. The driver slapped the car into gear and stepped on the pedal, throwing both men back in their seats as the vehicle zigzagged to the exit.

"On the perimeter road outside Heathrow airport." His call answered. "I'm...yeah, I'm fine. Had a bit of trouble, which is why I..." Boniface watched as the car drifted to the left, Barratt corrected, and then drifted to the right. Boniface checked his seat belt, braced his legs, and then looked away from the road. "Sorry, slightly distracted... Anyway, I had a bit of trouble last night so I couldn't call you back, but I'm fine. I don't have time to explain, but I need you to do something."

The car nudged the curb, a squeal of rubber and a jolt. "Sorry about that," said Barratt with a slight look of surprise on his face.

"You need to get someone, no make that several people, to Sherborne's place...yes Trumpeters' House. Real people, good people, people you trust, people who will ask questions and follow leads—and find out what happened there last night." Boniface listened to his former wife, then continued. "It was bloody. We left Sherborne and Ellen Armstrong there. They didn't look healthy, but I called an ambulance as we left."

Barratt jerked the car into the right-hand lane and followed the filter onto the slip road leading under the runway and into the airport.

"You had a reporter down there? Really? Nope. Didn't see the guy, but I'm guessing he's dead. Was he driving a Ford?" Boniface stared into the distance, not focusing on anything in particular as he listened. "Three things I know about Turgenev: He tries to be cautious, he's scared, and he's very good at killing people. Bring those three together, and if your guy was bumbling around outside Trumpeters' House, our Russian friend would have seen him and killed him. Probably killed him with his bare hands."

Boniface's eyes came into focus, and he shot out his hand to set the steering wheel straight. Barratt looked at him, his mouth open. He shook himself back to consciousness. "Sorry, Boniface, I er..." The car straightened.

"I'm about to lose you as we go into the tunnel," said Boniface. "Find out what's been happening and call me back when you have spoken to someone you trust. Last night's headline had enough mistakes for this week."

The phone went dead.

sixty-seven

Krylov answered before the second ring.

Grigorii Belotserkovsky, the swarthy driver, kept the gunmetal-gray Vauxhall Insignia moving swiftly, but with little finesse, toward Heathrow airport, passing along an anonymous strip of asphalt cutting between Victorian terraces built from sandstone-colored bricks, blackened through years of proximity to passing internal combustion engines.

"Yes Mister Kuznetsov, this is Krylov." Krylov sat up straighter in his seat and pulled his shoulders back. "Nikolay. Yes." The swarthy man turned to Krylov, with a questioning look. The older man drew his finger from his nose across his cheek as if to indicate a scar.

The swarthy man raised his eyebrows, mirrored the finger across his cheek, and mouthed "Nikolay," then returned his focus to the road.

Krylov listened, then continued. "Yes. I saw Nikolay leave yesterday. Mister Turgenev told me that I might have to send some items home for him." He jolted in his seat as if he had received an electrical shock. "My understanding was that Nikolay was going home... I didn't get a reason or an explanation. Yes... That was Mister Turgenev. Yesterday. Early evening. Maybe six PM."

The remaining color drained from the passenger's dull, pockmarked face, and he opened his eyes wider. "Gone? Turgenev disappeared... No, sir, I haven't heard from him since we spoke about Nikolay."

The swarthy man pointed to himself—the sound of his index finger hitting his chest audible above the sound of the engine. Krylov looked to him, and the other man mouthed, "I saw him."

"Sir. Grigorii saw him after that." He turned to the swarthy man. "You were behind the desk in reception were you, Grigorii?" The other man nodded. "What time was that?"

"He went out on his bike at around eleven. I don't know—we don't note his movements. Said he would be back soon, but he hadn't come back when I left at midnight."

"And you haven't seen him since?" The swarthy man shook his head. Krylov pulled the phone closer to his ear. "No, Mister Kuznetsov. Grigorii last saw Mister Turgenev at about eleven PM and hasn't seen him since."

A plane passed overhead, its undercarriage dropped, ready for landing. Krylov acknowledged the other man's questioning look, pointed in the direction of the plane, then pointed back at the road, which had now broadened into a three-lane highway with light industrial buildings— most displaying the logos of international freight couriers—set well back from the road. In the distance, a row of hotels sat, each looking the same, only differentiated by the neon sign displaying the name of the chain. The pockmarked man waved his hand in their direction, and the driver accelerated.

"Yes. We're close to the airport now, sir." He listened. "Maybe five minutes... Boniface. Boniface. Right. You'll send a picture... I understand. Not in public. We will, sir."

Krylov hung up and cracked his window, taking a lung-full of oxygen infused with aviation fuel, then turned to his driver. "Well, Grigorii Belotserkovsky. You may have only been working with us for a few days, but there has been a significant change. Apparently, as the cowboys would say, Turgenev walked off the reservation yesterday. It seems you were the last person to see him."

"But that was only a few hours ago. Isn't it a bit early to be worrying? Hasn't he found a woman or something?"

"Grigorii. You're young, and you don't know better, so I'll forgive you this once." He scrunched his face, then released quickly, his image returning to its usual lifeless state. "When you were in the army, loyalty was a matter of life and death. For Mister Kuznetsov, loyalty is more important than that. You do not, and will not, have a disloyal thought. Turgenev understood that."

He paused and looked out the window, then turned back to the driver. "If Turgenev has been gone for this long, then he's either dead or gone. And if he isn't dead, then he will be dead as soon as Kuznetsov knows where he is."

A silence hung between the two men, broken by the pockmarked man's phone beeping. He looked down at the phone, then back to the driver. "The boss is angry, and we must fix it. He knows we didn't cause the problem, but he'll blame us for not fixing it. There's no one else to hold responsible—Turgenev has gone, Nikolay is missing. His session with his trainer must have made him even angrier, and he's taking all his rage out on us."

"So why has he sent us to Heathrow?"

Krylov sighed. "He thinks Turgenev might be there."

"But we'll never..."

"I know. And Kuznetsov understands. But he wants us to be close. He wants us to look, and if it goes wrong and we're here, then we've got a problem." The driver made a noncommittal sound, acknowledging that an order had been given. "And he also wants us to look for someone called Bonny-something." He looked back at his phone. "Boniface, that's it."

"Who?"

"Someone with expensive suits and soft hands who was doing something with some dead professor that Kuznetsov is upset about. Kuznetsov seems to think this Bon...Boniface...is with Turgenev or has helped him to escape."

The driver snorted. "Turgenev? Take help from someone who works in an office? Someone who uses hand cream and probably moisturizes?" He shook his head, sneering.

"I know. But he wants us to look for him, and all we've got is his photo." He held his phone out. "Turgenev will be expecting us, and so he'll hide. Kuznetsov reckons that this Boniface man will be much easier to find, so we'll go after him."

"Let me see the picture," said the driver, pulling Krylov's hand holding the phone into his line of sight. His eyes flicked to the screen. "I know him." He released the other man's hand. "I saw him yesterday. He met with Mister Kuznetsov. I'll recognize him."

sixty–eight

"That lane."

Having given the order when the gouged black Mercedes emerged from the tunnel and joined Heathrow airport's inner ring road, Boniface pointed in the direction of the terminal three road. The car drifted across two lanes as Clive Barratt moved without looking and without noticing the chorus of angry horns behind him.

The car jerked to a halt in the drop-off line outside the terminal, no apparent effort having been made to pull up to the curb. "Well, sir, thank you. You saved me; you got me here. Give me your card, and I'll call to arrange dinner, where I can explain the whole story." He offered his hand, the two men shook, and Boniface was out of the car and into the terminal building.

He was scanning across the rows and down the columns of the arrivals screens when his phone rang. "Montbretia, hi. Where are you?" He turned away from the screens, nestling the phone into his shoulder. "Passport control... In a long queue... Not an EU National... Right then, I'll get a cup of tea... Yes, very English... Call me when you're in the baggage hall... No, I'm sorry, Ellen...couldn't make it. She says 'hi,' but she had a life or death issue that needed to be dealt with... No, everything's fine." Boniface scrunched his eyes shut. "Anyway, you've got me as your host this morning, so give me a call when you're sure you're not going to be deported."

He hung up and sighed deeply, bowing his head, lost in silent contemplation. A small pink plastic suitcase on wheels knocked his ankle. His eyes followed the lead from the case to a small girl, no more than four years old, with blond hair tied back in a neat ponytail, pulling with both hands to free her luggage from his ankle. "I am so, so sorry," said the woman standing next to the child. Her look was similar, but her shade of blond tried too hard and seemed to suggest envy of the child. The iron grip around her collection of itineraries, booking details, and passports, coupled with a mis-buttoned blouse, all pointed to someone who wasn't a natural organizer.

Boniface squatted down and looked directly at the girl, unhooking the case while keeping a look of deep concern on his face. "I'm sorry. Did I get in your way?" She pushed out her bottom lip and nodded vigorously, her face breaking into a smile as she took back control of the case. He stood and looked at the mother's apologetic face. "It's not a problem. Really, it's fine," he said and then turned back to grin at the child, trying to ignore his vision of how her mother would spend the next several hours transferring all of her pent-up stress to the little girl. He couldn't, so he turned away, looking to see which of the cafés offered internet access.

Ye Olde Londone Coffee House seemed to fit the bill, even if the name made Boniface cringe with embarrassment for his city. At the top of the stairs he turned into the café and found himself looking at the food. Picking out a shrink-wrapped bacon sandwich, he joined the queue. "Cup of tea and this...please." He grabbed a tray, dropped the sandwich onto it, and placed the two next to the cash register.

One of the servers sneered, filling a cup of hot water and dropping a tea bag onto the surface. Boniface felt the unique disappointment that comes from the expectation of poorly made tea. "Heated?" asked the man behind the register, wiping his nose on the back of his latex-gloved hand.

"The tea?"

"The sandwich."

"Oh. Sorry. Please. Yes."

The disapproving tea-maker placed the cup with the floating tea bag onto the tray and picked up the sandwich, ripping open the plastic and flipping it into a microwave. Boniface looked at the water in the cup; a small trail of brown was starting to seep from the tea bag, but without any apparent desire to impart any flavor.

The nose-wiping cashier put a small stand holding the number 17 on the tray. "Seven pounds thirty."

He tried to hide his shock as he offered a £10 note. "Milk?" The nose-wiper tilted his head toward the end of the counter, dropping the change and a receipt onto the tray as he turned to address his monosyllabic question to the next person in line.

Boniface picked up two small plastic milk pots and three sugar packets from the end of the counter and made his way to the row of two old and battered computers standing against a wall at the far end of the café. He picked up one of the coins from his change, dropping it into the slot while he continued to unload his tray. He squeezed the tea bag, placing it on the tray, then added milk together with twice his normal amount of sugar.

He flipped his phone and checked the message received a few hours ago. With a few clicks on the computer, he was back in Nigel's online storage, downloading the photos. He took a sip of his tea, winced, and put it to the side. It was at least twelve hours since he'd had anything to drink, but even he couldn't drink that.

"Number seventeen!" a voice shouted across the room. Boniface contemplated whether he was brave enough for a second sip. "Number seventeen." The voice seemed weary.

"Here." Boniface raised his hand. Surely a premade bacon sandwich had to be better than a bad cup of tea. The nose-wiper carelessly dropped a plate with his sandwich in front of him. Boniface spent a moment or two assessing the risk of food poisoning before the need for food kicked in. He took a large bite and stared back at the screen.

With a few clicks, he opened his email. He had last checked his messages shortly before he had left for his meeting with Kuznetsov. Since then, he had received around five hundred emails, and only about half of those were spam. He could deal with the technology, but he needed someone to help him with the organization. He ignored the unread mail and started a new message. After attaching the photos he had downloaded from Nigel's online storage, he hit the send button.

sixty-nine

The gunmetal-gray Vauxhall Insignia sluggishly crawled past the long-term parking lot on Eastern Perimeter Road and turned onto Northern Perimeter Road, leaving the row upon row of abandoned motor vehicles, and followed the high barbed-wire fence around the runway, which was surrounded by young men in cheap weatherproof clothing carrying binoculars, cameras, and notebooks, all pointing excitedly at each arriving plane. "You don't think this guy will be camouflaging himself as a plane spotter?"

Both men scanned their surroundings like paranoid owls who had drunk too much coffee, the driver gripping the steering wheel with his left hand and scratching his nose with his right.

The phone rang. Its owner answered it before the second ring. "Krylov." He stiffened. "Sir... Terminal buildings. Fast!" He pushed his phone into his jeans as the car sped up, moving into the right-hand lane. "Boniface's phone signal has been tracked in terminal three."

The driver held the wheel tight, throwing the car to the right, then cut across two lanes to get to the left lane, took the ramp down, and turned left at the scale-model Airbus to follow the road to the terminals. "Hurry up!" he shouted at the bus in front of him as a minicab blocked him on the other side. "Are we sure this is Bonny-whatever-his-name-is?" He hit his horn and veered toward the minicab beside him. The minicab driver responded with his horn, but when the swarthy man didn't seem to yield, braked to allow him into his line.

"We're sure it's Boniface's phone." He sighed, grimacing. "And even if we're not sure, we're sure—Kuznetsov has told us we're sure. It could be Boniface, it could be Turgenev with Boniface's phone—we don't know anything except that we have orders to look."

The car shot out of the tunnel into the jumble of roads that fanned in front of them, before then contracting as the inner ring–road traffic joined the flow. "There." Krylov pointed at the sign for terminal three, and the driver accelerated, cutting across the traffic, daring anyone to get in his way as he followed the road.

"If you've seen him, then there's a chance Boniface can recognize you, so go to a gift shop first. Buy yourself a hat and some sunglasses. Look like a tourist, not like..." He looked the driver up and down. "Well...do anything but look like you. We want to find this guy and figure what he's up to. We don't want to scare him and make him run."

"But we can scare him later?"

"Oh yeah. Scare him a lot. It'll be easy—I'll rip his suit a bit. That'll make him cry. But first we need to know what he's been doing. Other people have made mistakes...big mistakes, so we can't afford to. This is all about being quick and quiet. We need to find and follow—if he's dead, then we can't ask him questions. But once we've got his answers...then we won't need him alive."

The car continued to accelerate, tires screeching through the next bend. It pulled up with a skid, throwing both men forward and then back into their seats as the vehicle stopped. Each rolled out, slamming his door behind, and started jogging toward the terminal.

seventy

As the email he had promised to send to Ellen started to lazily pass its cargo across the wires, Boniface picked up his bacon sandwich and took another bite. Given its provenance, it was surprisingly good and was consumed in three further bites as the email finished sending.

The nine photos on Nigel's online storage stared back at him. He created a new email addressed to himself and then stopped, falling back into his seat and softly muttering, "Don't need to do that—I've got a copy of the email I sent to Ellen."

Staring at the nine thumbnails as he chewed. "Gotta do it," he muttered and selected the nine photographs before hitting the delete button. He watched as the online storage showed a graphic display dragging each individual photo file to a bin until eventually the folder was empty.

He logged out and then went to the files he had copied to the local machine, deleted them, opened the recycle bin, located the nine files he had just deleted, and deleted them from the recycle bin. "Vanya will be pleased," he said softly, standing.

As he reached the bottom of the stairs he walked to the arrivals area, looking for somewhere to stand where he could see and be seen. He wondered whether he should make a sign so that Montbretia would find him.

The contemplation was disrupted by his phone. "Hi. How are you doing?" Boniface stopped walking. "You've got your luggage and you've just come through customs. That was fast...you're nearly here." The flood spilling from arrivals walked around him as he talked. "So what am I looking for?" He listened, repeating fragments. "Five-nine, shoulder-length brown hair, rucksack, white shirt, jeans, desert boots, pretty scuffed, phone in hand, standing in front of me if I lift my head..."

Boniface's vision found the sandy-colored desert boots laced up above the ankles, disappearing under the end of a pair of jeans, faded and close-fitting without being skintight. As he lifted his head he saw the white cotton shirt, which looked incredibly fresh, a tailored fit with brown buttons and sleeves neatly folded back. His gaze passed the rich brown hair lying over the rucksack straps and found the broad grin, the strip of freckles over the small nose, and the dark-green eyes. "Good to meet you, Boniface."

"But..."

"I recognized you from your website, although...you did seem to have a better suit on for those photos." Self-consciously, Boniface looked down at himself, pausing to notice his scuffed, dirty shoes, the large patches of mud on his suit, the shredded tie, and the crumpled shirt. "Rough night?"

"Rough night, long story, and needing a dry cleaner and a good bath are the very least of my problems. Let's get out of here."

"Sounds good to me." Montbretia was still grinning.

"Can you drive?" asked Boniface.

"Of course."

"Then let me take your rucksack, and follow me," said Boniface, turning and bumping into a tall man with about ten days' growth on his head, wearing jeans and a leather jacket. "I'm…" Boniface stopped, mouth open, color draining from his face as he took in the pockmarked skin. He looked again. "I'm sorry…I…I thought you were…someone else."

"No problem," said the stranger in an accent with a distinct Russian flavor.

Boniface took the rucksack. "This way, Montbretia. Let's go somewhere and get you a decent breakfast, and I can start to explain."

The bus followed its circle route between terminals, finally dropping them at the long-term parking lot. After some time looking for the parking ticket in the trunk and then paying the equivalent of what it would cost for dinner in a Michelin starred restaurant to get out of the parking lot, Boniface handed the keys to Montbretia who cautiously drove the Ford with Boniface sitting silently to allow her to concentrate. His only communication was the occasional hand gesture to suggest direction and a few ambiguous comments when Montbretia asked about her sister.

"I hate stick shifts."

"It's a family failing," said Boniface. "Left at the end here."

Montbretia pulled out and joined the flow of traffic. "Is that the Thames?"

"Yes."

"And do people live in those houseboats?"

"On some. But it gets a bit cold in winter." Montbretia's head flicked to look at the river before she returned her concentration to the road. "So where to?"

"Our destination is in sight," said Boniface.

"I see a wall. Bit of an old wall, if truth be told."

"Beyond the wall." He paused. "At the roundabout, turn right, then take the entrance on the left with the animals on top of the pillars."

Montbretia followed the instructions, slowing as she turned into the gateway. "Wow. I mean wow, wow, wow! This is proper, proper England. Is this…"

Boniface felt like a proud parent, keen to brag to all his friends about his child's achievement. "Yup. Hampton Court Palace." He turned to

Montbretia. "And by the way, it never ceases to amaze, however often you come here." The car behind honked. "Park up... It's on the left here."

The two stepped out of the car into the sun. "Do you want to start taking some pictures while I get the tickets?" Montbretia opened the back door and rummaged through her rucksack while Boniface stood at the back of the car, admiring the rear wing refashioned by Clive Barratt.

"Ouch," said Montbretia, walking around to join him.

"Mmm." He continued, his voice distracted. "I'll get the tickets and find you somewhere around there."

"I'll be waiting."

He watched Montbretia walk toward the Great Gatehouse, her camera swinging from her hand, before he turned into the ticket office. It was an old building—new by Hampton Court standards, but old by everyone else's. The inside had all the lack of charm of a heritage center that could be found anywhere in the UK: large, dark porcelain stone-effect tiles on the floor; varnished oak tables that were still oak-colored, resembling the contents of a Swedish furniture store catalog, not having had the time to darken like the blackened, untreated oak in the Palace. Each table was covered with a range of cheap and dog-eared publications highlighting other English heritage locations for the uninspired tourist. Boniface bought two tickets and winced at the price.

The ring of his phone told him that Veronica was calling. He answered, slinking into a corner of the room, looking to confirm he wasn't overheard. "Talk." The color slowly drained from his face, dragging his soul and spirit with it. He felt himself go weak and started to wobble, landing in a nearby cheap oak-framed chair with fabric-covered padding, his head resting on his knees.

seventy-one

Boniface sat up. Feeling his eyes burn, tears streaming.

He wiped his eyes with the back of his hand, unsure of how long he had been sitting in the ticket office or who had been watching him.

After several deep breaths, he slowly got to his feet, taking his first few steps with the precision of a dizzy child. There was an exit sign above the door. He fixed his sight on the sign and tried to walk with purpose, picking up speed until he was outside and able to breathe fresh air again.

He took several gulps of clean oxygen, tugged his lapels to straighten his jacket, tucked his shirt in, and ran his hand through his hair, picking out grass, mud, and cow shit before wiping his eyes again and going to search for Montbretia.

Turning the corner he saw the figure: desert boots, jeans, immaculate white shirt, shoulder-length chestnut hair recently cut, engrossed in capturing the majesty of Hampton Court palace from every angle and in the changing light as the clouds moved across the fresh spring sky.

Boniface stepped onto the main drive leading up to the Great Gate-house, relieved to be able to stroll along the length without urgency. Even more pleased that he wasn't being chased by a homicidal Russian.

He caught up with Montbretia. "Hey Boniface. Why the police cars and the crime-scene tape?"

Boniface looked back to the guard hut, now surrounded by police crime-scene tape vibrating in the breeze. He didn't want to lie, again, so he did his best to brush off the question and shrugged nonchalantly.

Montbretia, looking irrepressibly happy, like a puppy, seemed content with the unspoken answer. "I've got a load of photos. They'll be great for the blog, and Ellen will love what I'm going to say. So where does the tour begin?"

Boniface cocked his head and pointed away from the Great Gate-house. "This way."

They followed the path through the kitchen garden—going against the flow of tourists heading for the Great Gatehouse and Anne Boleyn's Gate—and then along a quieter path.

Montbretia looked at the sign. "What's a tiltyard?"

"Where they tilted," said Boniface flatly. His companion looked confused. "Jousted," he added, leaning forward as if holding a lance.

Silence fell between them again. Boniface pale, his eyes still stinging, feeling sick, but not feeling anything that couldn't be blotted out by taking up drinking again.

"You look like shit." Montbretia broke the wordlessness as Boniface let his eyes point to the path they should follow. "No...I mean, when you met me at the airport, you looked like shit, and that hasn't changed. But there's something more now; you look worse, and more than ten minutes worse. And you've gone quiet—I know you were quiet when I was driving—but this is break-up-with-your-girlfriend quiet. What's up?"

Past the end of a wall, they moved out of the direct sunlight into a quiet, secluded area, away from the main features drawing the visitors. Boniface ignored the keep-off-the-grass sign, walking until the two were a distance from the path in a corner formed by two Tudor walls. He sat down on the grass, still damp with the previous night's dew, unworried by his wet ass or any damage to the suit, and motioned for Montbretia to join him.

"You do know that it's humor that gets a girl into bed, not wet grass," said Montbretia, sitting opposite him, resting against an old twisted tree. Boniface looked up, allowing her to see his bloodshot eyes with tears starting to flow. Her face fell, taking a look of concern.

"Your sister and I had a bad night last night. We saw things that we never wanted to see."

"Long story," whispered Montbretia.

"Long story." Boniface nodded. "Let me get to the important part that you need to hear." He wiped a tear that was trickling beside his nose. "You've heard of her publisher, Richard Sherborne?"

"The fat one with the harem? Is it still a harem when all the members post-menopausal?"

"That's the one." Boniface paused. "After you spoke to Ellen last night, we went to Sherborne's house. Again, long story. While we were there, we were held at gunpoint by a man called Turgenev."

"You're just making up Russian names to make your story sound more adventurous." Montbretia smirked, dropping the mirth when Boniface didn't reciprocate.

"The guy is dangerous." Nothing registered on Montbretia's face. "The crime-scene tape around the guard hut inside the gate?"

Montbretia bobbed her head once, seemingly apprehensive about agreeing.

"I'm guessing he killed a man last night. There." Boniface watched the shock on her face turn to fear. "And that wasn't the first nor the last person he killed yesterday."

"This man was holding you at gunpoint?"

Boniface flicked his eyelids closed to acknowledge.

"You and Ellen."

"Yeah." Boniface's voice faded, his words communicated through aspiration. "Sherborne took a chance. He has a collection of antique flintlock pistols. I don't know where he got the gunpowder or when he loaded it, but he tried to defend us. Ellen tried to stop him. Turgenev knew you were coming and threatened you. She wanted to protect you."

Montbretia trembled.

"The gun misfired."

Montbretia gasped, putting her hand over her mouth. "Tell me Ellen's alright."

Boniface slowly shook his head. "Ellen was hurt, badly. She was taken to hospital. She didn't recover and died two hours ago."

She laughed. "This is a great joke. Awful joke, but I almost believed you. Russians... Antique guns..."

Boniface shook his head, tears streaming down his cheeks. He reached and grabbed Montbretia, holding her while she sobbed.

seventy-two

"Where is she? I need to be with her." Montbretia pulled back from Boniface and tried to stand, falling back to the ground, clutching at Boniface and sobbing. "I need to be with my sister. She can't be alone."

Boniface awkwardly reached into his pocket and pulled out his handkerchief. Before last night it was clean and white. Now it was creased and stained with mud and blood, and Ellen's tears. He offered it to Montbretia. "I'm sorry, it's all I've got."

She took it, looked for a less dirty patch, mopped her eyes, and then looked up at Boniface, two sets of bloodshot, tear-stained eyes making contact. "I want to be with my sister, Boniface. I want to be with her."

"I know. But she's being looked after now." He lowered his head, his voice a whisper. "And there's a legal process...but she's being looked after."

"It was an accident, can't we just..."

Boniface wiped his eyes with his thumb and gently shook his head. "I'm sorry. There are legal processes. But I've talked to a friend who's a newspaper editor, and she has got some of her journalists on it—they'll be able to find out much quicker than we could. She'll make sure that you're the first one to know when anything happens."

Montbretia contemplated Boniface's dirty handkerchief, rejecting another dirty patch. "Tell me the whole story. Tell me how this happened. Why are you alive while my sister is dead?"

He could see the rage and the impotent frustration building. "I'm alive because I was on one side of the room, and she was on the other. If we had swapped places, I wouldn't be here. You can't even blame the Russian; it was simply an accident."

"An accident? My sister's dead, and you say it was an accident." Montbretia stared at Boniface, silently accusing him as the tears flowed, her voice breaking. "Why didn't you stay with her?"

Boniface hung his head, tears rolling down each side of his nose. "I wanted to. Really I did. But I was in handcuffs, and Turgenev had a gun. I didn't have a choice. The only thing I could do—the thing I did do—was call the ambulance."

"And what about Sherborne? Is he dead, too?"

"Not yet. But he wasn't that far from death before we began." He looked up, with the slightest hint of a twitch at the edge of his mouth. "Sherborne is fat. Not just a bit overweight. Not cuddly. But out-and-out obese. That's one of the main reasons why he was already so close to death." He shook his head slowly. "Turgenev punched him. If Richard hadn't been so fat, the blow would have killed him, but as it is, his blubber provided some sort of padding."

Montbretia smiled. "Well, can we go and see him?"

"Soon. I'm sure the redoubtable Ada is with him, tending to his every need." He looked up. "But there are other things that need to be done, and you're not going anywhere without me being there next to you."

"I'm a big girl, Boniface. I can handle myself."

Boniface could hear the offense in her voice. "I know, but..."

"It's a long story. I get that. My sister spends a night with a homicidal maniac, and all you can say is it's a long story. Well, I'm ready for the long story now, Boniface."

The silent expectation, laced with anger and blame, froze both of them. "You will hear the story. I was there, I saw what went on, and I want you to hear everything, and you will hear it from me." He weighed how to phrase his next remarks. "But there's something I need to do first. We're both still in danger."

Montbretia jolted. "Why am I in danger? I've only just arrived."

"Because your sister was in danger and you were threatened last night." Boniface bowed his head with a small smirk. "Long story..."

"Now you're being silly, Boniface. There's no danger."

"Perhaps you're right. In fact, I hope you are, and that I'm wrong. But I've seen too many people die in the last few hours, and I'm not taking any risks. I'm going to the source to make sure that I am safe and that you are safe. The order of priority for me is one, deal with the danger, then two, explain." He held her stare.

Montbretia broke first. "Then I'm coming." She went to stand.

"Nope." Boniface left no room for discussion. "You are going to stay here where I know you're safe. I can't think of a better place to be: There are loads of cops around, and Mister Turgenev certainly won't be returning to this crime scene for a while. And if you're here, you won't get caught in any crossfire."

She still looked unconvinced as he continued. "Ellen wanted to bring you here; we talked about it last night. It's one of the most gorgeous places in the country. Take some time, walk through the grounds, have a look in the buildings. Here..." He reached into his pocket and pulled out a ticket. "I did get the tickets, before...before...before I got distracted." He looked at her. "You've had awful news. You've had news that I don't know how you ever deal with." He saw a tear start to form in her eye. "Take some time, sit with your memories of Ellen. Be patient. I'll be back as soon as I can."

Boniface started to stand. "How long will you be?" asked Montbretia.

"An hour there, ten minutes meeting, an hour back? Maybe some delay—I've got to get the train. Certainly less than three hours. I'll be here for lunch. And after lunch we can check out the Maze. I'll race you to the middle, so no cheating and checking out your route while I'm gone." Montbretia tilted her head. "Deal?" He held out his hand to shake.

"Deal," she replied, taking his hand and pulling herself to her feet.

"You've got my phone number, so call if you've got any problems, but I'll be back as soon as I can." He reached into his pocket and pulled out his wallet, handing her all his cash apart from one bill. "Just in case."

seventy-three

Grigorii Belotserkovsky remained at a distance, scratching his stubble and watching the man called Boniface with the younger woman he had met at the airport.

Boniface had taken the woman to a secluded area and had made her sit on the grass with her back to a tree before he talked to her. From the way she reacted, it had been bad news.

He then went to leave, although she appeared to not want him to depart. But he had, and before he left he took something from his pocket and gave it to her—the swarthy man guessed this was cash. But why bring her here, upset her, then give her cash?

Her blouse—which had been white when he first saw her at Heathrow—was now marked with mud and grass stains, but that didn't seem to concern her as she sat on the damp ground, weeping.

In the quiet between the passing airplanes, and when there weren't any children running around shouting, he could hear the occasional sob and snivel, punctuated with gasps for air before she put her head down, wailing, with her whole body shaking.

He watched, waiting.

Slowly she lifted her head and looked around, wiping her nose on her sleeve. He started walking toward her, careful to make enough noise that his approach would be heard.

"Please. Sorry disturb. You are lady with Mister Bonny?" Inwardly he cursed his lack of fluency with the English language—he was a soldier; he had never thought diction or translation would be important. She looked up at him, staring blankly through bloodshot eyes. "Please, Mister Bonny need you help." He held out his hand to her. "Quickly."

She remained impassive, staring up at him. "Who are you?"

"Mister Bonny need you help, now." He reached forward, putting his hands under her arms, and gently lifted. Reluctantly she stood, wiping her eyes and contemplating the Russian.

"What's happened?"

"Please now." He tried to keep the aggression out of his voice.

"I'm calling him," said the woman, reaching into her pocket and pulling out her phone.

Belotserkovsky took one step to stand square to her and smashed his arm down just behind her ear. As she made contact she wobbled, then started to fall away from him. He took two quick steps, lowering his back, then grabbed her, pulling her weight over his shoulder.

He stood straight, his victim flopping over his back, and started to walk with intent, scanning to make sure he wasn't being watched.

seventy-four

Boniface left Montbretia sitting on the damp grass, resting her back against a large tree. Her formerly crisp white blouse was now far from pristine, having become muddy when Boniface held her as she screamed, and grass stained as she lay on her side sobbing.

He walked back from the far side of the Palace grounds to the Great Gatehouse, turning onto the central drive leading to the outer gate. The memory of driving along the track last night with Ellen was clear, but he couldn't remember anything since he had left Montbretia. Logically, he knew where he had been and the route he would have taken. He was sure that he would have seen other people, but he couldn't bring the image of the route to mind or recall any faces he might have seen.

He had been running on autopilot, lost in a trance.

He stopped abruptly. Someone was blocking his way. He looked up and recognized the form—highly polished boots, jeans, well-worn leather jacket—but couldn't call to mind a name attached to the lifeless pockmarked face glaring at him.

"Mister Boniface."

Boniface stared. A flick of recognition. Of course, this was one of Kuznetsov's men—the dress code, the military stance, the invasion of personal space, and the accent told him that, but there was something more. Sure, he had more than a passing resemblance to Turgenev, but probably so did half of the former Spetsnaz members now working for oligarchs around the globe.

"Mister Boniface. Alexander Boniface."

Boniface gave up trying to remember where he had seen this face. "Just Boniface." He took half a step backward. "I'm sorry, I can't remember your name."

"Mister Turgenev has been your guardian angel. He's rather busy today so has asked me to come and have a word with you." The Russian pointed in the direction from which Boniface had just walked. "Please. Walk with me."

Boniface remained impassive, swaying on his feet, unable to assess what was being asked of him or whether he should oblige. He took a deep breath and held it before he started to talk. "Look..." He was lost again in contemplation. "Look. I've gotta get to see Kuznetsov. There are some things he needs to hear...directly...in person...you know, confidential stuff."

He started to step forward. The pockmarked Russian did not yield, but leaned toward Boniface and quietly mumbled, "Don't make me upset Mister Kuznetsov by killing you in public." He pointed back in the direction from which the Englishman had walked.

Boniface slowly turned and started to walk, the Russian immediately behind and to his right, talking into the Englishman's ear. "We're going somewhere quiet for a pleasant little chat, and if you don't want to chat..." Without looking, Boniface could feel a grin spread over the other man's face. "If you don't want to chat, well...let's get away from these people, and I'll explain."

The two proceeded, turning out of the main flow of people converging on the Great Gatehouse, and following the path through the kitchen garden, through the outer grounds of the palace, toward the tiltyard.

"So this is where Henry VIII lived? He was the big fat one? He liked eating but was less worried about CCTV cameras."

Boniface stopped. The Russian's shoulder knocked into his. "Stop. Stop playing. Stop trying to intimidate me."

The big man's face maintained its palsy-like state. His unblinking eyes locked on Boniface. "Very brave. But remember, you're here because Mister Kuznetsov didn't want us to spill blood in his office. Now walk."

The two men held their stare. The Russian threw his head to the right, and Boniface started to walk in the direction indicated. "And as we walk, Mister Boniface, you talk." The Russian walked in lock-step diagonally behind and threw his shoulder forward to knock Boniface's. "Understood?"

"Understood."

"So start with your friend, Mister Turgenev."

Boniface stopped, spinning to face the larger man. "He's not my friend."

"And yet you spent so much time with him yesterday and you're still alive. What other conclusion am I meant to draw?" The Russian stepped forward, his glare fixed on Boniface, grabbed the Englishman's crotch, and squeezed. "I'm sure your friend Turgenev—or would you prefer me to call him your co-conspirator, Turgenev—led you to believe that we're all pussycats."

Boniface felt the growing pain. Unable to twist away, he remained motionless.

The Russian didn't deviate. "If that was the case, then I'm sorry for the misunderstanding, but I'm not cuddly like he was, and I've got a much more volatile temper." He increased the pressure in his right hand— Boniface whimpered. The Russian leaned closer, assaulting Boniface with his raw breath. "There's no point pretending you don't know what I'm talking about when I know that you do."

Boniface tried to make a sound.

The Russian continued to grip Boniface, who tried to speak, tears starting to form in his eyes. "But I don't..." The pressure increased. Boniface whispered. "I didn't..."

The Russian lifted his hand, and Boniface stood on his tiptoes. "So why has Mister Turgenev let you live? That's Turgenev who's on his way to Paraguay, by the way."

"Because," yelped Boniface. "Please." He flapped his hand, and the Russian loosened his grip slightly. "Because I lied to Turgenev." His speech became a fast hiss. "He had a gun on me. I had to get out. So I told him a lie. I let him think that I was giving him something to barter with Kuznetsov. Something that he could use to guarantee his own safety and retire. If he's sitting on a plane to Paraguay, that means he hasn't reached a computer and found that what I gave him was..." Boniface modulated his voice, "junk. A few low-grade, blurry, underexposed images that no one can read."

The large Russian smirked. "You fooled Turgenev?" Boniface gave the smallest of nods, trying to blot out the memory of the second thumb drive that Turgenev took. "He'll kill you when he finds out. You do know that?" The Russian released his hand; Boniface fell to his knees, taking large gasps of breath. "Keep talking." He lifted Boniface by his collar— there was a soft ripping sound as Boniface raised up. "And keep walking. Now explain about your girlfriend. Remember, if you don't talk, I'll hurt you, and then I'll hurt your pretty little friend."

Boniface stopped. "Leave her out of this. You've done enough to hurt her and her family. Take me, but leave her."

The Russian's face fixed again in its palsy-like state. His unblinking eyes locked on Boniface. "Very brave. Very honorable. And if you want, we can talk about it. But by the time we've finished the conversation it might be too late. My friend Grigorii was never a sensitive lover. Enthusiastic, yes. But far less tender than I am. He's a very vigorous young man."

Boniface stiffened. "Who's Grigorii? What's he doing to her?"

The pockmarked Russian remained impassive. "I don't know. You're the one that wants to spend his time talking."

Boniface started to sprint toward the tree where he had left Montbretia.

"Where is she?" he gasped to the Russian jogging behind him as they reached the tree.

The Russian raised his eyebrows and started walking. Boniface followed, running to catch up, his breathing becoming labored. The Russian left the path and headed toward a groundsman's shed—a rough shiplap-clad building with reinforced metal corners holding it together like an overstuffed packing crate, except this would probably fit two cars.

He held back as they reached the double doors, as if to allow Boniface to enter first.

Boniface looked at the padlock. The lock was fastened shut, but the screws holding the hasp in the second door had been forced out. The Russian pulled the door with the padlocked attached: "In."

Boniface stepped in front of the other man and felt a blow on the back of his head.

seventy-five

There was a rasping sound. Not fast. Stone scraping on metal. Slow, consistent, deliberate, focused, with a regular rhythm.

The grinding fought its way through Boniface's ears, stabbing into his brain as he started to come around. His head throbbing and bones aching, reminding him of the physical beating his body had taken over the previous 12 hours. Cautiously, he opened his eyes, keeping his focus narrow, wincing with the pain at the back of his head as he tried to locate the sound of scraping. With each rasp he felt an involuntary spasm, and the pain of movement as his body jolted.

He tried to focus in the gloom inside what he presumed was the shed he had been led up to, but movement was hard now; his wrists and ankles had been bound, and his body seemed to have been thrown on the ground with his hands bound behind his back.

The grinding was relentless as his blurred vision flicked around the shed. Gardening tools hung on the walls—forks, spades, several bow saws, hand saws, pruning saws, loppers, and shears—and the shelves were stacked with string, tins, and packets. On the floor of the shed were two lawnmowers, a roller, and several other pieces of large gardening machinery that he recognized but couldn't put a name to, along with piled bags of fertilizer, grass seed, and old sacks.

In the half-light, as his gaze moved toward the door, he saw a man sitting on an upturned wooden crate with a shovel laid across his lap. The swarthy man was focused on his task, rubbing something in his hand over the edge of the shovel. Boniface shifted his weight, scraping the floor as he moved. The man looked up from his shovel. "Sergey."

There was a low groan from the hinge as the door moved. Boniface struggled as his eyes adjusted to the light now streaming in. Regaining focus, he could see that the pockmarked man who had persuaded him not to leave Hampton Court was now in the shed and had picked up the shovel that the other man—a swarthy man Boniface thought he might have seen at the Silver Spike—had been crafting. The pockmarked man ran his finger across the shovel's newly sharpened blade as if he were stroking a newborn kitten and turned to Boniface. "It's like a compulsion for Grigorii. He's like one of Pavlov's dogs—you give him a shovel, and he sharpens it. He won't stop until it's sharp enough for him to shave, and as you can see, he needs to shave very often."

He turned to the swarthy man. "This is good work. Are you going to shorten the handle?"

The other man stood, took the shovel, and walked over to the saws. He selected one and rested on the wooden box he had used as a seat as he started to cut the handle.

"It's his training. The only weapon you ever need is a shovel." Boniface frowned. The taller Russian moved another crate closer to his captive and sat before continuing. "Every soldier in the Russian army has a shovel, but he relies on his gun. In the Spetsnaz, you have a gun, but you rely on your shovel—it is your weapon."

The other man finished his cutting and passed his handiwork to his senior. "I'll be outside," he said and left, pushing the door behind him, returning the shed to gloom. The pockmarked man tried the weight of the short-handled sharpened shovel in his hand, then tossed it several times, spinning it and catching it by its handle.

"You see, this is sharp. Sharper than an axe. You can use it as an axe, but the sharpness makes it more effective than a knife. A knife might be, what, twenty or thirty centimeters long? This is fifty. For hand-to-hand combat that extra reach gives much better range than a knife. Plus it's heavier, so if you hit someone, you can do more damage. Hit them right..." he stared at Boniface, resting his thumb on the blade, "and they lose a limb if you're being kind. If you feel unkind, you split their head like a log. And, of course, you can throw it." He snapped the shovel back, ready to throw, and laughed, watching Boniface flinch and wince in pain as he moved.

"Why not use a gun?" asked Boniface, his voice straining.

The Russian dropped the shovel back onto his lap. "Guns are for amateurs. Guns run out. Guns miss. Guns make a noise. You don't miss with a shovel, and if someone shoots at you, you can defend yourself."

He watched Boniface, seemingly letting the implicit menace distill into fear before casting a look of disappointment. "We had our fun and games outside, but now, if you don't tell me what I want to know, then I will give you a demonstration of what I can do with this shovel that Grigorii has so kindly crafted for me."

Boniface tried to sit up but found it too hard to move—his head throbbed and his limbs ached from too much travel in the trunks of cars.

"I need to pee." It was a female voice.

Boniface spun his head and looked into the dark corner of the shed behind him, beside a pile of grass-seed sacks. "Monty? I didn't see... What... How...?" He turned back to the Russian. "You've done enough to hurt her. Let her go; I've told you everything you've asked, and I'll tell you exactly what you want. Just let her go."

"Oh, Mister Boniface. I know you'll tell me what I want to know. While she's here, you will tell me everything." He lifted the blade of the shovel, again admiring the result of the other man's labor.

"At least let her piss. Then we can talk."

The Russian stood. "Grigorii." He stepped toward Montbretia with his shovel and pointed to her knees. "Open." She pulled up her knees and spread them, separating her ankles by a small amount and putting the tape binding the bottom of her legs under tension. In a blur, the Russian struck with his shovel, cutting the tape before returning to his seat. She held her taped wrists in front of her. The Russian looked, then shook his head.

The swarthy man came into the shed. "Take her for a piss." He jabbed his finger. "Round the side, then straight back here." The swarthy man turned to face the young woman who had rolled onto her front and was trying to stand.

Pulling her knees under her, she pushed herself up, reaching an unsteady standing position. She took an uncoordinated step backward to steady herself, and—with her wrists taped together—she continued to move, lifting her right elbow, jabbing it into the swarthy man's nose.

Boniface heard the crunch and saw dark liquid flow. Unbalanced, the man threw his leg to steady himself as Montbretia turned, lifted her foot, and stomped on the side of his leg, her boot connecting directly with the side of his knee, projecting her full weight through her foot.

There was a dull crunch, a muffled shout from the Russian, and he fell to the floor.

Before she could stand straight, the pockmarked Russian knocked her to the ground, pulled a roll of tape from his pocket, cut the tape holding her wrists, then bound her hands behind her back before rolling her over to bind her legs.

Boniface caught her eye. "He hit me. A girl's gotta get even. If I'd had more space, his days as a father would be over." The Russian finished binding her legs and tore off a short strip of tape, which he slapped over her mouth.

The crunch of cartilage in her nose was audible as his hand made contact.

He turned and shouted at the swarthy man in Russian. The swarthy man blushed and tried to move away. He shouted for a second time, and the other man was still.

"Mister Boniface. Now we talk." He stood up. Montbretia's body spasmed as he kicked her while moving back to the wooden box in front of Boniface. "A few more simple questions."

"I'll talk. But there's a lot of stuff that happened last night, and all you're doing is delaying the information getting to Kuznetsov. I was going to see him when you stopped me."

"Boniface, Boniface. You've got an answer for everything, haven't you? You're not going anywhere until I'm happy that you've told me everything. That way, if you have, shall we say, an unfortunate accident, then I will be able to tell Mister Kuznetsov the details you want him to know. It's much safer that way, isn't it?"

"But..."

"These images you gave to Turgenev."

"You mean..."

"I mean you don't answer my questions with a question of your own." The pockmarked Russian stood and kicked the elbow Boniface was leaning on. He fell, cracking his head on the concrete floor before the Russian placed his boot over the Englishman's throat. "Has anyone ever told you about our interpreters in the Spetsnaz?"

Boniface opened his mouth, gasping for air. The Russian rocked back and forth, adjusting the pressure exerted by his boot.

"Our interpreters aren't like the interpreters attached to Western armies. They are soldiers. Proper soldiers who fight with us. And why, why are these well-educated men integrated into the army?" He paused, staring into Boniface's eyes and holding the pressure through his boot. "Because they can speak the language of any...guests...we find along the way. If they can speak the language, then they can make them more comfortable."

He released his boot, dropping to sit astride Boniface, facing him, and crushing his bound arms under him. "So that means our interpreters are experts in motivating people to talk." He sneered. His hand flashed forward, coming into contact with Boniface's mouth, which opened as the Englishman went to scream at the pain of his head slamming back onto the concrete floor.

The Russian pushed his hand into the open mouth, reached, and grabbed Boniface's tongue, holding it firmly. With Boniface's jaws wedged open by his fist, the Russian felt in his pocket with his other hand and retrieved a pair of pruning shears. He opened and closed the shears, the spring squeaking and the blades scraping.

"Let me tell you something I learned from our interpreter friends." Boniface tried to pull back. With each movement, the Russian pushed his hand farther into the other man's mouth and gripped his tongue more firmly. "To help people talk, our interpreter friends like to make a snake." He pulled Boniface's tongue and thrust the open shears into his mouth, one blade above and one blade below his tongue, and started to squeeze. "Do you want a forked tongue, Boniface?"

Boniface tried to scream but was only able to expel air.

There was a click, and the shed darkened as a figure entered, pointing a gun at Boniface's tormentor. "Enough."

seventy-six

Montbretia tried to twist, delicately, feeling each bruise as she struggled to control the pain caused by her spine flexing over her wrists, which were taped together behind her back. She rolled—her back spasmed, and she flinched in pain, coming to rest with her spine jamming into her wrists, bone-on-bone-on-bone on something else really hard and uncomfortable that she was lying on.

She ached.

Her spine ached—each and every vertebra. Her wrists ached. Her arms ached. And her nose ached. She snorted, forcing drying blood out of her nose to ease the sole passage of oxygen while the piece of tape—so unceremoniously slapped in response to the demolition of the swarthy man's knee—remained firmly over her mouth.

The man by the shed door was dressed incongruously. From the waist down he was dressed as the two Russians: jeans and once-shined boots that were now muddy and scuffed. The top half of him was different—a red woolen sweater, which looked new and still had a price tag attached, and an improvised blue bandana.

Ignoring his sartorial choices, his intent seemed clear from the gun he held across his chest—pointing in Boniface's direction—as he peered around the edge of the door, apparently watching the two men he had just sent away.

He came inside and started fiddling with the phones he had taken from the two Russians. He pocketed the SIM cards and dropped the remaining electronics to the ground, crushing each under his boot, then grinding the pieces as if he were milling flour.

There was a sound of shuffling and moaning, and Boniface slowly levered himself into a sitting position, rocking forward with his hands behind his back. "Mister Turgenev. This is a pleasure; I wasn't expecting to see you for at least a few weeks."

There was no attempt to conceal the sarcasm, even though this was apparently the man who had held him and Ellen at gunpoint for much of last night. The man whose actions had led to a situation that brought about her sister's death.

The man she now knew as Turgenev ignored Boniface and continued to grind the phones with his heel while keeping the gun—the obvious indication of his violent tendencies—loosely trained on the Englishman.

"Why did you let them go?" There was incredulity in Boniface's voice. Almost anger in the slap-back echo of the shed. The Russian knocked the last few pieces of pulverized phone from his boot and ignored the question.

Boniface exhaled loudly. "Can you let them live? I mean..."

"They're not in a good state," said Turgenev, raising his head to look at Boniface and removing his bandana, his skull backlit by the ajar door, the sunlight halo around his features contrasting with the scowl they lit. "They are not a threat to me."

Boniface cocked his head.

"Once you tell Kuznetsov that I let them go, he won't be able to trust them. If he can't trust them, then they're not a threat." The Russian seemed pleased with his logic, or perhaps he was even more pleased that he intuitively understood something that Boniface didn't.

"Why the wooly jumper?" asked Boniface. "Is that what they're wearing in Paraguay these days?" He had a look of distaste as he surveyed the Russian.

"So they did know," muttered the other man. "Disguise. You think I'd dress like this for any reason but disguise? This was all I could buy at the airport, and I knew they wouldn't look for me dressed like this."

Boniface waited a beat. When he continued, his voice was quiet, his attitude approaching conciliatory. "So why are you back here? Why did you disguise yourself, then come here?"

The Russian looked straight at the other man. "I saw you walk into Sergey, and then they followed you." The Russian seemed almost friendly as he recounted his decision. "They were at the airport, so they must have known I was there. That means they would have someone waiting for me in Paraguay, so I couldn't get on the plane, and I needed to make sure you stayed alive long enough to pass on my message to Mister Kuznetsov." He paused. "And while I'm here, I can get my bike."

Turgenev ducked his head out the door, then stepped back in. Taking a step to Boniface and grabbing the tape holding his wrists, he lifted. Boniface let out a low yell as his shoulder joints were flexed, but leaned forward to release the tension on his arms as he reached his feet.

As Boniface found his balance, the Russian grabbed the shears on the floor and cut the tape around the Englishman's wrists, then stood back, training the gun on him again.

Montbretia watched Boniface as he shook out the tension in his muscles and examined the marks around his wrists, and turned to the Russian who was holding—for Boniface to see—what looked, in the gloom of the shed, like a small cylinder of plastic.

In his other hand, the gun was now pointing directly at her.

She tried to scream with her mouth still taped.

Boniface's head spun to look at her, then flipped back to the Russian.

"I never trust computers." The Russian's voice was heavily accented but calm and controlling. "We're at Hampton Court—go and find me some original documents. Fast." He moved his gun toward Montbretia.

Boniface lunged, making a grab for the piece of plastic the Russian was holding.

He missed but knocked it out of the Russian's hand.

Montbretia watched as the plastic spun toward her, bouncing on the ground and coming to rest about 12 inches from her feet. She lifted her legs—taking the weight of her body through her back onto her tied wrists underneath—and dropped her feet onto the plastic, listening to the satisfying crunch as it shattered.

Boniface and Turgenev stood silently, looking at the site of the destruction.

"Whoops," said Montbretia with no sincerity.

Slowly, a goofy grin spread across Boniface's visage.

When he spoke, there was anger in the Russian's voice. "You'd better run and find those papers."

"Not going."

Turgenev turned and pointed the gun at him.

"You need me alive," said Boniface.

The Russian stared blankly.

"That thumb drive that just landed under Miss Armstrong's boot was the last copy of the photos."

The Russian kept his stare fixed on Boniface.

"I doctored the pictures on the original thumb drive I gave you. Have a look—all you'll see are blurry images of some old documents, and the text doesn't make sense if you actually read it."

"Give me your phone." It was a command from the Russian.

Slowly Boniface opened his jacket, reached into his inside pocket, and pulled out his phone. He held it between his fingertips, offering it to Turgenev. "If you want the password, there's no point. You saw me at the airport, so you should know that I went to the internet café, where I deleted the online photos." He smirked. "They're all gone."

The Russian snatched the phone and pocketed it, keeping the weapon pointed at Boniface.

The Englishman's tone was controlled. "Here's how it goes: There's no evidence anymore, but I know what you know. Kill me, and Kuznetsov doesn't know why you need to stay alive. Let us live—both of us live—and I can make sure Kuznetsov understands the danger in not leaving you alone."

The Russian stood in silent contemplation.

Turgenev's fist connected with the side of Boniface's skull, a bright slap jerking his head. The Englishman's body fell backward, slamming into the side of the shed, making the wooden panel creak and the whole structure vibrate, before collapsing where he had previously been tied.

"I've wanted to do that for hours. That man talks too much." The

Russian looked away from Montbretia, stepped toward the inert mass of humanity lying in a heap, and checked his throat for a pulse.

He stood and moved toward Montbretia. "You understand that I can't have you following me." His voice softened. "I hope you will agree to hand over your phone without complaint, and that you will accept a few pieces of tape to restrict your movements until Mister Boniface comes round."

seventy-seven

"Ow." Boniface looked up from his tea. "My tongue hurts, and this tea is hot." Unconsciously, he touched the bruise on the side of his head.

"Stop being such a baby!" snapped Montbretia with mock exasperation, as she picked up a napkin to wipe a drip of blood that fell from her nose onto the easy-wipe plastic surface of the café table.

"But he cut me," said Boniface. "Look." He let his tongue flop out of his mouth.

"He cut you because he was clumsy taking the pruning shears out of your mouth when Turgenev came in with a gun. He didn't actually..." She opened and closed her first two fingers as if snipping with a pair of scissors. "He didn't make a snake. You don't speak with a forked tongue."

She looked at his tongue, which was still hanging out, and winced. "But that is an unpleasant cut. When did you last have a tetanus shot?" He shrugged, replacing the lump of flesh in his mouth.

He gingerly sipped his tea at the side of his mouth, shifted slightly, and winced as his back twinged. "I don't think I've got a muscle that doesn't hurt." He looked up to Montbretia. "And you must hurt more. He hit you pretty hard."

"But that Greek-looking one is going to need surgery. I'll take a broken nose for the pleasure of hearing his knee crunch." For the first time since he had told her about her sister's death, Boniface saw Montbretia smile.

"Are you sure your nose is alright?"

Montbretia delicately repositioned the ice wrapped in a tea towel. "Do you think they..." she flicked her eyes to the counter, where two disinterested teenagers were serving a group of mothers with small children, "bought the whole I-tripped-and-hit-my-nose thing?"

Boniface leaned back; looked down at his suit, noting each rip and tear, the bloodstains on his shirt, and his grimy tie; then looked to Montbretia, who looked like she hadn't washed either herself or her clothes for several weeks. The only thing fresh about her were the duck tape adhesive residue around her mouth and her new cuts, bruises, and gashes.

"Do I think they bought our story?" He felt the muscles in his face relax. "No. Do I care? Even less. Am I glad it's over?" He slowly nodded, careful not to cause himself any further pain.

Small children, with the joy of being alive, ran up and down the broad passages between the tables. The boys mostly imitated noisy cars, and the girls pushed their dolls in miniature baby buggies, while the more boisterous of both genders raced each other on scooters. The mothers clustered around the room, all overweight, badly dressed, and stressed. All seemed desperate for any human contact; the noise of happy children sufficient to ensure their primeval instinct to protect didn't kick too hard.

"So what just happened, Boniface? How did we get out?"

"We got out by luck, and we got out because we need to strike a deal. Or rather, we got out because Turgenev needs to believe that we're going to make a deal that will keep him safe."

"So you literally talked our way out of there?" Montbretia frowned. "Talk. That's all you did?"

"For the record, I've got skills. I didn't want to hurt those guys in front of you. I felt you had humiliated Russian manhood sufficiently for one day. That's the only reason I let Turgenev punch me." He delicately felt the side of his face, touching the swelling where the Russian's fist had most recently connected.

"Well, I'm in a weakened state at the moment, Boniface, so if you can keep your skills under wraps, that would be appreciated. But tell me, are we going to do a deal?"

"Oh yeah... We're going to do a deal," said Boniface calmly. "Just not the deal Turgenev wants."

"What deal are we going to do?" She began hesitantly and then changed tack before Boniface could answer. "And why do you keep saying *we* are going to do a deal? How does this involve me?"

Boniface took another sip of tea and winced as the hot liquid hit his injured tongue. When he started talking, his voice was somber. "Last night, Turgenev threatened you. That may have been an empty threat to scare your sister, but it was a threat."

"And now he's gone, Boniface." Montbretia seemed ready to move on.

"Now. But what about tomorrow?" His tone invited no response. "Mister Kuznetsov's employee threatened you. If Mister Kuznetsov wants our future cooperation—and I'm sure he will—then I require that Mister Kuznetsov extend the courtesy of his protection to you."

Montbretia stared at Boniface but made no sign that she wanted to demur.

"The second reason you're involved is that I'm presuming you can access Ellen's email."

With a small nod of her head, Montbretia affirmed.

"When I arrived at the airport this morning, I emailed copies of the images to Ellen." He waited, watching Montbretia's seeming internal confusion. "In other words, you've got everything that Turgenev wanted, so you're as dangerous to Kuznetsov as Turgenev thought he was. The difference is, you have the photos, and since you broke that thumb drive, all he has are some doctored images."

"Yeah, I'm sorry about that," said Montbretia, seemingly trying to stop the look of a naughty schoolgirl spreading across her face. "It seemed like a good idea at the time. You grabbed for the drive, he dropped it—my boot stopped you squabbling."

"Unfortunately, there is a price that comes with this information." He grimaced. "We have to do a deal with a rather dangerous oligarch." Boniface kept his face still, calibrating Montbretia's response, then softened. "The price is simple: silence."

"Silence about what? Ellen's death?" She frowned, twisting her head away while keeping her eyes locked on Boniface's.

"No. The police already know about that, and Kuznetsov had nothing to do with that."

"So what am I keeping quiet about? Whatever it was is connected with my sister's death." She dropped the volume of her voice. "I've been taped up and beaten by three Russians. Are you saying that my reward is a cup of coffee? I think I deserve more than that."

"You do." He sighed. "Kuznetsov is pretty mercurial, more so when he thinks people have let him down."

Montbretia laughed. "Don't patronize me, Boniface. I told you I'm a big girl. I can look after myself." Her eyes bored into him. "Ask the guy with the snapped knee."

Boniface flushed. "I'm sorry... I'm..."

"It's alright," she mouthed, her face softening. "Tell me what I'm keeping quiet about."

Boniface pondered for a moment or two, his mouth moving, silently beginning sentences, until he sat still. "Kuznetsov's weakness—which even he doesn't know about yet."

"Which is?"

He cocked his head and began. "I'm sure Ellen explained the basic history behind Nigel's book."

"Mmm."

"So you understand the basic idea—Wolsey, in collusion with Anne Boleyn, killed Henry." She bobbed her head. "When the murder happened, Henry had an illegitimate son, Henry FitzRoy, who was about twelve—he was Wolsey's godson. The first thing Wolsey did—and there was already plenty of historical evidence to substantiate this before Nigel came along—was to arrange a wife for young FitzRoy. At the behest of Anne Boleyn, FitzRoy married Anne's cousin, Lady Mary Howard. This was 1533 or sometime around."

"So they were both dreadfully young," said Montbretia.

"Fourteen," offered Boniface, looking at Montbretia's shocked face. "Maybe thirteen." She twisted her face, looking as if she had tasted something unpleasant. "But it kept FitzRoy occupied while Wolsey did whatever it was he did and Anne was occupied being pregnant with Elizabeth, who was born around that time. However, three years later everything had changed, and Anne Boleyn was starting to cause trouble for Wolsey, so she was beheaded."

"A very efficient way of dealing with the person who knows all your secrets. Let's hope Mister Kuznetsov is kinder with us."

"Precisely." Boniface hesitated, realizing what Montbretia had suggested. "But, Wolsey didn't kill FitzRoy. I'm going to start speculating about his motives, but maybe Wolsey did have some scruples and couldn't kill his own godson. However, he needed him out of the way to ensure there would be no competing claim on the throne. So two months after Anne's beheading, Wolsey arranged for FitzRoy to be disappeared."

"I thought he died from tuberculosis. Was I told the wrong story?"

"TB would be far too routine for Wolsey. No, Wolsey arranged for FitzRoy to change his name to John Stephens and to disappear. The story about the illegitimate heir dying of a childhood illness was concocted by Wolsey as a cover. John Stephens, as he became, grew up and became a wealthy landowner and happily lived out his days doing whatever it was that wealthy landowners did."

Montbretia's mouth fell open. "Oh, Wolsey was good. Do you ever feel you could have learned something from him, Boniface?"

"A lot. If nothing else, I would love his administrative skills. I've got about a thousand unopened emails, all mixed up with spam offering me length and girth enhancements, not to mention several weeks of bills piled up, and I haven't filed a single piece of paper since I took my new office. But I digress..."

"You do." Montbretia tilted her head, seemingly waiting.

"John Stephens, FitzRoy under his new name, lived out his life, doing all the things that rich landowners did, including getting married and having children. Those children had children, and with each successive generation, the family mythology grew that they were not only connected to royalty, but that they were royal."

"Which they were."

"They were. But no one had records—Wolsey made sure all the documents were hidden—no one could prove anything, and over time it became part of the family story, and no one took it seriously. Well, no one took it seriously until two nights ago, when a small-time thief found some papers somewhere in Hampton Court Palace."

"Really! Where? Can we go and have a look?"

"I wish I knew where the document store is, but Turgenev's man shot the thief in front of your sister and me before he could tell us."

Montbretia's mouth fell open. "What were you two...?" A tear trickled down her cheek, washing a clean path as it descended. "What did you...?"

Boniface continued. "The man had been arrested by the police, and because Nigel was getting some publicity about his work with the publication of the book, the police called him when they needed a Tudor expert to assess some documents that someone had tried to steal from

Hampton Court. So that's how Nigel met Pete." He paused. "Pete was the thief's name."

Montbretia picked up a napkin and wiped the tears trickling down her cheeks, leaving parallel clean tracks streaking across the dirt on her face.

"Nigel's life's work was Henry, and he was particularly interested in an idea he had that Henry had been murdered. Murder-and-replacement was the most plausible way he could find to explain how the intelligent, articulate, thoughtful Henry at the age of seventeen became the obese tyrant in the history books. Obviously, he was interested in all aspects surrounding Henry and the other lesser-known descendants, but Nigel's focus had been on Henry and the murder, and this was the book that Kuznetsov had commissioned him to write."

"Makes sense," said Montbretia.

"Nigel wasn't shocked when he found that FitzRoy lived. However, he was surprised to find out about the change of identity and was then able to quite quickly trace the descendants because they were a family of good standing—it's just no one had made the link with Henry."

Montbretia listened intently, nodding as Boniface recounted the story.

"What stunned Nigel was the identity of the descendant."

Montbretia sat silently, patiently waiting, then snapped. "Come on, Boniface. Who?"

"Patience. It gets better. Your sister and I followed the trail and found that not only was there an heir, but the heir has a secret love child." He looked up, scrunching his face as if trying to recall a detail. "Do we still say love child, or is it becoming an archaic term?"

"Boniface. You know I can kick." Montbretia grinned. "Spill."

"Sherborne."

"No shit!" Montbretia slammed her hand over her mouth and whispered. "The kids didn't hear that, did they?"

Boniface shook his head. "Sherborne is the daddy, and the interesting detail is that Oscar von Habsburg is his son. You know Oscar? Son of Princess Heidemarie."

Montbretia sat with her mouth open.

"So there's the real irony. By pursuing the truth about the murder of Henry in order to show that the current royals have no legitimate claim to the throne, which was part of the mood music to kick off the referendum campaign, Kuznetsov has led to the uncovering of a true blood heir. And even worse for Kuznetsov, the heir is the man he has been butting heads with since he came to this country."

Boniface fell back in his seat to allow Montbretia a question she seemed to be intent on asking. "So why doesn't Sherborne make a noise about this? Has Kuznetsov got a hit out on him? Is that where those two guys have gone now?"

"In a word, proof."

"Really? I thought he owned a newspaper. Can't he make them print a story? Why not start a rumor on the internet?"

"He could, but there's a problem—or two problems—and those problems are Princess Heidi and Oscar. If the story breaks, then there's going to be quite a furor. For a start, Oscar's paternity will be made public. Sherborne's proud of his boy and wants to publicly acknowledge him. But for Heidi, there's the issue of lies that were told to cover a scandal twenty-plus years ago."

Montbretia frowned.

"When she became pregnant, her husband was in a coma—a coma that began about a year before Oscar was born and ended a few months before the birth when the poor fellow died. Newly widowed Princess Heidi claimed that there was no possibility that her friend Richard could be the father. She suggested that perhaps the coma hadn't been that deep all the time, or hadn't reached certain parts of his anatomy."

"Oh," said Montbretia. "So if the story breaks, she's got to admit that she lied."

"And if they admit Oscar's parentage but can't prove his direct link to a murdered King, then she will have lost twice: his royal connection by virtue of the man currently claimed as his father goes, and her reputation is trashed. So they need documentary proof before they do anything."

"Can't Sherborne get hold of the documents or whatever they are? He's a rich guy; he's got friends, hasn't he?"

Boniface sucked air through his teeth. "Too political. Too close to the bone. If he draws attention, there's a chance someone will leak the story—or half the story, the wrong half—to another paper. Plus, he can't be seen to have links to criminals, especially as the story relates to Heidi."

"So what's stopping us from going public?"

"Fear."

"Fear?"

"Yup." Boniface met Montbretia's stare. "You're one person. However many knees you fracture, Kuznetsov will always find more people to hunt you and kill you. And if he can't find you, then he'll hunt those that you love and will kill them instead. So we shut up and hope that he loses interest in the referendum. When he does, we're out of trouble."

"That's crazy. What happens if this gets out?"

Boniface looked down, then back up at Montbretia. "It won't. Apart from us two, Kuznetsov, Turgenev, and Sherborne, there is no one who knows about, and can explain, the documents. If the story leaks, Kuznetsov will know where it came from."

"What about the police? Don't they hold the documents as evidence?"

"Sure. But they don't understand what they've got. They think they've got historical artifacts. They don't understand the evidential value. And they're not going to." He chuckled. "Once we've explained the story to Kuznetsov, he'll set his lawyers loose so that they can rain down chaos. They'll tie everything in legal knots so that nothing happens. That way no one will do anything rash, like try to return the documents to their rightful owners. Or read them…" He exhaled. "And that is it. That is everything."

Montbretia looked accusingly at him. "Are you sure that's everything? There's nothing else I should know, is there?"

Boniface wrinkled his nose. "Well, there is one thing I haven't told you." Montbretia held her glare. "But we need to be in the middle of the Maze for that." Boniface stood, picking up the change. "Come on."

"Can't we go and search for some more papers?" Montbretia kept her face straight, the edges of her mouth starting to involuntarily lift as she caught Boniface's stare. "Alright, later, perhaps?"

They walked the short distance to the Maze. Boniface took out a coin and flipped it. "Call."

"Heads."

He showed the coin. "Heads it is. Your choice: Do you want to go left or right?"

"Left."

"That leaves me with right. Let's see who gets to the middle first."

seventy–eight

Boniface sat on the wooden bench in the middle of the Maze, enjoying the spring sun near the peak of its travel, undisturbed by the ebb and flow of children finding their way to the middle and then losing themselves on the way out. Oblivious to the shriek of their excited voices as they closed in on their target, unworried by their return to tell their valiant tale of far-off lands in the middle of the Maze.

"Hey! How did you get here before me?"

"Cheating." Boniface smiled. "How else would you expect me to win? Ellen said you would beat her, so I had to think a bit laterally."

"Uh huh..."

"All you have to do is say to a parent 'I've lost my kids; could you let me through the emergency-exit barriers?' and they'll rush you straight through, no questions. It's a nice sunny day, my legs hurt—who am I kidding? All of me hurts—and it seemed a shame to waste it walking around when I could be sitting here with the final piece of the puzzle." Boniface stretched back, soaking up the sun's warmth.

Montbretia made a sour face. "I'm still strong enough to punch you, and I won't feel any remorse."

"Then I won't explain." Boniface shielded his eyes and looked up. "Sit down and relax in the sun while I finish the story."

She sat next to him on the wooden bench.

"There's one thing that's missing. One thing unaccounted for. The cornerstone of every good murder mystery."

Montbretia looked at Boniface, frowning.

"The body." Montbretia relaxed her frown as Boniface continued. "Without a body there can be no real proof of murder. And equally, by finding the body, you can prove murder. So how did Wolsey dispose of Henry's body?"

"I don't know." Montbretia screwed up her face. "He dug a hole?"

"He probably did dig a hole, but you're missing the point. If you've just murdered the King of England and you're trying to convince everyone that you are actually the man who you've just murdered, then you never, ever want the old King's dead body to turn up. It would raise too many questions."

Montbretia nodded at Boniface's logic.

"Now if you're Wolsey, pretending to be the King, you can't simply dump the old King's body, because then it might be found. And anyway, where do you take it? The only answer is to hide it. And hide it somewhere close so you can keep an eye on it and make sure it's not disturbed. And as the owner of Hampton Court Palace, Wolsey had ample space to bury a body in his grounds."

Montbretia brightened. "Of course."

"But if you're Wolsey with all these grounds, you also have a lot of gardeners." He paused. "But hopefully not the sort of gardeners who try to cut your tongue in half." He paused again. "You see, gardeners are the sort of people who habitually dig things up, like dogs looking for bones, so you need to put the body somewhere where they won't dig. Today it's easy; you bury someone in concrete under a road, and the body is effectively lost forever. But in Wolsey's day, it was harder. Particularly when Wolsey kept expanding Hampton Court and building new buildings."

"So what did he do?" asked Montbretia.

"As you've probably heard from your sister, the official version as they will tell you on the guided tour around Hampton Court is that this Maze was planted in sixteen-hundred-and-something, maybe even early seventeen-hundred, for William of Orange."

"And?" said Montbretia, exasperated.

"Possibly to replace a Maze that Wolsey may have planted while he still owned the Palace."

"That sounds like a rumor."

"It wasn't." Boniface was definite. "There was a Maze."

"Boniface, you're like an over-excited child who's about to wet himself. Where is Henry buried?"

"Here." Boniface spread his arms. "The Maze was planted on top of Henry's grave. That way Wolsey could be confident that Henry's grave would not be disturbed. Your sister and I saw the proof last night in Sherborne's house."

A huge grin broke out across Montbretia's face. "You are kidding me, Boniface. You're making this stuff up to make me feel better."

"Apparently Nigel had his suspicions years ago. Historically, it didn't make logical sense to him that there was a Maze here, on this specific spot. It made even less sense to him when he looked at the size of the Maze. So he did...I don't know, he did something that made him even more suspicious."

"Very scientific," sneered Montbretia.

"Anyway, whatever he did made him certain that there was something under here, and then a few years ago he found that there were bones." Montbretia looked slightly shocked. "They were doing an architectural history program for the telly, and the crew were using radars, or whatever they use to check out buried foundations. Nigel played nice, and one of the guys scanned this area for him, and hey presto, he knew there were bones."

"That'll teach me for being such a skeptic."

"Now, of course, he didn't know whose bones they were or when they were buried, but he already had his murder theory kicking around, and so he put two and two together but only got three because he couldn't prove anything. And because he couldn't prove anything, he was unwilling to go public and push for a formal dig. If he'd been wrong..."

"He would have looked like a complete..." Montbretia half-finished Boniface's sentence.

"Yeah, a complete dingbat. And it would have completely undermined his reputation. So he spent years looking for any evidence to prove that the bones were Henry's, and two nights ago, when a long-haired man got stuck in a hole, Nigel found his proof."

Montbretia looked over at him. "Nigel was patient."

Boniface's tone was gentle. "He was. And that is the end of the story. When your sister and I were chasing down Nigel's leads yesterday, she said she wanted to bring you here. She couldn't, but I'm pleased that I could."

He reached into his pocket to pull out a handful of clean napkins he had taken from the café and wiped his eyes. He turned to Montbretia, whose eyes were welling, and passed her several napkins. "When you're ready, we had better go and talk to the police. They're going to need our help, and I've got some explaining to do."

Montbretia nodded, wiping her nose.

"And there's the slight matter of the stolen car you've been driving, which needs to be returned to its owner."

"That car was stolen?"

"Yup. But don't worry; I'm fairly sure I know who owns it... Fairly sure."

Note from the Author

The locations in this book are, mostly, based on reality. However, I have taken liberties with the internal architecture of many of the buildings mentioned.

The Silver Spike—a Russian oligarch's vanity building in the West End of London—is entirely fictitious. It stands where Centre Point presently stands. Those who know Centre Point will understand my desire to replace it. St Giles' Circus exists, but not as an island. At the time of writing this note (May 2014), the area is shrouded behind hoardings while the Cross Rail project is under construction. How it will look when complete is a mystery, but I think we can be certain it won't be as I have described it.

There is no crack in the wall—that I am aware of—in Hampton Court Palace. However, the signs of each new resident's desire to impose their will on the building are evident. If you do find any gaps where different styles of architecture meet, please don't try to clamber through in search of old documents, however winkle-like you may be. If you do visit, then admire the Great Hall and the splendor of the Palace. And should you want to dig up the Maze, then I suggest you run it over with some ground-penetrating radar...just to make sure Henry's bones really are there.

Thames Ditton is real. Thames Ditton Island is real and occupied; however, I feel I may have painted some of the residents in an unflattering light, for which I apologize. I have also taken some liberties with the bridge to the island. Kingston's one-way system is, regrettably, not a fiction, and the architecture of Ellen's house is not consistent with the properties on that edge of Ham Common.

Further down the River Thames, although Richmond Palace no longer exists, The Wardrobe does and is now private residences. Trumpeters' House is not one dwelling, but as I understand, is four apartments.

If you want to know more about the locations featured in the book, I have posted some photos and videos on my website. You can find them at simoncann.com/henry-background

Boniface Books

You can check out the latest Boniface books at simoncann.com/boniface

Pollute the Poor (Boniface #2)

The first Boniface knows about the dead body in the next room is when he is arrested for murder.

The lack of evidence against Boniface doesn't seem to concern the police—they are sure they have the right man—they just need to prove his guilt, and while they do, Boniface is bailed allowing him to return to work with his client.

His client, a shipping company, couldn't care less that Boniface is distracted. The client has its own problems: News is about to break that one of its ships dumped toxic waste in East Africa, leading to painful and lingering deaths, as well as widespread disability and illness. While the company privately acknowledges its role in the dumping—and its ongoing responsibility for the welfare of the victims—it is insistent that Boniface keeps the story out of the public domain until it has fully assessed how it can most effectively deliver support to those affected.

Boniface knows he has been set up for the murder—and that somebody is trying to destroy him, his business, and everything he holds dear—but he doesn't know who has set him up, or why. He strips back the layers, discovering who the dead man was, why he was killed, why the body was dumped in his office, and why he was set up in such a clumsy manner until, he finds who has endangered his livelihood, his liberty, and his friends.

This leaves Boniface with only one conclusion: He must neutralize the threat, permanently, while at the same time trying to protect anyone affected by the dumping.

Tattoo Your Name on My Heart (Boniface #3)

Although past his mid-thirties, the teenager that lives inside Boniface's head can't believe his luck when he is hired to help one of his rock idols, Danny Featherstone, and his ex-glamour-model wife, Dawn.

Danny and Dawn are the target of an anonymous internet hate campaign that has led to poor ticket sales and lost television work. Broken contractual terms brought to light by the hate campaign have led the management to freeze the band's assets, cutting off the couple's source of income.

And then Dawn disappears.

Boniface searches for Dawn but uncovers small-time crooks looking for money and excitement who think Boniface has something they can extort. Making his search even more complicated is an angry son looking to destroy the parent he believes abandoned him, and embittered, poverty-stricken musicians trying to regain their former fame and get a slice of the income that was only ever theirs in their dreams.

But most worrying, Boniface finds a husband who loves his wife, unconditionally, and who will do anything to protect her.

About the Author

Simon Cann is the author of the Boniface series of books.

In addition to his fiction, Simon has written a range of music-related and business-related books, including the How to Make a Noise series, the most widely ready series about synthesizer sound programming, and Made it in China, about entrepreneurs building businesses in China. He has also worked as a ghostwriter on a number of books.

Before turning full-time to writing, Simon spent nearly two decades as a management consultant, where his clients included aeronautical, pharmaceutical, defense, financial services, chemical, entertainment, and broadcasting companies.

He lives in London.

Keep in Touch

If you want to know more about Simon, his books, the background to his books, and what he's up to, then check out:

- His website: simoncann.com
- His Facebook page: facebook.com/simoncannauthor
- His Google+ profile: google.com/+simoncann
- His YouTube channel: youtube.com/simonpcann

The swiftest way to find out when Simon's next book will be published is to join his mailing list at simoncann.com/mail